21
QUESTIONS

21
QUESTIONS

A NOVEL

ALEXANDRIA ROSE RIZIK

SparkPress, a BookSparks imprint
A Division of SparkPoint Studio, LLC

Published by SparkPress, a BookSparks imprint,
A division of SparkPoint Studio, LLC
Phoenix, Arizona, USA, 85007
www.gosparkpress.com

Published 2021

Printed in the United States of America

Print ISBN: 978-1-68463-087-5
E-ISBN: 978-1-68463-088-2
Library of Congress Control Number: [LOCCN]

Formatting by Katherine Lloyd, The DESK

For my first love, thank you for being my muse.

To my mom, thank you for being there
every time he made me cry.

KENDRA

I always knew I wasn't meant to be a human. I thought of myself more as a mermaid—maybe even closer to a dolphin. But definitely not human. At least that's how I felt every time my toes touched the water.

Its salty flavor filled my throat as it collapsed over me. *It is what it is*, I repeated to myself as the overwhelming wave fumbled me around, somersaulting me to shore. It was the mantra I chose when angst tried to creep its way into my mind.

I started to panic as I lay on the sand, trying to catch my breath, eyes shut. Thoughts of doubt cluttered my brain, but I pushed them away, focusing on inhaling and exhaling, reminding myself, *I can breathe*. The anxiety wasn't always bad, only sometimes. Never while I was in the water—mostly when the waves plummeted me to shore, forcing me to face reality again.

A shadow cast itself over me. I opened my eyes to find Coach Harkins standing above me, his wet, blond locks dripping onto my face.

"Come on, Ken! You need more explosive maneuvers."

I sat up and nodded my head. He was right; he was always right. I paused before grabbing my surfboard and heading into the water. The ocean felt like home. If only I had gills, I'd probably never touch the earth's land again.

I paddled out past a few small waves, then sat on my board waiting for a larger wave to form as Coach Harkins stood on the sand. I took in the sun's rays beating down on my skin.

"This one, Ken! Come on," he yelled to me.

I eyed the wave coming toward me, unsure if we were friends, but I knew I could easily introduce myself. The water was the one place I didn't question myself; there was no time for awkward silences or prying thoughts of uncertainty. I knew how to flow with its currents and tides.

I paddled a ways before hoisting myself onto my board. My adrenaline surged as I attempted to nail a backside air reverse in the water. I could hear Coach Harkins screaming when I landed the move perfectly, my board gliding against the wave and then launching into the air, landing a perfect 360 back down onto the water, surfing the wave to shore.

I walked up the beach where he was waiting for me.

"Rough start, but good work today," he said.

I was preparing for the quarterfinals in the USA Surfing Prime West.

We always ended practice with a five-minute meditation. Coach taught yoga part time—something he had discovered after a terrible car accident. He'd been drunk driving and was told he'd never be able to walk again, let alone surf. But he'd proved the doctors wrong.

What I admired most about him was his honesty regarding his struggle to become sober. Although it sometimes felt repetitive listening to his frequent lectures on staying away from "that crowd," I appreciated his sincere concern. But believe me, I knew firsthand all about "that crowd"—they'd been a permanent fixture in my house during most of my childhood, along with the substances they brought and the death of my brother that followed. The thing was, they weren't bad people.

No. They were lost people—at least that's how my dad always explained it.

Coach was the one who introduced me to meditation, and it changed my entire mindset. My dad had tried family counseling and shrinks—one who diagnosed me with a type of anxiety called panic disorder. They even put me on a small dose of medicine for a while when I was twelve, but it didn't work. The side effects were too overwhelming—nausea, joint pains to the point where I couldn't even surf. But the worst were the night terrors. Thankfully, I met Coach, and he sparked my interest in utilizing the Eastern approach to managing anxiety. Not just in surfing, but in most aspects of life, from school to just overall facing daily fears. I used to have panic attacks quite often, but learning how to control my breath really changed things for me. I didn't think it would ever be truly cured, but at least it could be managed.

Coach and I sat across from one another on the sand in a shaded area. My eyes fell upon his throat where a trach scar from his accident remained. Coach seemed like a completely different person than he was before, from the stories he'd told me. It's weird to think though that scars are always there to remind you of who you once were.

"All right, close your eyes," he said.

I closed my eyes, focusing in on my third-eye chakra, trying to clear my mind of worrying about school and everything I had to do. It took me out of my head and into the moment.

"I want you to take a deep inhale through your nose for five seconds," he guided me. I inhaled. "Now hold that breath for five seconds . . . three, two, one, and exhale for five."

I let out a heavy breath through my nose. I could feel it in the back of my throat as we repeated the exercise. It felt good. I began to feel lighter, my body naturally and unconsciously swaying back and forth as if I was going to float away.

"Exhale an audible breath out of your mouth," he said.

I sighed as I let my breath go.

"Remember you can always come back to this place. Whenever your mind wanders away, come back to the breath. It allows you to be present—and really, life can only exist here in this moment. So, live it. Breathe it. Be it."

I welcomed the smile peeking through as Coach's words resonated with me.

"Gently open your eyes, Ken."

I slowly allowed my eyes to open, the sun somewhat overwhelming. I caught sight of the hills covered in houses beyond the fog. Laguna Beach was magical, especially in the morning.

"How do you feel?"

"Amazing."

Coach stood up and stuck out his hand for me to grab. I held on as I lifted my calm body back up. I was in a whole different space. I stood there, taking in the breeze. The ocean. The sun. The sand between my toes. Everything around me.

What I loved most about my bike rides home in the morning was watching all the cafés open up down South Coast Highway. I loved the smell of coffee brewing and the sound of forks clinking against plates. I could hear the waves crashing from a distance, the ocean calling me to come back with every crash and roll of its tides. What I would've given to be able to surf all day, every day.

My stomach gurgled as I passed by all of the bakeries tempting me with their fresh pastries sitting in the front windows. I was famished.

Thankfully, when I got home, there was food waiting on the table.

"How was practice, doll?" Harry asked.

Harry was my dad's fiancé and, in a sense, a maternal

figure—being that I didn't have one. I mean, he took responsibility for all the obligations that a mother would normally have.

"It was good. I'm starved."

I devoured the food—I swear I could have eaten the plate itself. Harry handed me a glass of orange juice as his phone rang. He checked the caller ID and silenced the call.

"It's Zola . . . too early to talk business."

Zola was an old friend of Harry's who he'd met back in cosmetology school when they were in their twenties. Now they were opening up their own salon together.

"Have you told your parents yet?" I asked.

"About the salon?" He shook his head, clearing his throat as he redirected his gaze to the ground. I felt bad for bringing it up.

"They won't talk to me, Ken. You know that."

I nodded.

Harry's parents were very old school and could never quite come to terms with the whole "gay" thing. They thought my dad and Harry were destined to go to h-e-double-hockey-stick—total opposite of my dad's parents. And no, I didn't cuss. I know I was sixteen and that seemed weird, but I just didn't like it. When I heard other people swear, it sounded so vulgar and dirty. I tried to do everything the opposite of my brother, except for surfing. He swore a lot.

My dad walked in the house from his morning run, sweat dripping from his naked head down to his nose.

"Morning, sweetheart." He greeted me with a kiss on the forehead.

"Hi, Dad."

He walked over to Harry and gave him a kiss.

"Bruce, we need more bacon."

"I thought you went vegan?" he asked as he replaced his prescription sunglasses with his regular bifocals.

"Yeah, that didn't work out too well," Harry said, stuffing a steaming hot sausage into his mouth.

My dad laughed. Harry went through many phases; last week he bought a ten-class package for a Pilates studio. He went one time and was too sore to even sit the next day, so he decided that the owner was a "narcissistic b-word" and that Pilates was a total scam. In his words: "Working out is supposed to invigorate you, not disintegrate you."

Skittles, my Pomeranian, ran into the room, barking.

"Morning, Skittles!" I fed her a sausage.

"Ken, no human food," Harry lectured. "She'll shit all over the house, and I'm the one who has to clean it while you're at school."

"Speaking of school, I have to go or I'm going to be late."

I threw my bag into the basket of my bike and started for school. When I got there, all my friends were sitting in the courtyard.

"Hey, Ken!" Ashleigh came up and hugged me. I noticed she was wearing the bracelet I got her for her last birthday.

"Cute bracelet. Who got you that?" I teased.

"Some bitch."

We walked over to the rest of our group. They were all circled around Ashleigh's boyfriend, Ashton, and one of his soccer teammates. The two of them had their fingers pressed up against each other's necks.

"Uh, what are they doing?" Ashleigh yelled.

"Playing the pass-out game," our friend Taylor replied.

"They're going to hurt themselves!" Tiny Ashleigh walked into the middle of the circle and pushed them apart. Ashton accidentally hit her in the face when he jerked his hand back.

"Ashton! My nose!" she said, flipping out. Ashleigh swore that her only insecurity in life was her nose. She thought it was too big for the rest of her face. But I didn't see it. I mean, *maybe*. The only flaw I could see in it, really, was a small bump that she said was from breaking it as a child. "Please, it's already big enough!"

"What are you doing, Ash?" Ashton snapped. I used to tease them and refer to them as Ash Squared, but they didn't get it. I personally thought it was adorable.

"You're going to kill each other, dumbass!" she scolded him. Ashleigh was like one of those Chihuahuas that thought she was a pit bull. Something that I wish I had more of in me. But I was more reserved. I guess we balanced each other out.

"It's just a game! You don't need to always butt in."

"Annoying bitch," Ashton's teammate muffled under his breath. Ashton and Ashleigh jerked their heads toward him.

"Hey!" Ashleigh whined.

"Don't call her that again, dick," Ashton defended her. "Or I'll make you pass out for real, next time."

The first bell of the day rang, giving us five minutes to get to our classes.

"Shit, I can't be late for chem again. See you at lunch, Ash." Ashton grabbed his bag, running off to class. He and Ashleigh had been dating on and off since we were in eighth grade. We'd all had pre-algebra together with Miss Benson. Ashton used the back of his pop quiz to write her a note asking that she meet him at the park after school—he said he knew he was going to fail the quiz anyway, so he didn't even bother turning it in. Of course, she made me tag along. They made out on top of the monkey bars, and I'd been third wheeling ever since.

Ashleigh and I walked inside together. Lockers lined the hallway.

"Are we doing a limo for homecoming?" she asked.

"I don't even have a date—"

"Ken, you're not backing out. Sorry. Not allowed."

I had hoped that I'd somehow be able to get out of going to the dance. I don't know why I'd even agreed in the first place. I would rather be surfing than at some school dance I wouldn't even remember in a few years.

"I know, I know," I said as I pulled *The Great Gatsby* and my study guide out of my bag. "I'll see you later."

I opened the door to my English class; only four other people were there so far. No one usually showed up until a minute before the late bell rang. I liked to be extra early, as just the thought of walking in late with a bunch of people already seated gave me heart palpitations. Mr. Paul sat on his desk at the front of the room, shuffling through his papers.

"Morning, Mr. Paul."

"Hello, Miss Dimes," he greeted me.

A few more of my classmates scattered in. I opened up *The Great Gatsby* to where my bookmark was stuffed between the end of chapter eight and the beginning of chapter nine. I skimmed through chapter nine as the door opened and twenty-something other people boisterously entered the room. The late bell rang as they took their seats.

"All right, everyone, settle down, please." Mr. Paul tried to be calm, but I could see his face flush, and he did this thing when he'd get angry where his chin jutted out.

When everyone sat down and faced the front of the room, Mr. Paul stood up.

"I hope you all brought your books and study guides. We're going to review chapter five and then go over the study questions."

"Can I look at your book with you?" Michael Bradley asked me.

"Yeah. Sure."

I scooted my desk closer to his so he could see. He smelled like a mix of BO and peanut butter, but I didn't want to offend him—I decided the only solution would be to breathe through my mouth for the rest of the period. It wasn't his fault he had football practice before first period. Michael and I had a lot of classes together throughout high school, but I didn't know much about him except that he was on the football team. I'd always been good at keeping people at arm's length. The closest friend I had was Ashleigh, although even she didn't know my past. No one in Laguna did.

"We saw a lot of themes coming out in this chapter. The theme of social class was a big one." Mr. Paul went on for a good forty minutes talking about social class during the 1920s while Michael was basically asleep on my lap.

When I looked up at the clock—which Mr. Paul insisted had to be analog because "these days, teenagers just have it too easy"—there were barely two minutes left of class. I drew the conclusion that time flew by when you read ahead.

"All right. Before I let you go, I want to cover a few of the symbols. One that stuck out was the green light." Mr. Paul glided between the aisles of desks.

"Miss Dimes, what would you say is significant about the green light?" he asked me.

"The green light represents a couple of things, one mainly being Gatsby's hopes for the future—"

The bell interrupted my train of thought. Michael jumped up out of his sleep, drool hanging from his mouth. Everyone swiftly packed up their bags, ready to bolt for the door.

"Hold on there! The bell doesn't release you, I do," Mr. Paul said.

The class settled back into their seats.

"Remember to read chapters six through nine this weekend."

He paused, looking around the room.

"You're free to go."

Everybody darted out of the room as I took my time gathering my things up and placing them into my bag.

"Thanks for letting me use your book, Ken." Michael smiled and winked at me.

I smiled back. "No problem."

As Michael started for the door, a mint container fell from his bag. I picked it up and hurried to his side. It was one of those red tin Altoids packs.

"Hey, you dropped these."

"Oh," he said, quickly taking the small container from me and shoving it back in the front pocket of his bag. I couldn't help but notice the way his face went blank. "Thanks."

He rushed out of the room without another word.

I turned back around to grab my bag from the desk and headed for the door. It was a relief to breathe out of my nose again.

"Good job, Miss Dimes," Mr. Paul said as I passed his desk.

"Thanks. Have a nice day."

BROCK

I hated Thursdays—they were so close to Friday but not close enough. I mean, it almost seemed like a pointless day, like the word *um*—why not just get to the point? The fucking weekend.

I let my cigarette hang from my mouth as I strummed a cord on my Fender—it was one of several guitars that hung along my walls. It wasn't my favorite, but it was still a beautiful piece—a '65 Stratocaster.

My thoughts drifted with the sound of each note.

Fuck school, my mind sang to the melody as I noticed the time on the clock; punctuality wasn't my forte. Then again, nothing that required structure really suited me well.

All teachers ever did was talk, talk, talk, blah, blah, bullshit. They never let us speak, only expected us to listen to their textbook theories on nothing. Music spoke *and* listened. It was a mentor and a student. It spoke a language that anyone could understand, and it understood what people had to say when they couldn't speak at all.

I was running so late that when I finally *did* decide to make it to second period, I figured stopping for a coffee wouldn't matter. I pulled up to the drive-through and ordered my usual: a hot coffee with a tablespoon of cinnamon, four sugars, and a quarter cup of cream. There was nothing better after smoking a morning bowl. It was, like, an odd counter-buzz.

I pulled up to school just as the bell rang, releasing everyone from their first-period classes. Before I got out of my car, I squeezed a drop of Visine in each eye. As I was walking through the courtyard to the front doors, Billy, the security guard, stopped me.

"You need to go through the office to get a tardy slip."

"Come on. Really, Bill?"

"Really."

I looked him up and down; he was your typical high school security guard. He was tatted from his neck down. He was probably in his mid-fifties and most likely just got out of jail or rehab. His potbelly stuck out past his toes, and his beard was full of cracker crumbs from the night before. I put my hand on his shoulder, looking him straight in the eye.

Without changing my gaze, I reached into my pocket and pulled out a bag of coke. There wasn't much in it, and it was cheap shit anyway. I was going to use it up later or try and pawn it off to this fucking nerd in my math class in exchange for completing my late homework.

I dangled the bag in front of Billy's face.

"This will be yours for free, if you let me through."

His eyes widened a little.

"What?" he said, playing dumb.

"Billy," I started, "how long you been clean for?"

"What? How would you know I—"

"You have the chemical compound for coke on your calf and *sober* tatted on your wrist."

His eyes were wandering all over the place until he snatched the bag out of my hand and stuffed it in his coat pocket. I proceeded to the doors. That was even easier than I anticipated.

"Have a nice day, Billy."

When I walked into school, it was still passing period.

"Hey, babe." Annie slapped my ass as she walked by.

I wanted to fuck her right then and there.

"You want to ditch second?" she asked as she stuffed something into my pocket. I reached in and felt a condom wrapper. One more period wouldn't hurt.

We walked outside, passed the football field, and headed for the baseball diamond. No one used it during school hours. We sat on top of the bleachers and started making out. She lay down and I lay on top of her. I unbuttoned her jeans as she worked her lips down my neck and pulled down my pants.

"I'm about to blow your mind," she whispered as she grabbed ahold of my most vital of organs. I was so hard. She worked her mouth down my chest to my stomach and then all the way. She knew all sorts of tricks—tricks I was more than willing to let her demonstrate on me.

She looked at me as she did her thing. It really turned me on when she kept my gaze like that. It was a sign of confidence.

She smiled this half grin that said, *Please fuck me*.

"Sit up, babe." She did as I said.

I quickly put the condom on.

She rode me fast and hard.

"Ah! You're so sexy, baby!" she cried. I had her moaning and groaning so loud that Billy came rushing over to the diamond. When he saw it was me, he turned around and ran off.

A whole class period worth of bleacher boning later, we finished.

I threw the condom in the bushes as she put her pants back on. I pulled my pipe out of my pocket along with a small bag of pot, lighting it up and taking in a long hit before handing it to Annie.

"You going to homecoming?" she asked me, taking a second hit.

"I guess so. Are you?"

"Yeah. I'm taking this kid from Saddleback."

"Cool."

She handed me the pipe. The good thing about Annie was that there were no strings attached. I wasn't big into commitments—they made me feel suffocated. The last time I had a girlfriend was in the eighth grade, and it lasted two weeks. I ended up hooking up with her older sister. The thing was it wasn't like I was a bad boyfriend. I just made out with other people sometimes.

"I've got to get going to class. See you later."

"All right."

She grabbed her bag and walked back toward the main building. As I took another hit, my phone went off. It was a text from my mom.

Call me.

I grabbed my bag and headed to my third-period class as I called my mom, taking one last hit for good luck.

The rest of the day went by super fucking slow, even though I ended up ditching two of my other classes. I went to my last period, though, music class. It was the only class I bothered to go to really—and the only one I enjoyed. Mr. Brawling was a bad ass, and he didn't give a shit about much. Like me. Plus, he never assigned homework, so he was automatically my favorite.

Today, he let me sit in the hallway and mess around on his custom Fender, while he played *The Godfather* in class and lectured on about the film score. The Fender had his last name written along the neck and everything.

We got to talking after class. He told me the guitar was from his rock band days when he toured in his twenties and Fender sponsored him. He seemed way too cool to be a teacher.

"You seem very passionate about music, Brock," he said to me as I started for the classroom door.

"Thanks. I am."

I may have loved music, but it was just a hobby. A *passion* as Mr. Brawling put it. But drugs and selling them were my world.

KENDRA

Friday wasn't my favorite, especially this Friday. Homecoming was tomorrow, and the thought of dancing—in public, mind you—made my palms sweat.

I walked out of history, my brain throbbing.

"Hey, Ken."

I looked to my right—Jason Wells was at my side.

"Hi, Jason," I said as we continued down the hallway.

Jason was a super-senior and captain of the football team. To most girls, he was the hottest thing to walk Planet Earth. He wore a frequent tan—the result of many days at his mother's tanning salon—that made his blond hair look even lighter. He had perfect teeth and perfect biceps. Everything he did was perfect really, minus his grades. I guess you can't have it all, right?

"Did you write down the trig homework? I wasn't in class."

"Yep. I'll give it to you later."

"Sweet. You excited for the dance tomorrow night?"

"Duh! Are you?" I lied.

"For sure. But I have a problem that I think you can help me with."

We left the building along with the rest of Laguna Tides High School, everyone heading for their cars.

"What's that?"

"I don't have a date."

"Isn't it a little late to try and score a date?"

"Yeah, totally. That's why I need your help."

"Most of the girls I know have dates, but maybe—"

"We could go together?"

My heart fell. Jason and I? We were just friends—and I wanted to keep it like that. He was cute and all, but I don't know . . . he was Jason. He flirted with anything that crossed his path. Plus, I knew he only wanted me to go with him because I'd never hooked up with him before. Supposedly he and the rest of the football team had a bet going on to see who could hook up with the entire junior and/or senior class first—and I wasn't about to be the girl who helped him win. At least, that was the story Ashleigh gave me, and usually her stories were only 50 percent accurate. The other half seemed to be lost or distorted through a game of telephone. But still . . .

"Oh, you wanted to go together?" I restated, the heightened pitch of my voice evident.

"Well, I figured since neither of us have a date and all."

I quickly searched my mind as if it was a filing cabinet and I had to scan all of the documents labeled "Excuses."

"That's nice of you to ask but . . . it's just such short notice." Lame excuse, I know, but it was all I could think of when he put me on the spot like that.

"Y-yeah, I get it," he stuttered. His bicep flexed as he scratched the back of his head, almost confused that I'd turned down a date with him. He was probably surprised. No one else in the whole school would reject the chance to be with Jason. In my opinion, the whole homecoming thing was overrated, and so were guys with muscles that big.

I wanted to get some practice in while the tide was still high.

"I'll see you later."

I walked over to the bike rack, throwing my bag in the basket as I headed for home.

When I walked into my house, Skittles greeted me with her yappy barking. I squatted down to her level and scratched the top of her head.

"Hi, baby! Did you miss me today?"

She licked my nose.

I could hear the sound of the sewing machine coming from the dining room. I followed it in there. My dad was sitting at the table, sparkly fabrics sprawled out all over.

He noticed me standing over him and quickly jumped up.

"You can't be in here! This is your homecoming dress. Close your eyes."

I shut my eyes as I sighed with frustration. My dad had always dreamt of being a designer, but it was something he did for fun just for my friends and me.

Any hope of backing out of homecoming was kiboshed now that my dad had spent the time, effort, and money into creating a custom dress just for me. He would be crushed. I was hoping he'd forgotten that I ever even mentioned to him that I was going, but he took these things to heart. He was always saying how he wanted me to get the "full high school experience." Did that mean I had to call Ashleigh about the limo? That sounded super tacky when it was only going to be her and Ashton—and me third wheeling (a sport I had exceled at during the course of their relationship).

"Okay, you're good, you can open now," my dad said.

The fabrics were cleared away, out of sight.

"How was school, honey?"

"It was good. Felt long."

"Are you going to the homecoming game tonight?"

"I should probably get some practice in for Primes. I need

to practice every chance I get." Plus, the thought of having to sit through two hours of rowdy shrieking and shouting while sweating my butt off due to an excess of human body heat sounded far from ideal. I'd much rather hit the water, come home, put my pajamas on, and cozy up with my dog.

"You need to go out and be a teenager is what you need to do. I'm taking your surfboard away for the night."

I laughed. What always surprised me most about my dad was that, despite Kyle's death, he always encouraged me to go out, be with my friends, and experience life. He never really tried to keep me in a box like you might expect a parent who'd lost a child to do.

"Okay. I guess I'll call Ashleigh to see if she'll pick me up."

I started for my room.

"Oh, and Ken?"

"Yeah?" I turned back around.

"Tell Ashleigh that I hemmed her dress. She needs to try it on at some point tonight."

"Okay. I'll tell her."

I walked upstairs to my room, Skittles following behind me, and set my bag on the ground. I pulled my cell phone out of my back pocket and dialed Ash's number.

"Hey, lovey," she answered.

"Are you going to the game tonight?"

"Duh. What kind of question is that?"

"Pick me up."

"Wait—Kendra Dimes is actually going out? Like on a Friday night? To have fun?"

"Funny, ha-ha."

"Be there around six."

"The game doesn't start until seven!"

"We have to get good seats! It's going to be packed."

"Fine. See you then."

I hung up, surrendering to the fact that I was going out tonight. My anxiety was starting to kick in at the thought of those claustrophobic bleachers.

BROCK

"You going to the game tonight?" I asked Nick as I took a hit. The two of us were sitting in my car, hotboxing.

"Yeah. Are you?"

"I guess."

I wasn't really into football, but whatever.

He stuck his hand out. I passed him the joint.

"Who you going with?" I asked.

"You, bro."

We both laughed—everything seemed funnier when we smoked together.

"I kind of wish I had a date to homecoming," Nick said, moping.

"You sound like a pussy." I laughed at Nick.

"I'm serious, man."

"That's the sad part."

Nick was such a bitch. He had to be a virgin. But he always told everyone this lame story how he got a BJ in the pool while on vacation last summer. I was calling bullshit though. No doubt. I just didn't buy it. The kid was way too into trying to score any girl that gave him minimal attention, and so far, since I'd known him, he hadn't even made out with anyone, let alone touched the cooter. Any guy looking for a "date" or a "girlfriend" was really just looking to get laid. That's fact.

I took one last hit before rolling down all of the windows. I threw the joint outside and drove off.

My phone rang. It was my father. I couldn't help but roll my eyes.

"Hello?" I answered.

"Where are you?"

"Uh, going to the football game."

"What football game?"

"The homecoming game tonight."

"Are you with anyone right now?"

"Yeah."

The line went dead.

I looked down at my phone and clicked the lock button as I shoved it back into my pocket.

"Who was that?"

"Just my father."

"So, what's the deal with you and Annie?"

"Nothing. Why? What have you heard?"

"That you two fucked on the baseball diamond."

"Who told you that?"

"She was bragging about it to all her soccer friends in class."

I stayed silent. True players don't kiss and tell—or fuck and tell, in this case. That was lame. I wasn't pissed, but how old were we? That was some middle school shit.

"So, did you?"

I just laughed. Nick joined in, picking up on the unspoken truth.

When we got to the football game, we were so late it was already halftime. Jason, the quarterback who was always hitting me up for coke, messaged me before the game. He was trying to buy. He left fifty bucks in the men's bathroom stall trash can in the building across from the field, and I left an Altoids tin filled with coke in exchange.

When I walked out and headed toward the bleachers, a girl passed by me, her fists clenched at her sides as she mumbled under her breath, "This is why I don't go to football games."

She collapsed down behind a wall where they were selling concessions.

"You good?" I asked her.

She didn't bother to look my way; she was breathing heavily in and out through her mouth.

So, I asked again, "Are you all right?"

I neared her as her eyes met mine. She looked like she was on the verge of tears.

"Yeah, I just get really nervous in big crowds like that when everyone is all smooshed together and on top of each other," she said, speaking with her hands in an exasperated manner.

"I get it. I'm not much into sporting events myself." I chuckled. She smiled and lifted her long brown hair off of her face.

"I'm Brock, by the way," I said.

"Kendra," she replied. The conversation ended there because her friend, who I recognized as Ashton's girlfriend, came chasing after her. I decided to continue on with my shit.

Anyway, I got a few deals in, so overall it was a successful night—minus the game. It was a major loss.

The next day was the dance. Something I had no fucking interest in, but my parents were making me go because it was a prime opportunity to get some deals in. Duh.

I looked in the mirror as I buttoned up my shirt. I couldn't lie—I was looking fresh as fruit.

My father walked in, a glass of scotch in hand.

"You look nice. You taking a date?"

I shook my head.

"What about Annie? Does she have a date?"

"Yeah, some kid from another school."

Annie's and my families were, well, family friends.

I threw my suit jacket on over my shirt, then headed over to my dresser to grab a watch. I wasn't really in the mood for the interrogations.

I turned back around to find a handful of mini plastic bags filled with cocaine inside of a larger plastic bag sitting on my desk.

"This is exactly ten grams. I want you to have exactly ten grams sold by the end of the night. Understood?"

I looked at my father—his eyes were narrowed in on me, like he was a camera trying to focus itself. We had the same eyes and that scared me sometimes.

"Understood, sir."

"And here." He tossed me the keys to the Ferrari.

"Really?" I looked at him.

"Sure."

I put the bag in my coat pocket as I left the room. I could feel my father's gaze searching me up and down.

I zoomed down Nick's street. He was waiting on the sidewalk. His jaw dropped when I rolled down my window.

"So fucking sick," he said as he opened the car door.

"My father's letting me use it for the night."

He got in the car and looked around, amused, touching the leather, the window, the roof. I laughed. He was like a kid in a candy shop for the first time. Such an amateur.

"Man, I thought your whip was sick. This is even cooler—no offense."

I shook my head. "None taken." But I had to admit, my car was pretty fucking awesome. It was a matte black Audi A8 with all black interior and custom rims. My family didn't come from that old money shit; I didn't grow up with all of these materialistic things. It was new money—money that was a result of a lot of dealing and shady shit. It came from taking risks and bent morals. This kind of money stemmed from the desire to have what we never did—and damn, did we have it all now.

"You ready to fucking dominate tonight?" he said.

"Hell, yeah. Look what I got." I pulled out another bag of cocaine from my pocket—my own personal stash.

"Oh shit!" Nick choked. "So dope!"

"So not dope," I said, laughing at my own pun.

Nick looked at me, clueless, his eyes empty.

I poured it onto the dashboard and hit a bump. I poured some more for Nick. He did the same.

"Now we're ready," I said.

We drove off.

The dance was lit. I mean, maybe I was just tipsy enough to enjoy it. I grabbed Annie by the waist from behind. She turned to face me, grinding on me from the front. She squatted down to the floor, circling her hips around. She smoothly made her way back up, gliding on my body. We began to kiss. She tasted like pot.

"Where's your date?" I asked in between kisses.

"Don't know."

And knowing her, she didn't give a shit either.

I let the music take me for a moment. Somewhere else. I closed my eyes, and suddenly I wasn't me, and I wasn't at the homecoming dance for Laguna Tides High School. I was elevated somewhere greater than this. I was digging on the dramatic minor chord progression. Super tight beat. I didn't know why my mind understood music the way that it did. But it did. It still does. I can recognize notes and chords and all that shit without even thinking. It's like second nature.

"Let's go to your car," she whispered in my ear, interrupting that melodic high and bringing me back to reality.

Before I could answer, I felt my phone vibrating.

"One sec." I reached into my pocket.

Ryan: Can u still meet up?
Ryan: Jason n I wanna buy
Brock: Yeah. Where you at?
Ryan: Drinks. . . .

"Be right back." I released Annie.

"Where you going?"

"Deal." When I said Annie's family and mine were "friends," I meant more like business colleagues.

She nodded her head and kept on dancing as I walked toward the beverage table where Ryan Decker was waiting with Jason Wells. They were regulars. I didn't know much about them except that they loved cocaine—and Jason was on the football team. Ryan looked anxious. Like super fidgety. Jason, on the other hand, already looked stoned. He was talking to some chick, totally distracted.

"Hey," Ryan said.

"Yo," I said.

He slipped a hundred-dollar bill onto the table. I grabbed it and replaced it with a small red mint tin, which contained a plastic bag full of coke. I only used the mint containers when it was a school deal going down. Otherwise, it didn't matter.

He nodded in thanks and walked off. I had more game than

I thought—three grams sold at the dance alone. That meant only seven to go.

I returned to Annie. She was dancing with someone I assumed was her date.

I turned around to find Nick trying to grind on some chick. She looked at him and rolled her eyes, crossing her arms as she scurried away with her friend.

"What?" he yelled to her over the music. It was a dope beat, but DJ Overdose never ceased to impress me. He was kind of one of my biggest inspirations.

Nick threw his arms up in the air. Some people have *it*, others don't. He was one of those others.

I walked up to him, pulling a flask from my coat. I took a quick chug, then offered some to him. He pounded it down.

"Wanna dip?" he said, exhaling a belch. I took the flask back.

"Duke is meeting us here. Let's wait for him."

Duke was my homie from LA—well, more like brother. My fuckin' ride or die.

Brock: U still coming??
Duke: Hell yeeeee . . . omw

He was going to shit when he saw the 'Rari. One time he and I jacked it for the night without my dad knowing and took it for a helluva joy ride through LA. But we got pulled over by a cop, and he called my parents for being out past legal curfew. If the cop had only known what my parents did for a living.

Anyway, my dad kicked my ass 1. For taking the car and 2. For getting pulled over in a car that was basically a dispensary on wheels. But he definitely didn't care about the curfew.

KENDRA

I stood between Ashleigh and Ashton—third wheeling as usual—as my dad and Harry snapped photos of us in our homecoming attire. For once I'd actually rather be third wheeling if it meant I didn't have to go with Jason. He'd approached me after the game last night to try and convince me again to be his date to the dance. His persistence was becoming annoying. At the same time, I felt bad for always turning him down . . . but not bad enough.

Anyway, the night I was dreading was finally here—and I was running very late. Honestly, I'll admit, it was my fault. I'd stalled as long as I could in hopes that Ashleigh and Ashton would maybe get in a fight that would prevent us from going. Or something of that nature.

"Come on! Bigger smiles!" Harry shrieked as the flash on his camera blinded us. I'm sure he captured my awkward face mid-blink as usual.

"Aw, you guys!" he said, pulling the camera away from his face to look at us. "Okay, okay, okay, for this one I want Ashleigh to—no, Kendra, stay where you are—Ashleigh, I want you back-to-back with Ashton. Okay, now face left—no, other left. Yes, yes! Don't move. Now, guns up!"

The camera flashed as we stood there like wannabe Charlie's

Angels, our suppressed giggles ruining the fierceness of the photo. Skittles barked in agreement at our ridiculous poses.

"You guys better get going," my dad advised as he looked down at his watch.

We all left through the front door. My mouth ached from smiling so much.

I paused to hug my dad and Harry goodbye.

"You look great, Ken," my dad said. I looked down at my dark green dress that sparkled against the light. It was a mermaid-style gown and, honestly, I loved it—despite the fact that it was for this hyped-up dance.

"All thanks to your designing skills, Dad."

Harry coughed, hinting for me to add, "And your hairdressing skills, Harry."

He smiled with satisfaction.

"You really do look gorge, Ken," Harry agreed.

We all climbed into Ashton's car. His dad let him borrow his Mercedes for the night.

"Bye, sweetheart!" my dad yelled.

"Please be careful!" Harry chimed in, sniffling.

We drove off. Ashleigh turned up the music. She started dancing all over the passenger seat, belting out lyrics in sync with the radio. She held out her hand with a clenched fist in front of Ashton's mouth. He sang into her fist as if it was a microphone. I couldn't help but laugh.

We pulled up to school, limos lined up in front of the entrance. Ashleigh turned down the volume.

"Woo! Party time!"

Ashton laughed.

We walked into the lavishly decorated auditorium.

"This is tight," Ashton said.

"Let's dance!" Ashleigh yanked Ashton and me out onto the dance floor. Ashleigh twirled me around as Ashton danced around us. My body stiffened right up, and I could feel sweat forming above my lip. I stood frozen in the center of Ashleigh and Ashton.

"Come on, Ken! Dance!" Ashleigh laughed at me.

I looked around; people were bouncing around and clapping and grinding provocatively all over each other. I clapped my hands together, laughing at my uncoordinated self, trying to get out of my head and just enjoy the moment.

I started to get claustrophobic in between all the people. The room felt hot, and my nerves began to kick in. Ugh.

It is what it is, I said to myself. I quickly started to focus on my breathing, blocking out the thought of how squished I felt. Concentrating on it would make me nervous, and I'd potentially forget how to breathe—which would be super embarrassing in the middle of this dance. Mostly because no one who has never dealt with anxiety would understand. That was really the worst part. They would just think I was crazy. Thankfully, I got ahold of myself before it accelerated.

A freshman girl slithered past Ashton, sliding against his body to get through the crowd. She smiled at him as she passed through. Ashleigh froze up mid-twerk.

"What the fuck, Ashton?" Ashleigh scolded.

"What did I do?"

"Are you joking? Grinding all up on that freshman slut!"

"*You're* joking, right? Like, I'm supposed to be laughing."

"Does it sound like I'm joking?" Ashleigh pouted off, Ashton chasing after her.

That was my perfect escape from the center of the dance floor. I made my way over to the beverage table. My friend Ella, even taller than her normal five-foot-nine self, due to her six-inch pumps, stood there talking to an unfamiliar boy.

"Hey, Ella."

"Hey, Ken! Cute dress!"

"Shpanks, girly. I like yours too."

"Thanks. It's couture," she noted, twirling in a circle. Ella looked like a high fashion runway model at all times, whether she was at a school dance or in the biology lab. She took a sip of whatever was in her red cup and then suggested, "Let's take a picture!"

She whipped out her phone and snapped a photo of us.

"Damn! It turned out blurry," she said as she zoomed in on it.

"Want me to take it for you?" the unfamiliar boy asked.

"Yes, please."

Ella handed him her phone.

"Oh, Ken, this is Brock."

Brock. I looked at him more in depth and realized he was the guy from the football game. How embarrassing, I hoped he hadn't remembered. I'd been mid-anxiety attack when he'd confronted me the day before. That was a part of myself I never wanted anyone to see. The anxiety. The vulnerability. The football game had been awful. I got so overheated and claustrophobic in those bleachers, I thought I was going to pass out. My heart rate started to pick up, which made me even more nervous because I was somewhat of a hypochondriac. So, I thought I was having a heart attack or something and ran right out of there at halftime.

"I think we met last night," he said, confirming my concern. My body tingled.

He smiled at me, taking the phone in hand. I observed him, forgetting what was going on in that moment, as if I was in some sort of slow-motion scene in a movie. His eyes gazed into my own and it was like, even though it was basically the first time, it didn't feel like it. I felt like a crazy person for what I was feeling for a complete stranger. Then I looked at his lips and the way he half smiled, the corners of his mouth lifted just slightly. My heart rate sped up, and my face began to sweat, which freaked me out because I didn't want my makeup to get ruined. The camera's flash blurred my vision, bringing me back to reality.

"Here you go." Brock handed Ella her phone without taking his gaze away from mine. No one had ever stared at me like that before. I had to look down. It was intimidating.

"Here, let me take one of you two!" Ella chirped.

Brock and I stood close together and he put his arm around me. My stomach fluttered.

"Okay, ready? One, two, three. Say penis!"

Brock and I both laughed as the camera flashed brightly. I could feel his hand squeeze my waist. He smelled like ocean and some sort of expensive cologne. I liked it.

I took a step back, studying him over again as he removed his hand. He smirked. It was weird—meeting Brock was like re-meeting someone I'd known before. Like we had this instant connection—or at least *I* felt connected to *him*. This sounds stupid, but have you ever been drawn to someone that you know nothing about? That's what I felt with one look at Brock.

A strong grip grasped onto my shoulder, making me jump. I turned around.

"Hey, sexy," Jason whispered in my ear. He reeked of alcohol.

I forced a smile. I felt my body turning hot and flushed.

"Do you guys mind if I steal her for a little bit?"

"Go right ahead," Ella replied. I kind of hated her.

I hesitantly took Jason's hand as he led us over to the dance floor. I looked back. Brock was staring, laughing as Ella stood by his side flipping me off.

"Lucky bitch!" she mouthed to me. She, like the rest of the teenage female population, was obsessed with Jason. But no one topped Taylor's craze over him. She may or may not have been the one responsible for jacking his jersey last year from the boys' locker room. She created a cult following in the downstairs girls' bathroom—that no one used—with a shrine including the jersey and an arrangement of photos that all of Jason's "fangirls" had collected over the years.

A slow song came on. Jason placed his hands at my waist, my arms around his neck. I could feel my shoulders tensed up to my ears. I gently relaxed them. But they worked their way back up as the song continued.

"You really do look beautiful," Jason said.

"Thanks, Jason."

He began to ramble on about something. I wasn't really paying attention. I searched the auditorium, looking to catch sight of Brock.

"Ken? Did you hear me?"

"Uh, yeah, sure."

"So you want to ditch this shithole and go somewhere?"

His alcohol-coated breath became warmer on my neck as he leaned in to kiss me. I placed my hand on his chest, pressing him away.

"Jason, you're a nice guy and all, but you and I—we're just friends."

"Yeah, yeah. No, of course."

He stepped back, releasing me. I walked back to Ashleigh and Ashton, who were now making out in the middle of the dance floor.

"Sorry to interrupt," I said.

They both turned to me, still glued together by their hip bones.

"How's your boyfriend Jason doing?" Ashton teased.

He laughed at his own joke. I nudged him.

"He's not my boyfriend."

"Hannah is throwing a huge party after the dance. You down?" Ashleigh asked.

I took a look at my phone to take note of the time. I had practice early in the morning. I mean, Coach wasn't going to be there. It was just me practicing on my own, but still. My commitment to this was everything.

"I should—"

"Ken, seriously, an hour of fun won't kill you. I promise."

I sighed.

"All right, why not?"

Before I knew it, the three of us were following the blaring music into Hannah's backyard. I was dreading every second of it and wondered why I'd agreed in the first place. Although, I wondered about Brock; would he be at the party? I wished Jason hadn't pulled me away at the dance.

We walked through the gate; people were stripping down to nothing and jumping into the pool, beer pong tournaments were set up on the basketball court, and people were making out everywhere. It was definitely out of my comfort zone, to say the least. I stood there and kept to myself, unsure of where to sit or even stand, really. I knew why people had to get completely blackout drunk to enjoy these things. Otherwise, what did you do besides stand around and look awkwardly for someone to talk to? Or maybe that was just me.

I felt a hand touch my waist. I jerked around to find Ryan standing behind me with two of his burnout friends.

"What up, Ken?"

He pulled me into him.

"You smell like weed, Ryan," I said, pushing him away in disgust.

"Oh, c'mon! Don't act like you've never tried it."

I walked away. I hadn't tried it—and I never planned to. All it took was one time for my brother, and he was hooked. He spent two years of his life chasing the next high and the next . . . until the high took him.

I took a breath, calming the chaos of my mind. *Inhale. Exhale.*

A loud, shattering crash drew my attention around the corner. A broken beer bottle lay at Ashton's feet. He and Ashleigh were at it again.

"I'm so sick of your BS, Ashton!" I overheard Ashleigh say.

"What do you want from me?" Ashton answered.

"Stop flirting with other girls or I'm done—for good."

"Calm down, Ashleigh! Who did I flirt with?"

"That foreign exchange student from Italy—Gina."

"What? No, I didn't. Ashleigh, honestly, you're psycho!"

"Wow, thanks a lot."

They continued to argue. I couldn't even keep track about what anymore.

A voice startled me. "They do that a lot, huh?"

I turned around to find Brock standing there in between two other boys—one taller who wore a hat that didn't seem to match his nice shirt and slacks, and the other, Brock's height with almond-shaped eyes.

I laughed as I felt my face turn flush again, embarrassed at my own awkwardness. Brock's shaggy brown hair was messier than when I'd seen him earlier. It was super cute. He brushed his hand through it, that same half grin painted on his face. His nonchalant composure appeared effortless.

"Yeah, they do." *Really? That's all you can say, Ken?* I thought to myself. Why did I have to be so uncool? Couldn't I be flirty and outgoing like all the other girls?

Jason stumbled toward us, a beer stain on his shirt, his face sweaty.

"Hey, Ken."

He offered me a beer.

"No thanks," I kindly declined.

"Jason! Come on, we're up at BP," Ryan called after him.

"All right. I'm coming," he slurred.

He turned back to me.

"See you later, babe."

He planted a sloppy kiss right on my cheek before proceeding to beer pong. I wiped the wetness off of my face.

"By the way, great shit, Brock!" he yelled to him as he approached the game with Ryan.

Brock nodded his head at him. I wondered what he was talking about.

"That your boyfriend?" Brock asked, followed by a strong sniffle. He rubbed his nose aggressively.

"Oh—nononoooo!" I talked fast when I was nervous. It was a bad habit of mine.

"You sure? He was all over you at the dance."

"Yeah, no. He's just a friend."

"Dude, she's way too cute for him," his taller friend interjected. He winked at me—or maybe it was a twitch, I wasn't sure. But his smile was warm and inviting. "I'm Duke, by the way."

He stuck out his hand for me to shake in a gentlemanly manner. I smiled at him, shaking it.

"I think he likes you," Brock said.

"Who?" I questioned.

"Jason."

"He's a womanizer."

"I don't know about that."

"He's not my type."

"What is your type exactly?"

"Yes, what is your type exactly?" Brock's other friend, the one with the almond eyes, chimed in as he slung his arm around me. He carried a slight accent of some sort. Maybe from New York or Chicago or somewhere like that.

"Oh, this is Ken, Ken this is Nick. But you can call him CB."

"CB?" I questioned.

"Cock block."

"Oh!"

I felt bad for laughing at Nick—but Brock's delivery made it inevitable. Brock joined in with a chuckle as Nick's face remained vacant of any emotion.

"By the way, Ken is just a nickname."

"I figured it had to be short for something. Ken is too much of a dude name."

"Yeah, I get that a lot. It's short for Kendra."

"That's a pretty name."

Why did he have to keep making me blush? I felt it come on every time he complimented me. I didn't want him to see me turn into a cherry red tomato, so I just kept looking down at my dress as if I was picking a piece of fuzz off of it or flattening it down.

"Shpanks."

"Shpanks? Shpelcome."

He totally thought I was weird. I could sense it. I had to change the subject fast.

"SohowcomeIhaveneverseeneitherofyouaroundschoolbefore?" I felt the quickened pace of my words, speaking so fast it felt like it all came out as one long gush of some foreign language.

"What was that?" Brock asked, his grin overflowing into a short chuckle.

I took a breath before speaking, reminding myself to consciously slow down as I spoke.

"So how come I've never seen any of you around school before?" It was the first thing that came to mind.

"Oh. I'm from LA, and my friend Nicholas here just moved from the East Coast—"

"And I go to The School of Hard Knocks." Duke spoke for himself. I wasn't sure what that meant, but Brock laughed at it, so I assumed it was a joke.

I nodded my head, trying to think of what to say next. The milliseconds of silence felt like hours. Duke's phone rang, forcing him to excuse himself from the small circle we had formed in the corner of the yard.

"I love this song!" I blurted out, unsure of what was even playing. It was some sort of EDM raver type of song. But the beat was surprisingly catchy. Maybe I did like it.

At the same time, I noticed the tattoo on Brock's forearm. It was black-and-white piano keys that evolved into a heartbeat.

"Yeah, it's gotta sick beat," Brock agreed. "DJ Overdose is my shit. He knows how to combine real instruments and beats like a total EDM god."

DJ Overdose? I felt my skin crawl at the word . . . *overdose*.

I saw Brock's eyes wander around the yard, as if he was searching for someone. I opened my mouth to ask him—

"I'll be right back," he said before I had the chance to speak. He walked off.

"So," Nick said. He inched his way closer to me. "I like your shoes."

I was half-confused with what he was saying and half-preoccupied spying on Brock, across the yard, talking to Annie Hamrocks. I didn't know her that well, but she was on the soccer team. Did that mean he was into athletic chicks? If so, then I might have stood a chance of crossing his mind now and again. But my mind explored a hundred different scenarios in which I wasn't his type.

"What are they talking about?" I asked Nick.

"How am I supposed to know?"

I checked my phone for the time. I hadn't realized how late it was.

"I have to go," I said.

"What? It's, like, only eleven."

"I have practice early."

"Oh, gotcha—"

"Could you, um—could you tell Brock I said goodbye?"

"Uh, yeah. Sure."

"Thanks. See you later!"

I began to walk away to find Ashleigh and Ashton.

"Nice to meet you, too."

I turned back around to face Nick.

"Huh?"

"Nice to meet you."

Nick stuck out his hand for me to shake.

"Oh, nice to meet you too."

I shook his hand, but he wouldn't let go.

"Nice to meet you."

I laughed nervously, unsure of how to respond. I pulled my hand back.

"You too. Bye, Nick."

Nick was quite the character. He might have been more gracelessly weirder than myself—something I didn't know was possible.

I spotted Ashton and Ashleigh making out on one of the lounge chairs by the pool. I walked over to them, wishing I could have unseen the number of times I'd seen them mauling each other in public tonight.

"You ready to go, Ken?" Ashton asked when he noticed my presence.

"Yeah, if you guys don't mind."

Ashton lifted tiny Ashleigh off of him. They both stood up, Ashleigh flattening down her dress that had risen up a significant amount since I'd seen them fighting.

We headed for the back gate that we had entered through. I took one last look at Brock, who was still talking—or flirting or something—with Annie.

"You coming, Ken?" Ashleigh said, already at the car.

"Yeah, sorry," I said, catching up to them.

BROCK

"Here," I said to Annie. I handed her a few bags of the cocaine my father had given me earlier. I didn't bother sticking it in an Altoids tin. We all had our thing—mine was the Altoids tins, while Annie stuck hers in those old-school Hubba Bubba Bubble Tape packages. She took them without any hesitation, quickly slipping them into her pocket.

"Thanks again," I said.

"Thirty percent."

"Excuse me?"

"You want my help or not?"

I let out a sigh of frustration. There went any commission I was going to make. Annie smiled, pressing her body against mine. She began to whisper in my ear, "I want to suck your . . ."

It was always the same shit. I turned around, not paying attention to what she was saying anymore. She had pissed me off about the 30 percent.

I looked around the yard. Kendra was gone. I pictured her face. She kind of looked like this chick I'd hooked up with in Rocky Point two spring breaks ago. Something about her eyes—but Kendra was softer looking. And she was curvier too—in all the right places. It made her appear more mature compared to the other girls. I wasn't biased in terms of blondes or brunettes, even redheads, but Kendra was the kind of pretty that made me say I was into brunettes.

"Who are you looking for?" Annie interrupted my train of thought.

"No one."

I spotted Duke and Nick on the patio, smoking hookah, and went over to join them.

"What up, man?" I said, taking a seat next to Nick.

"Not much."

"Where'd Kendra go?" She was a super chill girl. I was kind of bummed when I saw she wasn't around—and that never really happened.

"She had to leave."

Nick passed me the hookah hose.

"Why?"

"She had some kind of practice early in the morning."

"Huh. I wonder what kind of practice."

"She was a cutie for sure, dude," Duke added.

I nodded my head, agreeing. She was definitely hot. But definitely stiff or tensed up or something.

"You should hit that," Duke said.

"Nah, man. I don't know if I'm tryn'a get caught up with anyone."

Duke and I went way back, for real. Damn, did I miss those days. Rolling around with the squad, just enjoying life, smoking, crashing parties. My friends in the OC were cool too, but they lacked some real-life experiences that my homies in LA had. There was no way my buddies here could handle an LA party. Maybe Nick, but I wasn't even sure about him.

Duke was always raiding dances and hitting up after-parties because he didn't exactly have a normal high school experience. He was fucked up—like the rest of us. His dad was an alcoholic who murdered his mom. Duke witnessed the whole thing. After that, he dropped out of school and took off. He started dealing, eventually making enough bank to live a life of luxury on his own out in LA.

But he had this thing about treating women right, I think because of the way he watched his mother get abused for the majority of his childhood. He always fed me the same lecture: *If you're gonna turn her into dessert, at least take her to dinner.* I didn't really pay attention though, because what did it matter? But there was no denying that the ladies loved him.

I passed Nick the hookah hose and popped open a beer. Annie came over and sat on my lap.

"Where's your date?" I whispered in her ear.

"Oh." She giggled. "He left a while ago."

I was feeling pretty buzzed. Buzzed on coke, buzzed on drinks, buzzed on life, really. Annie wrapped her arms around me and began to kiss my neck.

"Can we go to your car now?" she whispered as she made her way up my ear.

I was still pissed, but whatever.

"Mmhmm."

I chugged the rest of my drink, and then she slid off my lap. We walked to the front of the house where my car was parked. I unlocked it, and she jumped into the back seat, basically already stripped down to nothing. I let her do her thing.

It was kind of quick because I was tired and stoned. As I was buttoning my pants, there was a knock at the window. I looked up. It was Duke, Nick standing behind him.

"What the fuck?" Annie wasn't feeling it.

I rolled down the window.

"Dude, let's go drifting in the 'Rari!"

"Fuck, yeah!"

KENDRA

Coach and I sat on our boards, waiting for a wave to brew. The chilly water sent goose bumps up my spine. It was already Monday, and I was still exhausted from Saturday night.

"So how was homecoming?" he asked.

I yawned.

"Well, I guess that answers that." He laughed.

I giggled. "It was fun."

"Stay out late?"

"Yes—well, late for me."

Coach laughed as he searched for a wave.

"Come on, let's catch this one," he said.

We both paddled against the water.

"Try not to pearl this time either. Ride it out, trust your instincts."

I nodded my head. We stood up onto our boards. Coach bailed as the wave crashed over him. I rode it out until it flattened close to shore. He came riding in a moment later.

"Woo-hoo!" he screamed loud enough for the people in Dana Point to hear.

He took my hand, raising it into the air.

"And the distinguished gold medal goes to Kendra Dimes!" he yelled in a deep, announcer-style voice.

He picked me up and ran around the beach, my body hoisted over his shoulder. I was laughing so hard I couldn't breathe.

"Now that's how you make the USA Surf Team!" Coach set me back down.

"Really?"

"Absolutely," he said. "I see how focused you are right now. Don't let anything distract you."

I smiled, looking out at the ocean—competing in Primes and even becoming a finalist was one thing, but Coach thought I *actually* stood a chance at qualifying for the USA Surf Team too?

I took my gaze up to the sun. Its rays beamed into my eyes, blinding my vision; all I could see was Kyle smiling down at me. My brother could easily have won it all. If only he had seen it that way too. I mean, maybe he did. But drugs ruled his world, so nothing else mattered to him.

I could feel my heart smiling the rest of the day. But I didn't want to get my hopes up too soon about quarterfinals. Hope is a glimpse of sun on a cloudy day—but just a glimpse. Nothing more, nothing less.

There were a lot of talented surfers out there, and Coach's opinion on my abilities was only one opinion. I mean, yes, he was a former professional surfer himself, so his opinion meant *something*, but there was still a lot of practicing to be done before the competition, and I was well aware of that. Being a competitive surfer wasn't as easy as people thought, either. The effort and time alone put into practicing was rigorous, and surfers didn't reap the same benefits as a lot of other athletes. There weren't any college scholarships associated with it, or any pathways to college at all really with surfing. So many young, competitive surfers dedicated their entire lives to the sport, they even chose homeschooling over traditional, and the sad reality was there were only a small percentage of them who would make it.

Qualifying for the USA Surf Team would open up a lot of doors for my future, leading to bigger competitions, sponsorships, and basically a surfing career! And that's all I could ask for. To be paid for doing what I love most.

I walked into the cafeteria, whistling a song I had heard but couldn't remember the name of, my lunch in hand.

Ashleigh came bouncing toward me, snagging the apple from my lunch tray.

"Did you finish the reading for history?" she asked.

"Yeah."

"Can me and Ashton look at your notes?"

"You mean you?" I laughed.

Ashleigh giggled.

"Hey! Blame Ashton, he wouldn't let me leave last night."

"Ashleigh!"

"What? You know I can't multitask."

I blocked out the crude image she decided to establish for me on why her homework was incomplete. I tried to laugh it off. Ashleigh laughed too—but she was actually amused. I wasn't.

I followed her to a table. She took a seat on Ashton's lap as I shuffled through my bag for the history notes.

"Hey, Kendra."

I looked up to find Brock staring at me as I handed my assignment to Ashleigh. .

"Hey." I felt a little taken off guard. I brushed my hair off of my face.

Brock looked over at the paper that Ashleigh was copying.

"Cheater," he said to her. "I approve."

She giggled proudly. "Ken's way smarter than me. Wouldn't

it make more sense for the less skilled person to look at her homework?"

Brock observed her blank worksheet intently.

He leaned into me and whispered, "Didn't we learn about the Trail of Broken Treaties in, like, elementary school?"

I giggled, not wanting to admit how right he was. Jeez, he was cute *and* seemed smart? What was the catch? I was scared to find out.

"Apple?" he offered, tossing the apple to me.

I smiled.

"Thanks," I said, and was about to take a bite into the apple.

"Wait, what are you doing?" Brock stopped me before I could proceed.

"Uh—"

"Are you eating that without yogurt?"

"Yogurt?"

"Here."

Brock snatched the apple out of my hand as he casually whipped out a pocketknife. I stepped back a significant distance from the table.

"Um . . ."

"Oh c'mon. Live a little," he reassured me. I consciously un-furrowed my eyebrows and stepped an inch closer.

Brock stuck out his yogurt-dripping apple for me to take. I took it, somewhat hesitant before taking a small bite.

"Not bad," I said, surprised.

"You, uh—" Brock motioned for me to wipe the side of my lip.

"Oh." I touched the corner of my mouth where I felt a clump of yogurt.

It was official: I was an embarrassment to society—if there had been any doubt beforehand. I felt my body turn hot as I quickly wiped the yogurt away, hoping somehow I could teleport to my room and hide in a ball for the rest of eternity.

"Hey, Kendra. I don't think I have your number," Brock said. Maybe I wasn't as mortifying as I thought, or maybe he just felt bad so that was his way of trying to make me feel better for being a total embarrassment!

He handed me his phone and I typed in my number.

When I handed it back, he said, "I'll text you so you have mine too."

I smiled. What was this? Did he like me? Why would he want my number? I resented my overanalytical thoughts.

"Nick, let's grab a drink," Brock said.

The two of them got up and walked over to the vending machines.

"You totally like him!" Ashleigh said loud enough for everyone to hear.

I bit my lip in an attempt to hold back the smile trying to break through. But there was no containing it. I giggled.

"Maybe a little." Or maybe *a lot*. But Coach said not to let anything distract me, so I'd keep on denying my quickening feelings until I believed it.

"You know he hooked up with Annie on homecoming, right?"

"Seriously?" I thought back to Hannah's party over the weekend.

"Yeah, but you're way prettier, so who cares?"

"I thought she had a date to homecoming?"

"Yeah she did—skankasorous rex. Did you see that huge hickey on her neck?"

"Ew! No!"

"Really? It was hard to miss."

I wondered if Brock gave her that hickey.

"Wait, so are they dating?" I didn't want to come off entirely nosy, but I couldn't help myself.

"She wishes," Ashton butted in. He loved being in the know with all of the latest gossip. When he and Ashleigh weren't fighting, they were probably gossiping.

"Friends with benefits would be the proper term," Ashleigh clarified.

"Got it." I wasn't sure which was worse.

"We're probably gonna go to the movies after Ashton's soccer practice on Friday. You wanna come?" Ashleigh asked.

"Aren't you guys sick of me third wheeling all the time?" I sure was.

"Don't think of it like that. You'd be like more of a spare tire. Ya know? If something happens to me, you have permission to date my boyfriend."

"You are so weird." I wasn't sure what other friend offers her boyfriend up in case of emergency.

"I know. Self-admitted."

"Ugh, I'll come."

"Yay!"

I looked back toward the vending machines and spotted Annie talking to Brock. That hickey *was* huge.

My phone vibrated in my hand.

Brock: Save this # ;)

Friday rolled around quicker than anticipated, and I was feeling overwhelmed this week between school and surfing and avoiding my desire to be antisocial.

I met Ashleigh at the mall after surf practice. She was trying to find Ashton a birthday present.

"I feel like we've been dating for so long, it's like I don't know what to get him anymore. Ya know? Like, I'm out of cute ideas."

"What did you get him last year?"

"A wallet with a picture of us in it."

"Aw. That's really cute."

"I know. That's the problem. The year before I got him a watch with our initials engraved on the back. How do I top that shit?"

"Hmm . . ." I brainstormed ideas. I didn't have much experience with boyfriends, but if I was Ashleigh, I'd get him something funny. Maybe socks with her face on it. I bet Ashton would've cracked up at that.

"What about—"

"Oh my gosh! What about customized condoms?"

"Uh—"

"I think he would really like that. Right?"

"Um, I mean, that wasn't exactly what I was going to say, but hey, you know him better than I do in that respect."

"Let's go home and get researching."

We walked out of the mall to the parking lot.

"His favorite color is green. And—oh my gosh, he loves apple pie. What if we do apple pie flavored?"

"Isn't the flavor more of your preference?"

"Yeah, true. But still, it's the thought, right?"

"Sure."

When we got back to Ashleigh's house, I sat on her bed as she turned on her computer. She continued to ramble on about her bizarre vision of custom-made condoms as I pretended to listen, going through the pictures on my phone when I stumbled upon the picture of Brock and me from homecoming. I smiled as I zoomed in on the photo, staring at his eyes. My heart palpitated. It made me cough. I held my chest as I choked back into real life.

"You okay?"

I looked up at Ashleigh.

"Yeah. Fine." I laughed. "Can you please get ready, though? It takes you, like, two hours to just find an outfit. The movie is at seven."

"Yes, fine. Fine."

Ashleigh rolled out of her bed and started rummaging through her wardrobe.

BROCK

I walked into my father's home office. A pile of Oxys sat on his desk. That was his own drug of choice. He looked up at me before crushing up one of the pills and snorting it off of his desk.

"Want some?" he asked.

"No thanks."

"What's up?" he said as he took to his computer.

"I was wondering if I could talk to you about something."

He kept his gaze on his computer screen.

"Make it quick. I have a conference call in five minutes."

I sat down in the seat opposite of him, already regretting this useless conversation.

"I was wondering if I could have a raise."

He removed his glasses, redirecting his stare toward me.

"A raise?"

"Yeah."

I tapped my foot against the cold, hardwood floor. He looked around the room. His eyebrows were furrowed, a smug half smile smeared on his face. He shook his head.

"For what reason would I give you a raise?"

"Because I've made you fifteen thousand in the past month, and I've gotten maybe a thousand bucks."

"That's not true."

I raised my voice. "Yes, it is."

"Bullshit."

He stared me in the eye. I stared back. It was total fucking shit, and he knew it. My eyes were beginning to well up from not blinking. I gave in, looking down at my phone. I had to be at the movies in twenty minutes.

I stood up from my seat, feeling my father's beaming scowl stuck on me. I walked out of the room. What a waste of time.

I walked into the garage, and my eyes fell upon the Ferrari: his most prized possession. I took my key and scraped it against the driver's side.

"Fucking asshole."

I hopped in my car and drove down the street at full speed. The stop sign became a suggestion sign as I cut off a cop.

"Shit."

I looked in my mirror. He slammed on his brakes, honking at me. He accelerated toward me. If I got pulled over, I would be *fucked*. My car was like a cartel on wheels. I pressed my foot all the way down on the pedal and turned down an alley, swerving into a parking lot that cut through to another main street. I sped off, taking a look behind me. The cop was gone, but I hoped he didn't get my plate.

My dad had put me in a shit mood. I couldn't enjoy the movie. I walked out of the theater with Annie, Nick, and Brody. The film was horrible, but the sex scene with Scarlett Johansson made me seriously hard.

The sky was overcast. The smell of semitruck and rain filled the air. I looked toward the mountains, and they were covered by fog. It was evident that a storm was approaching.

"Hey, guys," Brody said as he adjusted the turban that was wrapped around his head. Brody was Nick's friend. He was kind of effeminate, but he was chill. Brody didn't smoke or do any drugs for that matter, so it was always weird with him around when we were high. His family was Sikh and very religious, which was why he didn't smoke, or so he claimed that was why.

I turned to see who he was talking to. It was Ashton and Ashleigh.

"What up, man?" Ashton nodded at Brody.

I looked toward the ticket booth and smiled. I walked over to an oblivious Kendra, purchasing a ticket. I tapped her on the shoulder.

"Oh—hey!" she said, surprised.

"What movie are you guys seeing?"

"I don't know. Some scary movie Ashton wants to see."

"So, you're into horror flicks?"

"I guess tonight I am."

We both laughed.

"We just saw some weird independent film. Brody is into that stuff."

"You should come watch this with us, so I don't have to be a third wheel."

"I told you, Ken. You're a spare tire," Ashleigh corrected.

"Well, whatever I am." Kendra giggled. I wanted her to laugh again. It was really melodic, the way it started deep and the tone heightened. I wish I could capture it and re-create it as a beat. Did that sound tacky?

"Okay. I'm down." A double feature was fine with me.

I looked over at my crew.

"Guys, I'm ditchin' dinner. I'll hit you up later."

Annie gave me a look. I wasn't sure what it meant. I walked over to her and hugged her goodbye. Before departing, I slipped the bag of coke into Annie's hands as quickly as I could, hopefully without anyone seeing.

"Thanks again for your help," I mumbled.

"Yeah, no fucking problem." She glared at me, obviously pissed.

She took a step back, looking me up and down.

"What?" I mouthed.

She shrugged her shoulders and turned around, proceeding toward her car. I knew there was a catch. There always was.

She was jealous I was hanging out with Kendra instead of her. Whatever. I turned back around; Kendra was still talking to Ashleigh. She caught my gaze, and for the first time in my life, I felt nervous. Like, my stomach felt this fluttering I'd never felt before. It was weird. It felt exciting, but at the same time I felt like a total pussy. I rubbed the back of my neck, looking at her. I half smiled. She smiled back.

"Are we going to see this movie or what?" Ashleigh insisted.

"Let's go," I said, breaking the intense eye contact between me and Kendra.

We all walked into the theater.

We entered the crowded room, most of the seats already filled. The four of us walked up the stairs to the very back row. Ashton and Ashleigh were on top of each other before the lights even dimmed. When the theater finally went dark and the movie began, all I could hear was their slurping and moaning. I normally couldn't give two shits about that kind of stuff, but I actually really wanted to watch the movie. I pulled out my phone.

Brock: Can't hear the movie :/

I pressed *send* and a moment later Kendra's phone vibrated. I saw her smile from the corner of my eye as she typed back.

Kendra: Same

I laughed.

Brock: Wanna ditch?

Kendra turned toward me and quickly nodded.

We walked out of the theater. I threw my drink away as we passed a trash can.

"So glad we're out of there," I said.

"Seriously." Kendra giggled again.

We carried on down the sidewalk, no particular destination in mind. Kendra's gaze was on the concrete. It was the first time I noticed how perfectly sloped her nose was. Was that creepy?

"Now what do we do?"

"We could go for a walk on the beach?" she suggested.

"Sure."

We crossed the street to get to Main Beach.

We strolled along the edge of the sand. It was dark out, except for the moon lighting up the boardwalk.

I wondered what Kendra liked. My chest felt tight as I searched for the right words. I opened my mouth to make small talk—

"So what's the deal with you and Annie?" Kendra asked, disrupting the awkward silence. She spat her words out so quickly it took me a moment to comprehend what she had said.

"Annie? Nada! She's just a friend." With benefits of course, but Kendra didn't need to know that.

I looked at her. She nodded.

"What's the deal with you and Jason? And be up front with me now."

"Jason?" she asked, as if it was strange that I had even brought him up. "I really don't see him as anything more than a friend."

"He likes you."

"No, he likes the idea of getting what he wants only because he hasn't accomplished it yet."

"Nah, he likes you. I couldn't blame him though." I smirked at her.

Her stare found mine, her eyes questioning my words. When she couldn't handle the eye contact any longer, her gaze found the sand below us once again. I could tell I was making her nervous, which enticed me.

She chuckled, shaking her head. "He flirts with anything that has boobs and a pulse."

"He likes you," I insisted.

"All right, whatever you say."

We both kind of laughed.

"So, do you surf?" she asked.

"I do. How about you?"

She smirked, as if I had just asked the dumbest question.

"It's my life. I learned to surf before I learned how to walk."

"That's dope. You compete?"

"I'm actually competing in the Prime circuit right now. Getting ready for quarterfinals."

"Nice! What happens if you win?"

"Well, the goal is to qualify for the USA Surf Team."

"That's awesome. I bet your family is really proud."

"Yeah, my dad and his fiancé haven't missed a single competition."

"What about your mom?"

"Well—"

Her phone rang before she could finish her sentence.

"Sorry, let me just see who this is."

"No worries."

Whoever it was, they made her laugh, which made me smile. I quickly straightened my face, feeling like an emotional man-pussy.

"Ashleigh's wondering where we went. Should I tell her to meet us here?"

I paused for a moment before responding, pondering how we could make this more interesting.

"Wait! Let me see your phone."

I took her phone without a response. I typed quickly and clicked the send button before she could question it, then handed it back.

She looked down at the text.

"You told her we hooked up?"

I nodded.

"What exactly is *hooking up* to you?" she quizzed me, her arms now crossed against her chest.

"Probably not the same as it is to you." I winked.

Ashleigh responded in seconds—as expected.

"What'd she say?"

"She was like, 'What the H-E-double-hockey-stick?'"

I shot her a look, my eyes narrowed searching for an explanation.

"I don't like to cuss," she clarified.

I thought she was joking at first, but when I realized that this girl was really this innocent, I couldn't help but chuckle.

"Hell is a destination, my friend. Not a cuss word."

"Maybe so."

Duke texted me at the same time.

Duke: Dude, party tonight at my place. I got the MOLLY. Gonna be lit, brother.
Brock: Shit, I'm so down. I'm with some homies right now tho
Duke: Bring them

We stood there. My mind drifted back to Kendra's innocence. It kind of made me even more attracted to her—which was weird. At least for me. She had to be a virgin. Could that be? A sixteen-year-old girl this attractive? A virgin? It seemed impossible, but then again, maybe I just hung out with a more experienced crowd.

I knew it would be a bad idea to bring her to LA, at least not tonight. She seemed too stiff for my squad.

Brock: Damn, don't think I'll b able 2 make it 2nite :/ Let's sesh tomorrow. I got some dank kush comin my way.
Duke: Sounds good! Peace

Kendra snagged my shades from my back pocket, trying them on. Her phone rang again.

"They're heading over to the Shake Shack."

I stole my sunglasses back and jogged away.

"Let's go!"

She laughed as she chased after me.

I stopped before we made our way to the front of the building and looked to Kendra.

"To keep this going, we need a plan."

I brushed my hands through her hair, making a mess out of it.

"What was that for?"

"So it looks like we had a good time."

"You creep!"

We both laughed—and for the record, she didn't actually think I was a creep.

"You know you love it, Kendra."

"You know you can call me Ken."

"Yeah, but Kendra is pretty."

"Aw, well, shpanks." She spoke in a nasally tone.

"Shpelcome!" I winked. "Just look very satisfied and here—"

I took her by the hand as we walked to the front where the outside seating was filled with everyone from school, most of them my clients. That kind of sketched me out in public, but I played it cool. They eyed down Kendra and me. I nodded to a group of guys. I smiled at classmates who were whispering as we passed by. Mia and the rest of the soccer team were there. I was sure they'd be telling Annie. Not that I owed her any kind of explanation.

Toward the back, Ashleigh and Ashton were waving us over.

"Hey, movie-ditchers!" Ashleigh teased. "You guys actually hooked up? How far did you go? Did you do it on the beach?"

"Ashleigh, leave them alone!" Ashton shook his head.

"Oh, my gosh." Kendra nervously laughed, hiding her face in her hands.

"I knew you two liked each other."

I changed the subject. "So how was the rest of the movie, guys?"

Ashton and Ashleigh glanced at one another, not hiding their lustful smirks.

"It was, uh—"

"Quite a show!" Ashleigh finished off.

"I'm just thankful that I wasn't stuck with you two by myself this time." Kendra smiled at me.

The two girls got up to go get Ashleigh's order.

"What'd you get?" I asked Kendra when they returned, eyeing her delicious-looking chocolate shake.

"A shake." Her eyes stared into mine as her lips wrapped themselves around the straw. It kind of turned me on.

"I know that, smart ass."

Kendra laughed, handing me the shake. I took a big sip.

"This is bomb!" I couldn't help but suck down a little more.

Kendra stuck her hand out, wanting it back, but I decided to keep it, walking off as we all got up to leave.

"Hey, mister!"

I turned around, Kendra almost running into me, our bodies close enough to feel each other's warmth.

"What's in it for me?" I raised an eyebrow at her before handing her the shake. Her lips parted as if she was about to speak, but she was speechless.

We left the Shake Shack and decided to go kick it at Ashton's place. We all got into his car—even though his license was suspended. He was shit when it came to driving the speed limit. Kendra and I were in the back. I liked hanging out with her. She was cool.

Our fingers brushed up against one another's. I was tempted to hold her hand. But I wanted to play it right. Plus, hand-holding was super relationship-y.

Ashleigh blasted the radio, violently dancing all over the front seat. I leaned into Kendra.

"Those are some interesting moves."

She looked at me and laughed, nudging my arm. It started sprinkling outside, raindrops drizzling down on the windows. I saw a flash of lightning in Ashton's rearview mirror.

"You can be the rain and I'll be the lightning," I whispered in Kendra's ear. She turned to me and smiled. To get the ladies, you have to know the lines. *The* lines. That was part of Nick's problem—he never knew what to say. And when he did, he said it with such little conviction that it came off lame as fuck. Like he was reading lines he must've researched online and rehearsed a hundred times.

The rain. The windshield wipers. The sound of other cars. It all made for a song. I nodded my head to the beat of it, as if I was the only one who could hear the tune.

Kendra traced her finger over her fogged-up window, drawing a heart. I leaned over her, drawing a smiley face inside of the heart. She looked at me. We both smiled.

Annie texted me as we pulled up to Ashton's. I didn't want to open it with the chance of Kendra seeing. Who knew what Annie was going to say. I shoved my phone back in my pocket.

The rain picked up as we hurried into Ashton's house. Kendra's arms were covered in goose bumps.

As we walked inside and up the stairs to his bedroom, we passed by his mom. She seemed like a nice lady the few times I'd met her. Plus, she was a total MILF. My eyes automatically directed themselves to her hard nipples popping through her shirt. Her tits had to be fake. If not, she was a gifted woman. Her husband was blessed.

"Hi, kids."

"Hi, Mom."

"Don't make too much noise. Your dad is asleep."

"We won't."

"Ken, by the way, tell Harold that I called the other day. I need to get into the salon next week before I leave for Dallas."

"Okay! I'll tell him to call you."

I wondered why she didn't just call her hairdresser herself and, better yet, how Kendra knew him.

We followed Ashton upstairs to his bedroom. Ashleigh jumped onto the bed, pulling Ashton next to her. She sucked down the last of their shake. I walked over to Ashton's desk, where an iPod was hooked up to the stereo. I was shuffling through the playlist when Kendra walked over. She tapped the iPod, picking out a random song. I looked up at her and smiled. She smiled back. I grabbed her by the waist, about to pull her in, but my phone interrupted us. *Shit.*

"Sorry, I have to take this. It's my mom."

I walked out of the room into the hallway.

"Hello?" I answered. My mom was lecturing me on the other end on how I should be working and not "lollygagging around."

"Yeah, I can't really talk right now. I'm out with friends," I interrupted, hinting that there were people around.

"Be home by midnight."

"Yeah, I know."

"You have a deal early in the morning."

"Okay. Eight o'clock?"

"Yes. No more of this Friday night bullshit. You have a job to do."

"All right, yeah."

"Midnight."

"I know! Bye!" I was fucking agitated.

I hung up and walked back into the room. She fucking pissed me off. I sat down on the beanbag, my eyes squeezed shut in an attempt to control my anger.

"Everything okay?" Kendra asked. I opened my eyes and looked at her.

"Yeah, sorry about that. You know how it is with crazy mothers."

She slumped into the beanbag beside me, seemingly uncomfortable. I hoped she hadn't overheard too much.

Nick texted me.

"Hey, bro. Can Nick and Brody come over?" I asked Ashton.

"Sure."

I hoped they weren't still with Annie. That would be super awkward with Kendra here. I looked at her.

"I'm so fucking hungry."

"You didn't get enough of my shake?" She laughed.

I smiled.

"Nah. That sounds good though. With, like, some fries or something."

"Oh, my gosh, and a burger," she moaned.

"Damn. Girl with an appetite. I like it."

"Ugh, and with competitions coming up I've been trying to clean up my diet and it. Is. So. Boring."

I heard a door open downstairs.

"Hello?" Nick yelled.

I loudly quieted him down. "Shh."

Nick and Brody entered the room.

"What up, man?" Nick said.

"Where's hickey chicky?" Ashleigh asked. Nick and I looked at each other. I shrugged my shoulders.

"Who?" Nick asked. He was as lost as I was.

"I mean Annie."

"Oh, she went home. She has a soccer game in the morning," Nick told her. He looked at me. "Dude, she was so bitchy after you ditched."

"Yeah. She was acting like a bitch," Brody added.

"Whatever." I didn't give a fuck. Whenever she didn't get her way, she threw a fit. She'd be fine as soon as I texted her back.

"Yo, Brock, you got the stuff?" Nick asked, tapping his finger against his nose.

I reached into my pocket and pulled out the bag of cocaine.

"Not in my room, you guys," Ashton said.

"All right, let's go do it in my car," Nick suggested.

"You comin', man?" I looked at Ashton.

"No. Coach drug tests us randomly."

"Boner kill," Nick snorted.

"Be quiet when you go downstairs. My parents are asleep."

I nodded to Ashton. I looked at Kendra and rubbed her hand before standing up.

"I'll be right back," I reassured her.

Nick and I hurried out of the room. We walked outside to his car. It was dark and wet out.

When we got into the car, I emptied the bag onto his center console and snorted a line. Within five minutes, my heart rate picked up, my insides jittery as if my soul was going to jump right out of my own skin. I felt ready for the night!

KENDRA

I sat next to Brody as he screamed at the television screen, a video game controller in hand. The sound of bullets and explosions filled the room. I had this horrific pit in my gut. I couldn't believe Brock was into such hard drugs. I felt a surge of mixed emotions: anger, sadness, confusion, betrayal. Mostly anger. I didn't know why, either. I had just met him. But it hadn't felt like that.

I looked to Brody. I don't think I'd ever talked to him before, but I was pretty sure we had history together freshman year. He wore thick glasses that seemed a tad crooked. But I would feel too bad pointing that out.

"Have you ever tried drugs?" I asked him, grasping the fact that the only five words I'd spoken to him made quite the first impression.

"Nah, it's against my religion."

Well, jeez, whose religion advised it?

"Good for you."

"Uh-huh," Brody said. He couldn't be bothered though. "No! Shit! Die!" he yelled at the screen.

"Do they do that stuff a lot?" I didn't want to be nosy, but I was curious.

"Kind of."

"Brock didn't seem like the type."

"Oh, he and Aunt Nora go way back."

"Who?"

"Are you serious?" he yelled at the game.

He threw his arms up in the air, surrendering to the aliens who had just attacked the 2D version of himself. He looked at me.

"Come on. You don't know what Aunt Nora is?"

I shook my head, wondering, *Was I supposed to know her?*

Brody responded by tapping his nose. I didn't understand. I looked at him and scratched my temple, my head tilted to the side. I stopped. Cocaine. Brody winked when he saw that I'd picked up on his gesture. At the same time, Brock and Nick reentered the room, panting with laughter. Their clothes were stained with rainwater. Brock sat down by me on the beanbag.

"Sup," he said. He didn't even sound like himself. He put his arm around me. I shrugged it off. I kept my gaze forward, unable to look at him. Not this side of him.

"Come on! What's the problem, Ken?"

"You have powder on your nose."

"Wanna come lick it off?" he said, laughing with Nick. They thought they were *so* funny. I stood up. Grabbed my bag. Left the room, not saying a word to anyone.

What had happened so suddenly? We were having such a great time together, but he had to go ruin it. What a total letdown.

As I rushed down the stairs, I felt as if I was having an out-of-body experience. The night was taking me back in time. The first time I witnessed Kyle do a drug.

I was six years old. It was after we'd gone surfing one evening. His friends were there too—although, they weren't really friends. They were drug friends. There was a difference. One of them—I think his name was Will—handed him this pill. I watched as my brother hesitated. I don't think he really wanted to be a drug addict. Does anyone? He was a good person. He had a big heart and people who loved him. But he was just . . . weak, maybe? I don't know. I never really pinned it down why exactly he chose to ever start doing drugs.

I remember the way he looked at me and smiled.

"It's just medicine, KK," he said. That's what he used to call me. "I have a headache from the sun."

I believed him. I mean, what else was I supposed to think?

He popped the pill, chugging it down with coconut water. I don't know what kind of pill it was, and I didn't think much of it until it had become a problem down the road. The fighting. The tears. All of the problems. In and out of rehabs . . . and his passing.

That was why I hated drugs.

That was why I hated being surrounded by people who did them.

But what I couldn't figure out was why I cared so much about Brock Parker doing them more than anyone else. Maybe he had initially come off differently, and it was a massive disappointment. Or maybe it was something else. I wasn't sure. But I hated the way I felt whenever I pictured him pulling that disgusting bag of white venom from his pocket.

BROCK

"Ken! Wait!" Ashleigh yelled, running out of the room.

"They're just joking, Ken," Ashton said.

I heard her yell to Kendra from the top of the stairs, "Let Ashton drive you!"

"Shh! My parents!" Ashton said.

I faintly heard Kendra reply, "I'm fine. I'll walk."

The front door slammed shut as the thunder roared outside.

Brody paused the video game, the room silent. I think everyone was just as shocked as I was.

Nick asked the obvious question. "What's her deal?"

"Ken does not like drugs—at all," Ashleigh informed us.

"Why?" I couldn't help but ask.

No one had an answer though. Ashleigh eventually shrugged her shoulders.

"No one really knows the deal. We just know it was something bad, maybe with her mom? That's my guess, but I don't really know. Definitely something before I knew her. She's never talked to me about it—and we tell each other almost everything! It's just one of those skeletons in her closet that's kept private."

"Weird . . ."

Kendra's moody behavior was kind of a buzzkill. Wasn't feeling it. Didn't like it. If she had a problem with this shit, we were going to have a problem hanging out. That was fact. It reminded me of why I didn't do relationships—I wasn't the type to be controlled or told what to do.

"We should go smoke some hookah," Ashleigh suggested.

Us guys nodded in agreement, standing up to head outside.

We all walked outside to Ashton's backyard. He had a hookah set up on his back patio, covered from the downpour.

We sat, passing the hose around, except for Brody of course, watching the sky slowly press pause on the rain. Kendra's flat and tightened gaze flashed through my mind. I wanted to know what could possibly make someone hate drugs so much. Brody didn't do them either, but he didn't storm off every time one of us did.

"You guys want some beer?" Ashton asked.

He stood up to head inside.

"No thanks, man," I said.

It was almost midnight. I had to be home soon. Not that I really gave a fuck if my parents got pissed. They'd find something to lecture me about anyway.

"I gotta get going, guys."

"You need a ride?" Nick asked.

"No, it's cool. I can just call a cab." I had to pick up my car from the movies anyway.

"You sure?"

"Yeah. See you guys later."

I walked through the back gate to the front yard. I sat there on the lawn, waiting for my ride, debating whether or not to text Kendra. She was really upset. I decided to just leave it as it was.

The cab dropped me off at my car; the streets were dead compared to earlier. When I pulled up to my house, from the outside, it looked like nobody lived there. I walked inside; everything was pitch black. A light turned on in the hallway. My mom stood there in her pajamas.

"You're late," she said with her arms crossed in front of her chest.

I looked at the clock. It read 12:02. I walked past her to my room, ignoring her stupid comment. She was always looking for a problem.

I felt her eyes on me as I continued to my room. I shut the door. She was a bitch.

My eyes felt heavy—I could barely keep them open. I had no choice but to surrender to the exhaustion as I collapsed onto my bed, still fully dressed, falling asleep within seconds of my head hitting the pillow.

Monday rolled around and, surprisingly, I made it to school— but, obviously, not on time. The whole Kendra thing was still weirding me out. I wanted to know what her deal was. She couldn't still be pissed . . . right? The whole thing was odd, in my opinion.

I walked through the hallway, and I spotted her at her locker. She was talking to Jason, but she looked unengaged—as she always did when he was trying to spit game at her.

She looked my way and our eyes met. We hadn't seen each other since Friday, so this was going to be interesting.

She immediately looked away, avoiding me. Monday was already proving to be . . . well, Monday.

"Do you want to go out this Friday?" I heard Jason ask from a short distance as I approached them.

"Hey," I said, now standing at her locker.

Jason winked at me, walking away as he said, "I'll see you later, Ken."

"See ya."

She kept loading books into her bag, refusing to look me in the eye. I stood there and I wasn't going to budge.

"What happened the other night? Why'd you storm off?" I asked.

"I don't like being around that stuff," she said, still avoiding my gaze.

"By *stuff*, you mean drugs, correct?" I tested her a little bit. I couldn't help it.

She nodded.

"May I ask what caused such a loathing toward these—"

"If we're going to be friends, you can't do that around me, Brock." She cut me off, finally looking at me.

"Kendra, it was just a bump—"

"It doesn't matter."

I nodded my head, trying to understand as if we had compromised some sort of silent but understood agreement.

"Look, can I make it up to you this weekend?"

"Actually, my birthday is this weekend," she said.

She pulled out an invitation from her bag. I watched as she tapped it against her palm. She was hesitant, it seemed.

"See you there?" she asked, lifting an eyebrow.

I smiled at her, walking off to class, leaving her wondering.

I knew she was watching too. I knew how this worked. The game. I invented it. I took a quick glimpse back when I assumed she wasn't looking, but she turned and caught me staring. We watched each other for a moment, until Mia, one of Annie's annoying friends, opened the door to her class and it hit Kendra right in the face.

"Ow!" She held her head, her attention now redirected.

"Shit, sorry, Ken," I heard Mia say. Mia was such a dumbass. I'd hung out with her once while with Annie. During the span of the two hours we were together, she'd asked if Twizzlers grew on trees and if Hawaii was its own continent—and she was serious!

"You all right?" I yelled down the hall.

She looked back at me and laughed. "You didn't see that." She hurried into class. I shook my head and laughed. Kendra was really something.

Usually the weekends felt like a break, but this weekend was comprised of too many bullshit deals to feel relaxing.

Don't get me wrong, I loved the money. But sometimes I just hated dealing with people, especially the morons you encounter in this business.

I stood at my kitchen island, waiting for the espresso machine to turn on. A random number texted me.

949-555-9080: Can u hook me up wit sum candy?
Brock: Sure. How'd you get my #??
949-555-9080: Duke. Told me u could help me out.
Brock: Oh cool. Yeah, what time you want to meet?
949-555-9080: Around 8?

Shit, that was the same time as Kendra's party. That was okay; I could run and get the deal done and then hustle over to Kendra's. I was low on cash.

Brock: Sounds good.

I headed back to my room, a small cup of espresso in hand. I took a sip before setting it down on my desk. I grabbed my old bass that hung on the wall. It was probably my most prized possession, a '63 Gibson Thunderbird.

I strummed a few chords as I gazed out my bedroom window. I looked past the rooftops and down at the ocean. Damn. Made me want to smoke a bowl.

I hung my bass back up and opened up the window, letting in a crisp breeze. I opened up my nightstand drawer and pulled out a fresh bag of Mary J, opening the bag to take a whiff.

I lit up as I lay on my bed, gazing out at the ocean. I hadn't changed out of my sweats all day—and I wished I didn't have to.

I wondered how it could get any better than this—until the alarm on my phone went off, interrupting the chilled-out vibes.

"Shit."

I shut my window and grabbed my keys—and Kendra's gift—before heading downstairs.

"Where are you going?" my mom asked as I neared the door.

"I've got a deal. Gotta be there by eight."

"Okay, good. No going out after."

"Got it," I lied.

I snuck Kendra's gift under my jacket. I'd had it since she invited me on Monday. I walked outside to my car and threw the gift in the passenger seat, speeding off and not-accidentally knocking the trash can over at the end of the driveway.

I pulled up to the parking lot of this abandoned building where a grocery store used to be, right between Laguna Beach and Laguna Niguel.

A few minutes passed. He was late. I was getting nervous and began to question if this was a setup.

I usually wasn't skeptical if they were a referral from Duke, but these kinds of guys were never late because they knew there could be consequences if we lingered too long in these abandoned areas. I knew this one dude back in LA who was waiting for his client for a half hour, but next thing he knew a swarm of cops had pulled up. He's in jail now for the next twenty-five years. Basically, everything could go wrong if a client was late.

As I was about to text Duke to see if he knew anything, a truck pulled up a few feet away from me. I got out of my car and walked over to the driver's side of the truck, my hand resting on my back pocket just in case—I always kept my pocket knife in there.

The tinted window slowly rolled down, smoke emerging from inside. A large man sat in the driver's seat. He had tattoos all the way up his neck.

"Yo! You got my shit?" he asked.

"You got my money?" I shot back. Experience taught me the greatest lessons when learning how to handle these guys—and knowing how to handle them was key.

He pulled out a large stack of bills, handing them over to me. I began to count, making sure it was all there.

"It's all there. Just give me my shit, kid!"

I ignored him, finishing the count. I reached into my pocket for the bag when out of nowhere, from a distance, sirens began to sound.

"Shit!" he said, quickly shifting into drive. He flew out of the lot.

I sprinted to my car, taking off as fast as I could, my hand shaking on the steering wheel. I sped out of the parking lot and drove off, rushing as far away as possible from the area. I pulled down an alley and turned off my car, waiting until the sound of the sirens died down entirely. I hadn't realized that I was forgetting to breathe. I took a deep breath.

Damn, that could've ended badly.

I still had the drugs, though—at least I ended up with the cash. I collected the money that had scattered throughout the car, still overwhelmed. When I piled it all together, I stuck it in the center console. It felt good for a moment to just be alone in silence.

Shit. I'd totally forgotten about Kendra. I grabbed my phone.

KENDRA

I watched as the sun set low beneath the hills. I looked at my phone. Still no messages from Brock—and at this point, I wasn't expecting a message, either. He was totally bailing on me, and that was that.

Ashleigh caught me looking at my phone. "Haven't heard from him?"

How could I be so naive to think he would show up? "Who?"

"Oh, come on. I saw you hand him the invitation."

I bit my lip, unable to hold back a smile.

I looked around me. Music filled the backyard. Harry had gone all out on the decorations; the trees were covered in white Christmas lights, and balloons were tied all over the chairs. Paper lanterns hung from the tree house, where a huge banner had my name written in block letters.

My friends sat around the firepit, sipping on hot chocolate, while Ashleigh and I stood in the corner, gossiping about the people I was forced to invite out of guilt.

"Literally, who would even think of wearing Ed Hardy anymore?" Ashleigh whispered to me loud enough for Natalie Smith to hear as she refilled her cup of hot chocolate.

"Shh—she totally just looked at you when you said that."

"Good. Maybe she'll take a hint."

I giggled out of obligation and loyalty to my best friend.

I set my phone down on the patio table. It was time to stop worrying about whether he was coming or not and enjoy the night. I danced around the grass with Ashleigh. Ashton jumped in the middle of us, showcasing his incoordination. Ashleigh and I burst out into unbreathable laughs, tears streaming down our faces. Everyone got up and joined in. We sang at the top of our lungs. Surprisingly, none of the neighbors called the police about the noise.

Jason walked through the back gate with a big bouquet of flowers.

"Happy birthday, Ken," he said. His eyes were red and glazed over, but I appreciated the thought.

"Thank you, Jason."

I hugged him . . . and when I did, all I could think was *Why can't he be Brock?* But I felt bad for thinking that—when he was kind enough to even show up with flowers for me—and quickly blocked out the thought.

I walked into the house with the bouquet, Harry following me.

"Why don't you go out with him, Ken?" Harry whispered in my ear as I searched the kitchen for a vase.

"I just don't see him like that. He's a good friend."

"He's the star quarterback for God's sake!"

"Yeah. He's just not for me."

"You're too picky."

"Probably," I agreed.

I found a vase in the cupboard for the flowers, filled it with water, and set it on the kitchen island.

I walked back outside to Taylor doing backflips on the grass. I walked up to Ashleigh, who stood at Ashton's side while the rest of the party gathered around Taylor.

"Does she need that much attention?" Ashleigh said.

"She's just really into her cheerleading."

"Yeah, no shit. We all know it's because she used to be a total FFP back in middle school, and cheer got her in shape."

"A what?"

"Former fat person."

I laughed. I mean, it was true; Taylor had been a little bit on the hefty side back in middle school. But it was just baby fat.

My dad and Harry walked outside with my birthday cake Harry'd baked himself. Everyone began to sing "Happy Birthday" as they held the cake in front of me. I smiled, looking around me at my family and friends.

"Make a wish, Ken!" Harry said.

I closed my eyes and blew out the candles. Skittles barked, wanting in on the action. I picked her up as everyone clapped.

With quarterfinals so close, Coach had me on a strict meal plan: no sugar, empty calories, simple carbs, blah, blah, blah. But wasn't skipping out on your own birthday cake bad luck or something? I swore I'd heard that before. I couldn't resist a small piece.

As I took that first bite, guilt sunk in. I wanted to win so badly. I couldn't let anything or anyone get in my way. If it meant missing out on birthday cake, so be it. I tossed the slice of cake in the trash can.

I'd do just about anything to take home that trophy. For my brother more than anyone else. He'd been training for Primes before he died. It was weird to think that the last birthday of mine that Kyle was at was exactly ten years ago, and today I was turning the age he was when he died. Was he ready to go? Seventeen was so young when you were actually faced with it. When I was seven, he seemed so old. Now I realize, he had a whole life ahead of him, taken from him. I remember he took me surfing that morning. Getting to surf with him—it was always so intimidating. I'd fallen off my board, and a wave had rolled me to shore. I was so embarrassed in front of him. I started crying, but he followed after me and said, "Are you seriously going to let a little fall get the best of you? I don't think so."

That day, I would have never thought I didn't have even another month with him before he was gone for good. It always seems so impossible to lose someone you love until they're actually gone. And all you're left with are memories and reminiscing scents that occasionally cast themselves through the air. Like coconut sunscreen and chlorine.

I sometimes wondered what it would be like if he was still around. Would my mom be around too? What would my seventeenth birthday be with both of them there? Would I even live in Laguna? Would I know Ashleigh? Would I have met Brock? How would I feel about Brock when he walked inside with cocaine on his nose if my brother had never died from an overdose? I stopped guessing about the *what-ifs* as I sat down on a lounge chair by the pool with Ashleigh and Ashton.

"How done are you right now?" Ashleigh asked as she fed Ashton a piece of cake.

"So done," I said, my laugh evolving into a yawn. I hadn't realized how late it was until I looked at my phone—almost eleven. It was way past my old-lady bedtime.

"I gotta go, Ken," Hunter said, approaching the three of us. "Thanks for having me!"

"Thank *you*!" I said as I stood up. "I'll walk you out."

I said goodbye to each person individually as they departed. Ashleigh and Ashton stuck around to help me pick up the yard, littered with cups and paper plates, popped balloons and confetti.

I shut the door behind them when they made their way out, letting out a sigh of relief with recognition that I may have forgotten to breathe in between all of those goodbyes.

I said goodnight to my parents and headed up to my room. I collapsed onto my bed with Skittles, petting her.

"Well, Skittles, I'm officially seventeen years old."

She licked my nose.

Skittles and I had these conversations sometimes. She was the only one who would listen to me without interrupting. Just listened.

My phone vibrated. My heart fell when I saw the name Brock flash on the screen. I rolled over onto my stomach as I read the text.

Brock: I have a belated bday surprise for u, look outside.

I walked over to my balcony, looking down to find Brock standing in my yard, a bag in hand.

"What are you doing here?" I asked, annoyed (but I was totally melting inside . . . like, melting in a good way).

"I like to be fashionably late."

"Well, you're *too* late. If my parents see that you're out here—"

"Who says they have to know? Now, can I come up there, or are you going to come to me?" He smiled that confident smirk. He knew he had me from the minute he showed up.

"How did you know this was my room?" I asked.

He shrugged his shoulders and said, "I didn't. But I hoped it was."

Brock was courageous. Nervy. As if he didn't fear anything. Ever.

I glanced at him; he was slightly shivering. I felt bad as he stood there smiling at me, dangling the bag in his hand.

"I'll meet you in the tree house."

"What tree house?" he asked.

I pointed to the tall, ancient tree standing broad behind him.

When I climbed up, he was looking around at the pictures and all of the old toys and trinkets I'd left up there over the years.

"It's like a real, homemade tree house you see in the movies," he said.

"My dad built it for me when I was a kid . . . to make me feel better about moving in the middle of the school year."

I tossed him one of the sweaters I had in my hand.

"Thanks. I was freezing my ass off."

After he put it on, we were silent as he continued to look around. The air subtly whistled and the crickets sang their midnight melodies. It was . . . nice.

I watched the way Brock's eyes froze on the photo of my brother.

"Is this your brother?" he asked, as if he knew. It sent chills up my arms. "You guys have the same exact eyes."

I winced. "Yeah."

I avoided looking at the picture. Sometimes it was just hard. Brock finally turned to face me, sticking out the gift bag in his hand.

I was hesitant for a moment, our gazes locked. It was all so strange to me. *Why'd he show up so late?* I never really let my guard down with people. But Brock was seeming to tear down my walls. It scared me.

"I was going to get you a card, but come on, do people even read those?" he said. "Go ahead, open it."

I opened the bag to reveal a music box. A surfer spun around to a lullaby. The soft music filled the tree house.

I couldn't help but be completely mesmerized by the music box, as if I was lost in some sort of hypnotic trance.

"I know it's not a lot, but—"

"Are you kidding? I love it!"

As if it was a natural reflex, I wrapped my arms around him. I'm sure he wasn't expecting that. Honestly, neither was I.

"It was originally a ballerina spinning around, but I found the surfer piece at a kiosk in the mall and kind of reconstructed it," he explained.

I set the music box down on top of the shelf, resting next to the picture of my brother.

Brock and I lay on the wooden floor of the tree house, bundled up in the sweaters my mom had knitted years ago. We stared into the night sky, stars giving light to the darkness. We snacked on a box of Girl Scout cookies that had probably been sitting there for a year.

"I don't know what's more attractive, you in that gorgeous sweater or your amazing assortment of Girl Scout cookies." Brock chuckled.

I nudged his shoulder.

"Hey! My mom knitted these!"

We laughed together.

"Look, a shooting star." I pointed.

"Make a wish."

I shut my eyes tight, wishing upon a star like a child who may actually believe it would come true.

I opened my eyes, turning to Brock. He peeked one eye open and laughed when he saw me staring at him. Why did I always have to ruin the moment with my uncoolness?

Act normal, Ken, I told myself.

We laughed nervously in unison—well, mine came from a place of nerves. I only hoped his did too. But from what I could tell about Brock Parker, I'm sure he was not even fazed lying in a girl's tree house in the middle of the night.

"Want to play twenty-one questions?" he asked.

"Sure. How do you play?"

"We ask each other twenty-one personal questions. Here, I'll start."

Brock turned to me.

"What is more difficult for you: looking into someone's eyes when you are telling them how you feel, or looking into someone's eyes when they are telling you how they feel?"

What about "C. All of the above"? Was that an option?

I looked past Brock to the music box still playing on the shelf.

"I don't know," I said. "I guess when I am telling them how I feel." My words gushed out as one.

He laughed at me.

"You talk really fast sometimes."

I looked down. I could feel myself blush—if only there were a way to control it.

"When I'm telling them how I feel," I repeated, consciously articulating my words.

"Same . . . your turn."

BROCK

I really, really liked looking at Kendra. Was that superficial sounding? And her boobs looked huge from this angle. Damn.

"Where do you see yourself in ten years? Like, what do you want to do for a living?" she asked.

"I've always loved music," I admitted.

"So that explains the tattoo," she said as her gaze fell to my arm.

I lifted it up, staring at it. She took my arm in her hand to get a closer look.

"I like it." She released my arm, letting it rest by hers once again.

"But I'll probably just end up taking over the family business," I confessed.

"Why wouldn't you do what you love?"

"That's a good question." I laughed, pondering the question. It was complicated. When it came down to it, money was always the answer. Plus, I was really good at it. Why fix something if it isn't broken, right? Maybe that was me making up excuses because I feared the unknown, to be honest. I didn't know what world lay beyond dealing drugs. I wasn't sure I wanted to find out. It seemed rough. It would take me way out of my comfort zone too. Fuck, I didn't even know why I was thinking about it.

I opened my mouth to speak but couldn't quite form the right words. I was trying to decide how I should express this.

"Um—er—well, my parents have basically had a plan for me to take over the business since I was born. I swear they had me just to have someone they could trust take it over."

"What kind of business?" she asked.

Shit. My mind tried to grab ahold of something fast.

"Sales. Nothing special."

"Okay, then," she said, thankfully dropping the subject. "You said you loved music. Do you play any instruments?"

"Yeah, actually. I play guitar, bass, piano, drums—"

"What? How come I didn't know this?"

I smiled.

"I don't know. No one here really knows about that, actually."

Music was always my escape from all the lame-ass family drama. Something I was actually passionate about. But I hadn't had the chance to play a whole lot since we moved to Laguna.

"You'll have to write me a song sometime." Kendra giggled.

"I would love to," I said. "Do you play any instruments?"

"A month of guitar lessons in fifth grade is as far as my musical abilities stretch."

I chuckled. It was cool to be with a girl who could laugh at herself.

"So, you could be your own one-man band. Like, if the Beatles had been only one person, they would've been you."

"I'll take that compliment! There's no doubt that the Beatles were one of the greatest groups ever, but I can't lie, I low-key hate those people in our generation that act like they're these die-hard Beatles fans, but probably don't know the difference between John Lennon and John the disciple. Like they're trying to portray this certain hippie image."

"Seriously! All they want to do is post on Facebook about it, as if it's just a trend."

"Finally! Someone who gets me!"

Kendra was, like, the chillest girl ever. She was super innocent and sweet, but a total baddie at the same time.

"What do you want to be?" I asked.

"I want to be a pro surfer, but my first priority is college."

"Where do you want to go to college?"

"Hey, one question at a time," she teased.

"Sorry, you're just so interesting." I winked.

She looked at me, her eyes narrowing. She was trying to keep a straight face, but a cute smirk snuck through. I poked her side. We both gave in and laughed.

When our laughing ceased, only the melody of the music box filled the tree house.

"My dream school is Pepperdine. It's, like, the perfect location for surfing," she said, breaking the stillness of the moment.

"My old house was a half hour from there."

She perked up. "Really?"

"Yeah, Pacific Palisades," I said. "So, when are quarterfinals?"

"December fourth."

"I'll definitely be there."

"Oh, my goodness. No way!"

"Why not?"

"Because! That's so embarrassing."

"How is that embarrassing?"

"I don't know. It just is."

She was a shy girl. I didn't know much about those.

"What's the worst that happens? You eat shit in the water. Who cares?"

"Gosh, you remind me so much of my brother."

"Is that a good thing?"

I noticed how the lifted corners of her mouth faded into a straight line when she nodded her head. It didn't seem like she wanted to talk about him, even though she brought him up. I wanted to ask, but I thought back to the other night at Ashton's; if something was going to upset Kendra, I didn't want to mention it. I didn't want to get on her bad side like that again.

"So, where were you born and raised?" she asked.

"Born in Phoenix, raised mostly in Malibu. Lived in a few other places in between. Hopefully Laguna will be the final destination," I said with a yawn. I didn't realize how tired I was. But I was beginning to feel it. "What about you?"

"Born in San Diego and moved to Laguna when I was eleven."

I gazed up at the night sky. The moon was full and bright. It would look even doper if I was lit.

"Check out that moon." I pointed.

"Isn't it beautiful? It's a supermoon tonight."

"Wow, I'm impressed. You into astronomy?"

"A little." She smiled. "How cool would it be to go to the moon? Just escape everything for a night."

"Very cool," I said. "We should go someday."

She looked at me and smiled, blushing. I'll admit, that wasn't the first time I'd used that line, but it may have been the first time I'd meant it.

I noticed the pendant hanging around Kendra's neck that she always had on. Like, you know when you feel yourself staring for a while at something but don't actually notice it?

I picked it up, observing.

"You never take this off, do you?"

"No. Never."

"What is it?"

"A Saint Christopher necklace. It's supposed to keep surfers safe in the water. My brother gave it to me."

I took my eyes back up to hers.

"That's dope."

"Yeah."

We stared at each other, the silence calming—although, we had the sound of the music box in the background.

"What is your nerdiest secret?" she asked. I was taken aback.

"My what?"

"Nerdiest secret. Everyone has one."

I smirked, directing my focus up to the sky. Kendra Dimes was really something else.

I looked back at her and said, "Promise you won't tell." This was serious business. My reputation was on the line here. No one would want to buy coke from a guy who collected rocks.

"Pinkie promise."

She stuck out her pinkie and I interlaced mine with hers.

"I have a rock collection."

She exhaled a suppressed laugh, as if she couldn't control it.

"Hey, don't judge," I said, tickling her stomach. She laughed, grabbing onto where my hand was, our palms gliding against each other. I know she noticed. "What's your nerdiest secret?"

She bit her lip, hesitant for a second.

"Okay, don't laugh at me—"

"Because you didn't."

She shot me a smirk.

"Literally *no one* knows this. Nobody."

She took a deep breath, laughing before she began.

"Okay—sometimes I stay after school for math study group even though I don't need the help."

I propped myself up onto my elbows, shaking my head in disbelief.

"Okay, that's really weird when I hear that aloud," she said.

"Uh, yeah! That's crazy. Definitely tops mine."

"I just—I really love trig."

"And you're in advanced? You really are a nerd." I nudged her. "You win."

She let out a cackle.

"Shh," I said, still laughing. "Your parents will wake up!"

She nodded, getting ahold of herself.

I lay back down, next to her.

"What did you wish for on that shooting star?"

"If I tell you, then it won't come true!" she reminded me.

"Fine! Fine. But, if it does come true you have to tell me."

She paused.

"Deal."

I turned to face her, resting my head on my hand. I was really tired now. I let out a yawn. We stared at each other. Half of her face was shadowed by the night while the other half was lit up by the moon. I started to hear piano keys playing through my mind. Lightly. The whole scene was inspiring something. I wasn't sure what it was quite yet. I took my gaze down as I turned flat on my back.

"I, uh . . . I better get going."

Kendra looked down at her phone.

"Oh, my gosh, it's almost three in the morning."

"Damn. I gotta be up in, like, four hours."

"Why?"

I sat up, turning to face her.

"Just helping my family with work."

"Oh, gotcha."

When we stood up, Kendra shut the music box, silencing the lullaby.

We climbed down the tree house. I held my hand out for her as her foot reached down for the earth.

She led me to the back gate.

"I'm glad I came," I said.

"Me too. Thanks for my gift."

We stood there a moment. I watched Kendra's nervous quirks in full force—the way she bit her lip and tapped her pants with her hands, rocking onto her heels. Her gaze wandered from one side of the yard to the other. She laughed a laugh I'd never heard from her before. It lacked her sweet snort.

I decided to silence her internal thoughts that so obviously leaked out into her actions with a kiss.

I quickly pulled away. Her eyes were still closed, slowly opening as I looked at her. I wondered what she was thinking.

She opened her mouth to speak, but didn't. Instead, she looked at me, smiled, and did something I wasn't expecting— she walked away.

"See you later," she said. That was it.

"See you, Kendra."

As I walked away, I looked back one more time. Kendra was jumping wildly up her staircase in excitement, until she caught my gaze. She froze, and we both laughed. I proceeded out the gate and took off.

I walked into my house, gently closing the front door behind me. I didn't want to wake up my parents—less because I feared their lectures, but more that they were just a nightmare to deal with.

"Where've you been?" I heard my mother's voice coming from the living room. *Shit.*

"Um—"

My father interrupted me as he emerged from the dark hallway, a glass of scotch in hand—as usual. "Never mind that. Just tell me how the deal went. Did you sell it all?"

"Yeah—well, sort of."

"What do you mean *sort of*?"

I pulled out the money from my pocket. My father walked into the light, snatching the cash right out of my hand.

"He handed me the cash, we heard sirens, and he took off."

My father started to count.

"Should I call him now and—"

"No. I don't want you to have any contact with him. I have no patience for idiots like him."

I nodded as he handed me a few bills from the stack.

"I'm proud of you."

"For what?" I asked, puzzled.

"For making sure you get the cash first. Good work."

I didn't let my dad see me smile, but I felt happy. Like I had done something right. I'd pleased him. It was so rare that it felt like the reward I'd been working toward. Stupid, I know. But it was true.

"Go to bed and be up by seven, or consider this your last payment for a while."

I walked off, rolling my eyes without him seeing. He was never satisfied for too long.

"Brock."

I turned back around.

"Zero contact with him."

I nodded, continuing to my room.

He was so annoying. I mean, Jesus Christ, I heard him the first time. Continuously reiterating the same thing over and over didn't make me understand any more. That was the kind of shit that got on my nerves. He treated me like I was a dumbass. I'd been dealing this shit since I was fourteen—I'd known what I was doing by this point.

I hit up Duke when I got in my bedroom, secured and safe from the hell that lived below me.

Brock: I've been talking to Kendra . . .
Duke: Nice, man. She's a baddie for sure
Brock: How's L.A.? Needa make a trip out there STAT
Duke: For real my man. Come kick it. Mexico this week!
Brock: fuck, u just reminded me . . . fml
Duke: Gotta bring in that $$$$
Brock: we can't even party tho!

I lay in bed, unable to sleep. I turned onto my side. My alarm was going to go off in two hours to wake my ass up for more deals. It never ended. I wished there was just one weekend where I could sleep in. My body ached, and my head felt full of my parents' voices. Kendra's laugh intervened. Her sparkling brown eyes flashed through my mind. I smiled.

I turned over onto my other side, but it made no difference. The overhead fan spun around and around on full blast. I was still sweating, though. I ripped the covers off, stuck my hand down my pants, and worked my way to sleep. I imagined what it would be like to see Kendra naked.

I swear the week disappeared before my eyes. Like, literally. I was so stoned the past four days, I didn't even remember half the shit that went down. Except for the important stuff. I'd just got back in town, and I was pretty exhausted. My parents and I had spent the past week in Mexico with Miguel Morales and his family. He was the head of one of the biggest drug cartels in the world and the one that linked all of us together—my family, Duke, Annie's fam. He flew us out there on his private jet and put us up in one of the nicest homes I'd ever stayed in. Our families had become close friends over the years. We were about to lock in a huge deal with him. Basically, he would pay my parents a huge sum of money to deal his shit all the way up the West Coast, and then they could recruit people underneath them to make even more dough. Essentially, Morales was creating a drug-dealing pyramid scheme in hopes of taking over the world. It was going to be tough, but so worth it. We're talking hundreds of millions of dollars a year.

I sat at my desk, on my computer, with a couple hours to myself to work on some music—finally. If there was one thing I loved more than smoking a bowl, it was smoking a bowl while mixing beats. The perfect way to unwind on a Friday night. I grabbed my guitar off its stand and plugged it into my computer—it would be so dope with some strings. I strummed a really deep, sick riff. I sold my sounds online to make some extra cash. It wasn't much, but it was something I enjoyed doing. Less for the money and more, in a sense, for the validation that maybe my work was legit enough to be recognized and used. I really hadn't had the chance to work much on any music since our move, only here and there. This was the first one in a while that I was determined to finish.

My parents had no clue. I didn't think they even knew I played guitar—okay, that was a lie. My dad was the one who'd introduced me to music. It's weird—he'd changed a lot since then. Greed. It could consume a man. I'd witnessed it firsthand. I hadn't seen him pick up his guitar since I was a kid. Maybe ten years ago or so. It used to connect us. Now the only thing we were connected by was that, oddly enough, we had the same blood running through our veins. And work . . . That connected us too but not really in a powerful way. Only in a necessary way.

I was almost done recording when my phone rang. It was Nick. I wasn't really in the mood for anyone.

"Hello?"

"What up, dude? Where the fuck you been?" he asked.

"Uh, sick."

"What are you doing tonight? Let's do something."

"I don't know. I'm pretty tired."

"Shut up. Everyone is going to the scream park. I'm picking your ass up. Let's go. We can sesh before."

My mom walked into my room.

"We're going to dinner tonight with the McAlisters. They're a really important client. Are you coming?"

I was surprised she was giving me a choice. There was no way I could handle my parents tonight. I had just spent an entire week with them.

"All right." I gave in to Nick. "See you later."

I hung up.

"Sorry, I just made plans with Nick."

"Okay. Be home by midnight."

"Okay."

She walked out and shut the door behind her.

Duke texted me as she left the room. He'd been in Mexico too when we went, but he'd left early. He had to get back to LA for business. He was making so much money it was crazy. He was working his way up for sure. Morales loved him. Respected him, I guess would be a better way of saying it.

Duke: What r ur plans 2nite??
Brock: Going to the scream park . . .
Duke: Da fuq is that?

Brock: I honestly don't know.
Duke: Miss U brother. Let's kick it soon.
Brock: FOR REAL.
Duke: How's Kendra?

I realized I hadn't talked to Kendra since that night. I mean, she had my number too. She could've hit me up. I wondered what she was doing and if I should slip into her messages.

I wanted to kiss her again. Shit, I wanted to do more than that.

Brock: I haven't seen her in a few days but she's chill. Hot af
Duke: I'm tellin' ya man. She's worth committing for.
Brock: Hmmm . . . IDK bout that, fool

Duke was more of a "relationship guy"—and well, I was not. In fact, I was the opposite.

I pressed play on GarageBand to listen to my completed beat. I had to admit, it was trill as fuck. I took another puff from my pipe with satisfaction, nodding my head to the music.

KENDRA

The last bell of the day rang, which meant fall break was officially upon us. I walked out of history with Taylor and Hunter. The week had sped by, and I hadn't seen or spoken to Brock since last weekend. So confusing.

"Ken, we're all going to the scream park tonight if you want to go," Taylor said.

"Sure, sounds fun," I said, although I hated haunted houses.

As we walked down the stairs, we passed by Annie. Her already short hair was up in a ponytail, exposing the hickeys that stained her neck. It was as if she wanted everyone to see them—which was weird to me. The three of us were having trouble containing ourselves, our suppressed laughs exhaling out into what sounded like a group of dying pigs. When she was out of sight, we broke down.

"I counted four!" Taylor said.

"No six! Did you see the ones through her shirt?" Hunter added.

"Oh, my gosh, you guys!"

We laughed. I wondered if Brock gave her those hickeys. She was super skinny. Skinnier than I ever really realized. I wondered if Brock liked that. I think I loved food way too much to ever be that tiny looking. She seemed almost frail, like my brother at the end. And suddenly a part of me felt bad for her.

"BTW, she totally gave you the stink face, Ken," Taylor said. "What the hell? What's her deal?"

I hadn't even noticed her looking, but did that mean I was right—did she know about Brock and me? Was he spending his days with her and nights with me? I didn't like the idea of that. But I didn't want to confront him either, because first of all he wasn't my boyfriend, and second I didn't have enough evidence to say.

I walked out to the parking lot where Ashleigh and Ashton were making out by his car.

"Get a room!" I yelled.

Ashleigh looked at me and laughed.

"Why get a room when we have a whole parking lot?" she teased.

"You coming over, Ken?" Ashton asked.

"I guess so."

The three of us hopped in Ashton's car and headed to his house.

When we walked inside, Ashton headed straight for the bathroom.

"Thank God it's finally break," Ashleigh said, overly exasperated as she plopped onto Ashton's bed.

"I know, right?"

I pulled out the rubric for my English essay that was due when we got back from break.

"Ken!" Ashleigh yelled. I jumped.

"What?"

"You are not actually thinking about school and homework and all that other bull crap right now!"

"Sorry. I just figured we're sitting here doing nothing. I mean, I might as well get it over with."

"Shut up, you nerd."

Ashleigh ripped the paper right out of my hand and almost tore it in half.

"Ash!"

"Relax."

Ashton walked out of the bathroom, plopping down on the bed next to Ashleigh. They started to kiss. Their slurping made my body cringe.

"I'm still here, you guys," I reminded them from my usual position on the beanbag.

"Sorry!" Ashleigh laughed.

"Ken, have you talked to Brock at all?" Ashton asked.

"It's been a few days," I said. Not a single text since the tree house. It was weird, actually. I hadn't even seen him at school all week.

"And he never showed up to your birthday. So strange," Ashleigh said, unaware of the post-party encounter.

"Well—" I began.

"Well what?" Ashleigh asked, now fully alert.

"He ended up showing up after everyone left."

"Shut up!" Ashleigh jumped off the bed onto the beanbag next to me, Ashton now hanging off the edge of the bed. "Give me the deets!"

"He texted me after you guys all left and was, like, in my backyard."

"What?"

"Yeah. And then we hung out in my tree house until three in the morning."

"What the freaking fuck?"

"Wait, Ken, where was he before? Why didn't he show earlier?" Ashton asked.

"Actually"—I'd never even asked him—"I don't know."

Ashleigh nudged Ashton. "You're his friend. Why don't you find out?"

"We're chill with each other but not, like, that close."

"He seems the closest with Nick," I said. And Annie, but I didn't want to think about that.

"Yeah. I think he is," Ashleigh agreed.

Or maybe Brock Parker was the kind of person who was unable to get too close to anyone at all.

A couple of hours later, the three of us headed to the scream park, stopping at a convenience store on the way to get Ashleigh an Icee and a scratcher. It was her thing, but she could only buy scratchers when Jim was working. He didn't care that she was underage. And she swore he was good luck.

"Woo! Twenty bucks!" She threw the scratcher in the air as we drove down the road. I was hardly paying attention, though. I couldn't get Brock off my mind, and as time continued to tick, I grew more and more antsy, wondering *if* and *when* he was going to text me. But, I couldn't wait any longer.

I looked down at my phone, my thumb hovering over the send button. I just wanted to see what he was doing. I quickly locked my phone and shoved it in my pocket before I made a rash decision. If he wanted to talk to me, he would.

"I literally don't think I can handle this haunted house shit," Ashleigh said, sipping on her Icee.

"I got you, babe." Ashton kissed Ashleigh's hand.

The three of us had gone to a haunted house last Halloween, and Ashleigh basically peed on herself. Of course, she and Ashton ended up in a fight—I don't remember what it was about. I was surprised she agreed to come again. I think it was because she knew Ashton was going to go with his friends either way, and she always liked to keep an eye on him. *Especially* if she knew there would be other girls around.

We pulled into the scream park, Ashleigh hanging on to Ashton's side when we got out of the car.

"I love you, babe," she whispered to him as we walked to the ticket line where our other friends were waiting.

"I love you too." He kissed her forehead. This was a nice change of pace while third wheeling with these two drama queens.

As we moved up in the line, a phone rang. We all checked to see if it was our own, but it was Ashton's.

"Hello?" he said.

He ignored Ashleigh as she playfully poked at him.

"We're in line. Do you see us?" he said into the phone.

He hung up.

"Who was that?" Ashleigh asked.

"It was Nick and Brock."

My heart dropped.

"Brock's coming?" I asked.

"Yep!"

Ashleigh shot me a look as we approached the front of the line.

"Why wouldn't you tell us?" Ashleigh screeched loud enough to make the group in front of us turn around.

"I didn't think of it," he said, rolling his eyes.

"You're such a dumbass."

I wanted to sneak a glance over at the parking lot to see if Brock and Nick were close, but I didn't want to seem desperate. I looked from the corner of my eye.

"I said, next!" the cashier yelled.

I looked forward, making my way to the booth.

As the cashier, dressed as Freddy Krueger, handed me a ticket, I heard someone yell, "Hey, losers!"

I turned around—it was Nick. Next to him was Brock, who had stopped in line to talk to Jason. When he saw me, he pushed past the crowd of people and cut everyone in line to work his way to my side.

"Hey," he said.

"Hi."

I was super excited but also really mad at him. Why hadn't he texted me? It took all of five seconds to send a text.

Before addressing the fact that he hadn't taken five lousy seconds out of his week to text me, he turned to Freddy and said, "Can I get a four-house ticket?"

"Forty bucks," he answered.

"You're going into all four houses?" I was terrified just thinking about it.

"Why not?" He smiled. I looked away, avoiding his gaze. Ugh. His eyes did this thing where they smiled even when his face was completely serious and straight, and it, like, made me want to smile, and then I'd totally give in and probably make some sarcastic remark out of nerves and blow everything. Not that there was anything to blow. He didn't even look at me like that.

We made our way into the park with the rest of the group.

"You going in this one?" Brock nodded his head toward the haunted house that we were waiting in line for. It was hard to be mad at him. *Ugh!*

"Yeah," I said, giving into his unintentional charm. "Are you?"

"Well, if you are, then I am."

"That's frickin' gay," Nick interrupted.

"Says the kid who gets no ass," Brock shot back.

"You're such a faggot," Nick retorted.

"That's offensive and politically incorrect," I cautioned Nick. I couldn't help myself.

"What'd I say?" he questioned.

"Is there a reason your reference about a homosexual is aimed as an insult? Are you insinuating that gays are offensive?" Ashleigh butted in, right up in his face. Nick wasn't sure how to respond.

"That's what I thought." She turned around and patted me on the shoulder. She knew how much I hated those kinds of comments. I rarely spoke up about things and normally would let ignorant statements go, but that kind of obnoxious behavior, especially when it hit close to home like that—it set me off.

When I looked at Brock, his eyebrows were raised. A mix of confused and impressed? I wasn't sure.

"That's what happens when you shoot your mouth off like that, dude," Brock added.

Jason laughed, amused by all of this.

"Piss off, Jason! We all know you're a screamer," Nick said.

"No, I'm not!"

We cautiously shuffled into the haunted house, Brock behind me. A man dressed as a clown popped out. I was slowly but surely regretting this decision. I loathed clowns. Jason screamed at the top of his lungs as he grabbed onto Taylor's arm for protection.

"Told you, you're a screamer," Nick said.

"Fuck off, dude."

I shook my head at them, annoyed, and turned away as a door opened to the next room of the haunted house.

The door slammed shut, trapping us in a small, enclosed area, too dark to tell what it really looked like. Hunter and Jason screamed. I instinctively grabbed Brock's hand. I wasn't even expecting that. He held it—and suddenly I didn't regret this festive activity.

Ashton lit up the room with his phone to find the exit. He pushed a wooden door open, letting all of us out. We ran as fast as we could until a man popped out from behind the wall with a chain saw. *Holy guacamole*, my heart dropped down to the floor. We stopped dead in our tracks and I accidentally ran into Brock's arms. He smelled like that cologne again that I loved. You know that kind of "hot guy" smell you always imagine hot guys to smell like? That was it.

Brock grabbed my hand again. It sent butterflies flying through my stomach and into my heart. Then they circled around and flew down to my toes.

He led all of us out of the hallway, through another door, and outside. We reached the end of the course in one piece— thank goodness.

"That was no doubt the scariest thing I have ever gone through in my life!" Ashleigh said, catching her breath.

"Scarier than missing your period last month?" Ashton said, teasing her.

Ashton and all the guys laughed—but Ashleigh wasn't having it. Understandably. I mean, that was such a personal joke to make in front of everyone. Sometimes I just didn't understand guys.

She stormed off, Ashton chasing after her. The soap opera had begun.

"I swear those two are bipolar," Brock said to me.

"Tell me about it," I said. "You should have seen them during the car ride here. It was, like, the total opposite."

"Watch, give it two minutes and they'll be all over each other as if it never happened."

"Bet you five minutes," I challenged him, my eyebrow raised.

"The surfer likes a little competition, huh?" He smirked. "You're on."

"Loser buys the winner a Starbucks."

"Hope you have enough money for a venti."

"Oh, okay, Mr. Cocky."

"You're cute when you're feisty."

I almost pooped on myself when Brock called me cute. Was he just messing around and playing with my mind? It was a possibility . . . but I didn't want to know. I just wanted to replay his voice in my head over and over again.

"Are you two coming or what?" Nick interrupted once again. I guess there was a reason Brock referred to him as "CB."

"Where?" I asked.

"Where else? The beach."

Brock looked at me and asked, "Need a ride?"

"Yeah." I had no clue where Ashleigh and Ashton had wandered off to at this point. But I was perfectly okay being stranded with Brock.

Brock pressed the unlock button on his car keys as we approached the parking lot, the lights to an Audi A8 shining brightly in the dark of the night.

"Is that yours?" I wondered, pointing at the car.

"Yes, ma'am."

"An Audi A8? Nice."

"What do you know about Audis?"

"Enough. My brother's first car was an Audi."

"Your brother sounds dope."

"Yeah, he was. . . ." I mumbled under my breath.

While my mind wandered off into the past, Brock suddenly interrupted my déjà vu, taking my hand in his as we proceeded to the car. He walked me over to the passenger side door, and instead of opening it, he pinned me against the car, our lips close to touching. I froze up. There were people all around us and I wasn't into PDAs, but suddenly his mouth was on mine. It was longer than our first kiss. I didn't want to stop, but I remembered we were in public, and I quickly pulled back.

"I'm sorry. I just—I don't like PDAs," I admitted.

I watched his forehead furrow.

"Is this really considered a PDA?" he asked.

"I mean, yeah. It stands for public display of affe—"

He laughed and said, "I know what it stands for."

Brock took a step back, his eyes wandering the scream park.

"Whatever you say," he finally said, shrugging his shoulders.

He opened the passenger door for me, and as I sat down, I said, "Why thank you, Mr. Parker." I wanted to act normal as if the whole PDA thing wasn't a big deal. I couldn't read him though. I wasn't sure if he cared or not.

He responded with a smile, shutting the door. Okay, obviously he was still a bit taken off guard—at least, I think. Maybe he didn't even like me like that! Ugh, I don't know. My overanalytical thinking was going to drown my brain in my own thoughts.

Brock got into the car. It was just the two of us. I wanted to know what was going through his head. I wished I could go back in time and make out with him in public!

The first few moments of the car ride were silent. Not in a weird way, more like in a mentally preoccupied way for both of us. Or at least for me.

From the corner of my eye, I watched his hand on the center console, his fingers tapping to the beat of the song on the radio.

He cleared his throat; I looked at him and laughed.

"Are you laughing at me?" he said.

"Maybe."

"I'm glad I can be of entertainment to you."

He placed his hand on my knee, giving it a small squeeze. My eyes, staring ahead, widened.

Holy cannoli. He. Placed. His. Hand. On. My. Knee! It sent this tingly feeling up my entire body. I redirected my gaze out the window, avoiding any direct eye contact as I bit my lip, thinking. Wondering. Was I supposed to put my hand on top of his? I decided to just stay still. I didn't understand, though; he had been MIA all week and now he had his hand on my knee? What was his deal?

"So how come you never drive? You're always hitchin' rides with Ash?"

"I don't know how to drive," I admitted. I could feel my cheeks blushing as my internal body heat increased.

"Really? Why not?"

"I'm scared."

"Of what?"

"All the other cars on the road?" I stated the fact as a question in full understanding of how weird it sounded. But it was true. Harry tried teaching me before and, like, I always did fine in parking lots, but when it came to the streets—that was a whole different story. I felt like I was in kindergarten again trying to color in the lines, only the crayon was a car and the lines were on the road.

"Well, that's a problem," he teased, giving my knee another squeeze as we pulled up to the beach. My heart jumped like a reflex.

We walked down to where our friends surrounded a beautiful bonfire. Flames lit up the night, but I could still see the ember, even in the dark. We sat down on the sand, my shoes in hand at this point. Everyone was just hanging out: no worries, no problems, just good company.

"You know, we never finished twenty-one questions," Brock said.

Although I had lost count long ago, I said, "Let's play."

"You start this time."

I almost forgot that there were other people around us as I searched for a question.

ALEXANDRIA ROSE RIZIK

"All right, define your dream girl."

"That's easy. Spontaneous and wild yet reserved."

"Well, sounds like you've thought that one out."

"I have."

We looked at each other and laughed. It was like we could read each other's minds.

"All right, now you have to define your dream guy—and please don't say something cliché like Justin Bieber."

I giggled. "Mmmmm, I don't really know."

"You have to have certain things that make or break a relationship."

"I mean, I like a guy who knows what he wants in life like I do and respects me."

"I feel ya," he said.

He sneezed.

"Bless you," I said.

"Thank you." He looked at me, then back at the fire. "All right, hookups or relationships?"

My mind wandered off, deciding how this question should be answered. I had a strong gut feeling that Brock was more of a hookups kind of guy. I, on the other hand, never even had a boyfriend, but I wasn't the type to just go randomly making out with people either—but still, I had to sound somewhat experienced. "Depends on the person. If they are boyfriend material, then relationships," I said. "What about you?"

"I would have to agree, but most girls aren't girlfriend material, if you catch my drift."

I raised my eyebrows and shot him a look. I knew plenty of boys like Brock.

"Unreal."

"What? I can't help that I'm skilled in certain areas."

We looked at each other again and laughed. I didn't *want* to laugh, but I couldn't help it! Brock had this way of saying things with such—such honesty behind it that it was comical.

"I have a legitimate question for you," he said with all seriousness, still with a smile on his face.

"Okay."

"Why do you hate drugs so much?"

I looked at the fire as I opened my mouth to speak, but only breath came out. The words were there. The memories. I wanted to be honest with him—I wanted to tell him about Kyle. I mean, he at least deserved that, and I felt that I could trust him, but—I didn't want to talk about it. I couldn't talk about it.

A pair of arms wrapped themselves around my neck, interrupting my train of thought. It was Jason.

BROCK

"Hey, guys," Jason said, his arms wrapped around Kendra. I wasn't a jealous guy, but I didn't like him hanging on her—mostly because I knew she didn't like him. Okay, well, also because I kind of felt like another dog was trying to piss on my territory. But technically, I couldn't say anything—and I didn't have to, because Kendra cleared her throat in a passive-aggressive manner, deliberately shaking her shoulder so that his arm fell to the side. Still, his obliviousness irked my nerves. I couldn't help myself, so I said something.

"Come on, dude. You're always hanging on her. Lay off. It's rapey when you're constantly on a chick and she's pushing you off. Take a hint."

I normally wouldn't call people out like that in front of everyone—shit, who am I kidding? Of course I would.

"I'm helping you out," I added. I could see Kendra's mouth hanging open from the corner of my eye.

"Oh, okay. Sorry," he said. I knew he still didn't care. He wasn't even going to think twice about this conversation.

"Yo, man, do you have th—"

"Uh, not here." I quickly cut him off before he made Kendra hate my guts.

She wasn't an idiot, though. She knew something was up.

I could tell by the way she was intently observing the situation, her stare shifting from me to Jason and back.

"I have your football in my car," I said, quickly trying to save my ass.

"Aight."

He was just dumb enough to go along with it.

"Be right back," I said to Kendra

I opened my car door, pulling out the bag of cocaine. It was dark out, but I was still cautious. I looked around, making sure no one was around, and stuck out my hand for Jason to take the bag, pausing before completely handing it over. There were some guidelines I needed to establish with this kid.

"We keep this on the DL, correct?" I clarified.

"You got it."

"And please don't tell Kendra."

"No problem, bro."

I gave him the shit and shut my door.

"Do you have any pot?" he asked.

"Nah, man." The only pot I had was for personal use—we didn't deal that shit. Unless it was for bribing purposes.

We walked back down to the beach.

"And listen," I said, having forgotten to mention this before-hand. "If you ever get caught with my shit and they question you, you better not give my name."

Jason laughed as if this was some sort of joke. I stared at him, my eyes narrowing in on his. I knew how to scare the shit out of people without saying a single word. My dad taught me—silence is deadly. I kept my gaze still, his laugh evolving into a smile that turned into a frown full of fright. He stopped laughing real fast—and if he hadn't, the knife was next. I wouldn't actually *use* it. Just a little reveal, so that he knew it existed.

"Okay."

"One more thing . . ." I said. I couldn't help myself—it was still bothering me. "I'd appreciate it if you weren't all over Kendra."

"Are you guys together or something?"

"We're chilling."

Jason nodded. "Got it."

We approached the rest of the group back at the bonfire. I saw Jason flash the bag to Ryan as they disappeared into the darkness of the night. I snuck up behind Kendra, wrapping my arms around her waist. She jumped. I took a step back, observing her underneath the moonlight; her eyes lit up like sand glistening underneath a striking sun.

"By the way, Ashleigh and Ashton have yet to make up. Looks like I'm winning the bet!"

"Nuhh uhh! You said five minutes. It's been thirty."

"Yeah, but my number is closer," she said with a pinch of attitude. It was cute. We went into a staring contest—neither of us changing our gaze—testing each other until we both gave in and laughed.

"I was going to buy you a Starbucks regardless of if I won or not," I said.

Out of nowhere, flashing lights began to close in on the beach. Four cops jumped off their bikes, shining lights in our faces.

"Shit."

"What is it?" Kendra asked.

I had a bag of coke in my pocket and a car full of everything parked up the street. There was no way this could end well.

"Kendra, I have to get out of here."

"Why?"

"My car. I just—I have to go."

I fled away into the nightfall before any more questions could be asked. If I got caught with that shit, my life would be over. My chest ached as Kendra's startled eyes crossed through my mind; I felt bad leaving so abruptly, but I had no choice.

I ran a ways until I found a random set of stairs, hesitating before darting toward them. It was better than getting caught. I ran up the stairs, my heart beating so fast I could barely breathe. They led me back to the street. I looked right. Then left. I wasn't completely sure which way I had to go to get to my car, but I guessed left. As I jogged down the sidewalk, I spotted Ashton's car down a side street—which meant mine was right behind his. I slowed down to a walk, looking around me, alert of my surroundings before getting in. I turned on my car, but I was blocked in between Ashton's car and Jason's.

"Shit. Shit. Shit."

I reversed into someone's trash can and bolted, driving down South Coast Highway at full speed—my adrenaline high as a fuckin' kite. When I turned into my neighborhood, I was finally able to catch my breath. I pulled up to my driveway and just sat there for a moment. I liked a thrill, but that was full-on sketchy.

"Dammit!" I punched my steering wheel, making the horn honk accidentally. Within seconds my mother came rushing out in her robe, her eyes heavy. I hadn't meant to wake her up, but I was so pissed. It was the small moments like this that I wished I could live a normal life, or at least knew what a normal life felt like. I didn't want to leave the beach. I didn't want to leave the bonfire. I didn't want to leave Kendra.

My mom made her way over to my window.

"What the fuck?"

"Sorry. It was an accident."

She rolled her eyes, walking away.

The next day, I decided to call Kendra. I paced my room, hitting my phone against my palm, trying to decide what I would say when it came up—and it *would* come up.

I pressed her name without thinking . . . the phone dialing.

My heart skipped a beat when I heard her voice. I was convinced she wouldn't answer after last night.

"Hey. What are you up to?" I said into the phone. I lay on my bed, strumming my guitar. It calmed my nerves. Not that I really had nerves. But . . . well, you know what I mean.

"Just finished up surf practice. What are you doing?"

"Just now getting up," I said, chuckling, trying to keep the convo light. But the other end was silent. I cleared my throat. "Hey, sorry about last night. I didn't realize the time. Way past my curfew." Yeah, that was realistic.

"You don't seem like the type to have a curfew."

"Um, well, last night I did."

"Oh."

Shit, she was pissy—and totally not buying it.

"Can I make it up to you tonight?" I said—and in that moment I was confused with what I wanted. *Making it up* to someone meant you gave a shit if they weren't going to talk to you again. Did I want Kendra? Did I want a girlfriend? The idea was suffocating, yet it was worse thinking that if I didn't lock her down eventually, she would be with someone else. Someone like Jason. Fuck that.

I heard whispers in the background. I assumed they were coming from her girlfriends or something, telling her that I should fuck off.

"Depends. How?"

"You remember my boy from LA, right? Duke?"

"Yeah."

"He's throwin' a rager tonight. You down?"

"I don't know—"

"Plus, you did win that bet, so I still owe you a Starbucks."

She paused. She was either going to hang up on me or—

"Okay. Fine."

"Sweet. Pick you up around seven."

"All right. When will—"

"Brock!" my mom yelled.

"Shit. I gotta go. See you tonight."

I quickly hung up and headed downstairs.

My mom was in the backyard, sipping on a glass of wine as she watched our gardener plant. Her face was hidden behind sunglasses and a large, floppy sun hat.

"Since when do you grow pot? Are we dealing marijuana now?" I was somewhat puzzled to find pot being planted throughout the yard.

"And downgrade?" She rolled her eyes. "It's for us. I'm over buying bad shit. So I figured, why not just grow our own?"

She took a sip of her wine.

"What do you have for me?" she asked.

"Duke Larson is throwing a party tonight in LA. I have a few customers there."

"Wonderful."

She chugged the last of her drink and handed me the empty glass. I headed inside for the refill. Sometimes I looked at my mom and wondered what she was like as a kid. I had never met any of my grandparents, seen any old photos, or even visited my parents' hometown. I knew she and my father met in high school and got into dealing back then, but I didn't know anything else, really. Just drugs. That was their identity to me.

Sometimes it scared me to think that was going to be my identity too.

I mean—it didn't *scare* me. But I'd been thinking. Just about the world and how there is so much more. Especially since meeting Kendra. She made me realize how much I loved music. How badly I wanted it. Don't get me wrong—I liked dealing and shit. It was the reason we were able to live the way we did. But sometimes—sometimes I wondered what it would be like to achieve other things. Other dreams.

I poured my mom a glass of whatever white wine was sitting on the counter and walked back outside.

"Thanks, hon," she said as I handed it to her.

Tonight was going to be a huge commission night. It was going to be kind of hard with Kendra there, but I knew I'd manage.

When I headed back to my room, my phone was blowing up with texts.

I was shocked to see Jason hit me up after last night. Nick told me that he and Ryan were arrested after that little bike cop mishap. Thank God I managed to get the fuck out of there before it all went down. I just hoped Jason knew to warn Ryan about throwing my name around too.

Jason: Hey . . . out of jail. Bro bailed me out.

Brock: That sux dude. Nick told me this morning what happened. Remember, keep my name out of it.

Jason: Ya of course.

Brock: Not even a word to ppl at school . . . & erase these texts. Tell Ryan 2.

Jason: Got it.

I also erased them on my end before opening up Nick's message. In my head, I went through a list of people I had sold to at school: Nick—but that barely counted—Ryan, Jason, a few of those athletes, some referrals from them. . . .

I was wishing and praying that no one would open their mouths. What if it got back to the school administration? I was going to have to be careful now and stay super low-key. No selling to the teenagers for a bit. It was okay though, because it would force me to challenge myself and hit up that middle-age target Morales was shooting for.

> **Nick:** me n Brody r going 2 the mall if u wanna come
> **Brock:** Sure. Pick me up.

I set my phone down on the nightstand and threw on a pair of jeans. I had hat hair from the night before, so I kept the trend going with a black cap.

It had been a minute since I last went to the mall. I was too busy. But I just got a phat paycheck and was considering how to splurge.

When I heard Nick honk his horn outside, I grabbed my wallet and dipped. He and Brody were waiting in the car, the music on full blast. He was into that screamo shit. I hopped in, Nick speeding off before I even shut my door.

"What up?" Nick said as he turned down the radio.

"Not much. What are you guys getting?" I asked as I pulled out my wax pen.

"I need to find a birthday present for my mom," Brody said, looking back at me. His glasses were crooked as usual. Normally, I would have told him, but it didn't seem to make a difference.

"Dope."

I sat back in my seat and relaxed, puffing out of my pen.

"Hey, let me have some," Nick demanded.

I handed him the pen and he took a hit before handing it back to me.

"Yo, can I plug my phone in? You gotta check out this sick beat I looped together," I said.

"Yeah, here." Nick handed me his auxiliary cord. I plugged my phone in as he turned the volume up.

The bass blasted through his speakers.

"Siiiick," Nick said.

I nodded my head to the music, impressed with my own skills.

As we passed by Main Beach on the way, Kendra's laugh made its way to the forefront of my mind. I smiled. I was excited to see her tonight.

KENDRA

I sat in front of my bathroom mirror, my cell phone on the counter next to me with Ashleigh on the line.

"Ow ow ow ow!" I yelled as I plucked a hair from my eyebrows. It left a red mark on my skin. I hoped that would go away before tonight.

"What? What happened?" Ashleigh freaked out on the phone.

"Nothing, stupid tweezers."

"Wait? Are you actually tweezing your eyebrows?"

"Uhmm—"

Ashleigh shrieked with such excitement, I thought my eardrum burst.

"Holy shit! Is my little Ken growing up?"

I smiled at myself in the mirror.

"Stop."

"Wait! Why are you getting all dolled up? I thought we were having a girls' night."

"Oh . . . uh, I forgot to tell you, Brock sort of—"

"Holy tits, you guys are hooking up? I knew it!"

"Ashleigh—"

"You guys are perfect for each other—"

"Ash—"

"And you'll have the cutest freaking babies—"

"Ash! It's just to a party, nothing big—"

"You're right. It isn't big, it's freaking huge!"

"We are just friends."

"Really? What about that kiss on your birthday?"

My lips tingled thinking back to Brock's mouth pressed up against mine that night.

"Yeah, but he disappeared for a week. What if he was trying to avoid me?"

"He wasn't trying to avoid you, dork."

"And what about last night? The way he just took off as soon as the cops came. That was odd, right?"

"Well, if you're so concerned with all these *signs*, why are you going out with him?" Ashleigh made a valid point. I looked at myself in the mirror. I had no clue what I was doing with my makeup because I never wore this powder and foundation-y stuff. Did I have on too much blush? I hadn't been wearing any makeup the night he kissed me. Should I take it all off? Why did he keep hitting on me and then disappearing? *Was* he hitting on me? Was he just another flirt?

My body stood frozen, paralyzed by my overanalysis as I tried making sense of all these mixed signals he'd been giving off.

"Do you think he likes me, like seriously?" I finally spoke into the phone.

"He invited you out to a party with his friends. He must have some feelings."

"What do I do if he—"

"Ken—you got this! You take on ten-foot waves."

I took a deep breath. She was right.

"Okay, okay."

My dad and Harry walked into the bathroom.

"Oooo, someone is excited for their date," Harry sang, picking up the curling iron plugged into the outlet. He intertwined it into my hair, curling it perfectly—unlike my attempt that resulted in wavy kinks.

"That's what I said too, Harry!" Ashleigh yelled out on speaker.

My dad spoke in a more serious tone. "By the way, we heard about what happened last night at Main."

Ashleigh and I were both silent.

I looked up at him. If there was one person who hated drugs more than me—it was my dad. Hate isn't even the proper term. There may have not been a word for his feelings toward abused substances.

"Yeah. It was awful. Poor Jason and Ryan," Ashleigh finally said.

"I don't want you hanging out with those boys anymore, Ken," he said emphatically. His voice was deep. And direct.

Ashleigh didn't know anything about my brother—nobody in Laguna did—so I knew my dad wasn't going to say much.

"Everything is okay, I promise." I tried to reassure my dad.

He nodded at me.

Last night had been pretty crazy. It all happened so fast; just as Brock had abruptly taken off, the four cops were suddenly standing before our bonfire—Grumpy, Happy, Sleepy, and Dopey. Grumpy had a permanent scowl while Happy had a permanent smile. Sleepy just stood there, yawning. And Dopey didn't seem mentally present at all. But either way, they had the authority over us.

"Okay, let's wrap it up, you guys are being too loud," Grumpy, the dumpier-looking one of the cops, said.

"Excuse me, officer, are we under arrest?" Ashton asked, cluelessly concerned.

"No, just keep it down next time, all right?"

"Where are Jason and Ryan?" Ashleigh whispered to me.

The police surrounded the bonfire as everyone began to head out.

An obnoxious howl of a laugh came from the darkness—it was Jason, Ryan by his side. They were super hyped up.

"I told you! He's got top-notch shit," Jason yelled loudly.

The police noticed them. "Hey! We said keep it down!"

Jason and Ryan put their hands up in the air, and a bag fell from Jason's hand.

"Stay where you are, both of you," Happy, the best looking of the four, said.

"Shit," Ryan said.

The cops descended upon them, Grumpy picking up the bag from the sand.

"Look what we have here," he said. Cocaine.

"On your knees now!" Sleepy ordered.

My heart fell down into my stomach as Jason and Ryan fell to their knees. My knees felt weak, my hands trembling. Brock's white-powdered nose on that rainy night at Ashton's flashed to mind. I swallowed down the ball forming in my throat. Then Kyle flew through my mind and I couldn't keep the tears from coming down. Silently. But still, they streamed.

Ashleigh rubbed my back. "You okay, girl? They'll be fine. Dumbasses did it to themselves."

She always picked up on when I was feeling anxious, and although she was aware that I had terrible anxiety, I never told her *why*—I didn't have any intention to tell her about my brother. Ever. Moving to Laguna was a chance for me to start over and leave the tragedies of my past behind. When we still lived in San Diego, once word spread about what happened to Kyle, everything changed for my family. At school, kids whispered . . . I was the girl with the dead brother. The school counselor constantly called me out of class to see if I needed to "talk" about anything. Then, eventually, I was the girl without a mom. I wanted to block it all out. Lately though, Brock Parker was making that quite difficult.

Before I had time to process the night's events, Jason and Ryan were being handcuffed, their hands behind their back. It made me wonder. Did they regret their choices now? I had trouble understanding *why* they had to do that. *Why?* I couldn't imagine feeling dependent on anything that would take me out of my own mind.

"You have the right to remain silent when questioned. Anything you say or do may be used against you in a court of law."

Kyle, please! We can help you!

Kyle! Open this door right now!

I shut off the voices in my head. My insides were shaking. I tightened my body up to prevent myself from full-on convulsing. I tried to restate my mantra over in my head. I was in the midst of a panic attack and couldn't find my breath. I remember all of the times that the police showed up with Kyle at our house. It started out with small things, like staying out past curfew, but eventually it got worse. The last time it happened, they pulled up to our driveway, forcefully removing Kyle from the back seat of their car. His bloodshot eyes hung low, and he was a mess. They'd caught him with heroin.

No punishment would stop him, either. Not even pulling him out of school, to get him away from "that crowd" as Coach would put it. He found a way to do his drugs regardless . . . and I think that is the most frightening part about an addict. They would do just about anything to maintain that high.

Anything. Even die.

I inhaled through my nose, letting out a silent sigh. With a few breaths, I found calmness—barely, but I did. I wanted to be far away from this nostalgic mess.

The doorbell rang from downstairs, bringing me back from last night's calamities and to the realization that Brock was literally at my house. Holy guacamole.

"Yay! He's here!" Harry rushed out of the room to go answer the door.

"Be cool, Harry," my dad reminded him, following behind.

"Wait, what? What's he wearing?" Ashleigh begged to know.

"I gotta go, Ash—"

"But—"

I hung up on Ashleigh—she would have kept going—as I frantically searched the room for my purse.

I hurried downstairs, concerned that so much could have already possibly gone wrong. What if my dad answered the door to Brock smoking a cigarette? Or what if Brock asked where my mom was or something stupid like that?

When I walked into the foyer, Brock was standing there. My dad stuck out his hand for him to shake.

"I'm Kendra's dad," he said.

"And I'm Harold."

Brock and I locked eyes, and he smiled. Ugh . . . my heart melted right into my gut.

"Hey, Kendra," he spoke from across the room. My dad and Harry turned around to face me as I entered the small circle they'd formed at the front door.

"You ready?" I asked.

"Yep."

"You guys all met?" I asked, looking at the three of them.

"Mmhmm," Harry said, his disdain apparent. Maybe I was being paranoid.

"Yes, princess. What time do you think you will be home?" my dad asked as they walked us out. I looked at Brock for an answer.

"I'll have her home no later than midnight, sir."

"All right. Have fun, kids. Be safe! That's my daughter in your car."

"You got it, sir."

Brock opened the passenger door for me.

"Precious cargo," he said to my dad and Harry.

The first minute of the car ride was driven in silence, until Brock broke the silence with a question I hadn't quite been expecting.

"Wait, so your dad, he's um—"

"Yeah, I'm sorry. I should have told you before. He's gay."

"No, no. I just wasn't sure."

"Yeah."

I wasn't uncomfortable or anything. I just never thought about it as *unusual*. I didn't think about it at all actually. To me, I had two parents: my dad and Harry. I guess it wasn't technically "traditional"—but come on. It was 2010. Was anything really normal anymore?

"One of my best buds is gay," Brock said. "Funny part is, bitches—I mean girls—dig on him so hard. They're always so bummed out when they find out he's batting for the other team."

I giggled.

"Coolest dude ever and rad fucking skater."

"That's awesome."

"Oh, here! I almost forgot." He handed me a Starbucks cup.

"Thanks. I thought we were *going* to Starbucks though."

"We *were* going to, but I promised a buddy of mine I'd be at the party early."

"Well, what is this?" I held up the cup.

"I call it a Sweet Tooth Slammer."

"What's in it?"

"A tablespoon of cinnamon, four sugars, and a quarter cup of cream."

"Um, can you say diabetes?" I set the drink back in the cup holder. "I can't be putting stuff like this in my body. I have quarterfinals coming up."

"Come on. Just try a sip and if you don't like it, you don't have to drink it."

I looked down at the drink, hesitantly picking it back up, wondering why I was going along with this when I had quarter-finals to be concerned about. I took a micro sip just to satisfy him, but it was actually *really* good.

"That's so good!"

"Right?" he said. "By the way, I guess Jason's brother bailed him and Ryan out of jail. Did you hear about that?"

"No, so they're okay?"

"I guess so. I mean, they'll have to go to court and all that, but at least they're not behind bars."

I wanted to ask Brock more about last night, and more importantly why he had so quickly vanished, but I felt that there had been too many opportunities before right now to do so, and dragging it on wouldn't do any good. So I let it go.

After an hour-long drive of mostly highway, we pulled up to a gate before a very long driveway.

"Are we here?" I asked as Brock typed a code into the key-pad. The gate opened.

"Yep! This is Duke's bachelor pad."

We drove up the mile-long driveway to the front of the mansion. I was so confused. Wasn't Duke around our age? Was this his parents' house?

We parked in the circular driveway, where an array of other foreign vehicles were parked: Mercedes, Bentleys, Jags, BMWs, you name it!

I had to know. "What does Duke do for a living?"

"He inherited some money from a relative who passed away."

"Did this relative invent the internet or something?" I joked.

Brock laughed, probably out of obligation.

"Not quite," he said, putting the car in park.

He reached over me to open my door.

"And they say chivalry is dead."

"Ha ha. Very funny."

"It's okay. I'm the kind of girl who prefers to open her own door anyway."

"Well, of course you can. But maybe I want to open it for you," he retorted.

We approached the front door, music blaring all the way outside. Like, literally, the ground was shaking. Brock paused as he grabbed the door handle and turned to me.

"You ready?" he asked.

I wasn't. At all. I was actually really nervous.

"Shouldn't we knock?" I asked.

He laughed at me.

"So I take that as a no?"

He extended his hand; I glanced at it before taking my gaze back to his. I placed my hand in his.

With that, we walked inside. The house was packed. Brock led us through the crowd of people hovering around the entrance, pushing through them. They were all nodding at him, shrieking his name in shock as if he was a celebrity and they were graced to be in his presence.

I held on to his hand even tighter, feeling more overwhelmed than I was expecting. There was a beer pong tournament set up in the dining room, where a group of guys stopped mid-throw to run over and greet Brock.

"Brock Parker! Holy shit!" one said.

"Hey, guys!" He let go of my hand to hug his buddies.

"Duuuude!" some random yelled from across the room, approaching Brock and fist-bumping him. "Los Angeles ain't the same without you, man."

"Damn, Pablo. Do you even eat anymore, man?"

"Down fifty-five pounds." Pablo flexed at Brock.

Then I recognized a face—finally. It was Duke. He walked toward us.

"Yo, bro. Glad you could make it."

"Me too, buddy," Brock said as they embraced.

"There she is!" He nodded his head to me, acknowledging my existence, before wrapping his arms around me in a full squeeze.

I didn't know quite how to respond, so I just kind of looked down at the floor. I wish I could've gripped Brock's hand right then.

"You guys, this is Kendra," Duke introduced me.

"Kendra, this is my ol' crew," Brock added. He sounded different around them. The way he talked. The way he moved.

"Nice to meet you guys," I said, way too fast for any of them to comprehend.

I did a double take when Annie came walking up to us. Why was she with Brock's LA friends? How was she so involved in his life? Were they more serious than I thought? I wondered where Mia and the rest of Annie's posse were.

"Shit," I heard Brock mumble underneath his breath. That didn't give me any more reassurance about his relationship with Annie. Was he nervous that both his girls were at the same party? Sometimes my life felt like a terrible movie cliché.

"Well, well, well, look who we have here. Laguna Tides High's new favorite couple." Annie smirked. She sized me up and down.

"We're not a couple," Brock shot back, and my heart shattered. I mean, yeah, technically we weren't an "official" couple, but come on! I thought this was a date.

"Oh, really? Then it wouldn't matter if I did this?" Annie pulled Brock into her and kissed him—hard. I winced, turning my head away. I thought Brock and I were on the same page but obviously not. I felt like the biggest loser in the world in this moment. Ugh. There I was, just introduced to all of his friends, and now he was making out with another girl in front of me and all of them!

I swallowed down the ball in my throat aching to burst out. To think that this was a date—what a joke. I shook my head, blocking it out, straightening my face. I was positive the night couldn't get any worse. And if it could—yikes.

"Come take a shot with me," Annie said to Brock.

"No thanks."

"Suit yourself."

She walked off, now eyeing Duke—which really confused me. Who did she want? Did she really want anyone? Was it all just a search for a cure for some sort of damaged childhood or something? More movie clichés persisted.

To say I was lost was an understatement. To say I was aching inside was an even bigger understatement. I honestly just wanted to go home at this point, cuddle up with my dog, and read a book or something.

"Well, if you don't mind, I'm calling dibs on that tonight," Duke said, patting Brock on the back as he walked off. "Come on, Brock. Grab a drink. There's some people I want you to meet."

"Aight."

Duke walked toward the living room area, Brock guiding me toward the kitchen to get a drink. I hoped they had Gatorade or something. I was feeling parched.

"You doing all right?" he asked as he grabbed a beer from the fridge. No Gatorade.

"Yeah," I lied.

"You sure?" he pressed.

"Yeah." It was quite clear that I wasn't okay, and it was concerning that he didn't know why—or if he did, he wasn't going to confront it. Which meant I wasn't going to either.

"Brock! Baby, I miss you!" A tiny tan girl with black curly ringlets interrupted our conversation, tackling Brock down with a hug. Was she another one of his girlfriends?

"How you doin', Kristy?"

"Doin' marvelous. Who is she?" Her words were slurred, her eyes hanging.

"This is Kendra. Kendra, this is Kristina. She's my homegirl from back in the day."

"Back in the day? We're still homies for life, fool. Just 'cause you're never around doesn't mean shit." She laughed. "I've known your boyfriend over here since we were in diapers."

"He's not my boyfriend," I said, hopefully giving Brock a taste of his own medicine. He shot me a look.

"She's got a habit of tampering with my ego," Brock said to Kristina.

"He's got a habit of having one."

I was on a roll and I wasn't going to let Brock's hotness stop it. He suddenly looked at me and smiled. As if, finally, he knew. He knew why *I was sure I was okay.*

"Oh. All right," Kristina said, sounding confused at all of it. She looked at me and shrugged her shoulders. "Hey, take a shot with me."

"I'm good with a beer right now," Brock said, lifting the bottle in his hand. "Kendra, why don't you take a shot?"

I felt my eyes widen. Why would he even bother asking that? And put me on the spot like that?

"No, no, no. I can't."

"Have a little fun." He massaged the back of my neck with his free hand. I think it made me tense up even more in nerves.

"I don't do drugs, Brock."

"Alcohol isn't a drug. It's a celebratory beverage."

"What exactly am I supposed to be celebrating?"

Kristina intervened as if she took offense to my question. "I don't know, a chill-ass night with some awesome people."

"Come on, don't your parents drink?" Brock asked.

"Well, I mean, Harry drinks wine sometimes."

"Do you know why he drinks wine sometimes?"

I wasn't following.

"To fucking relax!" he said. "Have a drink and just relax. I promise you will make it out of here alive. I wouldn't let anything happen to you."

And with that simple sentence—*I wouldn't let anything happen to you*—my insides liquefied. And I trusted him. When he spoke, he spoke genuinely. I hated and loved that about him. I felt like Brock Parker was a stranger to me that I'd known my whole life. An odd contradiction that made me feel like a fool yet so comfortable talking in a familiar manner about him.

Ew, I couldn't believe what I sounded like. It was like Ashleigh when she and Ashton first started dating. Now, they were like a married couple who'd been together for thirty years.

As I looked at Kristina, biting my lip, the thought of drinking *actually* crossed my mind. I mean, it was true, Harry drank wine once in a while. My dad didn't drink much. Only on special occasions. I guessed drinking was different than pot or drugs, right? I thought I'd even read an article once about the benefits of wine for your heart. At least alcohol was legal in all fifty states—that had to mean something. And if my parents could drink it, then I'm sure there was no harm in just trying some. I didn't want to be a complete prude loser in front of Brock. And this party was feeling tortuous at this point, so maybe a drink would help.

"Fine. But just one," I agreed.

"Yay! Let's do this!"

What had I gotten myself into?

We followed Kristina around the island, where she grabbed two red Solo cups.

"Whoa! Aren't those too big for a shot?"

Kristina laughed. "You're funny, bitch."

Brock leaned down, his lips at my ear level.

"She's not actually filling them up all the way."

She pulled out a bottle of rum from the cupboard and poured us two shots, handing one to me.

I took it, hesitantly, wondering what was about to happen.

"To being young, wild, and reckless!" Kristina yelled, downing the shot. How did she do that so fast? Did that mean it was my turn now?

I looked down at my own shot, sniffing it, then taking a tiny micro-sip.

"Honey, you best not be sipping that shit. Chug!" Kristina said.

I took another look at the shot before plugging my nose and downing it. I could not believe I had done that. I'd drunk alcohol. I wasn't sure what possessed me to do so. I'd hyped it up so much in my head for so long, that when it actually happened, and it didn't feel like anything, I was surprised.

Brock paused, looking at me, awaiting my reaction. I

couldn't help it—I stuck out my tongue, holding my chest as my face went sour. He laughed at me.

"So innocent," Kristina teased.

"It burns!" I said.

"You know what that means?" Kristina asked me as if I should have known the answer.

"What?"

"You have to do another."

Okay, one shot was all we were supposed to do. But I was sick of being uncool. I looked to Brock, searching for the right answer from him. Oddly enough, I trusted him, even with all of the reasons he gave me not to, because out of all of those reasons he had given me, there was always something he did or said to regain that trust—even dumb things, like how surprisingly delicious that apple and yogurt combination had been. Or the Sweet Tooth Slammer. Or even the way he ditched the beach last night, but he'd made sure to call and explain himself and even invite me out. I guess what I'm trying to say is, I felt the effort even when he messed up. That meant something. Or maybe I was just an idiot and I'd justify anything to make him Prince Charming, because you can't explain chemistry.

He nodded his head as if to reassure me that it was okay.

"All right. But just one more."

As Kristina poured the two of us another shot, I watched Brock slip away to Duke and a group of rowdy people sitting on the couch.

"I'll be right back," he said over his shoulder.

Kristina convinced me to break out of my "comfort zone" (as she put it) and try tequila next. I wasn't sure how much time had passed or how many shots we had downed, but, oh my goodness—the room was literally spinning. I couldn't feel my toes—and I sort of liked it. My body felt weightless, as if gravity was irrelevant. It made me wonder what boozing on the moon would be like. For once, I didn't feel constant angst creeping into my gut.

I looked over at Brock, hanging out on the couch. Holy cow, seriously, how cute was he? Especially when he wore his hat backward like that—ugh!

I let out a burp.

"'Scuse me." I giggled, holding my chest.

Kristina laughed like a hyena as she handed me another shot. I decided to stop myself from trying to figure out which number we were on. Seven? Maybe ten? I wasn't sure.

Coach's words flashed through my mind like a big red warning sign, but the faint burning, now sitting in my chest, demolished any thoughts at all. I was too numb to feel anything—even guilt.

"Woo!" Kristina yelled as she clinked her cup to mine. I downed it, my tongue indifferent to the taste.

"Oh, my gosh! I, like, really love you, Kristina!"

"Aw, girl, I love you!"

I looked at Brock again, my vision blurred. I closed one eye to see clearer. It looked like he was leaning over the table, but I couldn't really tell. I laughed, shrugging my shoulders to myself.

Curiosity struck me—or maybe it was Cupid who had sent daggers through my bones—making me wonder if he liked me. Because I might have lov—

I stopped myself before exposing alcohol-induced feelings and other things that I wasn't sure I even believed in.

BROCK

I sat on the couch with Duke and some potential clients he had been promising to introduce me to since they were moving to Orange County. Just ten minutes hanging out with them, and I thought I had made them regulars already.

It had been a minute since I had gone to LA—and I missed it. I missed the parties, the people, and the overall scene. It was the closest thing to home, I'd say the only place I really ever felt settled. Especially since Duke was there.

Duke basically ran LA these days—hence the new bachelor pad. Morales trusted him with all of Los Angeles County. His clientele started off pretty basic, typical high school cokehead shit. Now he was dealing with some of the biggest A-list celebrities in town. I don't know how he managed to pull it off, but he did. Just another reason I looked up to him. He was like a mentor to me—even though he was only a couple of years older.

"Dude, I noticed the new G-Wagon out front! So dope," I said.

"Right? Just bought it last week." Duke smiled as he leaned over the table to hit a bump.

Duke and I were in our element. Dealing, smoking, partying . . . Nostalgia wrapped itself around me. I didn't want it to end. It made me excited for the future too, for when Duke and I would be on our own. No parents. No Morales. No one in charge. Just us. As soon as we both built up enough of a clientele, it would happen. I was sure of it. One day.

I patted him on the back.

"Good times, buddy," I said.

"Hell, yeah. Love you, brother. Glad you could make it." He had his same old torn-up black baseball cap on. It rarely matched the rest of his outfit, but it wasn't meant to be a fashion statement—it was there to hide the big ass scar his father had given him as a child. Few have seen it, including me. And anyone who knew him well enough knew not to bring it up. Ever.

"Me too, buddy." I nodded at him.

"You hittin' that?" he asked as he lifted his head up.

I followed his gaze over to Kendra.

"No, no. She's not like that."

He laughed. "I swear every time you say that, I catch your ass in a closet five minutes later."

"No, I'm for real about this one."

"Shit, you must really like her. But, hey, good for you. It's 'bout damn time my homie finds his one and only baddie."

I couldn't help but chuckle. "That's the funny part. She ain't one of those bad bitches we're used to. She's actually really innocent."

"She's super cute. Make sure you're treatin' her right."

"I know. I know."

"Don't corrupt her too much."

Duke was perceptive about people. "What do I do though? She literally can't even handle pot, dude."

He nodded his head, contemplating. "Well, just respect it. It's that simple."

I saw where he was coming from, but it seemed more

complicated than that. Her issue was my entire life. My parents. My job. Me.

I inhaled a good amount of snow off of the table. I lifted my head back up, rubbing my nose to make sure there wasn't any white shit left.

I jerked around when I heard a shatter come from the kitchen. It was Kendra. She stood there hysterically laughing, standing over a broken shot glass.

"Woopsie!" she squealed.

"Party foul!" Kristina said, throwing her drunk party arms in the air.

I couldn't help but laugh. I got up and walked over to them as Kristina started to pour another shot.

"Don't worry about that," Kristina said, sweeping the glass under the counter with her shoe.

Kendra's words were slurred. "Oh, I love the Captain!" she said in a terrible British accent, lifting the bottle of Captain Morgan.

It was adorab—

I stopped myself. I was feeling like a pussy falling for her, as if I was under some sort of charm or spell. What was she doing to me?

"This bitch is a lightweight. We've barely had a dozen shots," Kristina slurred.

"I am not a shake weight!" Kendra said with uncontrollable giggles. It was pretty funny, yeah, but I figured it was best that I got her home.

"Come on, Kendra," I said. I took her by the hand, but she yanked it back.

"You can't tell me what to do! We're *not a couple*, remember?"

I looked at her. Her crooked smirk and drunken eyes. Her gaze never left mine. It made me smile. She was testy. But I knew how to handle her.

I lifted her up and hoisted her over my shoulder, carrying her out of the party.

"Yeah, buddy!" Duke yelled. People were cheering as I walked out of the house.

Annie was out front, smoking a joint. We didn't say anything. We didn't even make eye contact, but I felt her eyes boring through me as I walked down the yard to my car.

"Bye, Annie!" Kendra yelled, hanging over my shoulder. I held in my laugh—which was difficult. Kendra was way chill when she was hammered on hard liquor. I buckled her into the passenger seat. When I walked around to the driver's side, Annie was still staring. Didn't give a fuck though.

"Brock! You're like super cute," Kendra said from the passenger side, her eyes heavy and her lips curled into a permanent smile.

I couldn't help but laugh at her.

"Why are you laughing at me? I'm serious!"

I looked her way, my hands sturdy on the wheel, but my knees weak.

"You're really pretty."

"Stop looking at me while you're driving! Keep your eyes on the road!"

"It's your fault. You're distracting me!"

"Ow, ow, ow!" she whined as she ripped off her shoe and lifted it up to her face, observing it.

"What are you doing now?" I was hysterical at this point. Is this what I'd been missing out on? The wild and crazy drunk Kendra Dimes. A side I don't think she even knew.

"I think there's glass in my foot."

"You okay?" I asked.

The bass started bumping. I wasn't sure what the song was, but I liked it.

"Let's dance, Brock!" she said, turning up the radio. I turned it off.

"That's a bad idea." I smiled. Was this how I acted when I was fucked up?

"Whatever. Do you have any food? I'm hungry."

"We can stop somewhere if you want."

"Ugh! Yes! Please."

"Jeez, you're a totally different person when you're drunk!"

"Why are you laughing at me again? It's starting to bug me. And what does that mean—that I'm a completely different person? Do you like me more when I'm drunk? Or do you like me better sober? Should I take this as a compliment or insult? But either way, you're so cute that it hurts my brain."

We were stopped at a red light, my eyes on hers. My jaw had dropped somewhere along that spiel, and just as I thought I might have something to say, all that I could exhale was breath and an astonished chuckle. She was a very . . . theatrical drunk. This girl hadn't ceased to surprise me. She was different, and I think that's what I was beginning to fall for.

She blushed. "I'll just shut up now."

"I like you drunk and sober. And when I'm drunk. And when I'm sober."

Moments later, we pulled into a drive-through.

"What do you want?" I asked.

"The cheesiest of cheesy!"

"All right then." I turned to the speaker. "Can I get a cheeseburger with extra cheese and an order of fries?"

"Do you want onions on that?"

I looked at her for a response and she stuck her finger down her throat in a gagging motion. So I took that as a no.

"Will you be eating this in the car?" the woman asked through the intercom.

"Duh!" Kendra shouted. "What kind of question is that? Is there any better place to eat?"

I put my hand over her mouth, and in return she licked it.

"You sick ass." I laughed, pulling it back.

We pulled through the line to the window.

"By the way, I'm lactose intolerant," she decided to mention as I exchanged cash for our order, which I'd be shocked if they hadn't spit in at this point.

I handed her the bag of food and we drove off.

"Oh, my gosh," she gushed as she bit into a fry.

"Hey, give me one!"

She stuck out a french fry for me to take as I leaned my head toward her. When we approached the red light, she stuck it in my mouth, giggling, but I grabbed her hand before she pulled it away, sticking her entire finger into my mouth and sucking on it from top to bottom. I watched as she froze mid-chew.

"You're right, that is good." I winked. I released her finger as she swallowed her fry.

She pulled her hand back and into her chest. She was silent for a moment, biting her lip. Our eyes were still entranced in each other's.

"What? What're you thinking?" I had to know.

"So, I've, like, seen things like that in movies, where couples suck on each other's fingers, but I didn't think people actually did it in real life. Is that considered kinky? I'm not a kinky person. At least I didn't think I was. But oddly enough, that kind of turned me on. Maybe I am a kinky person?" She spoke so fast, but I was learning to keep up.

"You're a very vocal drunk person, huh?"

She shrugged her shoulders. It all seemed out of place. Her. The alcohol. This coke high didn't even feel like it normally did. I felt like the sober one right now, and I sure as fuck wasn't.

Out of natural reflex, I played with the small knob beneath the radio, turning the volume up. The stereo system blasted.

"I like this." Kendra began dancing to herself.

"You do?"

"Yeah!" she said, nodding her head to the beat, grabbing my hands and throwing them in air. I smiled at her. It made me happy—she was dancing to my own song.

"What?" She paused the dance moves.

"Nothing."

"Tell me." She turned the radio down.

"I made this," I admitted.

"No way! If that's true, then you have some serious skill, Brock Parker."

"Why do you say my first and last name?"

"You have one of those names."

"Damn, do I?"

"Maybe it's because it's like two first names."

"Huh. Never thought of it like that."

"I just can't believe you made this. You're amazing."

"Well, thank you."

She pulled her burger out from the bag and took a bite.

With food moving around in her mouth and slurred words, she said, "You're going to do something crazy."

That had taken me off guard. No one had ever said something like that to me before.

"What do you mean?"

She swallowed a not-fully-chewed bite of burger and continued on to say, "I mean, you're going to do something, like, super influential and crazy. Like, people everywhere are going to know your name one day."

I looked at Kendra. Did she really think that of me? I hoped she didn't. Because it wasn't true. Her perception of me was off—by a lot. I wished I could be who she thought I was, but I wasn't. Maybe I'd just keep playing along for now, though.

"Holy cannoli! So good," she said, devouring the burger.

"Whoa there, slow down!" I laughed.

We pulled onto Forest Avenue at the same time Kendra let out a burp, and when I looked at her, kind of shocked, she was already covering her mouth.

"Excuse me," she said. "Was hoping you hadn't heard that."

But I just laughed it off and said, "Very ladylike, Kendra."

"Could I be any more mortifying?"

"Definitely. You could be one of those girls that puke or cry when they get drunk."

We turned down Kendra's street. I could hear her stomach gurgle.

"You good?" I asked.

In response, puke spewed out of her onto the floor of my car. Now I felt bad for mentioning girls who throw up or cry when they drink.

"Kendra!" I jumped out of my car, and rushed to her side, opening the door. She was still bent over, chunks of alcohol-scented cheeseburger projected onto the car floor. I gathered her hair up to keep it out of the vomit.

She coughed, sitting back up.

"Are you okay?" I asked.

"Never better." She smiled. "Let me get a towel and clean this up. I am so, so sorry—"

"Oh, stop. I'll get it." I helped her out of the car.

She paused and looked back down at the car. "I'm cringing."

"Why? It happens! But I think you should probably stay away from the Captain for a while."

"Probably a good idea."

I could tell she was starting to sober up.

She persisted. "Brock, can I please go get a towel and clean this up?"

"Believe me, I've seen it all. It's totally okay."

She looked at me. "Thanks again for tonight."

"Thank you, beautiful," I said and kissed her forehead.

"Did you really call my hot mess of a self *beautiful*? Now I think you're the drunk one."

"No, I think that makes me the sober one, actually."

"Yeah, relationship goals: clean up each other's throw up. It's the new trending hashtag. Such a turn-on, I'm sure of it," she said. Then I saw the way her face fell, and she quickly corrected herself. "Not that we're in a relationship. Or anything of that sort."

"Right."

"But I have to admit, I do feel better after getting everything out of my system."

"Yeah?" I neared her.

"Yeah." She smiled.

I pulled her into me, avoiding breathing through my nose, or breathing at all for that matter, as I kissed her on the lips this time.

"Do you *want* to be in a relationship with me?" I pulled back, looking at her.

"Why would I want to date someone who lets random girls throw up in his car?"

"Yeah, fuck him. He sounds whack."

She just smiled, her eyes never leaving mine. It felt like something I swore I'd read about but never thought was real.

It scared the shit out of me, and suddenly I wanted to leave and never look at her again, but at the same time I never wanted to be away from her again. What the fuck? What was this girl doing to me?

"Do you need help getting inside?" I asked.

"No. No, I'm good."

"Okay, then—goodnight, Kendra."

I looked in my rearview mirror as Kendra stood there watching me as I sped off into the darkness, my engine roaring through her silent and serene suburban neighborhood. I was no genius, and I definitely didn't pay attention in English, but it seemed like a metaphor for a lot more.

When I got home, I decided it was a good time to play the drums that had sat unused in the corner of my room for much too long. I thought back to Kendra puking in my car and burst out laughing as I went hard, beating the drums.

My parents yelled from the other room to shut up, but I kept going anyway.

It was only nine in the morning, and I had already closed three deals. After spending all morning in my car, though, I myself was nauseated. It still smelled of Kendra's vomit from a whole week ago. I'd been putting off getting it cleaned, so I finally dropped it off at the car wash and called a cab to take me home. There was no way I had the attention span to sit and wait. The premium package took, like, two hours.

I walked into my house while I was on the phone with Kendra.

"You also didn't believe me when I told you apples tasted better dipped in yogurt," I said to her.

"Okay, that was one thing but seriously, peanut butter and bacon sandwiches? It sounds sticky and greasy."

"It is. And delicious."

"Can you believe today is the last day of fall break? I have that terrible Sunday feeling in my gut."

"I know, for real. I feel it too."

My father was on the phone in the kitchen.

"I gotta go. I'll text you."

I clicked off, trying to keep my presence under wraps, avoiding the constant barrage of questions.

"*Bueno, bueno*," my father said into the phone. He hung up. I tried sneaking past him without him noticing. I didn't feel like hearing about business.

"Brock, we have a shipment coming in from the border. I'm putting you in charge."

I yawned, giving him a thumbs-up, continuing on to my room.

"If you sell it all, I'll give you full commission."

I stopped dead in my tracks, unsure if I had heard him correctly.

"All of it?" I clarified. I turned around to face him.

"If you sell it all."

"How much are we talking here?"

"Ten kilos—"

"Ten?" I knew there was a catch. "That'll take months!"

"Then you better get working," he said with a cunning smirk, exiting the room.

Ten kilos? The motherfuck—that would be insane. It was no wonder he offered me full commission. He knew it would never happen.

There was no way I could let him get away with his typical bullshit. I was going to make sure that I sold every last gram of that shit. And I was going to do it fast. I pulled my phone from out of my pocket; desperate times called for desperate measures. I put the two hardest-working people I knew in a group message.

> **Brock:** Need your help...
> **Annie:** Of course U do ;)
> **Duke:** Whatever u need, dude
> **Brock:** 10 fucking kilos.
> **Annie:** 50%
> **Duke:** Come on, Annie.
> **Brock:** I'd rather die a virgin than pay you half of the commission on this.
> **Duke:** Now that's a blatant lie :D
> **Brock:** Okay, true ...
> **Annie:** Do U want my help or not?
> **Brock:** Yes ... but you're not getting 50%
> **Annie:** Fine, we'll figure out a deal later.
> **Brock:** Kk.

KENDRA

Monday was here and school was back in session. I usually didn't dread it this badly, but this week with Brock made me want to relive fall break over and over.

I woke up early to fit in a surf sesh with Coach. I walked into my house afterward, my body sore and still barely awake. I dragged myself into the shower, replaying the party in LA the whole time, fantasizing as if it was happening all over again. It was a magical night—from what I could remember. And minus the puke-y parts.

The hot water felt so good on my skin. I stayed in until it was cold, my thoughts consumed with Brock's voice. His smile. His laugh. His hotness. His coolness. His kisses. His everything. When I got out, I threw on sweats and a T-shirt. I looked at myself in the mirror, wanting to look cute for Brock. We'd talked every day since the party. No weird disappearances or sudden ghosting. I decided to change, wearing a pair of jeans I'd bought a long time ago but never worn and a vintage rock band T-shirt. I tied it at the bottom to make it tighter around my waist. Ashleigh would be proud.

I threw the other shirt in the hamper, too lazy to hang it back up, and I spotted the throw-up-stained shirt from the party underneath my dresser by my bed. I must've taken it off and thrown it on the floor. Thankfully I'd found it before Harry or my dad. It was best the evidence of last weekend's escapades wasn't exposed to anyone outside of Brock's car.

I couldn't believe Brock was even talking to me after that night. After he'd dropped me off, I crashed, and the next morning was shocked to wake up to a text from him—maybe miracles did exist. It was a picture of a towel covered in my throw up.

Kendra: You'll never let this one go, will you?
Brock: Nahhhh. ;)

I walked into class early, as usual, and sat down. It was just Mr. Paul and me in the room. The past week felt like a dream. I couldn't get it off my mind. As Mr. Paul continued talking about *The Catcher in the Rye*, I was more concerned with wondering where Brock and I stood. Sometimes, even during the best of times with him, it seemed I was in one place mentally, and he was in another. Also, a part of me *did* feel stupid, liking a guy who kissed another girl right in front of me. But I rationalized that technically we weren't together. Then I felt even more stupid thinking that.

"Ms. Dimes?" Mr. Paul's voice caught my attention along with his knee hitting the back of my seat. I jerked my head around to find my classmates seated at their desks. I hadn't even realized he was talking to me.

"Sorry," I said.

"Chapter nine, Holden gets off the train in New York. Who does he want to call?"

My heart dropped—I'd completely spaced on the new assigned reading during break.

"Umm . . ."

I bit the end of my pencil, looking around the room for someone—anyone—to save me.

"All right then." Mr. Paul walked away to his next victim. "What do you think, Mr. James?"

I pulled out my book and tried to skim through the pages. I read over the words at such a pace, my brain couldn't even process what I was reading.

As class ended, I was still trying to catch up on the assignment. I walked out with my head in my book, bumping into people. I had never missed a reading assignment. *Ever.* How did I forget? I walked to my locker, trying to finish up the chapter.

"Hey," Brock said. I looked up at him and smiled before taking my focus back to reading. "Did you hear Jason and Ryan are suspended this week because of the bust?"

"Really?" I kept my gaze down on my book.

"Yeah. They go to court this week. But I guess the principal found out and was considering expelling them. Thankfully, Jason's mom is on the PTO, and his stepdad donated a shit ton of money to the athletic department. So basically the whole thing was swept under the rug."

I nodded.

"What are you reading?"

I turned the book over to reveal the cover.

"Mark David Chapman—" Brock began.

"What? No, J. D. Salinger wrote it. Who's Mark David Chapman?"

"The guy who killed John Lennon. During his trial he read a passage from *The Catcher in the Rye.*"

"Really? I didn't know that," I said. It suddenly struck me that Brock Parker was a lot more book smart than he let on.

"Yeah."

I shut the novel, shoving it into my locker and reaching for my chemistry book.

"Hey, do you want to grab some ice cream?" he asked.

"What? We have class, I have—"

"Whatever you have probably isn't as much fun as ditching."

"Probably not, but it's more important."

"Don't be a pansy!"

"I am not a pansy."

The warning bell rang.

"Come on. You have two minutes to decide."

I looked at Brock. Ice cream *did* sound good. A smile snuck its way through my mouth. I shook my head and laughed.

"Fine. But *just* fifth period."

I followed Brock out of the building.

"So, like, how do we do this?" My heart palpitated. The most school I had ever missed was a week during ninth grade when I had the stomach flu. I'd never ever ditched class.

"Do what?"

I froze as the security guard neared us in his golf cart.

"Brock!" I loudly whispered.

"What?"

He looked where my gaze was focused.

"What up, Billy?" he said.

Billy nodded at him as he drove past us. My jaw dropped. How did Brock do that? I looked at the golf cart driving toward the football field. How did he know Billy, and why would the security guard let us off the hook like that? Brock kept walking to his car.

"Are you coming or what?"

Brock and I spent the afternoon on the beach, making a stop to get ice cream beforehand. At first I was paranoid about running into someone, or my dad and Harry finding out, but the nervousness passed. Whenever I was with Brock, I seemed to forget about the world around me.

As we strolled along, from the corner of my eye I caught Brock staring at me. I giggled nervously; I was uncomfortable with anyone just randomly staring at me like that without any words or reason. It made me feel insecure.

In response, he laughed at me.

"What?" I asked. I could feel my face turning flush.

"Can't a person laugh without having a motive?" he countered. He turned to me, taking my hand in his. "I've never noticed those freckles on your nose before."

I touched my nose instinctively.

"I like them."

I rolled my eyes, smiling at him.

"What?"

"I'm sure you say that to every girl."

"What's that supposed to mean?" he asked. As I continued walking, he dropped my hand.

I took a lick from my cone, avoiding having to respond.

"Hey." He caught up to me. "What're you saying?"

He seemed more serious now.

"I'm saying that I'm quite positive I'm not the only girl you've said that to. But don't get me wrong, it's a good one!"

"A good what?"

"A good line."

"Maybe you just don't know how to take a compliment."

I shrugged my shoulders. "Probably."

He quickly stole a bite of my cone and ran off.

"Hey!" I said, trying to keep up. And being the klutz I was, of course, I tripped over my own feet and dropped the rest of my ice cream on the ground. Thankfully Brock didn't see. I chased him down. He led me to a hidden gazebo with a view of all Laguna.

"Hard not to appreciate the moment here, huh?" he said,

gazing out and taking in paradise. He was right. It was hard not to. The sand. The water. The sun. The clouds. The hills. I closed my eyes and took in a deep breath, feeling all of it.

I opened my eyes. "This view is incredible."

"Right? I come here sometimes when I need to just escape. Parents. School. Life in general." He was serious at first, then he caught himself and looked at me and just sort of laughed it off.

He bobbed his head up and down, left to right. It aligned with the sound of the waves as if it was a song and he could hear the beat, crashing, rumbling, and roaring.

We leaned up against the gazebo, gazing out at the ocean below us. The moment was still. Silent. There wasn't much around us—no traffic or people. Just the waves and an occasional bird chirping in passing.

"Life goes beyond the textbooks, Miss Dimes."

This Brock, right now, right here—he was so different than the one I'd met that night at homecoming. I wondered which one of his personalities was the real one: the hard Brock Parker who snorted cocaine and was the life of the party, or the Brock Parker who loved the sound of ocean waves and was much softer-spoken than I'd realized. It didn't matter, because either way, I liked him despite his flaws. Something about him. Something.

I spotted a rock on the ground and picked it up. "Here you go."

"What's this for?"

"Your rock collection," I said, recalling his secret confession in the tree house.

He looked at the rock and suddenly dropped it down my shirt.

"Now it's my lucky rock."

"Brock Parker!" I said, grabbing onto my chest with both hands.

"I like when you say my full name like that."

He stuck the rock in his pocket. I shook my head at him, laughing. Okay, I loved it. I loved that it was now his lucky rock. I knew for a fact Annie had never given him a lucky rock before.

He stepped an inch closer to me.

Now there were no more inches that could be counted between us. Not even centimeters. He was so close to me that I could feel warmth radiating from his body. Ew, I sounded like the narrator from a cliché romance novel. But I loved it. Did he want me to make the move? Wasn't that, like, the modern thing to do? I mean, he'd made all the moves before this, so did that mean he was planning to again or that it was my turn?

He looked down as he took my fingers into his hand.

"Don't see too many girls walking around with those anymore." He tapped the watch around my wrist. "I'll be even more impressed if the time is accurate."

I followed his gaze down to my wrist.

"Oh, my gosh. It's already two o'clock. We were only supposed to miss fifth period!" Reality set in when I realized the time.

"Who cares. Live a little."

And then he made the move, closing any spare room between our bodies, wrapping his arms around my waist. Suddenly, reality was forgotten once again. I tensed right up, my arms glued to my sides like a soldier in the military.

My heart started pounding, not like racing, but *pounding*. To the point where I was scared he might actually feel it palpitating out of my chest.

"Am I making you nervous, Kendra?" he said, smiling and staring right into my eyes. All I could do was giggle and dig my eyes into the ground, avoiding any intimate eye contact.

"Your eyes are really clear," he said, taking my chin into his hand and lifting my eyes back up so they were looking directly into his.

"What does that mean, exactly?" I said, biting my lip.

"I don't know. Like you can see the coloring of your eyes so clearly."

"Thanks?"

My phone interrupted the moment. Lame technology.

I looked down at the screen. Coach.

"I really have to get going—I'm running late for practice!"

We pulled up to my house.

"That was fun today."

"Yeah. Thanks for playing hooky with me," he said, shooting me a wink. Ugh, he was so hot.

"I have to get going. I'm already a half hour late."

"All right."

I waited there a moment longer. I wanted him to kiss me so badly. Did that sound desperate? I sat there, twirling my hair around my finger, avoiding his gaze in hopes he would make a move. Meanwhile, his hand was moving a mile a minute texting away on his phone as if I was nonexistent. After the realization settled in that it just wasn't happening, I decided to stop being an awkward loser and open my door.

"See you later," I said.

I stepped out onto the pavement, starting for the front door.

"Wait," Brock said as he shifted into park. He ran to my side. "You going to Ashton's Halloween party this weekend?"

"Maybe. Are you?"

He stepped an inch closer to me, sealing the distance between our bodies as if we were on the gazebo again.

Kiss me. Kiss me! I sang over and over in my head.

"Well, I was going to say if you aren't, every year on Halloween my family takes our yacht out with a bunch of their friends if you want to come."

"So I finally get to meet the Parker clan."

"Yes, unfortunately. I need someone to keep me company while I listen to all of their boring, drunk friends blabber on about nothing. You down?"

"I'm straight up down." I wasn't sure where I pulled that out from, but I think it sounded cool.

"Sweet, 'cause I'm straight up up."

We laughed together, Brock interrupting my openmouthed giggle with a kiss. Before I had time to take it in, he was already proceeding to his car. I was stuck in place, time escaping from me. I was already late for practice. The sound of his engine startled my thoughts, bringing me back to real life—which was beginning to feel far from *real* these days.

As I approached the front door, my mind struck a blank wondering what had just happened in a matter of seconds. Before I entered the house, I looked back at him—and he was looking back at me. With a smile and a nod, he zoomed off. When I walked inside, I heard footsteps hurrying into the other room.

"Hello?" I said.

"In the kitchen!" Harry yelled.

I walked into the kitchen where Harry was preparing dinner. It smelled like his homemade Alfredo sauce, which was amazing. It was his mom's recipe. I think it was a nostalgic thing for him, especially since he didn't talk to his parents.

"It smells so good, Harry."

"I got an interesting phone call today."

"Really? From who?"

"Oh, nothing *too* important. Just your school informing me that *you were not in class today.*" He stopped what he was doing and looked at me with bulging eyes. I couldn't tell if this was a question or statement or even both at once due to his fresh Botox injections that made him hard to read. I stood there, unsure of how to explain myself, fumbling for the right words.

"About that—"

"Yes, I would love to hear more *about that*."

"Brock and I—"

"Brock? This Brock kid seems to be having a very bad influence on you, Ken. I wasn't too fond of him that night."

"It isn't his fault. We were just supposed to skip fifth and—"

"Listen, I'm not going to tell your dad this time. But seriously, I am going to advise you to maybe start breaking away from him."

"All right. Thanks, Harry."

Harry went back to his Alfredo when the sound of the garage door interrupted our conversation. Seconds later, my dad walked in the room. He kissed me on the head.

"How was school today, honey?" he asked.

"It was fine," I said, the pitch of my voice higher than I anticipated. Harry looked at me, acknowledging it. I hoped my dad hadn't noticed. He made his way over to Harry, greeting him with a peck.

"Zola and I put in our first offer for a space for the salon!" Harry said.

"Congrats, lovey," my dad said.

"I have to go. I'm running late for practice," I said, heading upstairs in case my dad asked any more questions.

Normally, I was a punctual person, but today I was the complete opposite. I ran onto the sand at Main Beach where Coach Harkins was waiting.

"Where've you been?"

"I'm so sorry," I said through my struggling breath. "I had this after-school thing for my chem class." All of this lying made my brain ache.

"It's all right, but you can't be this late again."

"I won't."

"You've still got a lot of progress to make in a short period of time. Let's get it together."

I nodded my head, agreeing with him.

"Cool. Let's warm up."

Coach had me do sit-ups, squats, arm circles, and quad stretches. The ocean's mist felt refreshing as my body heated up. I wondered what Brock was doing. I couldn't help but replay our kiss over and over in my head. It made my stomach flutter with nerves and happiness like butterflies were tickling my colon—which was not a good thing during surf practice.

"Ken?"

"Sorry, what?"

"Are you sure you're good?"

"Yeah. Why?"

"I've been saying your name for the last hour."

"Oh. Yeah. I'm good. Sorry."

We paddled out into the ocean. It was perfect out. I looked back at the shore, thinking back to Brock and me walking on the beach, ditching the movies. I got completely raked over by an unexpected wave while my mind was zoned out on the sand.

"You all right, Ken?" Coach asked when I popped my head above the water.

"Yeah."

It is what it is, I said to myself as I charged toward a wave. I stood back up, but it took me down quick. And hard. I was out of breath and already worn out, my anxiety relentlessly trying to worm its way through my thoughts, leaving me to focus on my breathing between waves.

From my peripheral vision, I saw Coach shaking his head. It made my body stiffen up with angst. After one last failed attempt, I paddled back to shore and walked up to the beach where Coach was waiting. It was an unsuccessful practice, and I could tell my lack of concentration was irritating Coach.

"What's going on today, Ken?"

"I don't know. I guess I'm just not focused. My head is in a gazillion other places."

"You know what, let's call it quits for today. Maybe you just need a day off. We'll pick up where we left off tomorrow, okay?"

I nodded, adjusting the St. Christopher pendant on its chain around my neck. I felt like I was letting Kyle down. At the same time, a cold breeze brushed by me, making me shudder. It was as if he was there with me, watching over me or something. But I quickly blocked the thought out of my head.

My chakras were all out of whack. I needed to go meditate.

BROCK

I parked in an alleyway between Laguna and Dana Point. It was that point at dusk where you couldn't see shit. Like, it wasn't dark out yet, but the sun had disappeared. A beat-up Mercedes that was, like, ten models behind pulled up. The windows were tinted. It had to be him.

I put my car in drive, pulling up so our windows were aligned. When I rolled down my window, the Mercedes reciprocated.

Morales had us dealing Oxys now. It was a big one on the market. An 80 mg tablet could go for as much as eighty dollars. I handed him the plastic bag of pills and he gave up the cash in return.

Normally I counted the cash before handing over the shit, but I was legit sketched out by this dude. Hopefully it was all there. He rolled up his tinted window and zoomed off.

I pulled my car out of the alleyway, looking right to make sure I could turn. Just past the tops of the buildings, the ocean sat calm. I admired its stillness. A smile made its way to the edges of my mouth, thoughts of Kendra rolling through my mind. I felt like a little bitch, but . . . whatever. I'd accepted it by now. I pulled out my phone and scrolled down my texts until I saw her name.

Brock: Hey cutie

Kendra: Hey there. What's up?

Brock: Wanna grab a bite to eat?

Kendra: For sure. Want to pick me up?

Brock: Yeah. Where you at?

Kendra: Right in front of the Chakra Shack.

Brock: Stay there. Be there in two.

Kendra: Warning . . . I have no makeup on & my hair is still wet :P

I pulled up to this place, the Chakra Shack, which I'd driven by a hundred times but didn't know what it was. Kendra was sitting along the curb, her brown hair in her face. Nightfall was here; I watched the house lights flicker on upon the green hills as the moon made its presence clear, shining bright above the ocean.

She hadn't noticed me, so I rolled down my window and said, "Hey there."

Then she looked up at me and threw her phone—what a spaz.

"Haaaa . . . iiii." She made a nervous laugh that somehow rolled into a "hi."

"Hop in, weirdo," I said, and she stood up, leaving her phone on the ground.

"You gonna bring your phone?"

She looked down at her phone that lay on the ground below her. Just staring at it.

I laughed. "Does it have leprosy or something?"

She finally picked it up and said, "To be honest, I was totally stalking your Facebook page when you pulled up and accidentally liked a picture from a long time ago."

She looked at me with one eye open and the other shut as if she was totally cringing inside.

"So just pretend that didn't happen, okay?"

"Did you really just admit that?" What kind of girl owned up to stalking your social media? It amused me. I liked it.

When she got into the car and shut the door, she took a deep breath, her eyes on me.

"Hey," I said.

"Long time no see!" she teased.

"Right? What's it been? Four hours?"

"How can you see right now with those on?" Kendra pointed out my sunglasses that I had on despite the darkness.

"I have many superpowers, Kendra."

"Oh, is that so?"

"Yeah. You think I was just going to reveal them to you all at once?"

She giggled.

"Where do you want to go eat?"

I placed my hand on her knee and gave it a small squeeze. She looked at me, her eyes widened. *Shit*, did that mean she was turned on? Or just full-on creeped out? She didn't push me away, so I took it she was turned on. I mean, we were past that point, right? I'd cleaned up her vomit.

"Umm . . ."

"I know where we'll go," I said, putting my car back in drive.

"Where?"

"It's a surprise."

"I don't know how I feel about that."

We were stopped at another light, and I asked, "What's in the bag?"

"Oh, I forgot about the sage."

"Sage? For what?"

"Burning."

"Do I have a crush on a pyromaniac?" I teased. "What does one burn sage for?"

"Cleansing and clearing the mind. I'm really into holistic approaches to managing my anxiety." She looked at me, but quickly turned away. "Sorry, I don't know why I'm telling you about all of this." She was flustered, moving her hands around as she spoke.

"No, no. It's cool. I didn't know you dealt with anxiety." I wanted to know more, but I also didn't want to press. I could tell she was nervous. I bet *vulnerable* would be the term Duke would have used.

"Yeaaaah. It's not a big deal or anything—like I don't want you to think there's something wrong with me. I'm really okay. I am." She spoke so fast I could barely understand her. "I've learned to manage it with yoga and meditating."

"You do yoga?"

"Yeah, my surfing coach is certified."

"That's dope. You should teach me some of your favorite positions."

Her eyes questioned my motives. I winked to explain them all.

"And by the way," I said, "I don't think anything's wrong with you."

She smiled.

"So do you believe in karma and all that shit?" I asked.

"Kind of. Do you?"

"Nah." I chuckled. "According to karma, I would've been fucked a long time ago."

She laughed, shaking her head, returning her gaze to the road ahead.

I slowed down, pulling into a resort.

"What are we doing here?" she asked.

"Dinner, of course!"

The valet opened our doors.

"Can you keep the whip up front?" I asked and tossed the guy my car keys.

"For sure," he said.

"My lady," I said in a British accent, holding out my arm for her.

She laughed at me, hesitating before wrapping her arm in mine as we entered the lobby. "You're a real character."

We exited the elevator onto the bottom level from where I could hear the waves crashing. I held Kendra's hand in mine as we walked to the front of the restaurant.

"Hello. Joining us for dinner?" the hostess asked. She had to be around our age, maybe a couple of years older. Her nametag read "Beverly."

"Yeah. For two," I said as I took a mint out of the bowl sitting on the counter.

Beverly was kind of hot, but I could tell her piercing blue eyes were fake. I looked at Kendra—she wore ripped jeans and a baggy T-shirt and somehow made it look sexy as fuck. Without even revealing a hint of skin. She was a natural kind of beauty.

"Follow me," Beverly said, two menus in hand.

We followed her to an outside spot that overlooked the ocean. It was perfect. I pulled out a chair for Kendra, taking note of how nice her ass looked in those jeans as she took a seat. I took the one across from her.

"Thank you," I said to Beverly.

"Wow, this is so nice!" Kendra admired the night. The moon lit up the water.

"Right? It's a good way to end the day."

"I would have to agree."

I looked at her. She intrigued me. I don't know—there was just something about her.

"You look pretty, Kendra."

"Aw shucks. Shpanks, Brock," she said in an adenoidal voice, her face scrunched up and blushing.

The waiter approached us. "Hello, my name is Wes. I will be your server tonight. Can I get any drinks started for you?"

I scanned the wine list before answering. "Do you guys have a good merlot?"

From the corner of my eye, I saw Kendra look up at me.

"Yeah. The Duckhorn merlot is a great choice."

"All right, then. I'll take a glass of that."

"Can I see your ID?"

I pulled out my wallet and handed him my fake. Kendra gave me an openmouthed smile, her eyes narrowed on me. I smiled at her as Wes checked out my New York ID. Morales had it made for me when I was fifteen. I looked at him as he looked down at me to compare my picture. I could tell by his eyes that he was questioning the truth. Out of protocol, Wes *had* to check my card, but out of deference to his boss, who was a close family friend—er, client—he had to risk his job since he knew that I was probably bullshitting him. But, hey, I was owed this favor.

"All right. Cool," he said, handing me the card. "And what can I get you, miss?"

"Actually," I interrupted, "fuck it. Let's get a bottle."

Kendra's eyes widened.

"Of course, sir. Are we celebrating anything in particular tonight?"

I looked over at Kendra as she held back a laugh. I thought quickly.

"Yes, actually." I placed my hand on top of Kendra's. "We just got engaged."

"Congrats!"

Kendra couldn't hold her laugh back any longer. She was uncontrollably hysterical, letting out a snort—which made me laugh. Wes looked at her. I'm sure he knew we were being complete assholes, totally fucking with him as if we were pulling it off.

"I'm sorry," she said, between the giggling. She couldn't contain herself. "I just still can't get over it. After all these years, he finally proposed."

Wes tried to force a laugh too, as if I was going to tip him more for acting amused at our nonsense.

"I'll be right back with that," he said.

Kendra wiped away her laughter-induced tears as she watched Wes disappear back into the restaurant. Her gaze quickly shifted to me when her mouth dropped, words stuck in her diaphragm, but a laugh escaped. It was like a giggle and sigh combined type of laugh. I wished she had included the snort. It was pretty fucking cute—at least on her it was. Did that sound weird? Sometimes the oddest things turned me on. Like Kendra's freckles.

She looked up at the sky and then back at me. "What the heck?"

"Come on, Kendra. I thought you realized I'm not that big on rules," I said, putting the mint in my mouth. I decided to leave out the minor detail that my parents were good friends with the owner of the hotel, Matt. Well, more like, he was one of their regulars. I also decided to leave out that I may or may not have texted him as we pulled up.

She gave me this testing half smile, but I could tell she was feeling it.

"What?" I asked.

"Nothing. But where's my ring?"

She lifted her naked hand up to face me.

"Babe, I'm sorry," I joked. "It's currently being custom made because a one-of-a-kind girl should only have a one-of-a-kind ring. You know I would only waste my money on the most precious and rare diamond for a gem like yourself."

Wes came back with the bottle of merlot.

He set two glasses down on the table, before opening up the bottle of wine for me to sniff. Once I approved, he poured a small amount into the glass, letting me take a sip. I nodded my head and he poured a full glass followed by Kendra's.

"Thanks, man."

"Of course. It's on the house for the newly engaged couple!"

"Aw. Thank you," Kendra gushed. She was in character now, going along with all the bullshit.

"Do you guys need another minute to order or do you know what you want?"

"Let me get us two filet mignons and an order of fries for the table."

He pulled out his pad of paper and a pen, quickly writing down the order, then took the menus and headed off. Wes would've done anything we said and just gone along with it. Matt was such a chill dude, he probably told him to take good care of us. I had to take advantage of that—at least for the night. When I thought about it, I'd never taken a girl out on a real date before like this.

I took a sip of the merlot. It tingled my tongue, but it was smooth. I liked it.

"I have a feeling you're one of those guys that gets away with everything," Kendra said.

"What makes you say that?" I said, already knowing the answer.

She looked at me because she knew I knew.

She leaned her head in closer to whisper, "They didn't even ID me."

"Of course they didn't." I winked and took another sip. "Aren't you going to have some?"

She shot me a probing look. I held my glass out.

"Cheers," I said.

She looked at it and then around the restaurant before finally raising her glass and clinking it to mine.

"Cheers."

She took a sip so small it didn't even count.

"What do you think?"

"I don't know how I feel about red wine," she admitted, a sour look on her face. She puckered her lips.

"It'll grow on you."

I aerated the wine, swirling it around the glass before taking another sip.

"So sophisticated, Mr. Parker," Kendra teased.

"It's a lifestyle."

I looked out at the ocean, the waves in sync with my breath. I turned back to Kendra, broadcasting my thoughts, louder than I normally would—as always with her. "You know what I was thinking?"

"What?"

"We should go surfing together sometime soon."

She smiled the kind of smile that made me want to smile. So I did. And without her saying yes, I knew she would want nothing more than to go surfing together.

KENDRA

Two glasses of this merlot stuff and I was already tipsy. It felt nice actually. The wine wasn't quite as nauseating as the Captain Morgan. I took a french fry from the basket sitting in the center of the table. Brock and I caught each other's eye, each of us mid-bite. The sight of us stuffing our faces made us both laugh.

"There's something about you, Kendra," he said to me, his eyes never leaving mine. "Just something about you."

Was it really Brock speaking or was it the wine? I was sure a slight combination of both.

"How we doing over here?" Wes asked as he approached our table.

"Amazing!" I squealed, lifting my wineglass. I could feel it in my toes. That buzzing feeling.

"Good. Let me know if I can get you two anything else," he said, walking back inside.

"Cheers," I said, lifting my glass again.

"Cheers," Brock said, clinking his glass to mine.

I interrupted him before he could take his sip. "Wait! What should we cheers to?"

"That's a good question." He stared off for a moment.

"Cheers to a forever long friendship!" he said, raising his glass again.

"Cheers to that," I agreed as our glasses touched. We both took a sip. Well, I took more of a *gulp*, finishing off the glass. A small burp fell out of me before it could be condensed and swallowed down.

I instantly covered my mouth as if it was a natural reflex. "Whoops. Pardon *moi*."

"You nasty ass." Brock threw a french fry at me.

Everything felt so perfect in this moment that it scared me. I'd always had this fear of things seeming too good to be true. Usually they were.

"Are you as stuffed as I am?" Brock asked, sitting back in his chair. He tossed the napkin that was resting on his lap onto the table.

"Yes. I'm really full. Gahhh." I stuck out my tongue.

"That was attractive."

I crossed my eyes and gave him a distorted face in response.

"Well," Brock said, looking at me.

"Well," I said back.

"What do you think about taking a walk on the beach?"

"I think that is a lovely idea."

"Great."

Wes and some of the other servers walked outside with a small cake. A candle in the center flickered.

"Congrats to the beautiful couple on their engagement," Wes said.

He placed the cake down in between us, and I burst out laughing. Brock put his hand on top of mine on the table.

"Blow it out! Make a wish," Wes said.

We looked at each other and blew.

Wes and his crew clapped together.

"Thanks, man. Hey, can we get a check too when you get a chance?"

"Of course. Enjoy! I'll be right back."

Brock took a spoonful of the cake. He stuck it out for me to take a bite. I awkwardly leaned over the table and took half the bite in my mouth, leaving the other half to fall off the spoon.

"Oh, my gosh," I said, my mouth full of cake. I covered it, hoping nothing else would fall out.

"How is it?" Brock asked.

I nodded as a response, giving him a thumbs-up, trying to chew. He took a spoonful for himself.

"Mmm," he moaned. "But, I mean, how do you fuck up chocolate cake?"

Wes came back with our check. I pulled out a twenty-dollar bill from my wallet.

"That's insulting. You better put that back."

He handed Wes two hundred-dollar bills.

"Keep the change," he said to him. I looked at Brock—he had to be joking. The bill was only, like, one hundred dollars, thanks to Brock being super likable or something. They gave us a whole bottle of wine for free! I didn't understand how he got away with everything.

"Thank you, sir. You two have a nice night. And congrats!"

"Thank you, you too," I said. It all felt real. I wanted it to be real—I mean, not the engagement part. But maybe the moments of being referred to as *you two*. Maybe.

Brock and I headed out of the restaurant, taking the resort stairs down to the beach. I took my shoes off before walking onto the sand, carrying them in my hand. My phone buzzed. It was my dad.

Bruce: Where are you?
Kendra: Just left dinner w/ Brock.
Bruce: Okay. Have fun. XO
Kendra: XOXO

"Well, thank you for dinner," I said to Brock.

"Thank you for the company."

We walked along the shore. It was silent—both of us living in our own heads. Or maybe I was presumptuous to assume that he was overthinking every moment like I was. Maybe this wasn't as big a deal to him as it was to me. I mean, Brock had been with plenty of girls, I'm sure. Maybe I had to snap out of the idea that Brock and I were an actual couple. A couple engaged and walking along the beach. Reality seemed to be calling my name, but I didn't want to respond.

Brock interrupted the silence by taking my hand in his. I looked down at our hands, now intertwined, and then up at him. He was already staring back when he kissed my cheek.

"I seriously want more of that wine," he said.

"It was so good!" I said, and at the same time I caught sight of three dolphins lit up by the moon, leaping through the water. "Oh, my gosh, look!"

"Damn," he said, mesmerized by the night. He squeezed my hand a little tighter and I laid my head on his shoulder, grabbing onto his arm. He kissed my head.

"Tonight has been really nice," he said, the moment soft. Serene. If this was a dream, I never wanted to wake up.

"Yeah. It has."

We leaned into one another, slowly meeting halfway until our lips touched. Slow kisses turned into making out. He pulled me into him.

"Your lips taste like merlot." He smiled at me, our heads touching. He licked my lips.

Somehow we ended up lying on the sand, his body pressed on top of mine. It was getting heated. More than ever before. I wanted it. And I think he could tell. He stuck his hand under my shirt and I didn't stop him. He kissed my neck and he lowered his hand down, making its way into my pants.

"Oh, my gosh," I moaned.

"Are you okay?"

"Yes." I hadn't expected it to feel that good. No one had ever touched me like that before, let alone touched me down there at all. I'd barely ever even touched myself. I tried once, but it wasn't as exciting as people made it out to be. But maybe I just didn't know what I was doing.

I closed my eyes, even though I could feel him staring at me still. You know that feeling?

"Brock!"

"What?" He froze. "What's wrong? Is this too far or—"

"That feels so good."

He chuckled as he kept going.

The sound of Brock's phone vibrating interrupted us. He stopped in the middle of everything to check who it was.

"I'm sorry, Kendra. It's my mom. I have to take this."

"Go ahead."

He stood up and walked a distance away to answer the call. "Hello?"

I could only faintly hear him over the sound of the waves crashing.

"I just grabbed a bite to eat with friends," he said into the phone. "All right. I'll be there soon."

He quickly hung up, and I had a feeling the night was over.

I started to button up my pants and Brock turned back around to look at me.

"Everything okay?" I asked.

"Yeah. I just have to head home."

"Okay." I said it without any hesitation or questions.

He stuck out his hand to help me up. We stood there, facing each other. He brushed his hand through my hair, kissing me again.

"I can't get enough."

"Let's go, fiancé," I said.

I ran up to my room, wondering *what* happened tonight and *how*. I didn't feel like myself at all. I mean, I wasn't the type to just let a guy get in my pants like that—but Brock didn't feel like just *any* guy. He was my fiancé for God's sake! Right? I dialed Ashleigh ASAP. I needed to confide in her experienced self.

"Hello?" she answered.

"Ashleigh," I said.

"What?"

I looked toward the hallway, afraid of anyone hearing. "One sec." I quickly shut the door.

"What is it, Ken?"

"He fingered me," I whispered into the phone.

"Shut the fuck up!" she shrieked. I wasn't sure if this was more of a scolding or if she was just completely dumbfounded. I, myself, was completely dumbfounded.

"I'm serious," I said, laughing. Although it wasn't funny. In fact, I was completely flipping out! Literally. The confusion and impulsiveness of the situation was settling in. I thought my heart was going to beat right out of my chest as my mind reminisced on what had transpired. It got me thinking. *Would this be it? Was that all he wanted from me? Just random hooking up and then done? Just like that?*

"Holy shit, my innocent little Kendra is growing up!"

"Don't tell anyone, please!"

"I would never." Yes, she would. She had the biggest mouth in school. "Wait. So what happened? Where?"

"Okay, so he picked me up to go get some food, and after dinner we went for a walk on the beach. We, like, totally started making out and then I don't know what happened, we ended up on the sand. He was on top of me and—ugh, it just happened!"

"Damn! Ashton's gotta step his game up." She was silent on the other end for a moment. "I'm actually shocked right now."

"How do you think I feel?"

"Did you like it?"

"Uh, yes?" Was that weird? I mean, he wasn't officially my boyfriend or anything . . . and would he ever be?

"Now you know why I'm such a fucking slut!" she joked, chuckling to herself on the other end.

"Dude, are you coming to Ashton's Halloween party?" she asked.

"I don't think so. Brock invited me to go on his parents' yacht. They have a Halloween party every year, I guess with all their friends."

"Well, that sounds fancy. If you guys are done early, come!"

"For sure."

"Wait, that's Ashton ringing in. Let me call you back."

"Don't worry about it. I'll see you tomorrow."

"Okay, bye!"

I yawned. My eyes felt heavy and my body fatigued. Maybe it was the wine.

Before I went to bed, I needed to do a five-minute meditation. I was feeling somewhat anxious. I wasn't sure why, because I actually was really excited. Happy.

I sat on the edge of my bed, my legs crossed and my eyes shut. I inhaled through my nose and with an exhale I let out a soft *om*. I repeated this a few times. It felt nice, like my body began to vibrate.

My eyes could barely stay open on their own. I pulled down my covers and quickly fell asleep, dreaming of Brock all night.

BROCK

When I got home, my parents were sitting in the kitchen weighing the shipment of coke they'd just got in from Morales.

"Where've you been? We're doing *your* job right now," my asshole father said.

"I told Mom. I went out to eat with a few friends."

I started for my room, but clearly getting off that easily wasn't a thing.

"We have to go out of town next week."

I paused. Out of town meant at least a week of alone time with my parents. Just me. And them. I could sense a headache already coming over me.

"Where?"

"Seattle."

"For what?"

"We're going to go look at condos."

My heart dropped. Were we moving again? Kendra's eyes crossed the front of my mind. "Why?"

"Establish ourselves there so we can begin to grow a clientele."

I felt my tensed body relax. It made me wonder, though: maybe I did want to make Kendra my girlfriend. If we were to move, she would be the only thing I actually missed. I mean, don't get me wrong, Laguna is fucking dope. I don't know how you could beat it, but I wasn't really *attached* to it or anything.

"Why don't you guys just stick to California for now?"

"Morales wants us all up the West Coast."

"Kind of stupid."

"Well, why don't you go get a job then and pay the bills?" My mom spoke the only sentence she'd said since I walked in.

And my dad couldn't help but add, "Or, you know, tell the Mexican drug lord that his idea is dumb."

He smiled like he was proud of his sarcastic comment and wanted to bathe in all of its (not-so) cleverness.

I rolled my eyes.

"Do I have to go?" I asked. Maybe I had a chance of getting out of this. What did they need me for? Wouldn't they rather have me stay and keep up the Cali sales?

"Yeah. You do. We're all going."

"Fuck."

"Bitch now, thank me later."

Every time my father opened his mouth, I wanted to fucking throw a rock at my own head. I was about to start for my room, but I decided to tell my parents about Kendra attending the party—partially because I knew it would piss them off. They weren't fond of outsiders.

"By the way, I'm bringing a friend to the Halloween party."

They both looked up at me, now fully engaged in what I was saying.

"A friend?" my mom asked.

"Yeah. Kendra."

"Oh, boy." My mom rolled her eyes. She always thought that dating in high school was overrated because "work was more important." And when I questioned why, she always gave me the same answer: "Because money will never fuck you over like a teenage girl will."

"Whatever. That's fine. I don't care what you do as long as you get your work done," my father said.

I went up to my room, fed up. My parents really knew how to kill the vibe. I sat down at my computer. I had to write an essay for English, so I opened a new document. I wasn't even sure what I had to write about. Something about the book we read in class, whose details seemed a little foggy in my preoccupied brain—er, well, technically I hadn't read it. Why would I? Unless you count the summary on the back. I stared at the blank page, my hands on the keyboard ready to type. I watched the cursor flicker as it anticipated becoming a word.

"Fuck it."

I shut my laptop down and grabbed one of my guitars hanging on the wall. I strummed a few chords, closing my eyes. Kendra's face appeared. It made me smile. There was just something about her. I couldn't figure it out. Or why it made me feel this way. It was nerve-racking and exhilarating all at once. And I know I kept saying that, but it's because it was true. It confused me. My own feelings were swallowing me fucking whole. So lame. I set my guitar down and pulled out my phone.

Brock: I had a really fun time with u 2nite

I went back to strumming my guitar. I had a sick riff going. It was too dope to be forgotten, so I restarted my computer and plugged my guitar in to record it. I nodded my head as I played it back. Sounded wicked tight.

Meanwhile, my overwhelming thoughts couldn't seem to leave me. I'd never felt this way about a chick before. I was used to hitting it with no attached feelings. But I wasn't even fooling around with Kendra and I was hooked. My phone beeped, interrupting my mental rant.

Duke: Come to L.A. for my Halloween party
Brock: Can't. Parents party. But still down to surf
Duke: Oh yeah, that's right.
Brock: I need to talk to you . . . thinking bout making Kendra
   my girl.
Duke: She's a dope chick. Do it. But remember, once you do it
   . . . don't be messin round w Annie

Duke valued women. Don't get me wrong—he valued a lot of women, but the thing was, never at once. When he chose to be committed, he stuck to his word. He wouldn't cheat. Ever. But he was also very upfront; if he only wanted to fool around with a girl, he'd warn her. That was fair in my opinion, especially since the girls went into it with hope, which meant he still got laid. But it was the first time in my life that his advice seemed to resonate with me. I finally got it. What he'd been trying to pull out of me all of this time.

I wanted to play around with this beat some more, but my bed was calling my name. I threw my shirt onto the floor and turned on the fan.

I checked my phone as I lay in bed. Kendra still hadn't answered. I assumed she'd fallen asleep—I needed to do the same. I set my phone down on my nightstand and turned out the light, instantly dozing as my head hit the pillow.

Friday I decided to ditch class and head up to LA for the day to kick it with Duke. We made a couple of deliveries, then got lunch downtown and made our way back to his pad.

"You got some shit?" I asked him.

"Hell, yeah."

He disappeared into his kitchen and returned with a bag

full of coke. He'd just been with Morales and had gotten a fresh supply.

"Dude, this is pure coke. Like real blow."

When I saw that thick powder dangling in front of my eyes, my adrenaline surged through me in a way that I anticipated love at first sight to feel like.

Duke poured it out onto the table in front of us. I rolled up a hundred-dollar bill and inhaled a huge fucking amount until my body began to jitter with excitement.

"Good shit," he agreed. "All you need is one hit. It's that strong."

But shit, I wanted more. It was an instant kind of high.

"Holy fuck!"

"By the way, what's going on with Kendra?"

"I invited her to my parents' Halloween party."

"Nice move, my man."

"Yeah."

"You like this one."

"Yeah. I do."

"I know I've told you already, but don't corrupt her too much, man. I can tell she's a good girl. I really saw it the night of my party."

I laughed at him. Duke was more the kind to ruin a shy girl. I was usually too preoccupied messing around with the ones that were already bad. Just like I liked them.

"Oh shit," he said. "I forgot to send you the link."

He opened up his laptop and logged on to some website.

"Check out this island, dude!" he said, turning the computer to face me.

"Sick!"

"Right?"

Duke and I were planning to buy our own island in the near future—sometime after I graduated. I was making enough with my parents to contribute, but Duke was making some real dough. Enough to buy that fucking island and live out our dream. We wanted to be retired by the time we were thirty.

"I can't wait, bro," I said. "I'm ready for it."

"Ditto. It's going to be amazing."

I wondered if Kendra would come with us to the island. Hey, there'd be plenty of ocean for her to surf.

"Duke?"

"What's up?"

"Do you ever second-guess this life?"

"What do you mean?"

"The drugs. Do you ever wonder if there's bigger dreams we should be chasing?"

"Shit, this coke is strong." He laughed but then realized I was being serious.

He looked down at the floor, his eyes focused as if he was trying to comprehend my question.

"I mean, yeah. I do. But I know in order to chase dreams, you usually need money, and this is our way of doing that."

I nodded, understanding what he meant.

"What's going on, buddy? Everything good?"

"Yeah, it's just . . ."

I sat up, rubbing my hand through my hair. I was about to sound like a total girl, but if I was going to sound like a chick in front of anyone, no one better than Duke.

"Ever since I met her, I feel like I want something bigger out of this life. I want to pursue my music full time."

Duke's eyebrows were raised like he was taken aback by my statement.

"Wow, I knew you were struck by her, but I didn't know it was like this."

"I know. It's so fucked!"

I threw my head back on his couch, my hands covering my eyes in despair.

"No, it's not fucked. It's a feeling, man. That's all we got are feelings."

I looked up at him. "And I thought I sounded like a girl."

He laughed. "Seriously, though, think about it. When we die, what do we take with us? Everything in this world is man-made: the cars, the houses, the expensive shoes. All we got are the feelings and memories. That's the only real shit."

"Damn . . ." He was right.

"I mean, don't get me wrong. The materialistic stuff is nice— I'm not complaining. But it's not everything."

"That's way too deep for me right now. I'm trying to block all this shit out."

He chuckled. "Just being honest with you since you brought it up."

"I think the drugs are speaking for you."

"Eh, maybe a little. But you know what they say. Stoned words are sober thoughts."

He shut the computer down, and we sat there for a moment in silence. I felt more confused than before. We needed to lighten the mood after that convo—plus we were on coke, so I needed to exert all of this energy somehow.

"Let's go fucking drifting!" I said.

"So down!"

We ran out of his house and hopped in his new McLaren. We needed to break this shit in.

On the way out, I decided to text Kendra, remembering that I hadn't talked to her today.

Brock: Boo! 👻

Kendra: Ha ha very funny, Casper

Brock: How's your day going? I'm a little under the weather but I'm excited to see U tomorrow

Kendra: Feel better! Yeah, I'm excited too

Kendra: By the way, is this a formal party?

Brock: Ehh ... Kinda

I shoved my phone in my pocket and rolled down the passenger window as we sped down Duke's empty neighborhood. His neighbors had to fucking hate us.

I ended up staying the night at Duke's house, and we woke up around six in the morning, hungover as shit. First thing we did was roll a fat blunt. It was tradition that every Halloween, Duke and I went stoned surfing. I don't even remember how this had begun, but we'd been doing it for years. I didn't surf very often—mostly because I didn't have the time—but when I did, it reminded me of how much I fucking loved it. I was definitely an adrenaline junkie, and the waves were supposed to be massive today.

We hotboxed in the G-Wagon, the windows rolled up and the car filled with smoke. I took the first hit. It was some good shit my parents had grown in our backyard. It was a type of sativa cannabis. Instead of sedating you, it lifted you up. I took a deep breath, taking it in.

With another hit, I felt the buzz. The ring. The thrill. The high. And with another, I was somewhere between numb and weightless on cloud nine and raging in the depths of hell, fire burning inside of me. With one more, Kendra's face lit up my mind. Her freckles.

When I handed Duke the blunt, he took a strong hit and immediately began coughing.

"That's some dank shit, right there!" he said.

"I'm so stoked," Duke said as we walked down Zuma Beach. It was the old spot we used to surf at in Malibu—most of the time when we should have been in class. Surfing was one of the rare times that I ever saw Duke without his hat on. I looked at the scar that traced a line from the top of his forehead down through his left eyebrow. I quickly looked away when he turned to me. It was something he was super sensitive about—which was understandable.

"Same," I agreed, exhaling a puff of smoke from my cigarette. "You should come tonight to my parents' party."

"I would, but I'm going trick-or-treating."

"You didn't really just say that."

Duke laughed. "What's wrong with that?"

"This must involve a hot chick."

"Of course."

We both broke into laughter as we planted our boards in the sand, Duke waxing his as I watched. I took one last inhale of my cig before tossing it.

"Don't tell me you're dressing up too."

"Uhh . . ."

"Fuck. She better be a damn supermodel."

I understood he wanted to make girls feel special, but come on—dressing up for Halloween?

He passed me the wax, and I rubbed my board down as I shook my head at him.

"Hey, don't spit up in the air too soon!" he said. "You're going to fall for Kendra hard and fast. Just watch."

I rolled my eyes at him, blowing off the comment, secretly freaking out that it had potentially already been the case.

When we entered the water, it was cold as shit. My balls shriveled right up.

"Damn!" I said.

Duke splashed water on me. "Don't be a bitch!"

Eventually we became numb to the cold, and a wave started to brew in the distance.

"Let's do this!" Duke hollered.

We charged toward it, the sun blazing down on us. It was so fucking early, my body was starting to feel the exhaustion.

The wave curled, and our stoned asses were taken down almost instantly. I popped up above the water, laughing, salt water draining from my nose down to my throat. It burned, but I was too hysterical to care.

Duke popped up a second later, also roaring with laughter.

"Let's do it again!" he said.

I shook my hair off my face, water flying everywhere.

We hopped back on our boards and rode the waves, one after the other demolishing us. But, I mean, that was kind of the point. When we were this stoned, it was fun.

We called it a day around eight and headed back to Duke's. What a morning. I could tell this Halloween was going to be lit already.

KENDRA

I rode my bike to the graveyard. The sun was present but block-aded by the clouds that painted the afternoon sky. My stomach grumbled, reminding me that I needed to eat. But I didn't have much of an appetite. Not this weekend. I couldn't believe tomor-row would mark ten years since he died.

I walked over to my brother's grave, taking note of the dates written across the stone. He was my age. As many times as I visited, it still always astounded me of how young he was—espe-cially as I got older. I kneeled down.

"Tomorrow's Halloween," I said, talking to the gravestone. I hoped Kyle could somehow hear me. His infectious smile flashed through my mind as memories of him danced around in my head like an old black-and-white film. I grabbed onto my necklace. He was the best big brother anyone could ask for and the reason I'm the surfer I am today.

"You wouldn't let me go with you last time." I laughed to pro-tect the tears that wanted to escape. I didn't want to cry. I didn't. Because once I did, I'd feel the pain. And I didn't want to.

"You were with your friends." Just hours before his last breath. I pictured all of their faces—"that crowd" that Coach always warned me about. My brother was "that crowd."

I looked down at the grass. It was so green. So alive.

"But you brought me back candy, like you promised." I choked on my words. "Dad and I really miss you."

I stood up as my cloudy eyes gave in to the rain, letting tears pour down my face. Salty drops of rain that kissed my lips. I wiped them away. "I love you, and I promise I'm going to accomplish all of your surfing dreams—for you."

I cherished his gravestone another moment before taking my gaze up to the heavens, knowing he was in a better place. He had to be.

On my ride back home, the wind blew against my tear-dampened skin, drying the tears up even as they poured. I took a deep breath, trying to put an end to the storm that had taken over my body. I had to compose myself. The day had to go on and it would go on, same with tomorrow—even though I wished I could just press pause on October 31 every year and pretend Halloween never existed.

When I walked into my house, my dad was in the family room, like I expected, watching *The Endless Summer*. It was Kyle's favorite. I let him be, heading up to my room. Today, I kind of wanted to talk about it. But I had no one to talk to, so I just cried for a while until Hunter, Taylor, and Ashleigh came over to help me get ready for the party.

Ashleigh rummaged through the clothes in my closet as Taylor did my makeup and Hunter sat on my bed, petting Skittles.

"Dude, are you nervous about meeting the 'rents?" Hunter asked, scrolling through Facebook.

"Duh, she's nervous," Ashleigh confirmed the obvious.

"Yes," I said. "I don't know anything about them. But, like, every time I'm with Brock, they call and make him come home. So I have no clue what to expect."

"I still think you should ditch and just come to Ashton's," Ashleigh said.

"Believe me, I'd much rather be with you guys."

"Seriously, like, it's Halloweekend. You should be with us!" Taylor agreed.

Ashleigh dressed me in a pair of jeans and an orange sweater that Harry bought me years ago but still had tags on it.

"Why don't you ever wear the shit you have in your closet?" Ashleigh whined.

"I do!"

"No, you don't! You literally wear the same shit every day, you beach bum."

She made a valid point—but hey, I spent most of my days at the beach. And beaches are for bikinis.

My eyes widened in hopes that I wasn't seeing properly as my dad and Harry walked in the room, dressed in grass skirts with matching grass crowns on their heads. That was it. Nothing else. I sunk down in my chair when I realized my vision was twenty-twenty perfect.

"Hi, girls."

"You guys look festive," Ashleigh said.

"What are you guys supposed to be exactly?" I asked, hoping they would confess it was all a joke.

"Adam and Steve," my dad said.

"We made them ourselves!" Harry said, excitedly.

They were so proud of themselves, I felt bad being embarrassed, but—ugh—I couldn't help it.

"You did a great job," I said, forcing a smile.

"What are you guys doing tonight?" my dad asked.

"Ashton is throwing a Halloween party at his place," Ashleigh said.

"And I'm going to Brock's family's Halloween party."

I noticed Harry's expression grimace at the mention of Brock's name.

"Sounds fun," my dad said. "Harry and I are going to a costume party down in Dana Point."

Dad always made a point of going out for Halloween. I understood the impulse. He had to get his mind off Kyle. We all did. I always wanted to retreat to my bed, as if sitting still all day would be the cure to the pit in my gut. But, as I learned the hard way, hiding only made things worse. So making an effort to get out and do something "fun" was a priority.

"Have a good time," I said.

"Make sure you set the alarm when you leave."

"I will."

They headed out of my room, and from the hallway I heard them yell, "Have fun, kids! No drinking."

"We won't," I said, hopefully loud enough for them to hear.

I wondered what my dad would think if he found out I *had* drunk before. I could only imagine what he would say if he found out I had been wasted.

We sat at a long table that overlooked the ocean. I had never been on a yacht before, and honestly, it was amazing. Breathtaking. Brock's parents seemed nice; they were your all-American couple, but they were people of few words.

His dad sat at the head of the table, his mother right next to him. They were surrounded by just over a dozen of their friends.

"So, Kendra, you probably know our daughter, Annie," one of the Parkers' friends said. She had introduced herself to me as Emmy earlier. She sat beside her husband, Martin. He was a hefty middle-aged man.

"You're Annie's parents?" Clearly, that was why Emmy looked so familiar. She and Annie were identical.

"Yes," Martin said. "Honey, we should've made her come tonight."

"She's young, she wants to go out and have fun," Emmy countered.

Martin and Emmy bickered about their daughter's attendance.

Did they know about her and Brock? And if they did, was it weird that I was his date tonight? I suddenly felt so awkward.

I leaned into Brock to whisper, "I didn't know you guys are family friends."

"They work together," he whispered back.

Emmy turned back to me and said, "Annie was going to come, but she ended up going to some party."

I bet it was Ashton's.

The servers walked out with appetizers, circling around the table, offering a serving to each guest.

"Thank you for having me, Mr. and Mrs. Parker."

"Please, it's Karl and Debby." Brock's dad smiled. He was charismatic the way Brock was when he spoke, that same half grin. I knew where he got it from now. But he had his mom's facial structure. I liked knowing where Brock came from. Who he came from.

"So what do you do for a living?" I asked. I hadn't said much so far this evening, or at least not *initiated* much, and I felt like I needed to make some sort of conversation. My dad always told me to never be afraid to speak up in social situations. But he never struggled with anxiety.

"We, uh—" his dad began.

His mother interrupted. "We do a lot of charity work."

His dad smiled and agreed.

They stuffed appetizers in their mouths, concluding the question.

"Aww. That's awesome," I said. I wished Brock had mentioned it before. I would have loved to get involved.

"What do your parents do for a living, Kendra?" Karl asked.

"My dad works in advertising and his fiancé, Harold, is a hairdresser," I said, taking a bite of the salad that had appeared in front of me.

Debby and Karl nodded their heads in unison, both sipping on their wine.

"Karl, what do you guys think about legalizing recreational marijuana?" Martin asked.

"I think it's great," Brock's dad said. "For the economy, especially. I mean, it doesn't affect me or my work in any way."

I noticed the way Debby looked at him. His face fell flat, and he choked on his bite of food.

"Agreed," Martin's wife, Emmy, spoke up. I was shocked by her and Karl's response. What kind of parents would support the legalization of drugs? I looked at her and then to Brock. He wasn't fazed at all. He caught sight of me gazing at him and smiled as he rubbed my leg.

"How can you be so accepting about the legalization of a gateway drug?" I couldn't help myself. It slipped out as if I meant to only think it, but it regurgitated verbally like the vomit in Brock's car.

Everyone paused, their eyes suddenly on me, and I regretted ever saying a word.

"Excuse me?" Karl halted his fork from entering his mouth.

This had to be one of the most awkward dinner conversations while meeting a guy's parents *ever*.

"Uh—it's just, I mean, I don't quite understand how you could be all right with recreational drug use, especially among young people." I spoke quickly, my voice high-pitched but soft. My face was flush, my palms sweating, and my heart rate rapidly increasing. I wanted to close my eyes and wake up from this horrible dream.

Debby raised an eyebrow at me. I fiddled with the napkin

sitting on my lap. Brock's grip on my leg was tight, like he was just as nervous as me. How could they judge me for disliking drugs? But I kept my thoughts to myself. Obviously, I should've beforehand.

"Weed has never killed anyone," Brock's mom spoke, her voice forceful.

"In fact, they say it helps cancer patients," his dad joined in. "And treating epilepsy."

And lastly, Emmy added, "In the Netherlands, marijuana is decriminalized, and they have the lowest rate of users. What does that tell you?"

I felt them all staring at me, even though my eyes were on my lap, focused on the firm embrace of Brock's hand.

I couldn't let it go. "But isn't it a gateway drug?"

Debby darted her eyes into mine. She cleared her throat passive-aggressively.

She spoke with venom in her tone. "Quite audacious for a guest."

"I'm sorry. I'm not trying to be rude, I just—"

Brock intervened. "I think everyone is entitled to their own opinion, Mother."

"I think your mother is just concerned that this is too political a conversation for the dinner table." Karl grinned a forced smile.

"Well, who started it?" Brock shot back.

"Watch it," his dad said.

"Excuse me?" Brock interrupted, setting his drink down. Oh, no. Why me? Why didn't I just keep my mouth shut?

I shifted in my seat, uncomfortably. All I could think was, *Someone rescue me.*

"Well, you know, that's what's wrong with society these days. Too many uninformed people about marijuana—" Emmy began.

"Are you guys serious?" he asked. Everyone went silent, redirecting their focus on Brock.

I nudged his leg under the table.

"Brock, just drop it," I whispered. I should've kept my thoughts to myself, but it was very hard for me when it came to the topic of drugs . . . and now it was too late to take it back. This had accelerated out of control.

"She doesn't like drugs. Respect that."

My heart started to quicken. I reminded myself, *It is what it is. It is what it is, Kendra.*

No one knew what to say. It was completely silent. Brock looked at his parents. I noticed the way his father eyed him back with narrowed eyes. As if there was some unresolved tension that had been brewing for a while.

His mother set her fork down, looked hard at Brock, and shook her head. I was unsure of what was going to happen next. The unpredictability frightened me. Brock stood up and took me by the hand; my body tensed up. I felt so on the spot, but I had put myself there. Ugh.

I stood up, following his lead toward the deck away from everyone else. This was the last thing I felt like dealing with. Especially today of all days.

He was quiet for a moment.

"You all right?" he asked me.

"Yeah. I'm fine." And I was.

"I'm sorry about that. Annie's parents are assholes. And mine—"

"It's fine. It isn't your fault. Do we—do we need to go back and sit down?"

I turned to face Brock. He hugged me tight.

"Nah, they're happier by themselves anyway. What's up with you today? You seem quiet."

"It's just—it's just a weird day," I said. I didn't want to get into the whole Kyle thing. Not now. Not here.

"I'll be right back," he said.

I looked out at the sunset. It was layered blue and orange like some sort of popsicle I enjoyed as a child. Brock returned with a bucket of candy in hand.

"It's not Halloween without this."

I forced a giggle as I stared into the bucket. My eyes immediately caught sight of the Skittles. That's what Kyle had brought home for me, ten years ago.

"Or this." Brock pulled a bottle of champagne out from behind his back.

I smiled at him. He was sweet. But I felt bad because I'd promised my dad that I wouldn't drink. But this evening, this whole day, was weighing on me. I figured a sip or two wouldn't hurt. That wasn't even considered drinking, right?

We sat down on the ground, resting our feet in the hot tub that looked out at the ocean.

"Twenty-one questions?" Brock asked as he popped open the bottle of champagne.

"You would think we'd be at, like, fifty questions by now!"

"I know, right?" He scooted closer to me. "Okay, do you prefer chocolate candies or sour candies?"

"I'm more of a sour girl. Sour Skittles are my favorite."

"Is that why you named your dog Skittles?"

"Yeah." Although, there was a lot more to it than that. But he didn't need to know *why* they were my favorite. Skittles was an emotional support animal that one of my previous shrinks thought would be a good idea. They were right. She helped me a lot when I was younger and first coping with all of the loss in my life. The grief. Dogs have a way of being there for people when people can't be.

He laughed at me as he rummaged through the bucket, pulling out two Skittles. He dropped one in my hand.

"Are you a cat or dog person?" I asked.

"Dogs for sure," he said, popping the Skittle in his mouth.

"Me too."

We looked to one another with a grin, neither of us breaking the stare until I giggled. It was one of those unspoken staring contests—which I always seemed to lose.

Brock laughed at me before facing me once again to ask, "Are you a virgin?"

I paused mid-chew. My heart felt pulseless now. No one had ever asked me that before. I just assumed that *they* assumed that I was.

The answer was simple yet it was complicated to spit out. But I finally admitted, "Yes."

He looked at me with smiling eyes that reeked of confusion. I know I sounded like a total prude. But I guess I was.

He finally spoke. "Wow. Good for you."

"Are you a virgin?" I wondered, although I was almost certain I knew the answer.

Brock looked at me with eyes that said, *You just proved there is such a thing as a stupid question.* Or maybe that's just how I interpreted it, based on how I felt after inquiring. He laughed, taking a sip of the champagne straight from the bottle, confirming my assumption without a single word.

"All right then." My mouth curled into an uneasy smile, still ruminating on my pointless question as I tried to think of a smooth change of subject. "If you could live anywhere in the world, where would you live?"

Okay, so it wasn't exactly *smooth*, but it did the trick.

"Anywhere?"

"Yes." I wished that I could have come up with more interesting questions, but I wasn't good with that kind of stuff. Especially when I pressured myself to think of something cooler—ugh, that's when my mind really went blank.

"The Caribbean."

"You've been there?"

He handed me the bottle of champagne. I took a smaller chug.

"Yeah. It's beautiful."

"Lucky. I wanna go!"

"You would love it."

"I bet."

I pictured Brock and me sitting on a tropical beach together, sipping champagne. I wanted to be there.

"The water is crystal blue," he said, interrupting the fantasy.

"Ugh, I can only imagine. I'm sure it's breathtaking."

"Duke and I have this plan for after I graduate high school. We're gonna take off and travel all of the islands and then buy our own to retire on."

I smiled. I liked dreaming. Even more so, I liked Brock sharing his dreams with me.

"Can I come?"

In that moment I was unsure if I'd said the right thing or if I'd crossed a boundary.

"Of course. We're gonna need some estrogen to balance things out."

"Your friend Duke is nice."

"Yeah. He's the shit. Closest thing I have to a brother."

"I can tell. He's your best friend, huh?" And Brock did not seem like he was close with too many people—even his own family.

"Nah. More than that. He's blood. I'd die for that kid."

"How'd you two meet?"

"Back in high school—before he dropped out. I was a fresh-man and he was a junior. Everyone wanted to be Duke, and still does. He was captain of the basketball team, he could get any girl he wanted, and on top of that, he's one of the most genuine dudes you'll ever meet. Wouldn't hurt a fly."

"Why'd he drop out of school?"

"It's complicated. He didn't live the most normal childhood. He came from a pretty abusive family, and uh, he just discovered bigger opportunities outside of the classroom."

"Like what?"

Brock sighed. "Business stuff. I don't know. . . ."

I nodded and took another sip of champagne during the pause of conversation before reminding him, "Your turn."

"Will you be my girlfriend?" he asked casually.

I looked up at him. Every bit of me was taken off guard. I bit my bottom lip and smiled. My heart pounded a little harder, my body buzzing. Brock Parker. My first boyfriend—though he didn't need to know that.

"I'm straight up up," I said.

He leaned into me, my body still frozen in thought. Our lips met just as the sun met the ocean, setting as nightfall quickly approached. Brock took my chin in his hand. It was so flippin' cute. I didn't want the moment to end. Ever. This was the best Halloween I'd had in a very long time.

I felt my phone vibrate mid-make-out sesh. We opened our eyes simultaneously, gazing into one another, leaving us with awkward giggles. I pulled back to look at my phone. It was my dad. I opened it up to find a picture of him and Harry at their party. I covered up my mouth as I let out a loud snort. They were such dorks.

"I love it when you snort," Brock said.

"Hey." I nudged him. "Don't make fun of me."

"I'm serious." His face was straight, with a hint of a grin. His eyes remained on mine, forcing me to look back down at my phone.

"Looks like they're having a good time," he said.

"Oh, I'm sure they are. My dad needs that today."

I went to my messages and realized I hadn't seen a text from Ashleigh.

Ashleigh: COME FUCKING PARTY BETCH!

"You know, we can still go if you want to," Brock said.

I was hesitant. I mean, I didn't want to be rude. But, at the same time, it wasn't like we were even around his family.

"I'll go if you want to," I said.

"Let's get out of here."

BROCK

I got Kendra and me a cab. I was still steaming about everything that had gone down with my parents and Annie's. But I wanted to put on a happy face for Kendra. Especially tonight. I could tell something was bugging her. I hoped she didn't let them get to her too much. I didn't want to mess things up. I needed her to teach me how to meditate or something. I could have used that breathing shit back at dinner. Especially since I didn't have any access to my candy at the time.

We pulled up to Ashton's pad. We could hear the music blaring from the car.

"Text Ashleigh and tell her we're here," I told Kendra.

"Okay."

We got out of the car. I took Kendra's hand in mine.

"We don't have costumes, though," Kendra said.

"Yes, we do. I'm Brock Parker. *The* Brock Parker. And you're professional surfer girl Kendra Dimes."

She giggled like a child. Like the kind of giggle that took you from reality and into some sort of holy promised land that reminded you that maybe, just maybe, everything was going to be all right. Did that sound super deep and cheesy? I guess it was. But I really liked this girlfriend. More than any other before. *Girlfriend* . . . I liked calling her that. I liked that I was *able* to call her that.

Ashleigh opened the door before we reached the front.

"Thank goodness you two are here!"

She ran up and hugged Kendra. She was carrying a bottle of vodka.

"What are you supposed to be?" I asked, looking at her up and down.

"Sandy from *Grease*! And Ashton is Danny."

"A couple's costume? Come on, you guys are cooler than that!"

Ashleigh rolled her eyes at me and continued into the house.

We walked inside. Our whole junior class was there. I was pissed I hadn't planned ahead—this party was prime sales material. If I'd known I was coming beforehand, I would've brought more coke. But in a way, maybe it was a blessing since the whole Jason and Ryan incident was still so fresh.

"Brock, man!" Nick yelled from across the room.

"'Sup?" I yelled back. We met in the middle, my hand still connected to Kendra's.

"Ken!" her friends yelled, all drunk out of their asses.

"Hi, guys!" she said, letting go of my hand so she could greet them.

"Nice costume, douchebag," I said to Nick. He was dressed like a priest.

"Thanks, bro. You know what they say?"

"No. What?"

"Priests smoke the best weed."

"Uh, actually, it's cops that smoke the best weed." He was such a dumbass.

Nick shrugged his shoulders. He didn't give a shit.

"Hey, guys," Ashton came up to us, all dressed up like a fucking fifties greaser.

"You fucking pussy! You did a couple's costume?" I couldn't help but laugh.

"It's fucking Danny from *Grease*. He's a total badass, and you know it."

"You got any beer, man?" I asked him.

"Yeah. Follow me," he said.

I followed him into the kitchen, where a group of people stood around playing flip cup on the island.

Ashton pulled out a six-pack, and when he shut the fridge, Annie was standing there.

I nodded a "What's up?" to her.

"Word travels fast. Heard you have a girlfriend." She grimaced.

"Yeah. So?" I said and walked away. From today forward, Annie and I were business colleagues, and that was it.

Nick and I walked outside to hit a bump of coke.

"Do I have anything on my nose?" I asked him before proceeding back inside. I didn't want Kendra to know. I *couldn't* let Kendra know.

"Nah. You're good."

The night was starting to pick up, and I was forgetting about my lame-ass parents. I sat down on the couch and pulled Kendra down onto my lap, my arms wrapped around her waist. Her friends all freaked when she took a sip of my beer.

"I. Just. Witnessed. Kendra Dimes. Take. A. Sip. Of. *Beer?* Am I drunk?" Ashleigh teased.

I looked up at Kendra, both of us meeting one another's gaze with a chuckle full of backstory. I liked the idea of a secret. Just between us.

Jason and Ryan came stumbling through the backyard door into the family room. They were dressed up as John Travolta and Samuel Jackson from *Pulp Fiction*. They looked fucked up, their eyes red and glassy. Last I heard, they both got off with a fine and also had to attend AA meetings once a week for the next six months, along with being assigned to weekly drug testing. Such dumb fucks. They were doomed to get more in trouble unless they had a way to get shit out of their system by the time they got tested.

"Brock!" Jason yelled. "Halloween dude! You know what that means?"

"What?"

"*Blow!*"

I gave him the eye to shut the fuck up, hoping Kendra was distracted enough talking with Ashleigh not to notice. Not that she probably even knew what blow was.

There was a group of us in the family room now, all hanging out when Ashleigh suggested we play Never Have I Ever.

"How do you play that?" Kendra asked.

"Everyone starts out by holding all ten of their fingers up, and we each go around saying something we've never done before, like, 'Never have I ever had sex in a hot tub' or something like that," I explained. "If you've done that, then you have to put a finger down. The person with the most fingers up last wins."

"Hmm, okay then," she said, although I was convinced she was still confused.

"Nick always wins," I teased.

"Ha ha. Funny, dude, fuck you," Nick said.

We all held our fingers up.

Hunter began. "Never have I ever had anal."

Taylor was the only one who put her finger down.

"What the fuck, Tay?" Ashleigh said.

"He was a really nice guy," she whined, her cheeks turning red.

"That's ratchet," Ashleigh said. "And that's coming from me!"

All of the girls laughed except Kendra. I bet she was already grossed out.

"Okay, never have I ever watched porn with someone," Taylor said.

I put a finger down, suddenly unsure if I really wanted to play this game in front of Kendra.

"Shut up, dude. With who?" Jason asked.

"Annie," I admitted.

I felt Kendra shift in her spot next to me.

"It was lame," I said, saving myself. "Never have I ever walked in on my parents."

Thankfully, everyone was safe there.

"Your turn, Ken," Ashleigh said.

"Okay. Never have I ever given head," she said.

All the other girls' fingers went down. They looked around, laughing at each other with pride.

"Ken, you slut! You got us all," Ashleigh said.

"Sorry," Kendra said, innocently.

I liked the fact that my girl was the only one at the table that hadn't done that yet. I mean, don't get me wrong, if she offered, I'd gladly accept. But it was cool to know that if she did, I'd be the first and only person she'd done that with.

The game was brutally interrupted when someone yelled, "The cops are here!"

Almost everyone darted for the back door into the yard, jumping over the back wall, except the usuals—Nick, Hunter, Taylor, Jason, Ryan, and obviously Ashton and Ashleigh.

I swear I'd had more close calls with the cops in the last week than I ever had in my life.

"Kill the music!" I said. This was a fucking shit show and none of these amateurs knew what they were doing.

"Shut the fuck up and no one open the door," Ashton loudly whispered. Everyone was silent.

"Laguna Beach Police, please open up," the cop said outside

of the door. His voice was deep and stern. Fuck. Thankfully, my car wasn't here. Who knows if they'd search cars or run plates.

I looked around the room; Ashton and Ashleigh were cuddled up on the couch. Ryan was sipping on a beer in the corner, being the weird loner fuck he always was. Jason and Taylor were whispering and Nick was actually getting the time of day from a girl, a.k.a. Hunter.

No one was moving an inch. We were barely breathing. But, of course, Jason couldn't hold in his nasty fucking burp. It was so fucking loud.

"Sorry," he said, without an ounce of remorse.

Ashleigh shushed him.

"You okay?" I whispered in Kendra's ear.

She nodded her head. Tonight was just not our night. I kissed the exposed part of her shoulder.

It was so quiet, I could hear the sound of Kendra's heart beating. She was shaking in my arms with nerves.

The other side of the door was silent, but flashlights blared through the windows as they tried to look into the house.

"Fuck," Ashton whined.

"It's cool, man. They can't do shit if you don't open the door. All they probably got was a noise complaint. Just *do not* open that door," I said.

I took Kendra by the hand and led her up the stairs to Ashton's spare bedroom.

"What are we doing?" she asked.

"I mean, we can sit out there and wait for nothing to happen, or we can cozy up in bed."

She didn't answer. She was still freaking out.

"What's wrong?" I said as I collapsed onto the bed and pulled her down too.

"If they bust this party, my dad will kill me," she said. "I'd get an MIC, and all hopes of having any scholarships for college would be shot! I might as well start writing my own epitaph!"

I could tell she was a wreck, not just by what she was saying but also by the speed with which she said it. I'd picked up on Kendra's quirks at this point.

"I'm telling ya. Halloween just isn't for us," I teased, although it was true.

"No kidding."

I stood up real fast to look over the staircase. Everyone was still silent. I assumed the cops had dipped.

We lay down, pulling the blanket over us, the house silent. It began to sprinkle outside, the sound of rain hitting the window.

"I'm really sorry about my parents earlier." It was driving me crazy. I couldn't get it off my mind, but I hoped Kendra had.

"It's not your fault. Really," she assured me, but I figured she was just saying that to be nice. "I should've just kept my opinions to myself."

"No, fuck that. Everyone is entitled to having a voice, and you were my guest. I think you need to teach me how to meditate. Like, how do you do it?"

"It's actually not as complicated as people make it out to be."

"Yeah? I'm curious if I'd be able to do it."

"All right." She adjusted herself next to me. "Close your eyes."

I allowed her to direct me, shutting my eyes with her instruction. I kind of wanted to laugh, but I didn't because Kendra was the type that would take it personally.

"Now take a deep inhale through your nose for a count of one, two, three. Hold it."

I did as I was told, not really feeling anything yet.

"Okay now, exhale for a count of one, two, three, and hold it."

There was no euphoric feeling of enlightenment, but, I mean, taking a moment to stop and consciously become aware of my breath felt good. Like a relief.

"How do you feel?" she asked, softly.

"I feel good." I smiled at her. Kendra had a heart. And that's what made her so special. I mean, yeah, everyone has a heart. But Kendra's heart was made up of *something*, and I wasn't quite sure yet what that was. I was one to believe that people's hearts were made up of different things. My father had a heart made of dust; it felt nothing and did nothing, only made up of a past that he let die inside of him. I felt like my heart was made of fire; although it kept me warm most of the time, it seemed to burn my soul once in a while. Kendra's—Kendra's heart was made up of something like flowers that lived to please others with their scent and provide oxygen with their existence. It was one of those hearts. I know that sounded tacky and cheesy and, like, so whipped, but it was true.

She snuggled into my chest. I could feel her heart beating against my body. It made me feel at peace. With life. And my parents. And all the other shit that pissed me off on a daily basis. Kendra didn't see me as the bad guy. The drug dealer. I didn't want her to see the messy parts of me.

"Wanna know something weird?" she said.

"What?"

"When we kiss, I can really see my third-eye chakra."

"Is that so?"

"Yeah." She giggled.

"Well, then. Let me help you out."

I kissed her. For the sake of her chakras of course.

Kendra beamed, trying to look through me, like many girls had before. But I wouldn't let any of them. And for some reason I let that guard down with Kendra. It was fucking freaking me out, but I loved it all at once. I'd never been myself this much with anyone else. I mean, besides Duke. But that was in a different way.

"Hey, girlfriend." I looked into her eyes, taking her chin in my hand.

"Hey, boyfriend."

Our lips slowly found home in a kiss.

"You're so sexy," I whispered in her ear. I kissed her neck, her collarbone and with it she shivered.

I unbuttoned her pants—and she didn't stop me, so I figured she wanted it.

She couldn't hold back a squeal.

"Here." I took her hand and put it down my pants. She began to stroke it. I knew that she'd never done this before, but I could also tell that she was a quick learner.

"Yeah, like that," I said.

It felt really good. Damn, I wanted her so bad. Holy shit.

"You're so hot, Brock," she said when I ripped off my shirt. It was getting fucking heated.

I took off her pants, tossed them to the ground, and found my way on top of her. My mouth worked its way down to her belly button before it hit her underwear. I pulled them down and threw those too.

She let out another yelp.

"What?" I jerked my head up, afraid I'd offended her or gone too far.

"Nothing. I just—I didn't know you were going to put your mouth there."

"Are you okay?" I was so hard, I felt like I was going to explode.

"No, but does it bother you? Like, pee comes out of there and yeah. . . ."

I smirked at her and kept going.

"You taste so good," I moaned.

I was so horny. Kendra turned me on more than any girl I'd touched before and any experienced chick who'd ever touched me.

"Can I stick it in for just a second?" I asked.

"What? Stick what where?"

"Like, stick *it* in."

"Oh," she said, suddenly frozen. My heart was pounding, my body on fire.

But she sat up.

"I'm sorry, Brock. I'm not ready for that. I kind of want to, um, wait. Until I'm older."

"It's okay, babe," I said, kissing her forehead. It was kind of a boner kill, and my balls were bluer than blue. Shit, they must've been black. "I can respect that."

I took a deep breath, trying to calm my body down. I had to change the subject.

"Shall we continue our game?" I asked, though I was sure we were way past twenty-one questions. But I liked playing. I liked getting to know Kendra.

"Yes. We shall."

"You go first," I said.

She took her sight up to the ceiling, the hallway light allowing me to admire the freckles on her nose. For a moment there, she was silent. But then she turned to me.

"Do you believe that stars aligning is what brings people together?"

"I do. I think that there's more to space and the stars and the moon that controls us down here on Earth. Do you?"

She grinned. "I want to think so."

The rain began to pick up outside. It was a Halloween storm.

"I hate the rain," she said.

"How come?"

"It's so dreary."

"Maybe it's symbolic of something bigger."

"What do you mean?" She looked at me, waiting for an explanation.

"I don't know—think about it. Maybe the rain is a sign from the universe showing us that even during the dreariest of times, there's growth. Flowers bloom from it, grass grows from it. The world needs dreary moments to survive too."

I didn't have a lot of faith in people—or our deteriorating society—but I did believe that the universe was constantly sending us signs.

"And maybe—maybe it's proof that even after all of that darkness and gloom, that the sun eventually shines again. No matter what." That was just the hope in me speaking, though, and once I realized how deep I just got with someone and how far I let her in, I immediately retreated back to my safe place. "But, yeah. It still sucks, and that's just a theory."

She gave me this *look*. This look of intrigue, like, now she was speechless, and somehow I had to change the subject or continue on down the path of emotional-and-sensitive Brock.

"What's that look?" I smiled at her.

"What look?" she asked.

"I don't know." I looked back up at the ceiling, and from the corner of my eye I could see the moon, glowing outside of the rain-covered window.

"You see our moon?" I said.

"Our moon?"

"Yeah. Our moon. Can you see the man sleeping on it?"

"Yes."

"Do you think it's God?"

"I'd never thought about it like that before. Maybe. It could be."

"Do you believe in God?"

"I like to think that there is a man or woman or spirit up there watching out for me. Rooting for me. Maybe it's just a feeling of hope, but I've always thought someone is up there."

I sat on her explanation for a moment, thinking about it.

"Do you?" she asked.

I was still silent, thinking. All of this was making me go so far beyond my normal thought processes.

"I don't know. I want to believe in him, but there's just too much madness in this world for me to understand that."

• How could someone like me, a fucking drug dealer, believe in God?

This game went from twenty-one questions to deep questions real fast. I was unable to help myself; this deep side of me that demanded to be heard was in full force tonight. Maybe it was because I knew Kendra had the kind of ears that seemed to hear without infiltrated judgment. Or at least it seemed. Or maybe it was just a mix of substances in my system that became exposed through my words.

I liked talking to interesting people, though—especially while intoxicated. People with depth and theories and ideas beyond what we see written down in class. Because most of that was made-up horseshit anyway.

"This is nice," Kendra said.

"I agree."

"I've had a nice night with you."

"Really? Even with all my family shit?"

"That really wasn't that big of a deal, I promise."

"Okay, good." Her indifference to the situation still didn't make it any less embarrassing though.

Her eyes began to shut. I pulled her into me. I wasn't tired—or at least I hadn't thought I was—but within a short couple of minutes, we fell asleep in each other's arms to the sound of raindrops.

Monday sprang on me quickly, and I realized I'd barely accomplished any deals over the weekend. I sprayed some cologne before I headed out of my room. I was already running late to pick up Kendra for school.

I stopped in the kitchen on my way out, opened the fridge, and reached for an apple, searching for a cup of yogurt to go with it.

"Do we have any more yogurt?" I asked my mom. She sat at the kitchen counter, staring at her computer screen with such intensity I thought her eyes might pop right out of her head.

"No," she said in her usual monotone, couldn't-be-bothered voice.

I closed the fridge, disappointed, but I had to get going.

"Where exactly are you off to?" my father asked as I headed for the door.

"Uh, school?"

"What are you talking about? I told you last week, we're going to Seattle."

"Fuck. Really? A twenty-four-hour notice would've been cool."

"Yeah. What's wrong with you lately? You've been slacking."

"What are you talking about? I'm the only one who makes deals! You wouldn't even be in business if it wasn't for me."

My father's eyes shot through me like a bullet . . . and I felt the pain.

"Is it that Kendra girl again? Is that what's going on?"

"What about Annie?" my mom intervened.

"What about her?" I asked. "Why are you two attacking me again?"

This was one of those moments where I wished I had a

delinquent younger brother or something that caused so many problems, my parents wouldn't even notice me.

What did they care anyway? It wasn't any of their business who I went out with. What happened to *as long as you do your job*? That's all my father ever said. That's all he ever cared about. There was no winning with him, so I started for the door again. But I was halted by a glass of scotch shattering against the door and at my feet.

"Clean it up," he said. "And pack your bags. We're leaving here in an hour."

I clenched my fists together and took a deep breath, remembering the meditation exercise Kendra had taught me—inhale and hold it. Exhale and hold it. It wasn't as useful as I hoped.

Hold it together. Hold it together, I thought to myself, trying to get in my head before my anger took over my entire being.

I untightened my fists as I walked back toward the kitchen to grab a towel.

"Go pack—now," my father said as he headed out of the room.

He was such a fucking dick. I hurried and wiped up the mess he made—like I was always doing—before texting Kendra. I'd have to make up a good excuse for this one.

My parents were silent in the front seat, my mom driving while my father answered emails on his phone. I might as well have gone crazy in a car with them for eighteen fucking hours. Kill me.

I watched as my dad placed his hand on her lap. They rarely showed each other affection. They were really more like business partners than an actual married couple.

"How you doing back there, Brock?" he asked. I was surprised he cared. Then I remembered how important a pack mule is to his cavalry and realized that's all I was to him—and that was everything.

"Bored as fuck."

"Watch your mouth."

"Then don't ask me questions."

He shook his head in the front seat.

"You'll thank me one day for helping you build a very successful life."

I rolled my eyes. And of course all my mom did was sit there mute. Did she have a voice of her own at all? I didn't want to hate on my parents, but they made it too easy.

"When are we going home?" I asked.

My father took a moment to say, "Friday."

"What's the point in driving eighteen hours just to stay a couple of days, then drive eighteen hours back?"

"Are you capable of going just an hour without bitching?"

"No."

My father left it at that. I was ready if he decided to come back with more.

I blocked out my anger with thoughts of Kendra. I thought back to Halloween, just her and me. Damn, she was so wet when I went down on her, it turned me on so much. Annie was never *that* soaked. A smile made its way through like no other girl could have ever caused. I couldn't help but let out a small chuckle thinking about how she freaked out about me putting my mouth where "pee" came out of.

"What's so funny?" my father questioned, bringing me back to the sad reality that I wasn't with her right now.

"Nothing."

KENDRA

"Are you sure you're okay, Brock?" I asked. I didn't know where I was. I thought it was school, but it didn't look like it.

His eyes were red and glassy. "Yes, I'm fine, Kendra!"

Jason appeared out of nowhere. "Hey, dude! You got the blow?"

"We do!" a familiar female voice answered. I turned around to discover Brock's mother, his father by her side. She held a bag in her hand.

She started toward us, reaching the bag out for us to take.

"It's for charity." She smiled.

I took the bag from her and opened it up.

My eyes shot open. I looked at the clock. Eight o'clock. Coach was going to hate me—I'd slept through practice *and* I was going to be late for school. I had a pit in my gut. How was I going to face him after all of the lectures he'd been feeding me lately about being focused and giving my all—ugh. All that work was feeling worthless.

And worse, that dream . . . or nightmare. I never got to see what was in that bag, and it bothered me, the whole thing. I threw the pillow over my face, frustrated with my current situation, and screamed into it.

When I sat up and looked at my phone, I noticed Brock had texted me. He was supposed to pick me up and was probably wondering why I wasn't answering. Not that he was ever on time.

> **Brock:** You'll never believe it! My parents surprised me with a last minute trip to Seattle! Crazy, right? Don't miss me too much my sexy girl;)

Seattle? That was super random. I mean, it was the middle of a school week. And he'd just missed a week of school recently too for being sick or something.

> **Kendra:** Aw how fun! Send lots of pics :* miss you already.

I got out of bed and quickly got ready for school. I was running so late, I felt discombobulated. Like, no matter what, I felt like I was forgetting something. Thankfully, Ashleigh and Ashton offered to pick me up, so at least we would be late together. I ran downstairs into the kitchen with one shoe on, the other in my hand. Harry was sitting at the island on the phone, probably with Zola.

I grabbed a cup of yogurt and an apple out of the fridge.

"Love you," I said and scurried out the door.

Ashton and Ashleigh were parked on the street, making out in his car. I guess it was better than the fighting.

"Hey, guys," I said as I hopped in.

"Where's lover boy?" Ashton asked.

"His parents surprised him with a last-minute trip to Seattle," I said.

"During a school week?"

"I guess so."

"That's really fucking odd. Why Seattle?" Ashleigh said.

"I have no clue."

"Ashton told me he's only been to Brock's house once but, like, they had to call his mom before they could go inside, and she wouldn't let them in for fifteen minutes. She wanted to *pick up a bit* before guests came in. I think they're sex junkies and have sex toys thrown all over the house."

I laughed at her ridiculous theories. "Oh, shut up, Ash! Maybe they're just private people."

"I didn't say that!" Ashton corrected her. "I said he was locked out and his mom didn't let him in for, like, ten minutes or something."

"Didn't I just say that, dumbass?" Ashleigh eyed him. Ashton gave up, silencing himself.

"Have you two done it yet?" Ashleigh asked.

"Done what?" I was lost.

"Boned. Screwed. Got it on. Whatever kids are calling it these days."

"Oh—no. We haven't."

"Only a matter of time," she said, with such conviction in her voice it made me wonder if she was right. We'd done everything but—did that mean sex was next? Did he expect that? Was I even ready? How would I know?

My phone vibrated in my lap.

Brock: How are you today?
Kendra: I'm good. Woke up too late ;P
Brock: How rebellious of you, Kendra ;)
Kendra: haha oh ya . . . so scandalous

I stuffed my phone back in my pocket as we pulled up to school. The late bell rang as I walked into the building. I walked as fast as I could down the hall, basically out of breath, and into Mr. Paul's class, tardy for the first time *ever*. It was kind of traumatizing.

"Thank you for joining us, Miss Dimes," he said.

I took the nearest open seat.

"Hi," I said, my voice quivering. Why did I have to be so awkward? I could have just slipped in through the back door and taken a seat without announcing my tardy presence.

I pulled out my phone, another thing I had never done in Mr. Paul's class.

Brock: I'm so bored. Let's play 21 ?'s
Kendra: K, u start
Brock: How are we going to make up for lack of time together when I get back?;)

I thought he was making sexual insinuations. I guess it was true—if you gave a mouse a cookie, he'd want a glass of milk.

Kendra: We should go surfing!
Brock: Yeah we should ☺

"Ms. Dimes, unless it's a book resting on your lap, put it away," Mr. Paul said, interrupting my game with Brock.

I slyly maneuvered my phone back into my bag underneath my desk.

It had only been a couple days without Brock, and I was going crazy. I totally sounded like a thirteen-year-old girl who was obsessed with her first boyfriend—which actually might have been the case. Or at least close to it. I felt all over the place, like I couldn't sit still, even when I *was* sitting still. I tried to throw myself back into surfing and practice, but even that wasn't helping.

One day, I convinced Ashleigh to come with me to an after-school practice.

I sat on my board in the water. Ashleigh floated on her board next to me.

"I literally haven't been in the water in forever," she admitted.

"I know, you never come anymore!"

"All right, ladies. We got a big one coming," Coach said.

We paddled against the current. I was surprised Coach was even talking to me, but I was thankful that he was. I needed him. I refused to let myself down and, more importantly, Kyle.

Maybe a week off from Brock was what I needed to get my head back in the game.

I stood up, and the wave began to curl over me. I rode it out. It took Ashleigh down, but somehow I managed to carry through, riding it to shore.

A hyperawareness jolted through my body with pure excitement. I needed that confidence booster.

"Whoooo!" Coach yelled. "That's what I'm talking about!" He raised his hand up to high-five me. "I got my Kendra back."

"You go, girl," Ashleigh said, carrying her board out of the water.

"I'm teaching yoga here tonight. Just a slow flow and guided meditation on the beach."

"We should go, Ken!"

"What time?"

"Seven."

"Okay. We'll see you tonight," I said.

We walked up the beach back to Ashleigh's car where our towels awaited us in her trunk. She threw one to me.

"Let's hit it," she said as we hopped in her car.

Ashleigh's driving scared me for a couple of reasons. 1. She was so short, she could barely see over the steering wheel. 2. She was Ashleigh.

Like I normally do while in her passenger seat, I looked down at my phone the entire time, praying that we would make it back home in one piece. Thankfully, I had a text from Brock to distract me. At least temporarily.

Brock: I think it's true.
Kendra: What?
Brock: Distance does make the heart grow fonder;) <3
Kendra: ☺ I think you're right.

"What are you smiling at?" Ashleigh asked as she looked over at me. At least we were at a stoplight.

I felt my skin start to burn, my face get hot, and my heart rate quicken. I just laughed; I didn't know what to say or how to express this feeling for Brock out loud without feeling totally embarrassed. It was weird for me, talking to anyone, even Ashleigh, about my boy stuff.

"Nothing," I said.

"It's totally Brock. You two are actually in love."

I smiled, gazing out the window. I wondered, was it love? Was it possible to even be in love at my age?

"Let's go get a scratcher and an Icee," Ashleigh said.

"Better hope Jim is working."

"We're totally blowing off yoga tonight, right? That sounds exhausting."

I laughed. "Yeah, it does."

We pulled up to my place at the same time as my dad and Harry. Ashleigh had her scratcher and Icee in hand. My phone rang in my hand. Brock was FaceTiming me. When I picked up, his camera was facing the view of city lights below him.

"How dope is this?" Brock said.

"Where are you?"

"It's the balcony of the hotel, with a view of all of Seattle."

"Oh, my gosh! I'm jealous."

"Who are you talking to?" my dad asked.

"It's her lover man," Ashleigh said.

I looked at Harry, who was rolling his eyes.

Brock flipped the camera, so that now it was on his face. I smiled when I saw it. I missed him more than I realized, and hearing his voice made me crave him.

"What's up, K Dawg?" He winked at me as he walked inside the hotel room. I saw his parents in the background.

"Who're you talking to?" his mom asked.

Without turning away from the camera, he said, "It's Kendra."

"Oh."

He looked back at his mom now, and in response she said, "Hi, Kendra."

"Hi," I said back. I wasn't really sure if she liked me or not. Especially after that Halloween dinner. Yikes.

"Brock, get off the phone. We're going to dinner." His dad's tone was firm.

Brock rolled his eyes. It was such a strange family dynamic, and I couldn't figure it out.

"I gotta go. I'll text you."

Ashleigh and I headed up to my room. We sat on my bed as she scratched out the pictures of dollar signs with a penny to reveal numbers.

"Can you believe my mom is out of town with her trainer again? I swear they're dating."

"Does that bother you?" I wondered.

"Barely. It's better than her trying to hang out with me all of the time. I swear she thinks we're the same age."

I laughed. I wanted to tell her she shouldn't take her mom for granted. I wished mine was around. It was a horrible feeling knowing my brother was gone and I could never talk to him again, but it was an even worse feeling knowing my mom was plenty alive and somewhere, maybe even close to here, and I was never going to see her again. She left us after my brother died. Apparently grief changes people.

"Did you hear Jason and Taylor are hooking up?"

"Shut up. How'd that happen? She's been in love with him forever."

"Uh, after they totally made out on Halloween."

"Wait, what?" I was shocked.

"Yeah, you and Brock had your little rendezvous upstairs while it was like a make-out party downstairs. Jason was with Taylor, Hunter was with that weird Nick guy. I don't even know who he is. Then there was Ryan, as usual, just watching like a creepo."

"I can't believe Tay finally got Jason."

"They're both narcissistic assholes, so it's the perfect match made in hell."

The real reason she hated her was because Taylor hooked up with Ashton when he and Ashleigh went on a break. But this was, like, all the way back during freshman year.

"I have to tell Brock about Nick."

"Why?"

I laughed, thinking of Brock always teasing Nick. "It's kind of an inside joke."

"You two are such dork heads," she said as she finished the last of her scratcher. "Fuck! Not even a dollar."

Kendra: Guess what . . . nick and hunter hooked up :P LOL.

Brock: Shit . . . maybe he's not CB after all :D

"Let's go steal a bottle of wine from my mom's cooler and talk shit about people—now that you're an alcoholic and all," she teased.

I chuckled, though I hoped she was joking about the alcoholic thing. "I'm down."

We walked back downstairs and got in Ashleigh's car. As we passed by Main Beach, I really missed Brock.

BROCK

It was finally Friday—my last day in Seattle. Thank God.

Surprisingly, my parents and I managed to get along for the majority of the trip, but honestly, the past day, I was starting to feel the effect of one hotel room. It had been almost a week since we'd left Laguna, and the walls were closing in on me, and my personal bubble had been popped somewhere along the way. I needed my room, my music, my own bed, and my fucking space.

I looked at the clock. It was only six. I grabbed my phone and headed downstairs to the lobby. It was raining, the sky mostly painted with clouds for the duration of the day. I walked outside and strolled down the sidewalk.

A sudden gust of wind exhaled against my face, tossing my hair off of my forehead. I tensed up with a shiver.

I hadn't talked to Duke in a minute, so I decided to Face-Time him.

"Duuuude, where are you?" He looked into the camera. Surprisingly he didn't have his hat on.

"I'm in Seattle, man. And it's fucking hell. Between the weather and dealing with my parents."

"When are you back? I'm throwing a rager tomorrow!"

I thought for a moment . . . I'd be back tomorrow, but

I wanted to spend my first night back with Kendra and I was pretty positive she wouldn't be down for another LA party.

"I get back tomorrow but—"

"But what?"

"I'm probably gonna be with Kendra."

"Daaaamn! Brock Parker falls in love! Who would've thought this was possible?"

I just laughed, trying to avoid the whole *love* word. I just didn't see much of a point in partying that hard when I had a girlfriend; nothing good could possibly come from it.

"Love is a big word, my friend."

"Obviously just big enough." Duke laughed at me through the phone.

"I asked her to be my girlfriend."

"Shut the fuck up! I'm here for it."

The connection was shitty and the FaceTime kept freezing.

"You're breaking up! I'll call you tomorrow."

"Aight. Peace."

A few minutes later Duke texted me.

Duke: Don't get too comfortable . . . we got an island to buy

Brock: She can come with

Duke: This the REAL DEAL.

Brock: F offfffffff

Before we took off for Laguna, my parents wanted to look at one last apartment. During the span of the few days we'd been here, we'd mostly looked at places, gone to a couple of business dinners with Morales's people, and drunk a shit ton.

I sat in the lobby while they took a tour because I didn't really give a shit what it looked like. It wasn't like I'd be spending time there. I was still confused on the whole Seattle thing to begin with.

When my parents and I got into the car and started for home, it was pouring rain.

"So, Brock..."

"What?" I asked. My father's voice was stern.

"We're thinking after next semester, you take over the Seattle accounts—"

"Wait, is that a joke?" Where were they pulling this shit from all of the sudden?

"Yeah," my mom said. "You and Annie. We were talking about it with Martin and—"

"Whoa, whoa, whoa. You want me to move again when I already have great, stable accounts in Orange County and just fucking pick up with Annie and dip to Washington? Oh, and it fucking rains there every day too to really top it off. Are you nuts? Why don't you move?"

"Brock." My father's voice was obnoxiously calm. "You're going to do what we say, whether you agree or don't. Nothing is final, but it's something Morales is pushing for right now. He knows how you'll thrive there."

I didn't respond. I wasn't going anywhere. Fuck that shit.

"You guys are whack."

I plugged my headphones in and, thankfully, Kendra saved the day with a text.

Kendra: When are you guys heading back?

Brock: We'll be back by tomorrow night!

Kendra: Thank goodness! Just in time for the weekend <3

Brock: Right? ;)

Kendra: :P kind of going CRAY without you.

Brock: Tell me about it ☺ Maybe I'll see you tomorrow?

Kendra: Hopefully!

I started to type and mention Duke's party but decided to let it go. I kind of wanted it to be her and me anyway.

I drifted off into a deep sleep, dreaming of the ocean and Kendra lying in it, naked. It was magical—and left me with a case of blue balls.

When I awoke, we were parked at a gas station. I looked out the window at my mom pumping the gas.

"What time is it?" I asked, yawning.

"Ten," my father said, looking down at his phone.

I threw my head against the seat.

"Don't be so dramatic. It's not like you've done any of the driving."

My eyes automatically rolled as I shook my head. It was like he got off on being a fucking prick. No wonder his parents disowned him.

My mom got back into the car. She yawned. I kind of felt bad for her. She was like my father's bitch, but I guess that was her own choice.

"Let's get going," my father said.

She nodded her head and started the ignition.

"Wait!" My father stopped her from taking off. "Brock, go hit that guy up."

By the entrance to the convenience store, a motley-looking guy was smoking a cigarette.

"Why him?"

"Just do it. You know what to say. It's quick money."

My dad had an eye for people; he was very perceptive, I'd give him that. He knew who was doing what, using what, and how they were using it.

"Why don't you pitch him?" I asked.

"You have youth on your side."

"What the fuck does that mean?"

"Just do it."

So, I got out of the car and approached the middle-aged man, who was probably actually younger than I suspected.

"Hey, man. You got any extra cigarettes?" I asked.

He looked at me for a moment before pulling a pack of cigs from his pocket and handing me one.

"Thanks."

He handed me a lighter too.

"What town are we even in?" I asked.

"Mount Shasta."

I nodded.

"Where you from?" he asked.

"I'm from Las Vegas," I lied. I'd never give my real info.

My phone began to buzz in my pocket. I fumbled to grab it, the small bag of coke falling from my pocket. It was my father calling; I swear he did this shit on purpose. The guy looked down at the bag, then caught my eye.

"How much?" he asked. I couldn't believe how spot-on my father was.

"A hundred."

"I'll take it."

He handed me five twenties and I handed him the bag. That was that.

We drove off into the night.

"Nice work, Brock."

I handed him the money.

"Let's split fifty-fifty," he said, giving me half the commission back. I was kind of surprised. It was like he actually liked me today.

I looked up into the rearview mirror; my mom kept widening her bloodshot eyes, struggling to stay awake.

"Want me to drive, Mom?" I asked.

"No. I'm fine." She yawned again.

I looked back out the window. The trees planted on desert terrain were lit up underneath the moonlight. I leaned my head against the window, my head bouncing as we drove down the rocky road. I wanted to be in my bed. Tree after tree after tree. I wished I could have fallen back asleep.

My father rolled up a joint in the front seat. He lit it up and took a hit, rolling down his window.

"Want some?" He handed it to my mom.

She took it from him, also taking a hit. They smiled at each other. It was love at first high. That was the one thing I *did* respect about my parents—they'd been together since they were my age. They'd basically grown up together. I wondered if that would be Kendra and me, but with the path I was going down and the one she seemed to be walking perpendicularly to me, I doubted that would be the case. Our roads seemed to be crossing, transcending into one, but I questioned for how long.

Hours passed, and the uncomfortable ride home left me with only occasional dozing. My back ached, and my head throbbed when I awoke for good.

The sound of the ocean became coherent from a distance. I felt so relieved to be back in my area. Home base. I rolled down the window, taking in the smell of the salty mist.

Brock: Finally back in Laguna!!
Kendra: yay!!
Brock: Y u up?? LOL.
Kendra: Surrrrf practice ☺

It was Saturday. Seven in the morning. When we pulled up to the driveway, I slowly got out of the car, trying to move my legs around. They had fallen asleep the last two hours of the car ride. I grabbed my bag and walked inside. It felt too good to be home. I went straight to my room and collapsed down on my bed.

KENDRA

I sat at my vanity in my towel, gazing out the balcony doors. It was sprinkling outside, the clouds covering the sun, night soon approaching.

My phone rang just as I was about to get up and put my necklace on. I set the St. Christopher pendant back down on my nightstand, reaching for my phone instead.

"I missed you," Brock said. It was nice to hear his voice.

"How was the ride back?"

"Boring as shit," he said. "What are you doing?"

"I just got out of the shower."

"Damn, you're turning me on." He laughed into the phone. I blushed, thankful he couldn't see.

"Shut up." I laughed.

"How was your practice this morning?"

"Good. I can't believe the quarterfinals are so close!"

"You excited?"

"Excited, nervous, overwhelmed." I sighed a deep breath.

"Let's do something tonight."

"I can't. I have practice at six tomorrow. Plus, my dad doesn't want me going out tonight." These next few weeks were vital for the competition. I was dedicating all my time and energy to it. I hadn't come this far to fumble at the one-yard line (that's what my dad always said).

"Oh, come on. I'll have you home by midnight. They won't even realize you left."

"Brock, that sounds sketchy. If my dad catches us, he'll be so pis—"

"Babe, trust me once in a while."

It was tempting. I hadn't seen him in what felt like forever. I guessed just a couple of hours wouldn't be a big deal.

"All right. Fine. But I have to be home no later than midnight."

"You got it," he said. "See you soon."

When we hung up, I walked toward the staircase. The TV was off downstairs, which meant my dad and Harry were probably in bed. I hurried back to my room, running on the tips of my toes, trying to avoid making any noise.

I threw on a pair of sweats, fully aware Ashleigh would be very disappointed in my wardrobe choice. Then Brock texted me.

Brock: Here.

Skittles began to bark just in time for me to get caught.

"Shhh, Skittles. Stop."

I grabbed her bone, which was on my bedroom floor, and threw it at her. She quickly shushed up and I shut my bedroom door, heading for the balcony.

When I shut the back gate, I made a conscious effort to close it gently. I walked down the driveway to where Brock was parked, waiting. His windows were so tinted, I couldn't see in.

When I opened the passenger door, I was greeted with a "Hi, beautiful."

We mutually leaned into one another, our lips locking like it could be the first or the last time.

"I feel like I haven't seen you in months," I admitted.

"Seriously, it's been torturous," he said as he took my hand in his and kissed it.

"What do you want to do?"

"Whatever you want."

There was a moment where only the car's engine could be heard.

"You know what I'm craving?" I asked as if he could read my mind. Sometimes I felt as if he could.

"What?"

"Red Vines and Coke." When I spoke, I wondered if I had to clarify, Coke as in *soda*—not the white powder

"Let's go get some!"

I'd eaten so healthy the last week. I deserved a treat.

Brock pulled down my street and headed for the liquor shop. When we pulled up, he handed me ten bucks so he could keep the car running as I ran in. I grabbed two Cokes and a bag of Red Vines.

"You get what you wanted?" Brock asked as I reentered the car. I felt pretty cool in his Audi.

"Yes!" I said, flashing him the bag of Red Vines.

He drove the car down the street a ways and parked in a secluded neighborhood that I didn't even know existed.

"Here you go, Mr. Parker," I said in my best British accent, handing him a soda can.

"Why thank you, Miss Dimes," he replied, also suddenly of British descent.

I popped open a can and set it in the cup holder so I could open my bag of candy. I took a Vine out and bit off each end before placing it in my Coke can as a straw. It was the only way to drink soda.

"What the hell is that?" Brock wondered, enthused by this concoction.

I sipped out of my Red Vine straw.

"Wanna try?" I asked him, holding out the bag of Vines for him to take.

"I guess," he said, tempted and confused at once. Still, he took the bag from me and imitated my straw-making method.

"I have my tricks too, Mr. Yogurt-Dipping Apple Eater!"

"I'm impressed!"

I nodded a thank you. We watched the moon hanging over the ocean, sipping on our sodas.

"You know where we should go?" He spoke to me as if I could read his mind. Sometimes I did. At least, I thought so. But now, I was mostly clueless.

"Hm?"

"Have you ever been to a drive-in movie?"

"No. That sounds like fun."

"Wanna go?"

"Right now?"

"Yeah!"

I hesitated, knowing I should be home. But, whether it was all the sugar that amped me up, or just being caught up in this moment, I agreed.

He placed his hand on my knee, right where it belonged, and drove off into the night.

We pulled up to an empty spot, parking closer to the back of the drive-in, the large screen illuminating the few dozen other vehicles. I looked around, my gaze searching our surroundings until it found its way to Brock.

"You want to get in the back?" he asked.

"Sure." I climbed over the seat and he followed.

We looked at the screen and then at each other.

"Hey, where's your necklace?" he asked, his eyes on my neck.

I grabbed my bare chest. "Oh, my gosh, I took it off when I was putting lotion on and forgot to put it back on!"

I was freaking out. I always wore that necklace. Without it I felt vulnerable, unsafe, naked.

Brock scooted closer to me, pulling me into him as our lips met, taking my mind off everything.

"I almost forgot," he said and got out of the car. He opened the trunk and returned with a bottle of Captain Morgan.

"It feels sentimental." Our drunken night at Duke's. I mean, *my* drunk night.

"Where did you get this?" I asked, laughing at the nostalgia of it.

"My buddy hooked me up." He handed me the bottle, encouraging me to take a sip. I wasn't really in the mood, but I did anyway.

"Ah, my chest," I said with one gulp.

"Bring back memories?" he asked, taking it from me and taking a sip himself.

I laughed.

"I missed that laugh." He looked at me. Deeply. Into me.

He wrapped his arm around me, took another chug of rum, then bit my ear, which I wasn't expecting—and even more so, I wasn't expecting to moan the way I did.

"You like that?" he whispered.

I responded with a kiss. We couldn't keep our hands off each other. The movie became background noise.

Brock pulled away to take another sip of rum as we finally started to get into the movie. It was nice to be back in his arms.

I felt something underneath my butt. I reached into my back pocket, realizing it was my wallet.

"Do you mind if I put this in your center console?" I asked as I was already sitting up and opening the console.

"Wait—"

"What?"

"I got it for you. Sit down and relax."

He leaned over, taking my wallet from me as I sat back down, confused, and placed it in the center console.

He sat back down, the movie screen lighting up half of his face, the other half shadowed—and that adorable smile.

"Twenty-one questions?" he asked. I nodded at that. "You start."

"What are you doing for your birthday? It's coming up, isn't it?"

"Kind of. It's January seventeenth."

"It's going to be your golden birthday."

"Golden birthday?" he asked, obviously unfamiliar with the term.

"Yeah. You know, like, you're turning the age of your birth date. Golden birthdays are special."

"What makes them so different from any other birthday?"

"You only have one."

"You also only have one nose. Does that make it special?" He tapped me on the nose.

"Well, I mean, kind of."

"You're quite strange, Miss Dimes," he teased.

"At least I admit it."

"That *is* the first step to recovery."

We laughed together at our senseless banter. Our eyes seemed to meet simultaneously until his stare shifted to my lips, then back up to my eyes again. With that, our mouths reintroduced themselves, allowing our tongues to connect.

"Brock." I spoke between kisses.

"Hm?" he said, his eyes still closed, invested in the moment, as I peeked mine open.

"Iwanttohavesexwithyou," I whispered at a rapid pace. I

wasn't sure what had come over me, or when I even decided that I was ready to be with Brock in that way. But I was sure I wanted it. I wanted him. Deeper than this. Harder than this. More than just this. I wanted to call him the one I lost "it" to, and when I was fifty years old and married with kids, a smell would cast itself through the air, and I'd think of him as my first love, and I'd laugh and miss him and wonder what he's doing. And maybe somewhere he'd be thinking of me too. Maybe not. But this was the chance I was about to take.

I felt the way his body froze, then his eyes shot open.

"I thought you wanted to wait?"

"I did. But . . . I really like you."

"I really like you too, Kendra," he said, and the conviction in his tone made me believe him. But then he reminded me, "You only have one first time."

"Those are pretty special."

We started kissing again as if there was no going back now. My hands slowly moved toward his waist like I knew what I was doing.

"Are you sure you want to do this, Kendra?"

I responded with more kisses. He pulled back to take another swig of rum before handing it to me. I took a sip too. A real one.

"Have another," he said.

I did as I was told and handed the bottle back to him. He set it down in the front seat.

I loved Brock—not just romantically, but as a friend too. I trusted him.

My neck. His lips. My shirt. Then his own. His lips were warm against mine, the taste of rum potent.

I slipped out of my pants and he slipped out of his. He was on top of me, a place I seemed to find him quite frequently these

days. His hands moved in a massaging motion over my underwear until he pulled them completely down. My body felt hot.

"Is that it?" I said, my breath heavy and my heart beating
fast. I was nervous I might start hyperventilating. But I didn't.

"No, that's just my finger," he said.

I was so anxious—my body trembled inside.

"You're so wet, baby," he said, then went down on me. It was
even better than the last time he did it. I grabbed onto his hair.
My eyes were closed and I swear I could see other galaxies. Holy
cow. It felt . . . I wasn't sure of the word, and even if I knew it, I
couldn't think of it because I was so tangled in whatever he was
doing to my body. I didn't want him to stop.

"Keep going," I moaned. I wasn't me anymore. I wasn't sure
who I was. I didn't know where I was. I just knew I liked it.

He lifted himself up, and his face was hovering over mine
again.

"Are you ready?" he asked with that confident half grin. I
thought back to the night we met. Back at homecoming.

I nodded my head, unsure if I really was ready. And then it
happened.

"Ow!"

"You okay?" he asked.

"Yeah," I lied. I didn't know it would hurt that bad.

"Damn, you're tight."

"Is that a good thing?" I didn't have a clue.

He looked at me and smiled. "Yes."

Brock Parker was literally inside of me. This was the closest
I'd ever be with someone, and it frightened me and enlightened
me all at once. I was falling deeper in love with him as he pen-
etrated deeper. He kissed my lips, and I didn't want him to ever
pull away.

"Kendra," he said.

"Yeah?"

"I really like you."

"I really like you too, Brock," I said back. I wanted to tell him I loved him. It was dancing on my lips, but I couldn't let it out. What if he didn't feel the same? I didn't want to be the first one to say it. I wanted him to tell me he loved me. I wanted to be loved by Brock Parker.

He sucked on my ear and it made me moan just like before.

My entire life, people had hyped up sex, like I should have expected fireworks to come bursting out of his penis or unicorns to fly through in the midst of it all. But it was much more magical than that. Sex with Brock was like walking on air without any fear of falling back down onto Earth. It was that kind of complicated simplicity. But it was also nerve-racking and new and scary. My vulnerability was what scared me the most. I'd never allowed someone this far in, but I also loved it. Would I regret it?

His lips floated over my neck and I could feel his rum-stained breath caressing me. I didn't feel like a girl anymore . . . no. Brock made me feel like a woman. An adult woman.

He made noises too. And they turned me on so much—I wasn't sure if I was supposed to let him know, but I got so lost in it all that I didn't bother.

"You're so sexy," he whispered into my ear.

Our breathing was synchronized, but when we looked at each other, we couldn't help but laugh. An awkward, nervous, confused, and stressed-out laugh.

Brock Parker tasted a lot like cigarette and trouble, but he smelled more like ocean and forever.

BROCK

I rolled off Kendra. She rested her head on my chest, both of us trying to steady our breathing.

"You all right?" I asked.

"Yeah. Are you?"

"Yeah."

I kissed her head.

I may not have been a virgin, but I'd never had meaningful sex. Not like that. The first time was just to get it over with—and Annie sure as hell didn't mean anything. Everyone else was always just a one-night stand or a hookup. I had never actually "made love" to someone. I mean, I guess that's what you would call it.

I looked at Kendra. At her freckle-covered nose.

"You're the fucking coolest."

She smiled at me with glassy eyes, which were either a result of first-time sex aches or too much rum—or maybe a slight combination of both. She was even beautiful with tears in her eyes.

"Not too bad yourself." She giggled.

I looked at the movie screen. The credits were rolling.

"I guess that's our cue," I said. Even though I wished I could stay here with her all night, cuddling and fucking.

"Yeah, we should get going."

We both got dressed and hopped in the front seat.

"Hey, do you mind if I smoke a cig real fast?" I asked.

She was hesitant; I saw it in her eyes. "Sure."

"Come stand outside with me." I grabbed a pack of cigs from my pocket.

We stood outside in the cold night air, most of the cars already gone.

"Do you smoke a lot?"

"Not really," I admitted. "Just once in a while."

Honestly, cigarettes were best when extremely inebriated or after sex. Strong facts. I'd been smoking more lately, though. Mostly just since Seattle. At night, when I didn't feel like hanging out with my parents in the hotel room, I'd go have a cigarette outside and just relax. Not think. Not talk. Nothing. Just me and a smoke.

"What kind of cigarettes do you smoke?" she asked.

"I like Marlboro Lights."

She nodded her head, her arms crossed around her chest. Her teeth chattered.

"Here," I said, the cigarette hanging out of my mouth as I wrapped my jacket around her.

"Thanks."

I kissed her, our eyes open this time. It was oddly dope as fuck. To watch each other kiss.

I pulled back to take another puff of my cig, blowing *O*s into the crisp night air.

"How do you do that?" she asked. I knew it'd impress her.

I winked. "It's just a little trick."

We looked up at the sky.

"Check out that moon," I said. It was full and bright.

She stared at it, almost in awe.

I continued, "I'd say our moon puts all the other moons to shame. Wouldn't you agree?"

"I'd say, our moon definitely does."

The smoke from my cigarette created a wall of fog between us.

"So mysterious," she said. "I'm not a fan of cigarettes or any of that, but I'll admit . . . you look pretty hot right now. Very James Dean."

"Oh, yeah?" I said, taking one more puff and then tossing it to the ground. I took her by the hand and kissed her hard one last time before getting into the car.

I buckled up the bottle of Captain Morgan like a child in the back before we left.

I felt the alcohol buzzing through me as we headed back to Kendra's. I wasn't worried, though; I swore my drunk driving was better than my sober driving. Maybe because I had to focus more. But I saw the way Kendra grabbed onto her seat from the corner of my eye. She was tensed up.

I placed a hand on her thigh.

"You all right?"

She smiled and nodded, but her eyes spoke differently. "Yeah. You're swerving pretty bad, though. Are you sure you should be driving?"

"Yeah. We're fine."

We were stopped at a red light. I leaned over to kiss her, giving her leg a gentle squeeze. My girl.

The car behind us honked when the light turned green, so I hit the gas, pressing the pedal all the way down.

"What the hell? Brock, slow down!" Kendra shrieked.

"Did you just say *hell*?"

"Brock, please—"

"You just said hell—"

"Brock!"

"Okay, okay, I'm sorry."

I grabbed her hand, looking at that perfect face. She was still irritated, her shoulders tensed up to her ears and her eyes appeared afraid.

"Come on, we're good. I'd never let anything happen to you, baby."

She looked at me, her shoulders now relaxed, but she still seemed frightened.

"I'm serious," I said.

I saw her chest rise as she took a deep breath in and started to calm down.

"Brock," she spoke, her voice soft.

"What's up?" I asked, taking a quick look at her.

"Can I ask you something?"

I was nervous where she was going with this. "Of course."

"I guess it's less of a question and more of a statement."

I waited for her to continue, but she paused a moment. Then she cleared her throat. She looked at me, and I tried to look at her too, although it was hard to watch her and the road when I was this tipsy.

"I think I'm in love with you."

My heart sank into my stomach. I didn't know how to respond, even though I felt it too. Shit, I was freaking out. I didn't think I'd ever told anyone I'd loved them before. Barely even my parents. Definitely not anyone in a romantic type of way. Time was running out—I had to respond somehow. Or else it was going to get fucking weird. Did I want this? Did I love Kendra? I knew I did, but how was I supposed to say it? Once I did, there was no going back.

"Hey," I began. "I love—"

"Brock!" she shrieked and grabbed onto me, her gaze ahead at the semi's headlights. Whose lane I was in. Fuck.

I woke up in an unfamiliar room. I looked down, my wrist was covered in hospital bands.

"Hello?" I yelled.

I sat up in my bed and a nurse came running in. I felt dizzy and light-headed.

"How are you feeling, Mr. Parker?" she asked.

"Where's my girlfriend? What's going on?"

"Let me get your doctor," she said.

She rushed out of the room and reentered with a middle-aged man dressed in scrubs by her side.

"Hello, Brock. How are you feeling?" he asked.

"Kind of sore, a little dizzy," I had to admit.

"Do you remember what happened?"

The doctor flashed a light in my eyes. So fucking obnoxious. I pushed it away.

"Where's Kendra? Is she okay?"

"Brock, I need you to answer the question."

"I don't know! I remember a truck, okay?"

I clenched my fists together, growing frustrated with the interrogation. Then I got nervous. Where was my car? All the drugs inside of it. Shit. I didn't have anything left in my trunk, but I knew there were still some mint containers in the center console. But only a couple. I was praying to whoever was running this shit on Earth that I wasn't going to get caught.

"So you remember a little," he said, writing. That's good."

"Can you please just tell me if Kendra is okay?"

"You both had alcohol in your systems during the accident. You're lucky to be alive."

I rolled my eyes. I wasn't in this situation because I was drinking—I was in this situation because a truck hit us head-on.

"Where are my parents?"

"We haven't been able to get ahold of them."

I ripped the covers off of me. "Can I please see Kendra?"

"You need to rest, Brock," the doctor said.

"I need to see her. I need to know she's okay."

I rushed up, almost passing out as the room around me began to spin. The doctor grabbed me by the arm.

"Sit down and rest. Now."

I removed my arm from his grasp, moving past him and darting into the hallway. I opened each curtain, none revealing Kendra.

"Brock! You can't do that," the doctor called after me, but I didn't give a shit.

I ran down the hall, opening curtain after curtain.

Then I heard a familiar voice say, "That can't be the case. My daughter doesn't drink."

I followed Mr. Dimes's voice down two rooms and opened the curtain.

"Kendra!"

She looked up at me, her eyes adjusting. She seemed really out of it. I started toward her, but her dad blocked my way.

His voice was quiet but strong. "You. Stay away from my daughter."

The doctor entered the room, seemingly out of breath, stepping between the two of us.

"You can't be in here," the doctor said to me. Fucking asshole. Was he serious?

"Mr. Dimes, I'm so sorry—" I tried to speak.

"I don't want to hear it. I should have listened to Harry about you," he said, but he wouldn't look at me. Couldn't look at me. I understood why. I did.

"Mr. Dimes—"

"Um, Dad—" Kendra said, her voice groggy.

"No. I've already lost one child. I'm not going to lose another. If you actually cared about Kendra, you wouldn't have put her in this position."

"What are you talking about?" I asked. What child did he lose? "Who died?"

"What happened?" Kendra asked. "Dad, let me see Brock."

Mr. Dimes shook his head but let me through. I sat next to her on the bed, taking her hand in mine. I kissed it. When I looked at her, in the eye, I wanted to fucking break down and cry. But I didn't. I felt so shitty right now. So guilty. Culpable. I was such a fuckup, and now it had affected Kendra. I wanted to go back in time and change it all.

"What happened?" she asked me. I noticed a long cut across her forehead. Everything went numb.

My foot bounced on the floor. I didn't want to tell her. Couldn't she just have amnesia from it and not hate me?

"We got hit by a truck." My hand squeezed hers tighter than I was planning to. But I was so nervous, waiting for her reaction.

"Because he was fucking drunk," Harry chimed in.

But she still wasn't comprehending anything. She was beginning to sit up when she cried out in pain.

I jumped up, afraid of what was going on. What had I done to her?

"Careful, Kendra," the doctor said. He helped her sit up. "You're pretty bruised up and may have a mild concussion. I also took a look at your X-rays." He tilted his head down. "Kendra, you have a hairline fracture in your left leg."

"What?" Her eyes were wide and glassy, and suddenly she was aware. "It can't be. No, no, no. I have a huge surf competition coming up—I can compete, right?"

"I'm sorry—" I tried to reach for her hand again.

"Don't touch me! This is your fault!" She looked at me, dead in the eye.

"Kendra, I'm sorry. I didn't—"

"Get out of here!" she sobbed. "I can't even look at you."

"Come on, Kendra, please—"

"What a joke," she said, tears falling from her face as she looked down at the hospital band around her wrist, fiddling with it. "All that hard work. All the time I devoted. Everything I worked for—destroyed."

Then she looked up at me to add, "And you don't even care."

I was going to start crying too. I'd ruined it. It was over. The only girl I'd ever loved. And I never even got to tell her. My mind raced through ideas of how I could change it all. Fix things. A time machine. Something! I needed a miracle. But the problem was, I didn't believe in those.

"I hate you."

I swallowed down all the pain she was throwing at me and headed out of the door. There wasn't anything left to say. Nothing left to do. When I was almost out of the room, she chucked a pillow at me. I deserved it. I deserved even more.

The hospital eventually got ahold of my parents. They showed up around six in the morning, and the hospital discharged me around seven. When they walked in, my mom—surprisingly—ran to my bedside and fell on top of me. I was surprised she cared. I placed my arm around her, unsure of how to take in this response.

"Brock! Don't scare us like that," she said.

"Sorry."

But my dad just stood there, shaking his head. Annoyed probably more than anything else. I'd gotten into trouble before, but nothing like this. I think it took my mom aback. It was nice to know she gave a shit.

I'd suffered a minor concussion, but that was it—thankfully. The doctors released me with strict orders to rest for at least a week and call if I started vomiting or felt off. They said concussions could take a while to heal, but I honestly didn't care anymore.

"Very smooth," my father said, sarcastically, as we walked to the car parked just outside of the emergency room.

"Come on, Karl. He was just in an accident," my mom shot back, her arm wrapped around me.

I was surprised again to hear my mother defending me. I think Karl Parker was a certified sociopath. Or just on too many drugs himself to think properly or be sane.

I didn't respond to him.

The three of us got into the car, exhausted. My mom exhaled a yawn. I felt bad for her. This morning more than ever.

"Listen"—my father shifted the car into drive—"you're going to be charged with a DUI no matter what, but the other driver is going to want to file a lawsuit against you. I think we should enroll you in alcohol classes so it looks good in court."

"Alcohol classes?"

"Maybe even stick you in a thirty-day rehab."

"Rehab?" He had to be joking.

"Yeah."

"But what about the deals?"

"The deals can wait. If you end up in jail, we'll be screwed over longer than just thirty days."

"I don't want to go to rehab."

He ignored me. "By the way, I hope you didn't have any cargo in your car."

"A couple of mint containers."

"Shit." He slammed the steering wheel, the sound of the horn making me jump.

"This is why you don't keep stock in your fucking car, Brock," he said, his tone firm. Like heat that felt so hot you think it's ice-cold.

"Well, where do you want me to keep it then, *Dad*? How am I supposed to get deals done? You never mentioned before that I shouldn't!"

"I guess I thought it was common sense," he said, the sarcasm dripping from his voice.

"What do we do, Karl?" My mom sounded worried.

He was silent a moment.

"I'll take care of it."

I wasn't sure what that meant and I was too exhausted to dissect it.

When we walked into the house, it was still and quiet. The most peace I'd gotten in the last twelve hours. I looked out the kitchen window, where the sun was just rising. I walked over to the refrigerator and opened it up in search of a water bottle. There was one left—I took it and cracked the top open, chugging it down within a matter of seconds.

When I collapsed onto my bed, I stared up at the ceiling, wishing someone could wake me up from this hellish nightmare. What the fuck? But it was my real life.

My head throbbed. A single tear streamed down my face. I wiped it away. I couldn't remember the last time I cried. How could this have happened?

I plugged my phone into its charger. When it finally turned on, I held it over my face, scrolling through all of the texts I hadn't seen yet.

Mom, Mom, Dad, Nick, blah, blah, blah. None of them were Kendra.

I threw it on my bed, dwelling on the ceiling as sunlight began to fill my room. I'd never felt so empty. So helpless. So shitty. I grabbed my phone and clicked Kendra's number. She hated me. She even admitted it. But I couldn't not talk to her. I typed quickly before thinking better of it. My finger hovered over the screen, time passing with each questioning breath. I pressed the send button. It didn't matter, anyway. She hated me regardless. I didn't expect a response.

I turned over on my side; I could still taste the alcohol in my mouth from the drive-in. It made me feel resentful. Toward myself, mostly.

I returned to my back and forced myself to fall asleep. Maybe I'd wake up and it would all be a really fucked-up dream.

Monday morning arrived and I was freaking the fuck out about running into Kendra at school. I was so nervous about it that I actually showed up to first period on time.

I looked in the reflection of the bathroom mirror during passing period, my face bruised up from the accident. It was a shitty-ass reminder of the weekend.

At lunch, I sat down at the table where Ashton, Nick, and Brody were already eating. I wasn't hungry.

"You all right, man?" Ashton asked. I heard him but didn't process his question. I was stuck in my head, figuring out how to go back in time and change the past forty-eight hours.

Nick waved his hand in front of my face.

"What's up?" I snapped out of it.

"You okay?" Ashton asked.

"Yeah. I'm great."

Kendra walked into the cafeteria, supported by crutches and a black boot. She caught my eye but immediately looked away, heading toward her girlfriends. I could feel my eyes welling up, so I started eating my apple dipped in yogurt. I hated this. I hated myself right then.

"Are you guys talking at all?" Ashton asked.

"No."

Basically the whole school knew that I got us into an accident, a DUI, and destroyed her surfing chances—what a shit show.

I considered whether or not to go up to her and apologize again. She hadn't even answered my text. Maybe I needed to respect her space. Her back was to me. I just wanted to be able to talk in person. Just five minutes.

Ashleigh approached our table. My heart leapt. It was my one chance to see if I could talk to Kendra.

"Hi, boo." She sat down on Ashton's lap.

"How's Kendra?" I asked her.

Ashleigh raised her eyebrows, taking a breath. "Honestly? A mess." Ashleigh spoke without a filter, and for once I was thankful for that. "What were you guys thinking?"

I looked down at the table. "I don't know. Do you think she'll talk to me?"

"Not right now, Brock. She's really upset. I mean, this weekend literally changed her life."

I understood, but why'd she have to say it like that? I felt like a monster.

Ashleigh turned away from me. She was pissed too. I know it was her friend and all, but shit, she really didn't have a reason to have something against me.

"You wanna sesh tonight, man?" Nick asked.

"Yeah. Sure." I didn't care.

"Brody wants to try it."

"Really?" I turned to Brody. I was surprised. It was, like, against his religion or something.

"Yeah. I want to experience it. You know?"

"Yeah. It's a good time," I said. "I'm supposed to drive up to

LA this weekend. You guys should come. My bro Duke has the hookup with some real shit."

"Right on," Nick said.

> **Brock:** Bringin some friends this weekend . . . that cool?
> **Duke:** For sure.
> **Brock:** Man, I really fucked up. . . .
> **Duke:** ????
> **Brock:** W/ Kendra . . . its bad.
> **Duke:** Even the finest knots can always be untied . . . remember that.
> **Brock:** Easier said than done.

Duke's advice was always reassuring, but I questioned it this time. She really hated me, and that was that.

KENDRA

I sat through chemistry, half listening to the lesson and half holding back tears. All I wanted to do was cry. All of the time. I wasn't sure who I was anymore. I was trying to be strong, but I could feel tears pooling in my eyes, one falling down my face to my lips. It tasted like the ocean—which made me want to cry even harder.

The doctor said the hairline fracture would take six to eight weeks to heal and that surfing could "hinder the healing process" or, worse, cause permanent damage. How I wished I could take it all back. But wishing was like hoping, and hoping never got anyone anywhere.

I could feel Ryan watching me. He was my lab partner for the day.

"You okay, Ken?" he whispered. I didn't want to look over at him. I didn't want to have to explain. So I simply nodded my head, yes—which was a lie. I couldn't surf. In fact, I could barely make it up a set of stairs. I was potentially going to face legal issues. And Brock and I were done. I was the furthest thing from okay. I was burning inside, full of anger and sadness, confusion and fear.

My dad was disappointed. We hadn't talked a lot since we got home from the hospital yesterday evening. Harry, on the other hand, hadn't left my side. And Coach . . . well, he was pissed at first. But now he wasn't leaving me alone, inviting me to meditation sessions and even offering to come to my house to do them. But I declined. I think he was worried I was now a part of "that crowd" that he'd always warned me about. I just . . . I didn't feel like talking to anyone about anything. I hated everything. Mostly myself. And there's no worse feeling than being the person you hate, because you can't escape yourself. It's physically impossible.

"Here," Ryan said to me. He smelled of marijuana and fast food. I didn't care. I was done caring. I finally looked to him as he reached into his pocket and pulled out eye drops. I took it from him. The label read, "Reduces irritation, dryness, and redness." Obviously, he carried these around for another reason, but, regardless, I took the hint and splashed a drop in each eye.

After class, I was walking down the hallway with Ashleigh when I spotted Brock talking to Annie at her locker. I swallowed down the lump in the back of my throat that wanted to explode. I was tempted to look back, but Ashleigh stared them down. Could he really have moved on that quickly? It wasn't even two days since the accident. Did he have feelings for Annie the whole time he was with me? My body shuddered at the thought of it all.

"Screw him, Ken. Come on."

We walked past them and out to the parking lot. The sky was cloudy and overcast.

I hopped in Ashleigh's car. Her radio blasted with the awakening of her ignition.

She blasted some sort of tacky breakup revenge song as we pulled out of school. I knew she was trying to make me feel better, but I didn't want to think about the fact that I wasn't with Brock. That he was with Annie. I'd never felt such a twisted and torn feeling of hating and loving someone so much, and it was killing me inside. On top of it all, I couldn't even do the one thing that would take my mind off of it all—surf. I felt empty inside. I didn't want to be dramatic, but I couldn't handle much more.

On the way to my house, we stopped at the drugstore. I'd told Ashleigh about how Brock and I had sex at the drive-in, and when she asked if we used a condom, I stayed silent. I hadn't even thought of that—and apparently Brock hadn't either. Ashleigh freaked out, insisting that I buy an emergency contraceptive pill. I hadn't realized how crazy expensive they were. But surely enough, I bought one. I couldn't imagine going through all of this agony to then also find out I was pregnant with my ex-boyfriend's baby. My life would be over, and my family would be mortified. Although both of those things already felt true.

"I know the heartache, Ken. I've been through it a gazillion times with Ashton," Ashleigh said when we were back in the car. The gray clouds hid the blue sky. It was almost too fitting.

I just stared at the Plan B box. I was hesitant to take a pill that I'd never taken before, so I stuffed it into my backpack and planned to read the side effects later. A tear fell from my eye and I quickly wiped it away before Ashleigh could notice.

"It's different, Ash," I said as I rolled down the window. I could hear the waves crashing from afar.

"I know."

"Ashton would never have put you in the position Brock's put me in."

"That's true."

We pulled up to my house. There were no cars in the driveway, so I assumed my dad and Harry weren't home.

"But don't forget you put yourself there too."

I wasn't expecting that.

"I'm not discounting that he's a total dick, but you made a

choice that night too. He didn't pour alcohol down your throat against your will."

I couldn't believe she was siding with him. Ashleigh, of all people!

"Thanks for the ride," I said, opening the door. I hoped she could feel the ice in my tone.

"Do you need anything?" she asked.

"No. I'm fine."

I got out of the car, my crutches supporting me, and Ashleigh pulled out of the driveway. Maybe I needed to hear what Ashleigh was saying, but I didn't want to.

I walked inside my house. Skittles was the only one to greet me at the door, but I couldn't bend down to pet her. I prepared myself to face the stairs with a deep breath before grabbing ahold of the railing, slowly limping up one foot at a time. When I finally made it to my room, I collapsed down onto my bed. I had piles of homework to do but wasn't in the mood to attempt any of it.

I heard the garage open.

"Hello? Ken?" Harry yelled. With each step they walked up the stairs, a squeak followed. Even *that* got on my nerves.

"We wanted to be home before you got here," my dad said, opening the door to my bedroom.

"We had to get a few groceries for dinner. We're sorry, hon."

"No biggie. Ashleigh dropped me off."

"How is your leg?" my dad asked. He was talking to me more today.

"It's really sore." The ice in my tone was apparent once again. I just felt like it was such a dumb question—obviously my leg wasn't okay. I could barely walk, let alone surf. So why did they ask? Or care?

"All right, we're going to start dinner if you need us," my dad said.

"Oh, wait!" Harry turned back around. He handed me a walkie-talkie.

"What is this for?" I asked.

"If you need us, we have the other one." He clicked the side button of the device and spoke into it. "Testing, testing!"

It sang into my talkie.

"I have a phone."

"Yes, but this is quicker and more convenient for the house," Harry insisted.

I shot my dad a look, arching my eyebrow. He shrugged his shoulders.

"Okay. Thanks." They disappeared back downstairs.

I finally had my room to myself. My space. Just me. And my thoughts. And Skittles, of course. I could breathe and hear myself thinking. I wasn't one to be constantly bombarded as if I was an invalid.

I grabbed the Plan B box from my bag and examined it. I started to read the side effects but then decided to just take the pill—nausea and a little dizziness sounded a lot more appealing than a crying baby. I hid the empty box in my backpack so I could throw it out at school tomorrow. Throwing it out in a garbage can at home was too risky. My parents would freak.

I walked over to my desk and sat down at my computer. Normally I started homework right after school unless I had practice, but today I continued procrastinating. It was kind of fun. I logged on to Facebook. First thing first: I immediately changed my relationship status back to single. As I scrolled through the news feed, I noticed Taylor and Jason were Facebook official. That had accelerated quickly.

I typed a *B* into the search tab but immediately backspaced. Ugh, the temptation was too much to resist, and I eventually typed in his whole name. Brock's page popped up onto my screen.

His profile picture was an old photo of him. It was the same picture he had on there since I'd known him. I scrolled down to view older posts and found a picture of us tagged in Ashleigh's picture from Halloween, his friend Duke wrote on his wall to call him, and then—there we were. At homecoming, the picture that Ella took when he and I first met. It was weird to look back at the beginning. How much had changed. Beginnings are beautiful and innocent. They're like blooming roses, so mesmerizing you don't even want to pick them but the attraction is there, so you do. Eventually the flower dies. I guess it would've ended either way.

I held back a smile and cried instead.

"Ken," the walkie-talkie said from my pillow. I rolled my eyes and walked over to my bed.

"What?" I said, quickly wiping away my tears.

"You have some visitors," my dad said.

"Who?"

Ashleigh and Ashton walked into my room.

"What are you guys doing here?" I asked.

"I could tell you weren't doing too well earlier," Ashleigh said, "so we wanted to come keep you company."

She plopped down on my bed.

"How are you?" Ashton asked, leaning against my windowsill.

Somehow I managed to hold myself together.

"Okay," I said. I dropped my head down, pretending to scroll through my phone to hide my welling eyes.

The room was silent.

"Ken, he is so not worth it," Ashleigh said. "Like, if he cared, he wouldn't already be back with that conniving whorebag."

"I know," I said, keeping my head toward the wall. "It's not just Brock, though."

"Ash, maybe she doesn't want to hear that right now," Ashton said.

People think girls can only be sad about guys and relationships, but I was hurting over a lot more than that. And Ashton was right, I didn't want to hear about how I deserve more and how I shouldn't be upset, because I was upset. Uncontrollably miserable and upset.

My adrenaline was running high, as if I was about to surf a wave I knew I couldn't handle. Tears began streaming down my face, like I had any control over it. Thoughts were convoluting my mind; voices were becoming louder in my head. Voices I had for so long pushed out. Kyle. My mom. His death replayed through my mind like the last scene of a movie. And when the audience realizes it's over, they wonder what the whole point was because now all they felt was sad.

"I can't surf," I sobbed. It was so embarrassing. I never cried in front of people like this. "I've worked my butt off to get to this point, to be able to compete and maybe even make the USA Surf Team. Now I can't. I can't surf. I can barely walk down the stairs on my own. And it's, like, knowing Brock is with Annie is the cherry on top of it all. And I just keep thinking about all of the things we said we were going to do together and never got to. It all just sucks!"

"Ken—" Ashleigh tried to intervene.

"And at the same time"—I was hyperventilating now—"I'm mad at myself for missing him. My chance at competing is completely shot. All because he drove. Because I let him!"

I was numb, like it was happening all over again. My mom crying and my dad pounding on the door. Kyle was on the other side, dying. It was like my brain was covered in fog. I was gone. Somewhere else. A different time. My limbs were useless, my stomach in knots. My breath was lost somewhere within my body. I was a prisoner of my own mind. There was no escaping—it was as if my soul was slowly suffocating me, and I wasn't sure how to snap out of it and return back to reality. Where had I gone? And how was I to return? Where was my mantra? And why could I not seem to repeat it over in my head? Where was my breath? And why could I not control it? I'd found myself in this place before, and I didn't think it would be of this severity ever again. I was drowning in myself. Was this the end? Because it felt like it.

I wanted someone to tell me it was all okay. I wanted Brock to say, "Who cares?"—his famous line. It was this awful torn feeling. I hated Brock. Genuinely hated him. But I missed him too. I craved him. I craved what *was*. I wanted to get up and punch him in the face, but at the same time I wanted to run into his arms so he could hold me and remind me I was going to be all right. Like he always did.

I squeezed my eyes shut tight, trying my hardest to get in my head. My strength had to be somewhere within reach. I couldn't let it destroy me. I *wouldn't* let it. I took my mind somewhere tropical, watching waves rise and crash, trying to emulate that sound through my breath. I finally caught it, slowly trying to grasp each inhale and exhale. I coughed.

Just breathe. I found the stronger of the two voices that resided deep in my mind. *Try. In. Out.* I found my breath and the voices became muted.

When I looked up at Ashleigh and Ashton, they were speechless. It was like I'd blacked out and forgotten they were there.

I slowed my breathing to calm the hyperventilating. I was home again. Inside of myself. But the hangover took its place—the vibrations that ran through my body, the tears imprinted on my face, and the racing of my heart still evident.

Ashton sat down next to me. "Ken, shit happens, and I know you're hurting right now. But, like, it's so not your fault. Stop blaming yourself."

"You're going to make me cry, Ken. I hate seeing you like this," Ashleigh added. I looked up at her and surely enough, her eyes were glazed over, as if watching me cry was going to make her tear up. I guess that was a real friend.

"And believe me, from a guy's perspective, he couldn't give two shits about Annie. That's called a rebound."

"Yeah, and nobody actually ends up with the rebound."

Harry's voice sounded from my walkie-talkie. "Everything okay up there?"

Ashleigh grabbed it and said, "Yes, but we seriously need a pint of Ben & Jerry's Half Baked."

Then to me: "Come on, what other men do you need besides them?"

I laughed through my tears. Ice cream was a temporary fix—but I'd take that right now.

"Aw, there's that pretty laugh I've missed!" Ashleigh said like she was talking to a puppy or a baby. She embraced me like I was a child.

We headed downstairs to Ashleigh's car and went to the gas station to get some ice cream.

For a minute there, my friends actually kept my mind pre-occupied. But every so often, Brock's eyes or smile or voice or promises seemed to storm through my brain, leaving me feeling helpless and confused. Why had I let myself make stupid choices because of a guy? I wasn't that kind of girl. Or so I thought. But Brock wasn't just any guy.

I looked down at my leg in the ugly black boot. He wasn't just any guy, but my dreams weren't just any dreams. I wondered what I'd be doing if I'd never met Brock, if I'd never known this kind of pain. But I also wouldn't have ever known this kind of love. This deep, infatuated, aching love . . .

I looked at my nightstand, where a half-empty pint of ice cream sat, and then out the window where the moon lit up the tree house. So many secrets hidden inside, along with so many firsts and so many lasts.

The week went by slowly, especially since I had a lot of time on my hands. I wasn't used to sleeping in and not starting my day on the beach. I felt like a fish out of water.

On Saturday, I decided to change that and had my dad drop me off at Main. I couldn't surf, but I could at least enjoy the view. I watched the early risers catch a solid surf and envied them. A young girl, much younger than I, was dominating a wave, but I watched as she curved her back foot. And as I expected, she went down.

I felt the angst inside of me for her. But she popped up out of the water and got right back on. I found myself completely entranced watching her, as if she was a reflection, and I was watching a younger me. A me I wish I could go back and warn.

This tunnel vision was interrupted by the sound of a cluster of male voices, forcing me to look up. It was Brock, Nick, and Brody. They all had surfboards. Out of the twenty-four hours in a day, and I chose this one to be at the same beach as Brock Parker. When he caught sight of me, he stopped. I couldn't even look at him. How could someone that once felt like your everything feel like a stranger basically overnight? I wasn't sure if I was more mad or sad; whichever it was, it formed a pit in my gut that worked its way up to my throat.

Brock waved at me, I'm sure waiting for a response. But at this point, I didn't have one. I just looked away. What was there to say anyway? *Thanks for ruining my life? By the way, how's Annie?*

I looked up at the sun, searching for answers to questions I hadn't quite asked yet, and when I looked back to where Brock had been standing just seconds before, he was gone. Nick and Brody were now in the water. He must have left. Should I have said hi? But maybe it was for the best. Brock and I were obviously better off as strangers. As memories. As anything other than people that could possibly exist in the present moment together.

BROCK

I usually loved the weekend, but this Saturday was already proving to be a nightmare. First, I saw Kendra at the beach, and it became evident that she was never going to talk to me again. Then I found out my Audi was totaled, so basically I was stuck with the spare car my parents let me use. It was a used 2007 Ford Crown Vic with the push bar still on it and a spotlight on the driver's side mirror. My parents kept all of the features on it from when it was a police car and used it for dangerous deals. Kind of like a disguise.

Seattle wasn't looking so bad after all.

When I pulled up to my house, I sat there for a moment, everything settling in. We couldn't even talk. We couldn't even look at one another. With each recollection of what we had, and how we lost it, it felt like a nail was being hammered into my stomach. My chest. My bones. Dammit, this girl had my heart. I punched the steering wheel and accidentally sounded the horn, which caused my parents to come running out. They were so fucking paranoid.

"What's wrong?" my dad said, standing outside of the car. I didn't answer. I just turned off the ignition and got out.

"Nothing."

I walked past them and into the house. They followed me in, and I wasn't ready for whatever bull they were about to spit at me.

"I took care of the car situation," my father said. I rolled my eyes because I didn't even give a shit at this point. Who knows who my father knew and what strings he pulled.

"And I talked to our lawyer. He said he thought the best way to go about this is to, obviously, plead guilty. We'll see what the judge offers, but because you're sixteen, it'll be a little different."

"What does that mean?" my mom asked.

"It means he probably won't be tried as an adult, especially since it's his first offense."

"First offense that they've caught," I said. I mean shit, I was a fucking drug dealer and these cops were having a heyday over a little DUI. Could you imagine if they knew the whole truth?

"Not in the mood for the smart-ass remarks today."

I shrugged my shoulders and headed to my room.

"Hey! You got any deals?" my dad yelled after me.

"Yep. Big party tonight. Same lame-ass losers, different night."

"That's what I like to hear."

Nick, Brody, and I were supposed to hit up LA to hang out with Duke, but they decided to bail on that arrangement, so we planned on going to an OC party instead. Lame. But whatever. I guess it didn't matter really what party I went to as long as I sold something.

When I picked them up that night, Nick was already drunk, slurring his words and drinking from a handle of tequila.

"Hunter is supposed to be there tonight," he said, his eyes half-shut.

"Dude. Calm down. Don't scare her off."

"She totally digs me, man."

A few minutes into the party and I'd already sold two of five grams of coke. I passed out a few extra Oxys I had on hand to get people hooked on those too. It was like a game I couldn't lose at.

I was surprised to see Ryan and Jason out after everything they'd gone through in the last month. But I also wasn't surprised. If those two were any dumber, you'd have to water them twice a day.

"Yo, Brock!" Jason always seemed to corner me wherever we were. Such a weirdo.

"Hey, what's up?"

"We should ditch and go hit up this new strip bar that just opened down in Newport. I heard they don't card."

This kid was such an amateur.

"No, thanks. Isn't your girlfriend here anyway?"

"I don't know. I dumped her last night."

"That was short-lived."

"Yeah, Taylor was just too clingy."

I wondered if he realized how he came off.

When Annie showed up, she didn't leave my side. Duke stopped by a little later too. The OG squad. The three of us headed out back to coke up.

I pulled the bag of cocaine out of my pocket. It was already chopped up so I spilled it onto the table and took a small bump. Annie scooped some up with her finger. She fed it to me and licked away any that was stuck to my nose.

She giggled. "Yum."

The night air was calm, but there was just something so uneasy about it. I watched as Annie bent over, holding her hair back to inhale the coke from the table. I didn't want to be sitting here with her. I wanted to be with Kendra, whatever that meant I'd be doing. Even if it wasn't this. She was so much cooler. So much more interesting and multidimensional. She wasn't another follower, just a part of the herd, trying to keep up with nobodies.

"I'm gonna get another beer," I said, lifting Annie off of my lap.

"I'll come."

"Can you get me one?" Duke said.

We walked through the back door, back into the house . . . and there stood Kendra. Me staring at her. And her staring at me. Both of us were stopped dead in our tracks, obviously not expecting this. Her arm was locked in Ashleigh's, who also froze when she saw me. I looked down at her leg, the black boot a painful reminder of what was stopping us from talking right now. Instinctively, we both turned around and headed in opposite directions. I hurried back outside. I couldn't deal.

"What the fuck is wrong with you?" Annie asked, following me out.

"What?"

"You saw that Kendra bitch and totally freaked out."

"Don't call her a bitch."

"Why?" Annie asked as she sat down on the chair. "She is one."

"Shut the fuck up, Annie. You're the bitch."

I grabbed the fifth of vodka sitting on the table and chugged it down. I needed to be numb. Gone. Disappear. And if I couldn't physically do so, I would have to mentally vanish.

"You good, man? You seem tense," Duke pointed out.

I looked at him and shrugged my shoulders. "No. I'm not okay at all."

"Dude, calm down," Annie shot at me. I wanted to fuck her right now, right here. Anything to diminish the thought of Kendra Dimes.

"Let's go have sex," I said.

"That accelerated quickly." Duke laughed. He stood up and walked over to me, leaning into me as if Annie couldn't hear.

"Man, that's not how you're going to get her back." He was drunk as fuck. I could tell.

"I don't want her back," I lied.

Annie and I went through the back gate and into the front where my car was parked. She was halfway stripped before we even got into the back seat. She undid my zipper and pulled out my dick, but when she tried sucking, I couldn't get hard. This had never happened to me before, and I was more concerned than embarrassed. I'd heard of whiskey dick before and I guess I was drunk but not blacked out or anything.

"What's wrong?" she asked.

"I don't know."

I sat next to Annie. The car silent. My heavy breathing settling down.

"That's never happened."

"Yeah, I'm aware," she said.

"Maybe it's the alcohol."

"And maybe it's her."

"Or a mix of both."

"Un-fucking-real."

We sat in the car for a few minutes. I tried jacking off, but nothing was doing the trick. We even looked up porn on my phone. Nothing.

When we finally gave up and walked back inside, Kendra was dancing, clumsily, on the table with Jason. His hands were all over her. It spiked my adrenaline, on top of being coked out. He handed her another beer and Kendra quickly shotgunned it down. I didn't even know she could do that.

My heart sunk and melted into my stomach. "Kendra."

She looked down at me. "Oh, hey there, Brocky Bear!"

Duke walked in behind me, resting his hand on my shoulder.

"Hi, Duke!" she slurred. "I bet you two are having a great

time together with all your little girlfriends now that I'm not around."

"Shit . . . you should get her out of here," he said.

This wasn't the most wasted I'd ever seen her—but damn close to it. Next would be vomit all over Jason, and that was a sight I'd honestly like to see.

"What are you doing? Get down," I said. She almost tripped over that big, clunky boot.

I wasn't going to let her make an ass out of herself. Or hurt herself even worse.

"No!" she yelled. "You can't tell me what to do."

"You're drunk."

"So?" she said, almost tripping over her boot.

"Kendra, this isn't you."

She looked at me, her eyes hanging and bloodshot. But I saw right through them, into the pain she was feeling. Because I was feeling it too. She redirected her gaze back to dumbass Jason, grabbing him by the neck and pulling him in for a kiss. I looked away.

"Come on, Kendra." I tugged at her side. I wondered where her "friends" were.

"Get away from me!"

"Ken, let Brock take you home," Duke said in his compassionate way.

"Leave her alone, bro," Jason said.

And that was enough for me to lose it—but I didn't. I just wanted her to get home safe.

"Shut the fuck up, you little bitch," Duke spat at him.

I tried to grab Kendra, but Jason jumped off the table. That fucking prick. He pushed me back. That's all it took. I completely blacked out. All I remember was somehow I got Jason on the floor and threw Kendra over my shoulder.

"What the hell are you doing? Put me down!" she yelled as I carried her out of the house.

"Brock!" Ashleigh yelled to me. "Put her down. Now."

I turned around, Kendra pounding her fists on my back, shouting and screaming at the top of her lungs.

"Well, do *you* want to leave and take her home then?"

Ashleigh looked at me. She was mad on behalf of her friend, but I knew the answer. She didn't want to leave the party, and she knew that I was a lot safer for Kendra than Jason. At least I cared about her and wasn't about to let him take advantage of her current state of inebriation.

"Make sure she gets home safely!" Ashleigh yelled at me as I buckled Kendra into the back seat of my car.

I drove as slowly and gently as I could. I knew from past experience she was a puker.

I pulled up to her house and put the car in park. When I turned around and looked at her, she was passed out.

I got out, shutting my door quietly to avoid waking her parents up. Her dad would literally shoot me if he saw me here. I carried her out and snuck through the back gate, up her balcony to her room—which was no easy task. Her damn dog came running in, barking. I threw a pillow at her, Kendra still slung over my shoulder.

"Skittles, shut up," she slurred. And the dog silenced herself.

I pulled down her blanket and laid her down, tucking her in. She looked so innocent, lying there like that.

"I miss you," I whispered, knowing she couldn't hear. And if she could, she wouldn't remember. Then I kissed her on the cheek and headed for the door.

"Then why did you do this to me?" she asked.

I turned back around, surprised she was awake and coherent.

"You act like I did it on purpose—"

"You kissed Annie on purpose."

"You're just picking out every reason to be pissed at me."

"Do you blame me?"

"No, I get it. But can we at least talk?"

"I needed to win for Kyle—" She choked up, unable to finish, and there came the sobbing. "I lost my chance . . . Kyle's chance."

"But who's Kyle?"

She wouldn't answer, just cried. I swear I remembered hearing that name before from her, but I couldn't recall who he was.

I looked down at the ground. I wasn't sure how many more times she would need an apology. Or if she'd ever accept one.

"You know how passionate you are about your music? That's how I feel about surfing."

I was taken aback. My music was such a private and personal thing. But I understood how she felt—I mean, to love something that much and carry it with your every thought. The guilt that I tried so hard to numb moved back through my heart, and it was there to stay. I felt myself go flush. I felt really terrible that I had taken that away from her. I really did. But how was I to go back and change that now? I couldn't.

"I'm sorry. I didn't mean for this to happen," I tried again.

"I know you didn't," she said, calming herself down. But still struggling to breathe. The room was silent, the sound of the trees blowing from outside. "But I kept asking if you were okay to drive and you said yes."

"I know. I know."

"Why do you do drugs?" she pressed.

What was I supposed to say? It was my lifestyle? My parents pimp me out to make bank off of people's addictions?

"I like the way they make me feel," I admitted. "They take away all of my worries and anxieties, so that I don't feel them."

21 QUESTIONS

"I just wish we could take it all back, because I miss you too."

I looked up at that moment. I wanted to frame her words and listen to them over and over because I was scared that her being drunk was the only time she'd ever say this again.

"But we can't go back in time," I reminded her.

"And I can't move forward with you, either."

She turned over onto her side, away from me.

I didn't know what to say or do, so I headed for the balcony door, shutting it behind me. It was best that I left.

KENDRA

I woke up with the taste of beer still in my mouth.

"Ugh," I said, turning over on my side. I ripped my blanket off to reveal I was still dressed in my street clothes. My body felt hot. The kind of hot that was rooted into your skin like a sunburn.

I grabbed my phone off my nightstand to check the time—it was already noon. I couldn't believe I had slept in so late.

Ashleigh: Did U mak it home sAfe?
Ashleigh: Txt me wheen U wake up.
Taylor: I literally cannot believe you, you bitch!

I wasn't sure what Tay was talking about, and I was kind of afraid to find out. My memory was fuzzy. I remembered drinking beer, but, apparently, not how many.

I got out of bed and walked out onto my balcony. I needed fresh air. The sun was shining bright, but there was a nice breeze to accompany it. I tapped my phone against my palm before deciding to call Ashleigh.

"Hello?" she answered, her voice groggy.

"Sorry, did I wake you up?"

"Uh, kind of, but it's okay. What's up?"

"What happened last night? I think I drank way too much."

"You think? You got fucking hammered."

"Taylor texted me this morning all pissy?"

"You made out with Jason!"

"Shut up. No, I didn't! No, I didn't!"

I totally crossed every boundary of girl code and with the most disgusting guy ever at that! I was mad at myself for even letting me get to that point of drunkenness. Why didn't anyone stop me? Not that it was anyone's responsibility, but as friends I wished they would've done something.

"Yes, you did!" She sounded more alert. "You really don't remember?"

"No! I'm mortified right now, Ash. Gag me!"

She chuckled into the phone.

"I need to call Tay now and apologize."

"Good luck. I'm going back to bed."

I hung up, still confused how even in my drunkest state, I could have made out with *Jason*. I wished I hadn't gone so overboard last night. I didn't know why I drank at all, actually. I just hated that none of this was me: the drinking and late nights, making out with my friend's ex-boyfriends, the fact that I couldn't even really remember most of it . . . all of it.

I hesitated before dialing Tay. She was going to be upset but—ugh—I had to. On the fourth ring, she picked up.

"Hello?" she said.

"Hi, Tay."

"What. Do. You. Want."

Her voice reeked of so much ice-cold, anger-induced hatred, I had to pause and collect my thoughts. I was unsure of how to approach the situation. Obviously, I shouldn't have been as drunk as I was. So either way, I was at fault.

"I'm . . . reallysorryaboutlastnight," I spewed out too quickly for anyone to understand. I took a breath in an effort to slow down my thoughts. "You know I would never intentionally do that to you. I was *so* wasted."

She was silent. I let it linger on only for a moment before continuing, "I totally get if you hate me but, like, I didn't even remember doing it until I talked to Ash this morning."

She let out a frustrated sigh before answering. "I'm really not *that* mad. I knew you were drunk. I mean, like, *really* drunk. And yeah, I was really pissed in the moment, but I know that you wouldn't be that mean to me on purpose. It was a really shitty thing to do, though."

"I'm really sorry."

"It's okay. I'm over him anyway. Honestly, I never really liked him that much."

"You didn't?"

"No, he was way too into himself."

I exhaled a relieved laugh.

"Holy shit, that's him clicking in right now," Tay said. "Answer! I'll talk to you later."

I quickly hung up, my tensed body able to relax.

I felt so gross; my breath tasted like alcohol, my hair was greasy, and I was congested. If I didn't shower in a matter of moments, I would lose it. I headed back inside and sat on my bed, attempting to take my boot off, then stripped my clothes off of my hot, sticky body and limped over to the shower. I tried to avoid putting any pressure on my leg. It was still so sore.

The steam felt good, like I could breathe again.

When I got out, I saw that Coach had texted me.

Coach Harkins: Short guided meditation @ 1:30 on Main if U want to come . . . would love to have you

I wasn't sure if I was ready to see Coach—he was as devastated as I was after the accident. And disappointed. Really, really disappointed. Even more so because I'd ignored all his advice. It was hard facing that. The disappointment I'd caused—that ached the most. I'd rather have someone scream at me than tell me I'd disappointed them, and seeing him would just remind me of surfing and everything I'd already lost. I wasn't sure if I could handle it. I waited to answer, uncertain if I had it in me.

In the meantime, I got dressed and put myself together so I felt like a human again. I lay on my bed, staring at the fan spinning around in circles. A flashback of last night consumed my mind—it was still fuzzy. Brock saying my name. But I couldn't see where. I remembered waking up in my bed, seeing him. He voiced a soft *I miss you*—I think. Maybe it wasn't him. Was it Jason? My stomach coiled at the thought.

I blocked out any other half-alive memories, because guessing which ones were real and which were not was too much of a struggle. Instead, I continued to stare up at the ceiling, watching one of the fan's panels spin around. And around. I couldn't bear to sit around any longer and dwell on everything that had happened—from the accident to last night. I needed to get out. Clear my mind. Go to meditation.

I asked my dad if he could drive me.

The car ride was mostly silent, my dad's window open and letting in the ocean air. I envied how freely it moved.

I miss Kyle, I thought. I wanted to say it aloud. I wanted to talk about it. But my dad wasn't capable. I wanted to talk about a lot of things lately. Things I'd been trying to bury inside for so long.

Why did Mom leave? I spoke again in my head, wishing my dad could read my mind. But he couldn't.

It was the first time in my life that I'd had time to think like this; it was the first time my thoughts were challenged and I wasn't fighting for a dream that may never have been mine to begin with. Surfing made me feel free—it was my life, and although I wanted to compete, I realized I was trying to win for unknown reasons. I was trying to make up for Kyle's losses, hoping that, in a sense, it would bring him back. And it wasn't going to.

"Do you believe everything happens for a reason?" I asked my dad.

My dad kept his gaze ahead, but I watched how his eyebrows furrowed and his lips crinkled, unsure of how to respond. Emotions worked their way to the forefront of his face.

I didn't want to dive right into talking about Kyle, so I clarified. "Like my leg. Do you think this happened for a reason?"

He sighed, waiting a moment to answer.

"Yes, I suppose things happen for a reason. Maybe you would've gotten hurt in the water and it would've been worse than your injury."

I nodded. Maybe he was right. But the problem is, I would never actually be able to find out. So maybe people always say things happen for a reason to feel better about what's actually going on. Maybe that's what I should have done from the beginning. But it was still hard.

Without my lead, he continued, "When your brother passed, I struggled for a long time. . . ."

I was shocked he was going in this direction without me touching on it first. I guess he could've wanted to talk about it too.

"I wouldn't wish that feeling of losing a child on my worst enemy. I felt angry and sad and guilty."

He exhaled, pacing himself.

"But one day, I was at the grocery store. It was some time after your mother left. I was grabbing cereal and I just lost it in the middle of the aisle, sobbing and all messed up."

Tears began to pool in his eyes, but they didn't seem to fall.

"This woman came up to me—to this day, I swear she wasn't even real. Like a ghost or something. Anyway, I spilled my guts out to her, and when I finally took a breath, she looked at me and she just . . . smiled."

"Smiled?"

"Yes, and she said something that always stuck with me. I never told anyone. She said, 'He's okay. He's here with you right now. And he wants you to know that if he hadn't gone like this, he would've suffered much more.'"

My father's words took a moment to sink in. Like, what was he trying to say?

"I know this sounds wild, but it gave me some sort of closure—maybe that's the wrong word. But I just always wondered if something terrible was on the horizon for Kyle. Maybe people die before their time is up because they're being saved from something much worse."

I swallowed down the lump in my throat. It had been so long since I'd even heard my dad say Kyle's name.

"So, yes, I suppose you could say that I believe everything happens for a reason. Don't doubt that. And don't be too hard on yourself for the things you can't change."

I wasn't sure how to respond, so I smiled, but less at my dad and more toward the beach that lay ahead.

My dad patted me on the shoulder when he stopped in front of Main.

"You okay?"

"Yep. I'm good. Thanks for driving me."

I didn't want to say that my dad's story gave me a feeling of resolution, but in a sense it was reassurance that maybe things *did* happen for a reason. But then I felt weird for thinking that because there never seemed to be a good reason to lose your loved ones.

"Hey, Coach," I said as I walked onto the sand.

"There's my girl!" He ran up and hugged me. "I'm so glad you made it."

"Me too."

"How's the leg?"

"Sore."

"I'm sorry about that. You know there's always next year, though."

"Yeah." I forced a smile as I looked away in case a tear tried to escape. I wished everyone would stop saying that—next year just wasn't enough. Even if things did happen for a reason like my dad said.

"Come on over," he said, leading me over to the rest of the group.

There were only half a dozen of us. I sat down on the sand next to an older woman.

"All right, today we're going to practice mindfulness meditation," he said, gathering all of our attention.

I looked out at the ocean. A wave began to form and then crashed down, the water almost working its way up to my feet.

"I want you to sit in a relaxed position—maybe legs crossed, maybe you sit on your knees. Whatever is most comfortable for you."

I sat with my legs straight out in front of me, because the alternatives would put too much pressure on my fracture and were too difficult with my boot.

"Now close your eyes. I want you to begin to focus on your breath. Stay aware of the present and everything around you, but anytime you become distracted by thoughts, a noise, anything, I want you to come back to your breath. Hear the breath. Feel the breath. Notice the pace of the breath. Notice the rhythm of the breath."

I began to breathe in and out through my nose. Something I may have forgotten to consciously become mindful of lately. Brock's smile. My dad's voice. My mom's tears. Kyle's shriek. It all tried swallowing me whole but instead . . . I took a breath and it was released. I let go. And when all of it tried to come at me again like a destructive wave, I heard the way my inhale and exhale mimicked it. It filled my ears and then my brain instead of all the clutter I'd been holding on to. I destroyed it before it could destroy me. For once, my breath was the wave, and my thoughts were the surfboard.

For so long, surfing had been the only way I could block it all out. Without it now, I was forced to face it. I wasn't sure if it was a blessing in disguise or just bad luck.

"There is a difference between being inside of your distractions and being aware of them. Choose to be aware but do not fall into them."

I saw Brock's eyes as my mind focused on *in, out, breathe*. I didn't want to see them, so I took a deeper breath to wash them away. I didn't want to even think of him. Or last night. Or the accident. The past month. Quarterfinals. Ugh. None of it. I didn't want to think.

"Your breath is the sea. With each inhale it rises and with each exhale it crashes."

The ocean in the background. Kyle's laugh. My mother's embrace. They all made their way through like clouds passing by through my mind. And I reminded myself: *Inhale. Hold the breath. Exhale.*

"Stay with the breath," Coach said. "It's not about blocking out these thoughts or sounds or sensations. It's about facing them while not letting them consume you. Be aware. Stay aware. But stay focused on the breath. Meditation can bring out some strong emotions, things that are hard to face. Look those emotions straight in the eye and keep breathing."

Brock's eyes crossed my mental vision once again. And Kyle's. They both held such character and emotion in their stare. I couldn't hold back the tears dripping down my face. But I kept breathing: *In. Out. In. Out.* I wasn't even sad about not being able to surf at this point. All of the grief I felt revolved around what the surfing carried. It carried memories of Kyle. It carried the things Brock and I never got to do. It carried all of my anxieties. And now that I didn't have it here to carry me along, I was left to hold everything myself. I didn't want to. So I took one more breath, a deep, deserved, and controlled breath . . . and I let it all go. The sadness and anger. The resentment at others and myself. All of the things I couldn't change. For my own sake.

"Now slowly begin to open your eyes," Coach said.

I allowed my eyes to open on their own. The sun was strong. It lay on my back, kissing my skin with warmth.

"Take a deep breath and sigh audibly out of your mouth."

Our whole group took a synchronized deep breath and everyone sighed together at once.

"Thank you, guys. I hope you enjoyed it. The most important thing is applying this meditation into the real world. That's where it really begins."

I pondered that for a moment, realizing that our breaths *are* like the ocean. And life is like the ocean with its constant rising and falling and ups and downs. And we just have to go with it and realize that everything happens for a reason.

I stood up, glad I pushed myself into coming. Coach spoke a lot of things that seemed to resonate with me.

"Thanks, Coach," I said, hugging him.

"Thanks for coming, Ken. It was so nice seeing you."

"You too."

I headed up to the sidewalk and texted my dad, letting him know I was done.

"Hey, Ken," Coach said as he passed me. "I know it sucks, but I'm sure you've learned something from all of this."

"I guess so," I said, feeling slightly embarrassed.

"I've been in your position before, only much worse. I know it sounds cliché, but I want you to know your thoughts are everything. You're going to go through things in life, much more than what you're dealing with right now. In all of it, remember that you become what you believe."

I nodded, unsure of how to respond.

"Remember, every day brings us infinite possibilities. Anything can happen."

I let Coach's words sink in a moment. When he walked away, I was left with my own thoughts. Were they negative? Positive? How did they serve me? I'd been in fight-or-flight mode lately, only assuming the worst was coming. But he was right, anything was possible.

It was time for a fresh start. A new beginning. A chance to forgive myself and those who'd wronged me.

I was also tired of rules. And always feeling the need to obey them. Even though breaking them with Brock seemed to get me into trouble, it also seemed to force me to face things. I looked out at the water, and a wave crashed on the shore. It was funny, a wave can crash and yet it keeps going. The water keeps flowing. It was in this moment, I decided I was going to participate in the quarterfinals and no one was going to stop me. Not even a stupid hairline fracture. I was going to keep flowing after this crash.

My dad pulled up. I got into the car and looked at him,

thinking back to what he said earlier. Things happen for a reason, and I was on a mission to find out why this happened to me. My phone vibrated in my pocket. Ashleigh.

"Hello?"

"Hi, bitch. Sorry I was half-asleep when I talked to you earlier."

"It's okay. I talked to Tay," I said. Thankfully my dad was on a call so he wasn't paying attention to my conversation.

"I feel so bad about last night. Thanks for making sure I got home though, girl."

"Uh, I didn't take you home, Ken."

"Wait, what? Then who did?"

"Are you serious? You don't remember?"

I whispered into my phone, "No, like, I was *gone*."

"Brock made sure you got home. You were, like, dancing on the table with Jason, who was disgustingly all over you, and Brock literally punched Jason and hoisted your ass down."

I was frozen, my mind blank.

"Brock?"

The blurriness of last night was coming back to me, triggered by Ashleigh. Brock laid me down on my bed. I remembered waking up and seeing him. All I could think about was his last words to me—*I miss you*—or at least the last words I could recall. According to Ashleigh and how hammered I was—and what she said about Jason—who knows what would have happened, if he hadn't seen me home safely.

I think I had spent too much time feeling sorry for myself and too much energy on hating Brock when in reality I wasn't all that innocent when it came to putting myself in this position. And turns out Brock might have been one of the only trustworthy people last night.

"I'm going to call you back, Ash."

"You good?"

"Yeah, just tired. Talk later."

I felt bad. I mean, Brock was in the wrong. But I'd been too. Coach had given me another chance and still believed in me and my future . . . so Brock deserved that from me as well.

BROCK

Monday morning had me feeling exhausted. I wasn't ready for the week to start. I got a few deals done at that party over the weekend until Kendra showed up. I thought back to her bedroom. I wondered if she even remembered. Probably not. She was so fucking drunk. Jason was such a douche dick. If he ever touched her like that again, I'd beat him until he had a brain—if that was even possible.

I had to meet a client before class, so I conveniently met him in the alley behind school.

"Yo, man," he said as he walked up to my window. He was a short, skinny Mexican guy with a buzz cut.

"Hey," I said as I grabbed his bag from the center console. It was oxy.

He handed me the cash. "Thanks." He walked away, already popping a pill in his mouth. I liked them quick and dirty like that.

I was running late for class, but I still had to talk to Mr. Brawling, my last-period music teacher, about making up my midterm from when I was in Seattle.

He didn't have a first period, so I decided to go see him.

He was sitting on his desk. "Mr. Parker. What can I do for you?"

"I wanted to talk to you about making up my midterm."

His phone rang, interrupting our conversation.

"Hold that thought. I'll be right back," he said, excusing himself from the room.

I sat down on the piano bench, my foot tapping anxiously on the ground. I looked at the piano. It drew me in as I played a melody over in my head. I lifted up the fallboard, revealing black and white keys. I couldn't help myself from punching them down, one at a time, as Mr. Brawling took his call outside.

That wasn't enough though—I couldn't resist. I turned to face the keyboard and started to play the chords I had put together the other night in my room. Kendra's Song.

I closed my eyes. My tensed shoulders fell from my ears. I felt it. I was somewhere else. Rescued. This was my meditation.

I lost myself in the music. The melody. Each and every note took me somewhere far away from the reality I was beginning to dread.

The first verse was my favorite. The first verse of any song usually captured me, though; it was like an introduction. The first hello—sometimes you know from that initial greeting that the someone you're meeting is special. Like Kendra. We connected instantly—there was no denying that. That goes the same for music. When that very first note says hello, you know how you're going to feel for the rest of it—or at least a general idea. Whether you're attracted to it or not.

The chorus was beautiful too. Shit, my own damn music swept me off my feet. Not to sound conceited or anything—but goddamn.

I was so entangled in the song that if the fire alarm were set off, I wouldn't even notice.

I played through verse two. The chorus again. A nice bridge . . . and the chorus. My foot rested on the sustain pedal, allowing the sound to fade out naturally. I removed my hands from the keys, the sound hovering in the room for another moment until I lifted my foot from the pedal and shut the fallboard.

"That was beautiful."

I jerked my head around to discover the female voice. Kendra.

"How long have you been standing there?"

"Not as long as I wish," she admitted. "I didn't know you were that talented."

I smiled, reflecting back on the inspiration and reminding her, "You told me to write you a song. That first night in your tree house."

"That was for me?"

She appeared taken off guard.

"Yeah."

I turned back toward the piano, my back now to her. I didn't know what to say, and I didn't want to say too much—I was surprised she was even looking my way at this point. It had been just over a week since the accident, and I hadn't expected her to ever talk to me again, let alone within just eight days. Surely enough, she limped over to where I sat and took the seat next to me on the bench.

"Kendra, I'm really sorry about the other night. I know I fucked up really hard. If I could take it all back, I would."

"You know, a week ago, I would've agreed. But, I actually wouldn't take any of it back. I mean, it sucks, but I think I needed this. I needed the accident to force me to . . ."

She paused for a minute, thinking. "Reevaluate things. That's what I'm choosing to believe right now."

I was so confused, I had no clue what she was talking about. I was just glad she was talking to me at all.

"By the way," she began. "Thanks for taking me home the other night. You know that isn't how I usually am."

"Of course. You don't have to thank me."

The room rested silently once again. I quickly tried to come up with something to say. I was never at a loss for words. Not like this. I cleared my throat, trying to make some kind of vibration through the room. But neither she nor I had anything else to say, so she stood up. It was over between us. I guessed it was time we both accepted that.

She turned around once more before leaving the room. "Brock?"

"What's up?"

"This is going to sound really weird, and I totally get it if the answer is no, but can you meet me at Main Beach tomorrow? After school?"

"Sure. Why?" My heart pounded with questions and nerves and fear for tomorrow after school.

"You'll see."

"Okay."

"Actually, can you give me a ride?"

I nodded and said, "Yeah, meet in the church parking lot? So no one sees."

"Good idea." She smiled and proceeded for the door, tripping over her boot but thankfully catching herself as she grabbed ahold of the chair in front of her.

"Hmph." She grabbed her leg and looked back at me with a smile, a failed attempt to hide her pain.

When she walked out of the room, my heart reflected a smile. And I didn't even care how cheesy that sounded. Feelings were meant to be felt. Something my parents never taught me. I turned back toward the piano and began to play the first verse over and over until—

Mr. Brawling reentered the classroom.

"Mr. Parker, you're really quite the pianist."

"Oh, uh, thanks, Mr. B," I said, nervous about showcasing my musical abilities. I liked to keep those private. To me, it was like knowing magic but only for self-use.

He walked over to me.

"You know," he said. "I think it would sound a little better if you took that G minor seventh chord to a G minor seventh first inversion."

I placed my hands on the proper keys and played—and he was right.

"Yeah, that sounds dope!" I said.

He nodded his head to me before pulling up a chair.

"Brock, I don't say this to really any of my students—in fact, most of them outright suck. But you really have honest talent. I mean that. Don't waste it."

I smiled at him.

"Thanks."

He stood back up and worked his way behind his desk, asking, "Now what can I do for you?"

"Oh, I need to make up the midterm."

"Oh, right. Well, can you take it right now?"

"Yeah."

Mr. Brawling handed me the test. It was only ten multiple-choice questions.

Question 1: The sharps or flats at the beginning of a line of music is called the . . . ?

I looked down at the four choices, but I was unable to focus because Kendra's smile kept flashing like a lightning bolt through my mind.

The next day, I waited for Kendra after seventh in the church parking lot across from school. No one really knew we were talking except for Nick. I assumed she'd told Ashleigh. She told her everything. But we figured it was best if we kept this low-key. I leaned up against the car. My parents were still letting me use the spare—not that they had a choice if they wanted me to rake in the dough.

Kendra approached the parking lot.

"Hey," I said.

"Hi."

There was a nervous tension in the air. Something unfamiliar. And something, quite frankly, I wasn't used to. She stood there, her eyes not directly holding my gaze. They seemed to look just beyond my eyes, avoiding direct contact. I understood.

"You ready?"

"Yep." I opened the door for her.

The first few minutes of the car ride were silent except for the constant voice in my mind asking, *What do I say?* Really fucking awkward.

It wasn't like things were the same. A lot had changed. I wanted to put my hand on her knee, and I couldn't.

"How was your day?" I asked.

"It was good. How was yours?"

"Good." I cleared my throat to pass the time that remained so silent that I thought I might just be deaf. "So what are we doing exactly?"

"What do you mean?"

"At the beach."

I looked at her and saw a smile peeking through. It gave me hope but, shit, hope was the most lethal of all emotions. And pointless at that.

She finally looked back at me and said, "I want to—I'm *going* to compete in the quarterfinals for Primes."

I felt my jaw drop.

"What?" she said, questioning my facial expression.

"Nothing. I'm impressed," I admitted, "and slightly concerned."

I looked toward the moving cars in front of us, then back to her.

"What about your coach? Did you ask him if—"

"He won't train me. I didn't even bother asking him. He would never go against my doctors. It was hard enough explaining to him that I couldn't compete. I need someone who will keep it all a secret for now."

I looked at her and again at the road.

"I'm proud of you. And I'm totally here," I said, afraid to actually look her in the eye when I said it.

"FYI, this is strictly professional."

Our eyes met and I could tell she was holding back her smile.

"Who you trying to convince, me or you?"

Was saying that too much for her to handle? Shit, I wasn't good at this awkward weirdness.

The car went mute again. I turned up the radio to block out the intolerable silence, tapping my finger on the steering wheel to the beat.

"Do you like trap music?" I asked, in an effort to make some sort of small talk. Kendra had always been someone that I felt comfortable talking to, but in this moment, I was trying to regain her trust. That made me nervous. Because I normally didn't give a shit what people thought of me.

"Depends."

"Yeah."

Was she nervous to be driving with me? I mean, I guessed I couldn't blame her if she was. The last ride didn't go too smoothly.

I really focused on the road, stopping completely at stop

signs and making sure to use my turn signal when I turned. The basics that I usually ignored.

When we finally pulled up, I helped Kendra out of the car. Our five-minute ride felt like an hour. We rented boards from the shop across the street.

We walked down to the empty beach. I carried Kendra's board. She sat down on the sand and removed her boot before stripping down to a one-piece swimsuit. She even made a fucking one-piece look sexy. I didn't think that was possible.

"What?" she said when she caught me gawking.

"Nothing. Nothing, I like your, um—" I motioned to her suit. She laughed and shook her head.

I pulled my shirt over my head, ripping it off. I noticed Kendra staring, and when my stare met hers, she quickly looked away.

"You ready?" I asked.

"For what?" she asked, staring directly at my abs.

"Um, I mean, to surf." I chuckled, scratching the back of my neck.

"Oh, right! Yes."

"What do you need my help with exactly?"

She sighed, moving the piece of hair that hung in front of her face behind her ear. I liked it hanging, though.

"Everything, really," she said, biting her lip. "I'm thinking we begin with some warm-ups."

"Okay, stand up."

She did as I told her, but her eyes squeezed shut in pain.

"You all right?" I asked, rushing to her side.

"Yeah, it's just a lot of pressure."

"Okay, here, sit back down."

I helped her to sit back down onto the sand and began to massage her leg out. I didn't really know what I was doing or what the extent of her injury really was, but, hey, massages help everything, right?

"Does that hurt?" I asked, pressing down on a specific spot, trying to get an idea if my treatment was helping or worsening the issue.

"No," she said.

I moved my hand down and pressed on another spot.

"Eek!"

"Sorry, sorry!"

"It's okay."

"All right, here." I stood back up and held my hand out for her to take, helping her to her feet.

"I think I should just forget about this. Maybe it's a stupid and pointless—"

"Hey!" I cut her off. "Watch out for those thoughts. They can make or break you."

She looked at me with this smile that I used to know and suddenly missed, even though right now I had it. It had been so long. Fucking mushy thoughts crowded my mind, but oddly enough, I embraced them.

"You're right, you're right!" she agreed. "I think I should try and learn to balance on my other leg. That way I can strengthen it, and worse comes to worse, I surf goofy-footed."

"See, you know what you're doing. You don't need me," I said, winking at her. I seriously had zero clue what the fuck I was doing. I wasn't a coach. I mean, yeah, I surfed, but not, like, professionally. But for some reason Kendra Dimes was looking to me for help with this. She was second-guessing herself and had sought me out.

This was my chance to make up for the past.

"Don't say that. I need you more than you realize. You push me."

That hit me like a ton of bricks. She needed me?

"I push you?" I instinctively asked.

"Yeah, like what you just said to me about thoughts. I need that. No one else is here to make sense of this, because it doesn't make sense."

I looked at her, unsure of how to answer such an honest response. It took me somewhat off guard. It seemed like it had been so long since we were this close—emotionally speaking of course. It seemed like I should be awkward, but it was more awkward that I didn't feel that way. It's weird how you could be so tight with someone and literally overnight, you're strangers. What the fuck is life?

"You just remind me so much of my brother . . . the way you—"

"Is that your way of friend-zoning me?" I teased.

She laughed, that nervous chuckle that was insecure but too cute not to notice.

"No! Obviously not—wait, I mean, but we are just friends but—um—"

"I'm just kidding, Kendra."

"Oh, okay."

Her flushed cheeks returned to their normal color.

She put all of her weight onto the right leg.

"Good, hold it there for a minute."

She lost her balance, wobbling as she tried to anchor herself. I caught her in time before another serious incident.

"Try using your breathing exercises you showed me. You know, the ones you do during meditation. To focus."

She nodded.

And she tried again, focusing on her breath this time. I thought the two words to myself, as if she could read my mind and I could read hers: *Inhale. Exhale.*

A part of me knew that we could read each other's minds. Was that fucking weird or what? Like, could two people be so connected that they knew the other's thoughts? When I was with Kendra, that's how I felt. It used to make me feel like a pussy, but now I craved it. I wanted it. I needed it. I needed her. Shit, there went hope charging through again, trying to destroy me.

"Cool, how do you feel?" I asked. If only she knew what I was thinking.

"Fine," she said as she set her foot back down.

I admired her as she breathed through the obvious pain she was enduring.

"Nice," I said. But I spoke too soon; her leg gave out and she fell down to the sand.

"Shit. You all right?" I collapsed down by her side, worried that I would be a part of another Kendra-related accident.

"Yeah. It's just not used to supporting my body."

"Let me massage it out and we'll try again."

We repeated this several times.

"You want to try standing on the board?" I eventually asked. She was hesitant, but agreed.

I helped Kendra onto one of the surfboards that I laid on the sand.

"Balance on that left leg again."

She grabbed for my hand as she put all of her weight on the fractured leg. When she did so, she instinctively bit her lip as her body wobbled slightly. I laughed at her.

"What?" she said. Her cheeks became ruby with uncertainty.

"Nothing."

"What?" she asked again, not giving up.

"You're just really cute."

"Shut up!" She laughed.

She didn't want me to shut up, though. I knew. I knew girls.

By the time the sun was setting, I could tell she was fatigued and her leg was bothering her—and I didn't want her to overdo it.

"Should we stop here today and meet again tomorrow?"

"Yeah. That sounds good."

"Sweeeeet."

Kendra put her clothes back on, followed by her boot. I grabbed both boards, and we headed back to the car. I had to help her maneuver into the passenger seat, moving it back so she had more legroom.

As I pulled onto South Coast Highway, driving in the direction of her house, from the corner of my eye I saw her fidget with the air vents.

"Do you have enough air?" I asked, adjusting the temperature.

"Yeah. I'm good."

Again, I was left clueless on small talk, so I turned up the music.

"Thank you," she said, keeping her gaze forward.

"No problem. I mean, it's really the least I could do. I got you into thi—"

"Don't say that. It's my fault too."

She looked at me as we approached a red light. I slowed down to a stop, looking back at her.

"It takes two to tango." She smiled. I smiled too.

"I'm glad we're talking again," I admitted.

She didn't respond at first, forwarding her gaze back onto the road that lay ahead.

She finally spoke. "I am too."

The light turned green.

The majority of the car ride was filled with silent thoughts and unnecessary talk radio.

"You can just drop me off here," she said as we pulled around the corner of her neighborhood.

"You sure?" We were a good three houses down from hers.

"Yeah, it's best if my parents don't find out about this."

"Okay." I stopped the car, putting it in park. I guess I understood why—I was the bad guy in the situation who had totally corrupted their daughter.

"Well, have a good night," I said.

"You too." She smiled. We were stuck on each other's gaze before Kendra opened the door and got out.

"See you tomorrow," she said. She shut the door behind her, limping toward her house. I watched her the whole way to make sure she made it in safely.

The traffic was shitty on the way home. It took fifteen minutes longer than normal before I finally pulled into my driveway.

I walked inside my house.

"Where've you been?" my father asked.

"A couple of deals," I lied.

"Oh, good."

I started toward my room. I desperately needed to shower.

"By the way, we're having salmon for dinner," my mom said.

"Okay. Sounds good."

I headed to my room, where I ripped my clothes off and hopped in the shower. A yawn escaped me, acknowledging my hidden exhaustion. It had been a damn long day.

When I got out, I had a text waiting from Kendra.

Kendra: Thanks again . . . for today
Brock: No prob. I'll see U tomorrow ☺
Brock: Need a ride 2 school tomorrow?
Kendra: I have court so I'm going late . . . :/
Brock: Oh shit . . . good luck. Let me know how it goes.

I threw my boxers on and lay down in bed while my parents prepared dinner. As I started to doze off, Annie began to blow up my phone.

Annie: Wtf! Y r u hanging out with Kendra again?
Annie: Fuck U
Annie: U fucking cock head
Annie: I can't believe U

I wasn't sure how she found out. Annie had never given a shit about me hanging out with girls before; we were nothing except friends with occasional benefits. But she knew how much I liked Kendra. And knowing how competitive she was, I knew it pissed her off. She liked being number one in everything—all the time.

"Brock, dinner is done!" my mom yelled from the kitchen. I didn't bother answering Annie. She was a bitch.

I threw a shirt on and walked downstairs. The three of us sat around the table.

"How was school today?" my mom asked as she took a bite into her salmon.

"Fine."

I was confused why she cared. It was almost worrisome.

"You look good today, son," my father said.

I paused as I was about to take a bite of dinner, setting my fork down onto my plate. I looked at my parents.

"What's going on with you two?"

They looked at each other and then back at me.

"You can give it to him, hon," my mom said.

"All right." My father got up from the table. He returned with an envelope in hand and handed it to me.

"What is it?" I hesitated to open it.

"Go ahead!"

I ripped open the envelope—several Benjamin Franklins stared at me. Was this really happening? I counted five thousand dollars in my hand. I distanced the paper from my eyesight to make sure I was seeing properly. When I realized I was, I looked at them.

"We got a big Morales payment today. We wanted to surprise you with a little bonus," my mom said.

Honestly, I was speechless and stunned.

"Thank you."

As reality set in, I wanted to know what the catch was, but I didn't question it. I set the envelope down next to my plate. No other words were spoken about the matter.

All I pictured was an island with a mansion facing the ocean, right on the Caribbean, Duke lit as fuck and Kendra by my side.

After dinner, I walked into the backyard to smoke a cigarette. It was so dark out, I hadn't realized my father was out there until I saw the spark of his lighter as he lit up a joint.

"Sorry, I didn't see you there."

He took an inhale from his joint. "How are things going?"

"Fine." I wasn't sure how to answer. My father and I never bonded, hung out, or anything like that. We rarely spoke about anything other than business.

"How are things with Annie?"

"We're not really a thing. She's kind of psycho."

"All teenage girls are psycho."

"True."

The sound of crickets singing in the night filled the air.

"Want a hit?" he asked, handing me the joint.

"Sure."

I exchanged my cig for his joint, and we both took a nice long hit of each at the same time.

"It's a nice night."

"Yeah, it is," I agreed.

"You doing all right?"

I was getting concerned about why he was talking to me so much, and even more, why he gave a shit how I was. He didn't even care when I was in a shitty accident. It seemed out of character. Maybe it was the big Morales check. Or maybe it was Mercury gone retrograde.

"Yeah. I'm good."

"I know I don't say this that often, but I'm proud of you."

At this point, I was full-on scared. What was going on? Was the marijuana that fucking strong? My dad was in his feels, and it was freaking me out.

"Uh, thanks. For what?"

"I know I push you, but it's because I know how good you are at what you do. I want you to meet your full potential. No one ever pushed me as a kid. I had to learn how to hustle on my own."

I nodded. That's all I knew how to do.

He patted me on the back, took one last hit of whatever that good shit was he was smoking, and walked back inside, shutting the door behind him.

Those four words replayed over in my head again: *I'm proud of you.*

It felt good to be recognized. I wanted to be closer to my dad, as rough as our relationship was. Maybe this was a start, but I wouldn't hold my breath.

KENDRA

I had court earlier, but thankfully I made it to the last half of my classes.

"I hope you learned a valuable lesson from all of this," my dad had said sternly as we approached the doors to the courthouse.

"Of course," I said, thinking about my upcoming surfing sesh with Brock.

The whole morning had been a blur, but I could still feel the butterflies that fluttered throughout my entire body as we entered that courtroom—from my toes to my legs up to my gut and into my heart. I'd never been to court, and the realization that I was going to be standing before a judge made me regurgitate into my mouth. I swallowed it back down, my hands shaking and my toes numb.

Overall, it was successful. Harry's work partner, Zola, was engaged to a lawyer, and he was helping out with the case. The minor in consumption charge was dropped completely. The lawyer said I was lucky that I was an underage female with no previous record.

"Why?" I asked him as we left the courthouse.

"There are two *justice* systems here," he explained.

"So do you think my friend will face anything?" I asked. Brock was facing a full-on DUI.

"If he was the driver"—his eyes widened—"he has a shit salad to deal with."

When I got to school, I ran into Ashleigh in the hallway.

"I literally hate Mr. Paul," Ashleigh said as we walked into the cafeteria.

"Why? What happened?"

"He gave me a D on the research paper! Like, seriously? What did you get?"

At that moment, we passed Brock and Nick. I wanted to stop and chat, but I didn't think it would be a good idea with Ashleigh around.

"Hey," Brock said.

"Hi," I said, keeping my focus ahead.

The butterflies tickled my stomach, making me blush. I hoped Ashleigh didn't notice.

"What the actual fuck is going on?" Ashleigh asked. I'd known better than to think that she hadn't caught on.

"Nothing. Why?"

"Um, that whole thing that just happened." She motioned with her hands. "Don't you, like, hate him now?"

"We're just being cordial with each other."

"Ken." Ashleigh stopped in her tracks. So I stopped too. "I've known you since we were twelve. Don't try and bullshit me."

She looked me straight in the eye when she spoke, and I tried for a moment there to keep her gaze but . . . she won. I gave in.

"No, seriously. I realized what he did for me the other night, you know? Like, if he hadn't taken me home, who knows what would've happened."

Ashleigh looked at me with suspicion. She knew something was weird about it all. I mean, technically I *wasn't* lying. I just wasn't telling her the *whole* story. She didn't need to know. Nobody did.

"Fair enough," she finally replied. I felt bad lying, especially since she'd been by my side through all of this drama. But I just wasn't ready for anyone to know I was seeing Brock outside of school. Just the two of us.

I nodded my head. There was nothing left to say. We parted ways for our classes.

My phone buzzed in my pocket.

Brock: Do you want to ride together? To the beach?
Kendra: Yeah. Sure!
Brock: Cool.

I felt like driving with Brock was like playing with fire; once you get burned the first time, aren't you supposed to learn your lesson?

It was just down the street, though, and obviously no one was going to be intoxicated in this situation. Maybe it wasn't smart to involve him in my plan to regain my strength for competing, but Brock had this thing about him. I didn't know how to describe it. But he was like Kyle in the way he believed that you could do anything if you put your mind to it—and that if you fail, you fail. I needed that right now. He was also the only person I felt would support this—the whole competing thing. I mean, it really was crazy. Oddly enough, Brock Parker seemed like the only person I could trust, especially with a secret.

Truthfully, maybe a part of me was trying to find an acceptable way for Brock and me to talk. Some sort of rationalization. This seemed like a good one to me. An honest one at least. It was an odd kind of feeling, the way you could hate someone so much yet crave their very existence.

At the end of the day, I needed Brock because I knew if I fell, he'd catch me—literally and figuratively—despite the past.

Kendra: Perf

I sat in class, tapping my pencil on the desk as I watched the clock tick. Each minute felt like an hour.

"Make sure your paper follows MLA formatting guidelines," Mr. Williams said.

When the bell finally rang, everyone jumped up and headed for the door.

"Have a nice day," he said.

I walked into the cafeteria, Brock and I crossing paths once again.

"Hey," he said.

"Hi."

We shuffled into a corner hidden away from the crowd.

"Same time today?" he asked.

"Yeah. I totally spaced out this morning and forgot to wear my bathing suit, so I have to run home after school."

"All right. Meet you in the church parking lot again."

"And maybe we find a different beach. Main is so open, I feel like someone will see us."

We looked in both directions before splitting. It was agreed that neither of us felt like dealing with the pressure of our peers interrogating us if we were spotted together. I walked over to where Ashleigh was sitting and sat down next to her. Hunter and Taylor were sitting with us too.

Hunter was concentrating on a sheet of paper on the table.

"What is that?" Ashleigh asked her.

"It's a list of potential themes for the winter formal. It's seriously stressing me out." She took her position as student government president very seriously.

"What are they?" Tay asked.

"The top three are Winter Wonderland, James Bond, and Red Carpet."

"They all sound lame," Ashleigh commented.

"Why do you think I'm so stressed out?"

"Ken," Taylor started, as she sucked down the rest of her protein shake, "why were you just talking to him? Isn't he the devil?"

"Talking to who?"

She leaned in to whisper, "Brock."

I felt Ashleigh's eyes darting through me—the whole table was silent, awaiting my response. I could feel sweat forming above my lip, like the Laguna sun was placed directly above me.

I stumbled on my words. "We're friends. It's nothing."

"Ken, come on. You hated him a week ago."

"Yeah, exactly," Ashleigh said in an icy tone. "But she's chosen to forgive and forget. How sweet."

I knew Ashleigh wasn't necessarily upset about me choosing to forgive Brock. She was pissed because she knew that something else was going on between Brock and me, and for once she wasn't aware of exactly what.

"I didn't *hate* him," I corrected them.

"Yes, you did," Ashleigh corrected *me*.

I shoved an apple dipped in yogurt down my throat so I didn't have to participate in this conversation for at least a few seconds.

Taylor and Hunter shot me a look. I looked at Ashleigh once again, hoping she'd start ranting about Ashton or something—something I'd never thought I'd wish for. But of course she couldn't do that the one time I needed her to, and now I was stuck.

"Okay," I said, leaning in closer to them. "Ihaveaconfession." I spewed out the words and then caught my breath that was stolen for a moment by nerves and angst. "But you have to promise not to say anything."

They stuck out their pinkies.

"Pinkie promise," Hunter said.

I locked my baby finger with theirs.

"Brock is helping train me so I can compete at the quarterfinals for Primes."

"Shut up!" Hunter said.

"You're not serious," Ashleigh said with an eyebrow raised at me.

"This is so Romeo and Juliet," Taylor cried in a dramatic cheerleader manner.

"It's so not, Tay!" Hunter scolded. "He hurt her! Both physically and emotionally!"

I tried to defend the situation. "No, it's not. It's not like that."

Ashleigh sniggered.

"What?" I said, defensively. *This is why I didn't want anyone to know.*

"Stop denying your feelings, Ken! We *all* know this is an excuse for both of you to talk and hang out."

I wanted to be mad at her for talking with such frankness, even though, I mean, she wasn't right, but she wasn't wrong either. I was glad this whole surfing competition thing gave Brock and me a reason to talk again, but I wanted to pursue my surfing regardless. I turned my body around in my seat, watching Brock as he talked to Nick at their table. He caught me gawking and smiled. I grinned at him, aware that my feelings toward him had escaped unscathed despite the accident.

Part of being a strong woman is being strong and forgiving people—and yourself. It's owning up to your own shenanigans.

I couldn't be mad at him forever. We both made decisions that night. To go out. To drink. To drive. To change our lives.

Ashleigh was short with me after lunch. I knew she was upset that I hadn't told her before. But what did she expect? It was a lot for me to handle too.

I texted her after school as I got into Brock's car.

Kendra: Love you!
Ashleigh: Luv u 2 but still think ur a dumbass

Brock ran me to my house, parking in the driveway of a neighbor who I knew was out of the country.

I walked into my house and changed, but as I hurried back downstairs, Harry stopped me.

"Hey, missy. Where are you headed?"

"Oh, Ashleigh and I have a history project due tomorrow. I'm going to her house to work on it. That okay?"

"Yeah. Be back by dinner."

"Okay."

I rushed out of the house with a stomach full of nerves.

Today, I decided I was going to actually get into the water, and so I did. The pain was still there but not as bad. Maybe all this training was helping to heal it. I was beginning to feel like I knew what addictions were like after all. Maybe they weren't just about drugs. Maybe some addictions came in the form of passions or even other people.

A long strand of seaweed had wrapped itself around my foot, so I grabbed it and threw it at Brock. I was laughing so hard my stomach hurt.

"So fucking gross," he said, laughing. He wrapped the seaweed around me, pulling me in close to him. Our bodies were pressed up against each other, and our laughing ceased.

Our eyes met like the sun meets the moon for a short period of time and forms an eclipse—it was that kind of stare. But just like the best of things in life, it didn't last forever.

"You miss it?"

"Huh?" I thought he was referring to us.

"I mean, surfing. Do you miss it? The water?"

"Oh, you have no idea."

I felt stupid for thinking he was referring to what we once were. I backed away, breaking the seaweed in half.

Probably to save the moment from becoming torturously uncomfortable, he said, "You did awesome today."

"Thanks. I can't believe I was able to stand up." I willed myself to forget any kind of feelings we had toward one another.

"I know. Crazy."

He opened my door for me, helping me in. When he got in the driver's seat, I was observing my reflection in the mirror with concern.

"How do I explain my wet hair?" I asked, giggling.

I pulled it up in a tight bun. I could feel Brock watching.

"I like your hair up," he said, pointing to his own head with a circular motion. "In that high, cauliflower-looking thing that girls put their hair in."

I smiled at him, unable to hold in my chuckle. "A bun?"

"Yeah, that!"

"Thanks."

Brock dropped me off at the corner of my street, as we decided that it was best that way.

"I feel bad watching you limp that distance home," he confessed.

"I'm fine, really."

I smiled at him before saying one last time, "Thank you, again."

We sat stagnant, neither of us willing to put our pride aside and make a move. I wondered if he wanted to kiss me goodbye. I thought if I lingered long enough, he would.

"Yeah, no problem."

"Have a good night. See you tomorrow?"

"Yes."

I got out of the car with the unfortunate realization that Brock wouldn't kiss me goodbye. I mean, was I crazy for wanting him to? Ugh!

He waited—as usual—to make sure I made it to my driveway before taking off. I heard him zoom away, old-school rap blasting from his car.

My phone buzzed as I got out of the shower.

Brock: Have U seen the moon 2night?

I walked out to my balcony to go see what he was talking about.

"Wow," I said to myself. A full moon lit up my yard.

Kendra: Omg so pretty ☺
Brock: ☺

I looked back up at the sky and then to the tree house. It sat there, empty, our ugly sweaters and Girl Scout cookies inside. Along with a handful of memories that would forever remain.

I let out a sigh. Why did that night have to happen? Why didn't I just stay home like I was supposed to? Why did I drink when he offered me the rum? I looked down at my phone as a plethora of *what-ifs* stormed through my mind like a tornado, and before my brain could comprehend my actions, it was up to my ear. Three rings in, I was going to hang up.

"Hello?" Brock answered.

"Hi," I said. I wasn't sure why I called. For a moment there, only time and heavy breathing became the conversation.

"What's up? Everything okay?"

"Yeah, everything's good. What are you doing?"

"Just about to go eat dinner with my parents."

"Oh, nice. What are you guys having?"

"I'm not sure yet." He laughed. "Have you had dinner yet?"

"No, not yet."

"Kendr—"

"Bro—"

We spoke each other's names at once.

"Go ahead," I said.

"No, no. Ladies first."

"I was just going to say thanks for helping me out the past couple of days."

"Of course."

"What were you going to say?"

"Uh, um—" He cleared his throat.

"Brock, dinner is on the table!" I heard his mom yell in the background.

"Never mind. I gotta go."

Was that a sign?

"You sure?" I asked.

"Yeah. I'll see you tomorrow."

"Okay, enjoy your dinner," I said. I didn't want this conversation to end. I was filled with suspense at what he was going to say to me.

"Thanks."

We hung up and I was left curious. I quickly blocked out my fantasies and hopes of what he might have said. I needed to stop being so . . . into him. There was no other way to put it.

Time passed. I stood outside at my balcony, staring out at the moon. I couldn't control myself, which seemed to be a common theme in regards to Brock Parker. I texted him.

Kendra: What are you doing?
Brock: Working on a beat ;P

I needed a legitimate reason to bother him since things weren't how they used to be and we couldn't just talk to talk anymore. Or at least that's the way it was in my head.

Kendra: Can U practice in the morning 2morrow?
Brock: Yeah. Pick U up around 6:30?
Kendra: Yes ☺
Brock: ;)

I wondered, *Was the winky intended to be that winky? How am I supposed to interpret that?*

I laughed aloud at my own ridiculous and overly analytical thoughts. They were going to drive me nuts.

The weekend flew by. Brock and I planned to meet again for another practice before school on Monday. I couldn't tell if my parents were becoming suspicious or I was just a nervous wreck when it came to lying. Harry was always asking where I'd been. My dad was pretty silent and unaware.

Brock and I walked down to the beach as the sun was just rising. I was determined to surf an actual wave today.

I yawned as Brock mounted the board into the sand.

"Tired?" he asked.

I nodded my head, exhausted.

We did our usual warm-up that consisted of ab work, balancing exercises, and calisthenics.

"You gonna surf today?" he asked me innocently. He knew how to trigger me.

"Duh."

We headed to the water, Brock carrying the surfboard. The cold water stung my feet at first touch.

"Freezing," I said as we made our way out to the knee-deep water.

He splashed the water my way, making my body automatically tense up from the bitter chill. I splashed him back.

"Meanie!" I said, but I got my revenge. He threw his hands up, covering his face.

"Okay! Okay!" He smirked. I think he liked it. The games.

I straddled the board, Brock doing the same. We faced each other, our bodies almost close enough to be deemed inappropriate for two ex-lovers. The water was calm, but my heart palpitations sure weren't. I was nervous and overwhelmed by the way Brock's presence seemed to fill me with sparks. Constantly. All the time. They exploded inside of me with each word he spoke. With every subtle grin he smiled. With every shared moment that I couldn't seem to shake from my mind.

"Quarterfinals are coming up soon!"

"I know," I said. "I'm nervous."

"Don't be. You got this."

I shrugged my shoulders and grinned, sighing out a brittle laugh—obviously filled with concerns.

"I don't know. We'll see."

"Hey, you won't get anywhere with an attitude like that."

Brock kept me in check. I needed that.

"Here we go, this is a good one. Try and put your right foot forward this time. Goofy-footed, like you said last time."

Brock hopped off of the board, allowing me to paddle. I propped myself up, making sure to bring my right foot forward.

"There we go! Keep the abs tight, weight in the front foot."

It was nice having Brock there to watch me from a third-person perspective to see the little mistakes that I couldn't from my view on the board.

I stayed with my breath as the wave curled over me, reminding myself to inhale. But on my exhale it took me down. I was scared at first, but when my lungs found air again, I came back to my breathing, trying my hardest to shake off the mental storm that could potentially end today's practice. I was more frustrated at this point than anything else. It overpowered even my deepest of fears.

Brock was waiting on the sand when I swam to shore.

"That was great—"

"No, it wasn't. It was awful."

There was no way I would be prepared to compete so soon. I gripped my leg, massaging it.

"It's getting worse, Brock. I can feel it."

I'd thought all the training would be good for my foot—despite what the doctors had said. It had felt good up until now. It was beginning to ache again and fatigue.

"Kendra, you should be proud that you're even out here right now."

"I know. It's just—I don't know."

"You're thinking too much," he said, his hand on my back.

"Maybe."

"Why don't we do some of that meditation? The kind you taught me on Halloween?"

He looked at me and I was lost in his eyes. How cliché did that sound? But it was true. Like my mind went blank. I nodded my head, agreeing with him.

The two of us sat beside each other on the sand.

"You lead us, Miss Meditator."

I couldn't help but smile.

"Okay," I sighed. "Let's close our eyes and just breathe. No specific pattern. Just in and out. But stay aware of the breath. The way it feels. Sounds. The pace."

When I spoke, I could hear Coach's voice. I mimicked his instructions.

Brock and I sat there, breathing. Together. It was kind of beautiful. To just stop and observe ourselves. To be that comfortable with someone. To become conscious of my breath. I'd never experienced a meditation like this. Where I was so invested in my breath that everything else became completely irrelevant. The waves didn't crash in my ears. The birds didn't sing. The cars didn't honk. It was pure breath.

I inhaled, my exhale synced with Brock's. Like magic.

We simultaneously opened our eyes, and when we did, our stares landed directly on one another.

He smiled at me. I smiled back.

"Thanks for teaching me how to meditate," he said.

And all I wanted to do was thank him for breathing with me. Was that nuts or what?

We pulled up to school, our hair still wet. What kind of idiot would repeatedly ride with the driver that got her into a car accident? This idiot.

I saw all our friends hanging out in the courtyard. There were only ten minutes until class started.

"I'll drop you off up front while I park."

I looked toward our friends and then back at Brock.

"No. Let's walk in together."

He raised an eyebrow, questioning me.

"Everyone is going to have an opinion, and I'm done worrying about what they might be," I said. Brock was a true friend to me. I wasn't going to be ashamed for hanging out with him despite the past. That would be the equivalent of not wanting to walk in somewhere with my brother just because he had once caused my family pain. I'd proudly walk in anywhere with him.

Brock smiled.

"Me too."

I realized that the moment we stop thinking about what *others* are thinking was when we truly begin to cultivate our purpose in this life. I wanted to live mine. I didn't want to worry about what others thought of it.

Brock parked the car and we walked in. Together.

BROCK

We walked into the courtyard where our friends were waiting before class. Nick looked up at me. He shot me a look—his face scrunched up in a quizzical expression.

"What?" he mouthed to me.

I shook my head as if to explain to him that this wasn't the time or place to get into it.

"Later," I mouthed back.

"Hey, guys," Kendra said.

Her friends didn't look *as* surprised. At least not as surprised as I expected or nearly as surprised as my buddies.

"Uh, hey, guys," Ashleigh said.

"Did you guys drive together?" Ashton asked.

"Mmhmm," Kendra answered.

They all kind of just nodded their heads, unsure of how to react. The warning bell rang.

"I've got to get to class. I'll see you later," she said to me.

She walked in through the doors. I liked this side of Kendra. It was refreshing. Different to say the least. She didn't give a shit anymore. I wanted to welcome her to the club.

"Seriously, what is going on? How did you get her to talk to you?" Ashton whispered in my ear. I'd be surprised if Ashleigh had known and he didn't. Maybe Kendra hadn't opened her mouth at all. Weird.

"Long story. Tell you later."

"Okay."

"I'm gonna head to class," I said, walking toward the door.

"See ya, man," Nick said.

As I headed to my first-period class, I made a detour to the bathroom. I waited until I heard the late bell ring before pulling out my rolling paper and some of that bud that my parents were growing in the backyard—which was some good shit. I had to give the 'rents credit where credit was due.

I felt overwhelmed today; I was going to have to leave early to meet someone for a deal, and I was already hanging by a thread with my English teacher. If I missed any more classes, he would probably drop me. I was gonna hear an earful from my father, but he couldn't have it both ways; hustlin' and good grades were like oil and water. I debated taking an Adderall that Duke had given me a while back. He was on it for legit reasons, but I took them once in a blue moon for recreation. He had given them to me, like, a year ago, though, and I wondered if that shit expired. I pulled them out of my bag but decided not to take one. Wasn't my style.

As I sat in the bathroom rolling up a joint, a nerdy motherfucker walked in. His shorts were too short, his hair too slicked over, and his arms scrawny as shit. I could smush him with one finger. He looked like a future frat kid at some prestigious UC school. He stood at one of the urinals. He was a weird motherfucker the way he was staring at me while taking a piss.

"Are those Adderall?" he asked.

"Yeah, why?"

Was this dude seriously trying to talk right now?

"My friend said you could hook me up with stuff."

"Who's your friend?" I asked, blowing smoke in his face.

"Well, he's not really a friend per se . . . but we have class together."

"I asked you what his name is."

"Ryan."

That douche needed to stop handing out my name. He'd already almost gotten me busted once.

"I'll buy that Adderall from you."

I raised an eyebrow at him. I didn't sell that shit. I only took it . . . barely.

"I'm failing my chemistry two AP class. I'll do anything." That made sense now.

"How much you willing to pay?"

"How about a hundred dollars?"

He pulled a hundred-dollar bill from his pocket and handed it to me.

An epiphany rained over me—Adderall for high schoolers. Why hadn't my parents or Morales thought of that before? These days, school involved a lot of pressure. Getting into college wasn't as easy as it once was. Kids didn't just *want* this drug. They *needed* it to succeed. The question was, did I sell it without my parents knowing and pocket the money myself or share my discovery with them?

"Here you go, buddy." I handed him the bottle, three pills inside.

"Thanks so much, Brock! I'll be hitting you up again soon."

"Aye," I said, as he was heading for the bathroom door. "Don't give my name out unless someone directly asks for Adderall. And tell them to call me Mr. A. Got it?"

He nodded his head and quickly left.

I think I just found a quick escape to Duke's and my island

without the attachment of Morales. I'm shocked I hadn't thought of it before. Truly.

I immediately messaged Duke.

Brock: I have a great idea....
Duke: Talk to me.
Brock: Dealing Adderall to high schoolers . . . these nerds eat that shit up.
Duke: Holy fuck. You're a genius. Count me in.
Brock: Hook me up w more of that sheeeettt . . . we gonna be $$$
Duke: This is dope.
Brock: No, this is addy ;) LOL.
Duke: Ahaha shut up ya lame ass
Duke: One problem . . . I don't go to high school.
Brock: True . . . but you still know plenty of high schoolers.
Duke: Okay, true. I'm stoked for this.
Brock: Island here we come!
Duke: BTW where've u been??
Brock: Helping Kendra . . . surfing.
Duke: :D Knew you'd revive and restore ur relationship with her. U guys have a special connection.
Brock: haha ok Romeo

I teased Duke for being so cheesy at times, but I liked the idea that what Kendra and I had was real.

A screeching alarm blared through the school. I jumped, realizing that I set the fucking fire alarm off while smoking up.

I tossed the joint into a toilet, flushing it down, then hurried out of the bathroom, mixing into the crowd rushing out of their classes to the football field—where we had to meet our home-room classes during a fire drill.

"Hey, dude."

I turned around. It was Brody.

"Oh, hey."

"I wonder if this is just a drill or the real thing."

"Probably just a drill."

We walked outside, where I spotted Kendra walking down the stairs to the field a few yards in front of me. I caught up to her, tapping her on the shoulder and running to her other side before she could catch me. She turned back around, confused.

"Hi," I said.

"Oh, my gosh, was that you that just tapped my shoulder?"

"Maybe." I snickered and winked as a subtle reveal. "Got you good."

She nudged me.

"I was literally in the middle of a pop quiz."

"So whoever this pyromaniac is saved the day?"

"Pretty much."

I leaned into her as we made our way onto the field.

"Good to know."

She looked at me, her eyebrows furrowed in confusion—and sparked a thrill in me. I walked away, heading to my homeroom teacher's spot on the field. Maybe the bad boy wasn't always the villain. Maybe he could save the day too . . . or at least save the princess from her pop quiz.

I couldn't help myself. I wanted to see her again before we separated for the day.

Brock: Can I give U a ride home 2day?:)

Kendra: Sure:)

I liked this idea of Kendra and me being friends. Although I craved more. I'd never really been "just friends" with a girl before. I guess that was proof that I really did like her . . . or even loved her.

KENDRA

It was a beautiful Friday morning—marking just over two weeks since Brock and I had first started training for the quarterfinals *and* our last official practice before the competition just twenty-four hours away. We took off most of last week. My family was getting suspicious, especially since I couldn't talk about school projects on the week of Thanksgiving. Although my family didn't do much for the holidays; it wasn't really our thing after everything fell apart.

The sun's rays reflected off the water onto our skin. It was warm, but the cool breeze against the chilly ocean dripping off of us balanced it out. It would make sense for me to start wearing a wet suit, but I guessed I'd rather freeze. Although I was going to have to wear one for the competition. Thankfully, the doctor said I didn't have to wear my boot anymore.

I swam a small wave to shore, reflecting on how much I'd improved since the injury first occurred—er, I guess it was less *improvement* and more just learning to overcome my thoughts. It was about just riding through the pain at this point. My leg was excruciating actually, but the hurting was way less important than winning.

I wondered if the past month was even real. It didn't feel like it. I'd been shoved out of my comfort zone and discovered a lot about myself along the way.

I collapsed down onto the sand, Brock lying down next to me. "Tomorrow's the big day," he said.

"Yep."

We both looked up at the sun, my eyes barely able to stay open as the fierce light pierced through my gaze.

"You ready?"

"No. But I'm excited."

Brock stood up, extending his hand to me. I grabbed ahold of it, and with his help, hoisted myself off the sand.

"Do you need a ride to school?"

"Uh . . . um, no, not today. I have to make a quick stop before, so I'm just going to walk. Enjoy the weather." I didn't want to share with him exactly where I was going. It was personal. Private. A place that made me feel my most vulnerable.

"All right," he agreed. In that moment, I looked into his eyes, and he looked into mine. A part of me wanted to reopen that door. He didn't know the story about my brother. Did I dare invite him with me?

"Well, see ya," he said as he turned around and headed in the direction of his car.

"Wait, Brock." I spoke before I had enough time to think.

He turned back to face me. "Yeah?"

"Will you come with me real fast?"

A surge of adrenaline flowed through my veins. There was no taking it back now.

"Yeah, sure."

I wanted his company. He was the one person that I felt comfortable enough to share all of these things with. That meant something.

We drove a few minutes down the road. I instructed Brock where to go. I stopped myself when I realized I was biting at my nails—a nervous habit I had sworn off some time ago. It freaked me out that I was doing it without any awareness.

"Turn here," I said.

We pulled up to the graveyard.

"This is it?" he asked, looking at the arrangement of head-stones that covered the lawn—I'm sure quite confused.

"Yeah."

He parked the car and asked once again, "Are you sure this is it?"

"Yes."

We walked through the grass until I stopped at the gravestone. I knelt down. Brock was slightly behind me. And Kyle was in front of me. I looked down at the date that was engraved on the stone: 1984–2000. He would've been twenty-seven years old. I wondered what it would be like if he was still here. Would our parents still be together? Or were they destined to be apart? Would we have moved to Laguna? If we hadn't, I would have never met Brock. I wondered what he would've thought of Brock—would they have gotten along?

I cleared my throat. "This is my brother."

I looked at Brock. The coloring in his face vanished as his eyes fixated on the gravestone. I looked back at Kyle's name on the stone. Chills shivered up my spine.

"Laguna Beach was his absolute favorite place to surf. That's why he was buried here."

Brock was silent. I was silent. The air was even silent.

"You wanted to know why I hate drugs. This is why."

I was surprised I didn't cry, nor did I feel it coming on. I didn't begin to shake or lose my mind or fall into a whirlpool of anxiety. I was calm. I felt at peace. I was here with my brother, even if he wasn't around. He was here.

"My brother, Kyle, he died. He overdosed on Halloween night ten years ago."

I looked to Brock. He deserved the story, and I wanted to share it with him. I'd never shared it with anyone else before. It was my secret because I never wanted to relive it.

"My mom pounded on his door. She was screaming and crying and losing it. My brother was on the other side, hysterical, and wouldn't let them in. He was only seventeen. My parents tried every tactic in the book, but he was so gone. So mentally gone. So stoned. Those drugs were embedded into his soul.

"I remember being seven years old, all dressed up, ready to go out for Halloween, just standing in the corner confused and lost as my parents desperately tried to get into his room. When there wasn't a response from the other side . . . We knew. My dad kicked the door in. I walked over to where my mother stood, holding on to the back of her leg. Kyle lay there, a needle in his arm. My mom collapsed to the ground, holding him with hope that it wasn't true. My dad just stood there looking down at his dead son and his inconsolable wife. Tears fled down his face. That was the one and only time I'd ever seen him cry. And I think the hardest part for me to comprehend is trying to figure out how a person could love something so much that would never love them back. No. It could only poison them. But I guess people do it all the time with other people, not just drugs.

"My mom took off after that. She couldn't handle it. She couldn't handle us, after that. I haven't seen her in years. My dad always said people grieve in different ways."

I finally took a breath and looked over at Brock. His eyes stayed on the gravestone.

"I'm so sorry, Kendra," he finally said softly.

"It's okay. It is what it is," I said, speaking my mantra aloud.

"Is that why you guys moved here from San Diego?"

"Yeah. My dad says he can feel his spirit wandering the beach sometimes."

"Kyle would be really proud of you right now."

"I hope so."

I surrendered. I leaned up against Brock, letting my head rest on his shoulder. He wrapped his arm around me as we sat there together. Silently. Words needn't be spoken, for it was tears and breathing and undisclosed thoughts that did all the explaining.

It started to sprinkle rain down onto us unexpectedly. Almost as if it was Kyle, cleansing us—the memories of us. The kind of cleansing Brock explained rain signified. We looked at each other. Smiled.

When I got home from school, Harry was just pulling in. Ashleigh dropped me off.

"Hi, hon. How was school?"

"It was good."

Harry unlocked the front door and we walked inside. Skittles came running into the front foyer, jumping on us with excitement.

"How was your day?" I asked him.

"It was good. I just had a meeting with Zola about the salon."

"How did it go?"

"Great. She's thinking that we'll be able to open up by the first of the year."

"That's awesome!"

"Yeah, it's exciting. I just feel so overwhelmed," he said, sitting down onto a kitchen chair.

"All that hard work will be worth it though."

"Very true."

I sat down on the chair across from him as my dad walked into the house.

"Hi, guys," he said, two brown bags in hand.

"What's that, sweets?"

"I stopped at the Armenian deli on the way home and picked up some food."

"Why don't we go have a little picnic on the beach?" Harry suggested.

"That sounds great," my dad agreed. They both looked at me for a reaction.

"I'm in," I said.

My dad smiled at this. "You're in a good mood today. Things are looking up, huh?"

I didn't want to give in and spoil the fact that I was preparing for quarterfinals with a hairline fracture—and, mind you, with the help of Brock Parker.

"Yeah, I think Coach's meditation class the other day really helped me. Changed my perspective." This was true . . . but just not the *full* story.

"Glad to hear that," my dad said and smiled even brighter.

I put Skittles on her leash, and the four of us walked down the street to the beach. We laid out a blanket and sat down just at the prime of sunset. The sky was layered pink and blue with the sun melting into the ocean. I could never explain Laguna sunsets, but there was something fantastical about them. They felt less like an ending and more like a beginning.

My dad pulled out to-go boxes full of food: chicken kabobs, pilaf, and spinach pie. It smelled amazing.

We all dug in.

"Those Armenians really know how to use butter," Harry said, chowing down on a spinach pie.

I fed Skittles a piece of chicken.

"How is your leg?" my dad asked.

"It's starting to feel better."

The truth was, I realized it was my improvement in attitude after meditation that seemed to accelerate the healing of my injury.

"If I ever run into that Brock—ugh," Harry said. "Lord help him."

My stomach turned.

"As long as he stays away from my daughter, I don't give a shit," my dad said.

I just wanted to enjoy the moment. Not worry about the past and every twist it had taken or even what turns the future potentially held. Just as we were in this scene of life. It was too perfect to take for granted.

"We should start doing this more," I said.

"I agree," Harry said.

"We've all been so preoccupied, we need to remember to slow it down," my dad counseled.

The sun fell down into the ocean, the moon replacing its presence. And when I looked at it, I thought of Brock. Our moon. It left me wondering if he was looking at the moon right then, and thinking of me too.

I was exhausted by the time we got home, and I had to be up early in the morning, so I decided it was best to stay in. It was an emotional day on top of school, and I was feeling the weight of it all.

I sat in bed, scrolling through Facebook, trying to distract my mind with something. My stomach had been in knots all day. I was a nervous wreck about tomorrow—the competition. I needed to figure out how I was even going to get there. Competition started at nine, so I had to be up by seven. Brock and I decided it was best we didn't drive together just in case my dad and Harry would see. It was the weekend, which meant they didn't work and were at home.

I shut my laptop and dialed Ashleigh.

"Hey, biatch," she said. She was crunching on something.

"What are you eating?"

"Chips."

"I have a favor to ask."

"You're still on my nerves about the whole Brock thing, but sure. What's up?"

"Is there any way I can hitch a ride to the Prime quarterfinals from you tomorrow?"

"I guess so. What time?"

"It's in Newport, so we should leave here by seven forty-five."

"Holy shit, it's Saturday!"

"I know. I know. I'd ask my dad, but he can't even know."

"I must *seriously* love you."

"Thank you!"

"If you don't hear from me by seven thirty, call."

She chomped on another chip.

"Okay."

"What are you doing tonight?"

"Nothing. I'm going to go to sleep soon, I guess."

"Shit, well, I guess I have to, too."

I laughed.

"I owe you."

"Shut up. I'll see you tomorrow."

"All right. Bye."

We hung up. I gazed out the window, the moon shining bright. Although it wasn't full, I could see the profile of a man's sleeping face. I approached the window, my eyes never leaving his.

"God," I began, unsure of where I was even going with this,

"if you're really up there, listening, please give me strength. Please help me."

I wasn't one to pray often. Not because I didn't believe, or because I wasn't spiritual. Mostly because it wasn't a habit I was accustomed to. But maybe I had to start praying more frequently. There was a lot to be thankful for—I was lucky to be alive after everything that had taken place. And even through all of the grim, the past, the bad . . . the sun always seemed to shine. Just like Brock said.

"And if you can hear me, give Brock strength too. He needs it even more than I do."

BROCK

I was low-key freaking out about court. I was supposed to appear for a preliminary trial in a couple weeks. My dad had reached out to Morales, and he referred us to a really great lawyer, but I was still trippin'. I had to find a way out of this. I had to. Thankfully, I finally made it out to LA to take my mind off of all of it. All the bull.

I felt like I hadn't seen Duke in fuckin' forever. There was no way I was missing out on another one of his ragers, but I was going to limit my alcohol intake because I wanted to be there for Kendra tomorrow.

Duke and I walked into his bedroom with a couple of hoes. I wasn't even that buzzed yet—despite the fact that Duke had convinced me to smoke this intense shit he just picked up on his last trip down south.

"Dude, I got the goods," Duke said, one of the girls nestled in his arms.

I was assuming he meant some quality coke, but then he pulled out a plastic bag of meth. Shit, I mean, I was into experimenting, but that was some hard stuff even for me.

I hesitated before answering. I didn't want to do it. I'd never done meth before and it kind of freaked me out. That was saying something.

I swallowed down my nerves, put on my game face, and finally replied, "Fuck yeah."

I wanted to do the right thing. I wanted to be the guy Kendra needed me to be. But I was still a drug dealer. That wasn't going to change anytime soon, because like all dealers, I was used to making a lot of money—and I'll tell you, *that* can be the worst addiction of all. My lifestyle revolved around this kind of shit . . . and this kind of people.

I knew Duke had done it a few times in the past, but it wasn't like he was addicted or anything. He was already gone, his eyes hanging more than normal and bloodshot like I'd never seen.

"You sure you're good, man?" I asked him.

"Yeah. Course."

Duke stood up, almost tripping over his own two feet.

"Here," he said, handing me a meth pipe. I was low-key concerned that he even owned one of those, but I was also not very surprised by anything with Duke.

I poured some of the crystal into the pipe, not wanting to bitch out in front of him. I was getting more nervous and as I lit it up, I had to control my hand's tremoring. This was a sketch-ass drug, but I convinced myself that it would be worth it to experience something new.

I was the first to tweak, taking a deep inhale. My pulse immediately spiked. Somewhere so high I couldn't feel much. It was a feeling of alertness and excitement. My adrenaline seemed to reach its highest point. Nothing could bring me down.

"Whoo!" I screeched, high on life.

Duke was next to take a hit. All of the sudden, his body started to convulse, his eyes rolling into the back of his head. I laughed, thinking he was just fucking with me.

But he wouldn't stop. His body shook like a fucking earthquake. It made my heartbeat quicken even more. The girls started crying and panicking, screaming at the top of their lungs.

"Duke!" I yelled. I looked to one of the girls. "Call someone! Get help."

They ran out of the room, the door slamming behind them. Foam drooled out of his mouth as I sat over him, trying to turn him onto his side. I remembered seeing that in a movie.

I tried pressing onto his chest. I poured water on his face. But he was frozen in time. I hit him over and over. He wouldn't wake up. He convulsed until I yelled, "Come on, brother. This isn't funny. Snap out of it!"

So he did. And that was it. His body went limp, finally still. I placed my hand on his neck. His heart was no longer beating.

Suddenly, my best friend was gone. I didn't want to admit, it couldn't be true. He couldn't be gone. A million memories tracked through my mind. Dreams.

"Duke! Come on, man. Please. Don't go," I cried. Tears fell from my eyes. I felt hopeless and confused. This moment couldn't be real. "What about the Caribbean?"

I'd never seen anyone die before. Not in person. If God really existed, why did he always take the good ones? The noble ones? The genuine ones? The real ones? Why Duke? I looked at the scar that was traced across his forehead. He deserved so much more than the shitty card he'd been dealt.

I sat over him until I heard sirens in the distance. I didn't want to, but I had to run. If I was caught here, I'd be so fucked— and I was already screwed with the DUI.

I jumped through the bedroom window and over the back-yard wall into a deserted area of land where only plants and night creatures resided. I ran as far from the incident as I could. I could hear tons of sirens driving toward Duke's. Thankfully— and surprisingly—I didn't know anyone at this banger, so worrying about my name being brought up wasn't an issue. I felt horrible for even worrying about myself in this moment. What was wrong with me?

I didn't want to believe that I was this selfish. I felt paralyzed in shock as I stopped, catching my breath and letting the past twenty minutes sink in. I squeezed my eyes shut, hoping that when I opened them, I'd wake up from this nightmare. But I didn't. Duke was dead.

I said it aloud: "Duke is dead."

That didn't even sound right.

My body collapsed down onto the ground, barely catching myself. Sitting there, alone, my thoughts began to slow down. I realized that life is full of moments. Most of which, we take for granted. But watching my friend lie there, breathless and gone, I realized that in a single moment, everything can change without any signs or warnings. Life is full of moments, and our job is to make the most of each one of them with the people we love. And I really hadn't been doing that.

During my cab ride home, I had to try and function with the pit that had formed in my gut like I'd never felt before. It was indescribable. I wanted to fall over and crumble into pieces. A part of me felt empty. A part of me felt guilty. It was people like me who changed lives—like Kendra's brother's. I was a monster. I was the villain in the story. The antagonist. My body was still but my insides raced and I couldn't catch my breath.

My soul felt numb, my heart frozen, and my mind lost. I hated everything. My parents. My job. And mostly myself.

I thought back to Duke on Halloween when he said all that shit about when we die we only take the feelings and the memories with us. Did he think when he said that, that his death was just around the corner?

When I walked into my house, my parents were sitting in the kitchen with Annie's mom and dad. It was poker night. I walked up to the table, none of them acknowledging my existence.

"Hello?" I said, interrupting.

My mom finally looked up as my father spoke. "Our delivery came in. Go wash up and then come back down here so we can talk."

I clenched my fists together tightly, trying to restrain myself from completely losing it. But then I saw Duke's limp body flash through my mind and Kendra's watery eyes reminiscing about the last memories she had of her brother—and in a sudden abruptness, I went mad. I was done being pimped out as my parents' fucking drug mule.

I shook my head and snickered. "Go *fuck* yourself."

"Excuse me?"

This got my father's attention, his gaze now stuck on me with crooked, glassy eyes. I got right in his fucking face.

"You heard me."

He stood up, our faces leveled.

"You better watch it."

My mom stood up, stepping in between us.

"Karl, settle down."

"I'm done working for you pieces of shit."

My father pushed my mom aside, punching me right in the face. I jabbed him in the gut, but it barely fazed him as he punched me back. I bent over, holding my stomach. He knocked the wind right out of me. I looked up, my eyes barely opened halfway, my body weak.

As I was regaining a small amount of strength, my arm swinging into him, Annie's dad suddenly grasped me, pulling me back. I pulled my arm out from his grip.

My father stood over me and spoke again, this time between

gritted teeth. "I *said*, our delivery came in. Go wash up and then come back down here so we can talk."

"You're such a greedy asshole!"

"How dare you after everything your mother and I have given for you—this life, a career—"

"This isn't the life I want anymore." I dropped to the floor, crying.

"Brock, what's wrong?" My mother fell to my side.

"He's fucking stoned, Debby."

My mother embraced me. "No, something happened. Something is wrong."

"Duke's dead," I sobbed into her shoulder.

"What?" My father sounded alert now.

"Duke. Is. Dead." I looked up at him. "He overdosed."

My father's eyes wandered all over the room.

"This isn't good. We have to call Morales. Someone needs to get on this and cover everything up. His phone records need to be erased, we have to—"

"Do you hear yourself? Duke is dead, and you're still more concerned about yourself. Your money. Your bullshit business!"

I stood up, facing my father.

He neared me, standing over me, and with that sinister smirk of his, he said, "I didn't mean it when I said I was proud of you. You're a lousy excuse for a son. And you're right—you're just a drug mule."

My heart was too numb to feel. I hated him. I hated this life he'd given me.

I spit on him, and before he had the opportunity to ruin me, I took off toward the front door.

My last words were "I'm not going to be responsible for killing people like Kyle."

"Who?" my mother screeched as I ran out of the house, my

whole body aching with all sorts of internal pains. Some resonated in the bones, others in the heart. It could feel again.

I hoisted my body into the spare car, my dad charging outside after me.

"You better fucking stop that car right fucking now!" he yelled loud enough to be heard through the vehicle. I wasn't worried, though. He'd never call the cops or anything like that—if that was the case, he'd basically be ratting himself out.

I sped out of my neighborhood, driving with no particular place in mind. One eye open, the other in too much pain to even blink. But my heart was hurting the most.

I pulled over down a side street. My breathing was heavy; I was about to burst. I opened up the glove box and grabbed the mint case that held my personal supply. It was empty. So I reached into the center console, hastily rummaging through, searching for drugs—pot, oxy, coke, anything! I'd had enough. My final breaking point. So much guilt sat on my chest.

I couldn't control Kendra or her surfing or the DUI or what happened or anything, but now I didn't even have my goddamn brother. What was there to even live for? The island was nothing without him.

I ripped the car apart, but no drugs. Nothing. I wanted them to take me too.

"Fuck!" I yelled to myself, hitting the steering wheel with rage. I turned to the only other thing that could potentially calm me down. I turned up the radio all the way. The bass blasted through the speakers. I slammed my hands on the wheel, my own personal drum set, my head bobbing back and forth so violently I began to sweat. But I couldn't stop. I was feeling the beat, the music, the melody, the vibe. I even began to sing along—and although I was a musician, I was no singer. But I sang and sang and sang until—

The talk radio interrupted it all, ending my jam sesh. I sat there for a moment in an attempt to calm down. I breathed—inhaling and holding. Exhaling and holding. Catching my breath. It made me think of Kendra. What do you do then? When something as necessary as breathing reminded you of a person?

I shook my head, disappointed and angry. Really, really angry.

I suddenly calmed myself—the breathing seemed to work. So much was traveling through my brain at this point in time, that when it all settled, I came up with a plan. I knew how I was going to change my life around and escape the DUI charges . . . hopefully.

It was a scary thought, but it was all I could do now. I didn't want to, but I was going to rat my parents out and Morales and all of his people to save my ass. Didn't they do that in mob movies? Like, they convince the guy who gets busted to wear a wire so they can bust everyone else, like the bigger people, and he gets set free or something?

I put the car in drive and headed toward the police station.

Things were about to change. Drastically.

KENDRA

As the competition was preparing to kick off, I stood on the beach, waxing my board. All of my friends showed up to surprise me—thanks to Ashleigh. I was surprised, being that it was so early in the morning. But Brock was still a no-show. I successfully snuck out of the house earlier in the morning, thanks to my parents' recent routine of sleeping in on Saturdays. I left a note on the fridge telling them that I'd gone to brunch with Ashleigh and Ashton.

"Do you know where Brock is?" I asked Ashton.

He shook his head.

"You haven't heard from him?" he asked.

"No."

I checked my phone again. Nothing. I sat down on the sand and began to massage out my leg. Angst was building up inside of me—and it didn't help that Brock wasn't around. In a way, I felt dependent on him. It would be comforting to know he was near.

I excused myself from the group and found a spot on the sand, shutting my eyes and taking deep breaths. I needed to focus.

"Ken, what are you doing here?"

I looked up. It was Coach Harkins.

I was slightly caught off guard. I didn't want to tell him the truth, but it was inevitable. I finally spat out, "I'm going to compete."

"The doctor said it was okay?"

"Not *exactly*."

He crossed his arms in front of his chest, his eyebrows furrowed in confusion.

"Listen, Kendra, I'm all for proving people wrong and chasing your dreams but—"

"All contestants, please approach the shoreline. We will begin in five minutes," the announcer (thankfully) interrupted.

I wasn't in any kind of mood or mental state to hear a lecture from Coach. I already knew the repercussions of my actions. I didn't need a reminder.

"I just really thought you were smarter than all of this."

I looked at him and swallowed down the sadness he just buried in me. He shook his head and laughed as he began to walk away, heading toward the beach.

He turned back around one last time to say, "But you know I'll be cheering you on, kid."

"Thanks." I forced a grin.

I looked out at the ocean. My stomach and a wave curled in time with each other. It was like trying to convince an old friend to hang out again.

"Have you heard from Brock yet?" Ashleigh asked as she approached me.

"No. Do you think he's okay?"

"He's fine. He probably just slept in or something."

"I hope that's the case."

I couldn't help but sense trouble. Brock was different lately. He wouldn't have slept in like that. Nobody else had noticed his transformation, but I had . . . and I had faith in him. Something else was going on. I could feel it in my gut, but I couldn't focus on that right now. I needed to get my head clear and not let whatever was going on with Brock distract me from this. He'd say the same thing, I knew. I had to try to focus in on what I needed to do, how I was going to conquer the water.

The announcer spoke again. "All right, surfers, take your places."

I wanted to throw up.

"Breathe, Kendra. Breathe," I quietly said to myself. I closed my eyes, taking in the moment, allowing myself to become calm. The cool water touched my feet, awakening me. I opened my eyes and watched the water inhale and exhale. I grasped my St. Christopher pendant in my hand, saying a prayer to God or whoever was listening up there.

"Good luck, Ken!" Ashton said.

"You're going to do great," Ashleigh squealed.

I headed toward the water, focused on my breath: *In. Out. In. Out.*

The whistle blew and there I went—into the water. My home. Such a familiar place, yet it was so frightening. It was like I completely blacked out and just went with the waves. I was nervous, but my confidence increased as I dominated the wave. I felt myself smile without any force. I couldn't help but embrace this moment, completely forgetting that this was even a competition. We competed in "heats" which included six girls at a time.

The joy was short-lived as I was quickly taken down. I came up for air and hopped back onto my board. Another wave was brewing from afar. I was having too much fun to even care if I was winning or not. It had felt like forever since I'd had a good surf like this. Years, maybe. It felt less like a chore and more like the days when Kyle and I surfed just to surf. It felt like my mom might just be waiting at the shore. Or at least at home with a hot, homemade dinner.

Fifteen minutes in, I stood up onto my board and let myself enjoy the ride. The wave curled over me and I kept my balance. I landed a pretty big maneuver on this one. I was almost there until the wave crashed on me and rolled me around. I'd put too much weight onto my left foot. The pain suddenly kicked into my leg. It was aching, and I realized this was it for me. I wasn't going to win. I accepted that.

As I limped out of the water, a déjà vu fell upon me, and I couldn't help but smile, remembering the first time Kyle took me surfing with him and his friends. I totally got thrown off my board and tumbled all the way to shore. I was so embarrassed in front of my brother and his friends that I started crying. He came rushing to my side and said to me, "Crying is for babies. You're not a baby. Are you gonna let a little setback set you back?" I guess he taught me well. Here I was—not letting a setback set me back.

My heart stopped when I saw my dad and Harry running toward me, my friends tailing behind them. How did they know to find me here? I swallowed down my nerves, unsure of what their reaction was going to be. Or better yet—how I was going to explain myself.

"Kendra, honey, are you okay?" Harry shrieked, wrapping his arm around me as support, walking up the shore.

"Yeah. I'm fine." But I was somewhat bummed that I hadn't qualified.

Ashleigh handed me a towel. I wrapped myself in it.

"You did amazing, Ken! Holy shit! I'm so proud of you."

I smiled, hoping they weren't just speaking out of pity.

"And I'm sorry if I was a bitch about everything before. You know I support everything you do."

I hugged her.

"Thank you, guys, seriously. For coming and supporting me."

"I wish you would have told us, Ken," my dad said only loud enough for me to hear. His arms were crossed against his chest, his head low. I knew he was disappointed. Not with the surfing. With the lying. A feeling of guilt sunk in . . . it weighed on my chest like a ton of bricks. I wasn't trying to hurt anyone. I was just trying to take a risk and accomplish something important to me. Important to Kyle.

I didn't respond, though. I didn't want to talk in front of everyone.

"We couldn't get ahold of you so we called Ashleigh," Harry said.

"Yeah, sorry about that, Ken," Ashleigh apologized. "I was so caught off guard, I didn't know what to say."

We walked up the beach, where I spotted Brock sitting by himself on a bench, smoking a cigarette. I'd never seen him wear a hat forward before. It looked good. Sunglasses covered his eyes as he basked in the sun.

"Hey."

"Hey, you did great," he said with that half grin as he stood up.

"Thanks."

Reality hit me when I realized my parents were right behind me. I knew this was going to go one of two ways.

"What is *he* doing here?" Harry asked.

"You," my dad said. He charged toward Brock. "I told you to stay away from my daughter—"

"Dad!" I cut him off and everyone's eyes quickly darted toward me. "I asked him to help me."

My father looked puzzled. Maybe even slightly embarrassed.

"Coach wasn't going to help me compete and Brock was the only other person I knew I could trust. It isn't his fault."

"*Trust*?" Harry asked.

Brock was standing now, eye to eye with my dad. Everyone else had slowly snuck away from the situation. Understandably.

"You hung out with this delinquent? You lied to me?" My dad's face was turning red.

"Dad, Brock helped me! You can't try and protect me from life forever. I'm not Kyle." It all slipped out so quickly, I hadn't even thought about what I actually said to my dad.

I could see the sadness in my dad's eyes, the vulnerability. He felt betrayed, and he couldn't blame anyone but me this time. And I knew from past trauma that when a parent had to blame their own child, they also felt responsible. I heard my dad talk about this many times with our family therapist.

My dad started down the beach. Silent. Harry looked at me and then followed.

"Bruce, wait."

They walked down a ways, leaving only Brock and me.

"Kendra, you better go talk to him."

"I know."

I waited another second, hoping, somehow, I could avoid dealing with these emotions.

"Dad?" I finally said, hurrying toward him as quickly as my sore leg would allow me.

I ran up to him and hugged him.

"I'm sorry for not telling you."

He stared at me a moment and then at the sand.

"Why didn't you just tell me how you felt?"

"I didn't want to disappoint you and I knew how much you hated Brock and—"

He finally looked at me. "No. I'm sorry."

"For what?"

"For trying to hold you back. I just—"

He began to choke up. My heart was heavy for him.

"After your brother, I've just always wanted to protect you, and I know we said everything happens for a reason, but I still feel so guilty. I know you're getting older but—"

I stopped him before he continued to torture himself. "I get it."

I gave him another tight squeeze.

"I love you, Ken."

"I love you too, Daddy."

Harry began to tear up, joining in on the group hug.

"You guys, I love you!"

We were a mess. But we were all we had.

My dad and Harry eventually let go.

"And I'm very proud of you, regardless of the situation. The lying. You had a dream and nothing stopped you from chasing it. I wish I was more like that at your age."

"Where do you think I got it from?" I smiled.

"No, that's not from me. That's from your mother. I spent a large portion of my life afraid to come out. Afraid to pursue designing. I love my job, but sometimes I wonder what my life would've been like if I hadn't been so scared."

His eyes wandered behind me, where Brock stood.

"I think Brock and I need to talk," my dad said.

"Mmhmm," Harry agreed.

My heart stopped again. That was the last thing I think anyone needed right now, but now here I was, in between my dad and Brock, their eyes locked. Harry stood beside my dad, his arms crossed defensively. I was so scared of what was going to come out of their mouths. By now, my friends had made their way to underneath a cliff ten feet away or so. The beach was rowdy, but the little circle we'd formed seemed secluded from it all.

"Mr. Dimes, I need you to hear me out," Brock began.

My dad cleared his throat and started with, "Listen, Brock, I don't want to *hear you out*. I understand you're trying here, and I appreciate that, as I'm sure Kendra does too. I'm trying to give her space and treat her as an adult, but I'm also not going to allow you to bring her down with you."

My heart sank into my gut. Brock's eyes were still focused on my dad's. Why did I have to be here for this? I wanted to melt into the sand.

"You're right, and I'm sorry about what happened. I know she deserves so much more. I know you don't like me—"

"I don't like *or* dislike you. I just want my daughter to be safe. And for your sake, I want you to get your shit together."

"Yes, sir."

I was cringing at this whole thing. What direction was this going in?

"Kendra, why don't you let us talk, man-to-man," my dad insisted.

I walked a distance away, but not far enough to where I couldn't eavesdrop.

"I really do love her," Brock said, and when he did, I felt butterflies dancing around my heart.

"Then do her a favor and let her go."

A huge wave came crashing down, so I couldn't hear what they said for a moment, but I tried to read their lips. Brock said something about "acceptance," and I saw my dad mouth something about "only child."

I turned around when I saw they were headed toward me.

"Have some fun tonight, sweet pea. Be careful. Use good judgment," my dad said. I was confused at his sudden change of heart. But I didn't argue it. What did Brock say to him?

"I will." I smiled, still anxious to see how this all played out.

Without another word, my dad and Harry headed up to the

street, back to their car. I turned to face Brock, who had closed the distance between us. He pulled me into him, and I felt so at peace with everything. I wanted to be like this forever.

"I missed this," he said, as if he was reading my mind. We embraced. It felt like home.

"Thank you," I said, pulling back to look at him.

"I want to eat your eyes right now." He chuckled.

"Is that a compliment?"

"Yes, the sun makes them look like caramels."

The moment was intruded on when our friends found their way back to us.

"Okay, seriously, who's bringing the beer tonight?" Ashleigh asked as we all stood around the beach.

"I got you, girl," Jason said, his words long and already slurred. "Right, Ryan?"

"Right, man!"

"Let's all meet at Main around seven," Taylor said. "Beach bonfire!"

Brock was quiet for Brock. When I looked at him, he wouldn't take his eyes off me. It almost made me uncomfortable.

"Everything good?" I asked.

"Perfect. I want to memorize that face."

"Shut up." I laughed, nudging him. He seemed off today, not in a bad way or anything. Just . . . off.

BROCK

Daylight quickly turned to darkness, but I still refused to remove my sunglasses and hat. Kendra and I stood around the bonfire with our friends.

"Who wants to plug their music in?" Ashton asked. He had brought a Bluetooth stereo with him.

"I will," I said. I uploaded some really chill beats that I'd made.

"I'm so glad you're all here." Kendra smiled.

"Of course! But really, you should have totally placed—I mean, you were crippled."

"Ashleigh, just—just stop!" Ashton intervened.

"Shut up, Ashton."

"You're such a bitch sometimes."

"Ugh!" Ashleigh stormed off, Ashton chasing after her as expected.

I wrapped my arms around Kendra's waist.

"And what do you think you're doing, Mr. Parker?" she asked, turning toward me. "Just because we're friends doesn't mean—"

"I don't want to be just friends." Our faces were so close, they almost touched.

She smirked at me, biting her lip as she took her gaze down.

I tried to learn every feature on her face. It was going to be the last night, and I wanted to savor her forever, her big round eyes against her tan skin. The freckles that covered her nose.

She looked back up and said, "Me either."

I leaned in closer until our lips met to form a kiss. I missed this. She was the closest thing to what Duke made me feel like—home. Like we were a part of something bigger, or somehow our dreams seemed to mesh. But it was different with Duke because he was like the family I'd chosen for myself. Kendra was a girl—she was *the* girl. But like all good things, this was going to come to an end—and very soon. I swallowed down the ball in my throat that tried to break through and replaced it with a smile that focused on the present. Right now I was with Kendra. That was enough.

I pulled back just far enough so that our noses still touched. But Kendra pulled me back into her lips. They tasted like salt. Like the ocean. I wanted to memorize each and every sense that involved her—the sparkle in her eye, the taste of her lips, the smell of her hair, the innocence of her voice, and the feeling of her head against my chest. I wanted to remember those long after tonight, and I had faith that I would. I mean, who could ever forget the girl that made them sappy in love, right?

Jason interrupted the moment. "Got the kegger!"

He and Ryan were coming down the beach with a giant keg full of beer.

"Whoo!" Taylor yelled.

"I bet with a little liquid courage, he and Tay will be hooking up by the end of the night. What do you think?" Kendra said.

"Oh, definitely," I agreed.

Kendra grabbed me by the hand, pulling me away from the bonfire. I was glad she did. I wanted to be alone with her, but it was also my first night sober. I hadn't had a drink, a hit of a joint, or even a bump of coke in almost twenty-four hours. I didn't want the temptation to haunt me while I was here with her, either.

"Can you take those stupid glasses off? It's dark out," she said, trying to pull them off of my face, but I beat her to it, holding them against my face so she couldn't grab them.

"All right, fine then," she gave in.

We continued our stroll down the beach.

"You impressed me today. Kyle would be proud," I said.

She smiled at me. I wondered if she believed me or thought I was just trying to be nice, so I added, "I'm serious."

"Thanks," she said, her voice soft. "So, what'd my dad say? How did you get him to let you around me again?"

It dawned on me in the midst of this tranquility that this was the end, at least for now. I had to break it to her. I didn't want to.

I stopped. I think she could sense that something was going on, but maybe that was just me being aware of the fact that there was.

"Kendra." I could feel my voice quiver. I looked down at the sand, uncertain of how to say what I needed to tell her. "I'm leaving."

She laughed. "Okay? Well, I'll see you tomorrow, right?"

"No, no. Kendra, I mean, ugh—" I paused, grasping my thoughts, growing frustrated with myself. "I mean, I'm taking off. Leaving now. I won't be back. That's why your dad agreed to let you see me again. Acceptance for one last night."

I watched her face suddenly fall. Her eyes, her mouth, her forehead sunk down.

"Why?"

"You were right. About the drugs. About everything."

I took off my baseball hat and sunglasses to reveal my bruised and banged-up face.

Her jaw dropped. I scratched my head, my shaggy and unwashed hair flopping around.

"Brock!" She caressed the bruise that covered my eye. I winced.

"I, uh—I need to start over, I need to turn my life around."

I could tell she was at a loss for words. I understood. It was confusing, and I'm sure she had a lot of questions.

She subtly nodded her head. I thought about my parents . . . if only she knew the truth.

"You'll understand it all soon," I said.

She shook her head, appearing clueless and taken aback. Again, I understood.

"Come here." I took her hand and led her farther down the beach. Just her and me.

I led Kendra away to our secret hideout—the same place we had gone when I convinced her to ditch class. We watched our friends party around the bonfire from afar. I wanted to tell her about Duke. She knew him and he really liked her. He thought she was, like, the dopest chick. But I didn't want to ruin the last few moments we had together with sad stories. We shared enough of those already. I had to hold back the tears that wanted to escape, just thinking about it.

"Can we finish our game of twenty-one questions before I go?"

"I suppose." She spoke with emptiness, as if her words had no meaning or feeling behind them. She was too preoccupied, thinking. Wondering.

She was upset. I could tell. I was too. But I just wanted to enjoy this moment with her.

"What's your favorite food?" I asked. It was a stupid question, but I wanted to lighten things up.

She was still zoned out.

"Kendra."

"What'd you ask?"

"Your favorite food," I repeated, this time making sure she was listening.

"Churros. The ones from Disneyland."

But her mind was somewhere else even when she spoke, like she was in a trance.

"What do your parents actually do for a living?" I think she was finally beginning to understand something was not right in my house.

"You'll find out soon."

"Why can't you just tell me, Brock?"

"Because." I raised my voice a decibel or two louder than planned. Mostly out of frustration. I wanted her to remember me as the hero she thought I was. The guy who saved her from Jason at a party. The guy who kept her surfing secret. The one she lost her virginity to. That meant something to a girl like Kendra. She would potentially hate me soon enough when she found out the truth. Everyone was going to find out. "Ask another question."

She faced the ocean, thinking.

"What was your first impression of me?"

I exhaled a quick "ha" as my mind seemed to wander back to that night. A night full of so many beginnings. "That you were intimidatingly beautiful."

She nudged me, sighing out a nervous chuckle.

"Liar."

"I'm being dead serious. You don't realize how pretty you are—inside and out."

"Aw, you're making me blush," she said in a mocking manner that only Kendra could pull off when she got nervous.

"What was your first impression of me?"

She pursed her lips into a cute smile. A shy smile. "You seemed very confident and sure of yourself."

"Would you say that holds true?"

She nodded her head.

"All right," I said. "Last question."

"Okay."

I looked at her, right in the eye.

"Will you be my girlfriend for one last night?"

Her eyes and mouth formed a smile in unison. "Yes."

I pulled her into me for a kiss, making sure it was a memorable one.

I heard a familiar tune playing off in the distance. Kendra must've heard it too, because she quickly said, "Oh, my gosh! Do you hear that?"

"Yeah."

I followed her gaze toward the bonfire, where the song was coming from.

"It's our song! From the first night we met," she blurted out, smiling.

"Oh, shit. You're right." I knew I liked that song.

I looked at her face, remembering my first impression, realizing that this was going to be my last impression of her. It wasn't enough in life that people recognized the final impression. Sometimes the last moments were even more important than the first, because those were the moments that you seemed to remember the best—oddly enough. All I could think of when I thought of Duke was his last breath. The seizing. The drugs. The end.

I wanted to make this ending feel like a beginning as much I could. For Kendra and me. We'd both already had to say so many unnecessary goodbyes. I didn't want our last moments together to include traumatic flashbacks or fear. No. This was going to be different. Different from our pasts. This was not going to be like Duke. Or Kyle.

This was not going to feel like an end.

She nestled her head against my chest, hugging me. I wrapped my arms around her too. Have you ever experienced a hug that felt more intimate than sex? That's what this felt like.

She spoke softly. "I miss you already."

I pulled back to kiss her forehead. I missed her already too. It sucked. It really fucking sucked. I was trying so hard not to think of tomorrow or a week from now or even a year from now, but each moment of right now made me want to forget it all or tell Kendra to run away with me. But I would never do that to her. She had too much going for her already. I didn't have shit to lose. Not family, not friends, not a job or some aspiring career— just her. But like her dad had said, I would only bring her down with me.

I looked down at her as she played with the St. Christopher pendant hanging from around her neck.

"What are you thinking about?"

She didn't take her eyes off the necklace when she said, "You. I'm thinking about where you're going to be. Are you going to be safe?"

She continued, "Are you going to remember me? Or will time make our memories fade into a blurry moment?"

"Are you serious? Of course I'm going to remember you." How could I ever forget the girl who saved my life?

"But just *one* moment of our lives is all this is going to be."

"Yeah. One *huge* moment."

She looked down at her necklace again and took it off, placing it around my neck instead.

"What are you doing?"

"I want you to have it. So your travels are safe."

"But your brother gave it to you."

"And now I'm giving it to you."

I was hesitant to accept something so symbolic.

"Think of it as an early birthday gift." She smiled.

I took her face in my hand and kissed her.

"It came true," she said.

"What?"

"The wish I made, that night in my tree house. You told me to tell you when it came true."

"On the shooting star?"

"Yeah."

What I would give to go back to that night; I would have stayed until the sun rose and said *fuck it* to my shit parents.

"What was it?"

"I wished for you to stop doing drugs."

"Why would you waste a wish on me?"

"Because," she said. She looked at me, smiling. "I love you."

"I love you, Kendra Dimes. Like a fat kid loves cake," I said, trying to keep the energy light. Goodbyes were already difficult enough.

She countered, "Like a penguin loves ice."

Our laughs became one, the waves crashing in the background—like music to our own personal movie. We hugged each other tight. I never wanted to let go. But I guess I had to . . . just like Bruce had said.

I walked Kendra home after the bonfire. We walked through her back gate and up to her balcony.

"Do you want to come in?" she asked.

As much as I wanted to—and honestly considered it—I couldn't. For many reasons—her parents for one. Plus, I had a big morning ahead of me. After I reported my parents and Morales last night, everything suddenly became real. The detectives at the station formulated a plan where I would go back home—so I did—and they were going to use me to fake a drug bust. Basically, I had to act like I was dealing an undercover cop some coke, and then they were going to raid the house. I had to wear a wire too, just like that guy in that Tarantino movie *True Romance* when they wanted to bust Christian Slater's character.

When I went home last night, my father was thankfully asleep, but when I woke up this morning, I took a brutal verbal beating. I almost wasn't capable of following through with the whole plan. The reason they devised it this way was because I was a minor and they wanted to get more info while I was wearing the wire. More evidence. And they sure fucking did.

"I better get going," I said to Kendra.

"Can't you just stay? You can live here, and we can figure it out! Whatever it is—"

"Kendra, you're a fixer—and that's a good thing—but I'm a broken toy with missing pieces. You can't put me back together."

"But you're not broken . . . you're just rearranged differently than others."

That was what I loved about Kendra most: her ability to see the best in situations and people who didn't deserve it.

"I wish I could stay."

She nodded her head, trying to be understanding. And I was too.

"I had a really nice night with you," I said.

"Me too."

We embraced one last time.

"I'll always love you, Kendra," I whispered in her ear.

"I love you too. Always."

We unwillingly released from each other.

"Oh, I almost forgot," I said, reaching into my pocket. It was the letter. I handed it to her.

"What is this?"

"Just read it whenever you get a chance. Not right now, though."

"Okay."

Our lips met once more in a synchronized manner as if this was our last hit before going sober. But the clock struck midnight and our time was up. It wasn't that kind of fairy tale, though. There wasn't some fucked-up lady in a dress with a wand who could promise us forever or even the next day, but in a way, our story was a hell of a lot better. Because it was the kind of love that we seemed to fall for like the stars in the sky fall for the earth, leaving us with wishes. And I would wish for nothing more than to see her again. One day. Somehow. I believed it could be possible if the universe wanted it to be.

Kendra headed up the balcony as I headed for the back gate.

"I'll see you later, Kendra."

I didn't like the word *goodbye*. It seemed too permanent.

"See you," she said. And there we departed for the night and maybe even for good—a new beginning ahead.

I walked home, enjoying my last night of potential freedom. Who knew what my world would be like after tomorrow?

When I got home, my parents were awake. No surprise. They sat in the kitchen watching TV, smoking a joint.

"Where were you?" my father asked in his bitter tone. We weren't recovered all of the way after last night's episode.

"I was out. Lot of deals at this bonfire," I lied.

"Your mom and I discussed it, and you won't be receiving a paycheck for a while."

"Okay," I said. He looked at me, I think surprised that I hadn't argued. I looked at him too. In a way, I was sad. At the end of the day, that was my mom and dad. The only ones I had. But maybe after all of this, I would save them. This wasn't a life anyone needed to live. I went upstairs and lay in bed. I couldn't sleep all night. I was so fucking nervous. I even had to get up to shit a few times from the nerves. My soul was full of fire. I looked over at my Gibson hanging on the wall. It drew me over. I sat down and started to play a few chords.

When I finally did doze off, I dreamt of the bonfire and Kendra. Duke came to me in my dream too. A lot of it was blurry, but I remember him saying, "I'm okay, dog. I'm on the island. This is paradise."

And I hoped that was a sign. I also hoped I would find my paradise after all of this . . . soon.

KENDRA

When I woke up, I felt hungover even though I hadn't drunk. Maybe I was drunk on love last night or life or surfing. I wasn't sure. I looked at my nightstand where the letter Brock had given me sat, waiting to be opened. But I wasn't ready yet. I wasn't ready to face the truth that this was the end of him and me. That he wouldn't be back. That I wouldn't be hearing from him potentially ever again.

I walked downstairs, still in my pajamas. It was the first time since the accident that I was able to get downstairs without my boot, but I still used the railing. I kept my gaze down to make sure I didn't fall. I noticed a long scar across my shin from the car wreck. It was crazy to think that no matter how much time passed, that scar would remind me of this period of my life. Scars were funny like that.

I'd slept late. The last twenty-four hours felt like an odd dream that had left me with questions that would possibly never be answered.

"Morning, sunshine," Harry greeted me.

"Morning," I said.

I let out a loud yawn as I stretched my body.

"Would our surfing champ like a fresh bagel?" my dad asked. My parents weren't as upset as I thought they might be today. In fact, it was the opposite. Everyone was in quite the cheery mood. Yesterday needed to happen. It was a break-through. A new start.

He tossed me a bagel, and I took a bite as I sat down at the table.

"How was the bonfire last night?" Harry asked.

I couldn't help but smile as visions of Brock's warm eyes lit up my mind, stimulating me with a sense of alertness that felt awakening. Was that crazy sounding?

"So fun."

My dad and Harry looked at each other with an all-knowing smirk. But my phone buzzed on the counter before I was able to retell the events of last night. It was Ashleigh.

"Hello?" I answered, taking another bite of my bagel.

"Ken."

"Hey. What's up?"

"You have to turn on channel twelve. Now!"

"Why? What is it?"

I hurried to the living room, searching for the remote. Ash-leigh's voice sounded urgent. I immediately turned the television on and flipped to channel twelve. Footage of Debby and Karl Parker—Brock's parents—being arrested was on the screen.

My dad and Harry ran into the room as photos of Annie's parents flashed onto the screen underneath the Parkers. I turned the volume up.

". . . local drug dealers who used their children to build up a high school clientele," the reporter said.

My heart dropped. Brock.

"Officials believe this may be tied to the recent death of Los Angeles native, Duke Larson."

Duke's face popped up on the screen. My heart sunk. I wanted to throw up. I couldn't believe he was dead. I felt so bad for him. For Brock. For everyone in the situation. I thought about Brock telling me about their island.

"These locals are also supposedly linked to Miguel Morales, a key player in the drug—"

I turned the TV off; I knew what I needed to know and didn't care to hear the gory details. Not yet at least. It wasn't hard to figure out at this point though. Brock Parker was a drug dealer for his parents, and for some reason, he'd ratted them out. Maybe he really did want to change. That gave me hope. Looking back, it all made sense. They were this rich family with their rich friends on that yacht. And Brock was always disappearing. That night at the bonfire when he took off when Jason and Ryan got busted. The red flags were there. Maybe I'd chosen to ignore them; maybe I just didn't care to look. Either way, I was glad that I hadn't noticed. Brock and I changed each other. For the better.

"Wow," I said into the phone.

"Right? And Annie too," Ashleigh said.

"I gotta go. I'll call you in a little while."

I hung up the phone. I had to sit down.

"I always knew he was bad!" Harry insisted.

"Yeah, but he didn't want to be," I said.

"You're right. No one wants to be," my dad agreed. I think we telepathically knew each of us thought of Kyle in that moment. He didn't want the demons he had, either.

"I think it's best though that he's gone for now," Harry said.

"That's true," my dad agreed. The room was silent, but I was too deep in thought to care or pay attention.

"You all right, Ken?" my dad asked. I was collecting my thoughts.

"Yeah, I'm fine," I reassured him. But I needed to escape. "I'm going to go hang out at the beach for a little bit."

"All right. You sure you don't want to talk about it?" my dad asked.

"Yes, but not right now."

"All right. Be careful."

I got dressed and headed outside. I hopped onto my bike, the ocean calling my name. The sun's brightness was peeking through the overcast clouds.

I approached Main, riding onto the sand, and let my bike fall to the ground. My first instinct was to check Facebook and look up Brock's profile. But it had been erased. Chills danced up my arm and down into my spine. He was gone in every sense.

When I sat down on a bench facing the ocean, I pulled the envelope Brock had given me out of my basket. I'd been putting it off, so far doing a pretty good job of numbing myself. I didn't feel like crying. I didn't feel like being sad. But I couldn't escape the pain forever. I knew from history that hiding from the things that hurt us only piles on the discomfort until our hearts explode. So I opened it up, colorful Skittles falling all over my lap. It made me giggle as I picked a red one up off the sand and stuck it in my mouth. I reached into the envelope and pulled out a CD. Who even used CDs anymore? Just another reason I loved him.

In black marker it read, "Kendra's Song: Play Me Whenever You Miss Me." I set it down next to me and opened the letter, bracing myself.

I'm sorry that I left like this. But sometimes we have to be selfish and do things for ourselves. If it is fate, our paths will cross again. I'll always remember the night I met you at the homecoming dance. I'll always remember how you never let your injury stop you from doing anything. I'll always remember that when I was having a bad day, just hearing your voice would cheer me up. I'll always remember how you changed my life and how much you taught me. I will truly never forget you. I love you, Kendra, and I hope you never forget me too.

I looked out at the ocean. I didn't cry. I didn't even shed a tear. I smiled.

EPILOGUE:

KENDRA

(11 years later)

Unlike most, I like the rain. I like the smell of it, the feel of it, the way it comes with this sort of nostalgic feeling—although it isn't attached to any certain memory. Maybe just a plethora of special ones. Especially a rainy day at the beach. However, what I love most about the rain is what it signifies: the sky may temporarily shed its tears, but eventually the sun shines through. That means something to me. Someone important taught me that long ago.

I walk up the shore, already soaked in cloud water. There is something magical about surfing in the rain. Refreshing, even. I look up at the clouds and smile.

I sigh aloud. No one is around . . . just me.

Shit, I didn't realize how late it was. Well, not late, but I'm running late. A reporter for *Surf Magazine* is going to be at my house within an hour. I wish I could just postpone the interview, but with my schedule for the next few weeks, it's best to get it over with now.

I head home, shower, and put on something presentable—but most importantly, comfortable. I don't bother blow-drying my hair or even wearing shoes. Screw it.

I prefer bare feet to heels, walking to driving, sand to snow, and bikinis to dresses any day of the week.

I have to finish picking up this damn patio. My boyfriend, Robert, threw a party here a few nights ago, and it's been left a mess. Of course, my doorbell rings just when I start to gather the trash. I'm not sure if it's worse that it's a mess outside or that I don't feel bad about it. Life gets messy, and sometimes we don't get to clean it up.

I open the door to a finely dressed man in a collared shirt with slacks and a sports jacket. His hair is dark and slicked back with some sort of gel. I suddenly feel underdressed.

"Hello. Nice to meet you," I say. Sometimes I get sick of all the photo shoots and interviews and blah, blah, blah. I wish surfing was just surfing like it used to be. But I also feel bad thinking that way, because very few people in this world get to make money living out their dream. I guess it's just part of the deal.

"Good afternoon!" He smiles. "I'm Eddie. It's a pleasure to meet you."

He sticks out his hand, and I meet him halfway with a shake. It's almost uncomfortable for a moment when his stare through his thick, Coke-bottle glasses lasts longer than what might be considered normal.

"Come in, Eddie," I say, finally taking my hand back. "Do you mind if we sit outside?"

"No problem."

"I love the rain."

"Me too," he says.

I walk outside. When I turn around, Eddie is still inside,

admiring all of the memorabilia and awards that sit upon my shelves. Sometimes I'm tempted to take them down so people don't feel obligated to stare. Like, I wonder if they actually find them interesting or if they just feel that they need to look. Like they think it's the nice thing to do or something.

"Sorry." He smiles and rushes toward me outside.

My back deck overlooks the Pacific Ocean. It's the kind of beautiful that you don't get sick of, no matter how long you've lived there. We both take a seat on the patio chairs, shielded from the now-ceased rain. The sun is just beginning to peek through.

"Can I get you something to drink?" I ask.

"Sure."

As I head inside, he stops me by saying, "I'm sorry."

I turn around, confused.

"I'm just such a huge fan. I'm so nervous right now."

This happens every time. At first, I was flattered by it; by the tenth time it made me nervous—probably more than the "fans." Now, I know exactly how to handle it.

"Don't be nervous." I smile. "We're just two friends having some tea on a rainy day, discussing life."

His eyes sparkle. Eddie is honestly adorable. The kind of adorable like a gay best friend that you want to tell all your secrets to.

I disappear into the house, leaving Eddie to himself as I warm up some hot tea, nothing too fancy, just a nice English breakfast with some honey. Perfect for the inspiring gloom that awaits me outside. When I walk back out a moment later, Eddie is incessantly tapping his pen against his coffee-stained notepad. It makes me smile. I always thought that if I hadn't become a surfer, I would be a writer. Maybe. I'm not sure. It just seems like such an escape in the same way surfing can be. Plus, I've always loved reading. Maybe I should start journaling.

"Hot tea with honey," I say as I place two hot mugs onto the table, steam rising from them.

"Thank you."

He takes a sip out of the cup.

"So." I pause to take a sip of tea. "What kind of interview is this again?"

"Think of it more as an autobiography really—not that you're old or anything, of course."

I can't help but chuckle at Eddie's nervous humor. He joins in, laughing at himself. I love anyone who can laugh at themself.

"It's just—people, well fans, want to know more about you. Your struggles, hopes, dreams, anything that can give the public an idea of who you were before you were 'Kendra Dimes.'"

"I'm the same girl I've always been. It's true, really. I'm just a normal girl who has an abnormal passion for the ocean and two dads instead of one. Everything else is basic and not very exciting, if you ask me. That's the way it's always been. I feel like people who have the drive to achieve a certain goal or dream aren't very exciting because they're so busy chasing something that it's like, when do you have time to do anything that exhilarating besides achieving that dream?"

"You know what I mean. Before you were *the* Kendra Dimes, the face of Nike, the winner of the three ESPYs, the woman who was seen on a date with Hollywood's most eligible bachelor, for crying out loud!"

I smirk at Eddie's admiration. It makes me unwillingly blush.

"I'm afraid I'm not too good a read," I explain, giggling to myself.

"That's because you're a book without any pages!"

I gaze out at the sun beaming down at the ocean. Home. I watch as leftover raindrops drip down from the roof. It reminds me of someone. Brock Parker. I smile, forgetting anyone else is even around. Now that's a story, but it's our story. Do I dare share it? I hadn't thought back that far into time since . . . jeez, years. Eddie is bringing something out of me that was oddly relevant to the rainfall today. Brock is the one that taught me about the rain. How it isn't depressing. It's cleansing.

"Come on," Eddie says. "There's got to be something that you can share. Family stories, relationships—"

"I did deal with quite a bit of anxiety as a teenager. I still do. I don't think things like that ever go away." I speak my thoughts aloud, not meaning to interrupt Eddie. I was more talking to myself. "I have a lot of trauma from my past that occasionally resurfaces, but when I was sixteen, I met a boy."

I look off into the distance as memories parade around in my head. I smile at some and wince at others as they infect my mind, taking me back in some sort of chaotic time warp.

"He was that guy that I was kind of an idiot for. . . ."

"I think we've all been there." Eddie laughs.

"I agree."

"And there she goes! Now we're getting somewhere," Eddie says, as he types on his computer.

"We used to play this game," I admit, redirecting my attention back to Eddie. I'm not sure if I want to go down this road—memory lane. But I continue to without much thought.

He leans in closer, ready for the details.

I gaze out beyond the wooden deck that stands tall over the trees, at the waves forming and crashing.

Without changing my stare, I say to Eddie, "You can title this, *Twenty-One Questions*."

After an emotional hour of reliving this story and an era that felt so long ago, the sun is shining ever so brightly—almost blinding my vision—as if the rain is now just a figment of the past. As if it never happened. How ironic.

By the end, Eddie is hysterically crying, unable to contain himself. I rush to his side in an attempt to reassure him. Can you say interview gone wrong? I can see the press headlines already: "Kendra Dimes Brings Reporter to Tears."

"You still love him," Eddie sobs.

"Eddie, don't cry. I've moved on. He's moved on." I'm not really sure where Brock Parker is, but I know anything is better than where he had been.

"That's the end?" he says in between hyperventilating. "He just left and that's it?"

Brock's beautiful brown eyes dance through my mind. That half grin. Jesus Christ.

That last night we were together. He was all bruised but still so perfect. Gosh, when I was younger, it really didn't seem possible that a "love story" with such raw emotions attached could have ended with an ending. At least, not the kind of ending that lasts forever.

"It wasn't a movie. I didn't get to choose how it ended."

I hand Eddie a box of tissues sitting on the table between us as I rest my hand on his knee, trying to be comforting. He pulls one out to blow his nose, tears flooding into his cup of tea. I'm sure it tastes quite salty by now. The truth is, I know what he is feeling because I once felt it too. I spent so many nights crying myself to sleep, wondering about Brock, if he is okay. . . .

"Those teenage feelings have evaporated into the air." I spit out another line in an attempt to calm Eddie down.

His eyes continue to rain down tears, heavier than the rainfall earlier. He knows just as well as I that feelings like that don't just evaporate.

"You up for a break?" I suggest.

He pulls out another tissue, blowing his nose so hard it sounds like a dying cow. He nods his head.

My driver, Jacques, pulls up to the driveway. Eddie and I get into the car. He sniffles in silence as Jacques drives down South Coast Highway.

"Why didn't he come back?" Eddie directs his gaze to me.

I look down at my fidgeting hand and shake my head.

"I don't know."

"How could you both just move on?" he asks, exasperated, as if he found out his favorite on-screen couple was just killed off the show or something.

"Because that's just life?"

"Have you tried reaching out on Facebook? Are you friends on Facebook?"

"No, I don't even have a personal Facebook account anymore. It just—it wasn't our fate, Eddie. Life took us down two different paths . . . for the best."

My body officially feels flush. I have to roll down this damn window.

When I do, the air leaks through, cooling me off, and I can hear the ocean from a distance. I close my eyes and take in the breeze.

We finally pull up to the coffee shop. Seriously, what a relief. I need a break from all of the emotions.

Eddie and I walk inside, his eyes now puffy and red.

"What can I get for you, ma'am?" the cashier asks as I approach the front of the line.

"I'll have a large coffee with a tablespoon of cinnamon, four sugars, and a quarter cup of cream."

"Will that be all?"

"I'll have the same," a familiar voice says from behind me.

I quickly jerk my head around to confirm it's just who I think it is. Brock Parker. A much scruffier and older Brock Parker. But his eyes are the same. And inside of them I see so many memories that I have forgotten. In this moment, I feel so small. Vulnerable. Like a teenager.

He pulls out his wallet and hands a twenty-dollar bill to the cashier.

"I see you're still hooked on those Sweet Tooth Slammers."

"Brock," I say. My voice quivers. We smile at one another, the world around us melting.

ACKNOWLEDGMENTS

Where do I even begin? This book has been in the works for a decade. There are so many people who have helped me along the way. This story started as a way for me to cope with a breakup, my first real heartbreak, when I was seventeen. Writing has always been therapy for me. There are so many people I want to thank, starting with my mom. She has been by my side through it all. She's caught every tear that's fallen from my eyes as I wrote this story and lived it in its entirety. I'm so grateful to my dad for always supporting my sisters and I in chasing our dreams (even though he had hope we'd all be doctors. . . sorry dad!). I also want to thank my three sisters, Mikaela, Angelica, and Julia, as well as my cousins Sabrina and Samantha for reading and loving *21 Questions* through all of its versions and evolution.

I couldn't have done this without the amazing editors I've had along the way and I'm beyond appreciative to my publisher for believing in my story and these characters.

I'm so grateful to my friend, Zach Figures, for being a part of this story, especially in its early stages when it was a screenplay. Also, thank you for bringing me pizza and wine when the muse behind this story made me cry.

I have to thank my friends who inspired so many of these characters. This story is so near and dear to my heart because it is a fictionalized version of my life. My experiences. Our experiences. Youth. First loves. Friendships. Nostalgia. The times we take for granted and look back on with a smile.

I come from a big, crazy Armenian family who have always supported me and stood by my side through thick and thin, and for that I am blessed and thankful.

As always, I have to thank Howard Falco, my life coach, who has taught me that no dream is too big and coached me through my anxiety when it was crippling. Thank you for teaching me that life is full of infinite possibilities.

I'm so appreciative to Tess Booth for allowing me to pick her brain about the surfing world. You're such an inspiration and I hope you accomplish all of your dreams!

As crazy as this sounds, I have to thank my two main characters in this story, Brock and Kendra. Even though they are fictional, they got me through so much when my heart was broken. . . for that I am forever grateful.

I want to thank anyone and everyone who has been a part of this story, its journey, development, and now the publishing of it! I couldn't have done it without you.

Lastly, I want to acknowledge the person who inspired this story. Who broke my heart, time after time. Thank you for the inspiration. I guess it's true, when a writer falls in love with you, you can never die. Our story will always live on these pages.

For the readers who can relate and connect, I'm grateful for you and your support. This story is for you.

God gave me a talent and a love story and with that, this novel came about. He got me through heartbreak and I couldn't have written this without Him guiding my hands along the keyboard.

ABOUT THE AUTHOR

Photo credit: Michael Franco

Alexandria Rizik is an award-winning film-maker and the author of two books, the poetry collection *Words Written in the Dark* and the children's book *Chocolate Milk*. She was born and raised in Scottsdale, Arizona, where she was brought up by a large Armenian family. She received her bachelor of arts in English literature from Arizona State University. Alexandria's love for writing began when she was a young child: her aunt bought her a journal and told her to write her a story, and the rest is history. Her favorite part about writing is being able to write the *happily ever after* that doesn't always happen in real life. Besides writing, Alexandria loves yoga, wine, and family time.

SELECTED TITLES FROM SPARKPRESS

SparkPress is an independent boutique publisher delivering high-quality, entertaining, and engaging content that enhances readers' lives, with a special focus on female-driven work.
www.gosparkpress.com

The Goddess Twins: A Novel, Yodassa Williams. $16.95, 978-1-68463-032-5. Days before their eighteenth birthday, Arden and Aurora's mother goes missing and they discover they belong to a family of Caribbean deities. Can these goddess twins uncover their evil grandfather's plot in time to save their mother, themselves, and the free world?

A Song for the Road: A Novel, Rayne Lacko. $16.95, 978-1-684630-02-8. When his house is destroyed by a tornado, fifteen-year-old Carter Danforth steals his mom's secret cash stash, buys his father's guitar back from a pawnshop, and hitchhikes old Route 66 in search of the man who left him as a child.

But Not Forever: A Novel, Jan Von Schleh. $16.95, 978-1-943006-58-8. When identical fifteen-year-old girls are mysteriously switched in time, they discover the love that's been missing in their lives. Torn, both want to go home, but neither wants to give up what they now have.

The Frontman: A Novel, Ron Bahar. $16.95, 978-1-943006-44-1. During his senior year of high school, Ron Bahar—a Nebraskan son of Israeli immigrants—falls for Amy Andrews, a non-Jewish girl, and struggles to make a career choice between his two other passions: medicine and music.

Attachments: A Novel, Jeff Arch, $16.95, 9781684630813. What happens when the mistakes we make in the past don't stay in the past? When no amount of running from the things we've done can keep them from catching up to us? When everything depends on what we do next?

Charming Falls Apart: A Novel, Angela Terry, $16.95, 978-1-68463-049-3. After losing her job and fiancé the day before her thirty-fifth birthday, people-pleaser and rule-follower Allison James decides she needs someone to give her some new life rules—*and fast*. But when she embarks on a self-help mission, she realizes that her old life wasn't as perfect as she thought—and that she needs to start writing her own rules.

CPSIA information can be obtained
at www.ICGtesting.com
Printed in the USA
FSHW010715290421
80764FS